The Lost Manuscript
of Martin Taylor Harrison

G·K
Hall
&C<u>o</u>

Also published in Large Print
from G.K. Hall by Stephen Bly:

Hard Winter at Broken Arrow Crossing
False Claims at the Little Stephen Mine
Last Hanging at Paradise Meadow
Standoff at Sunrise Creek

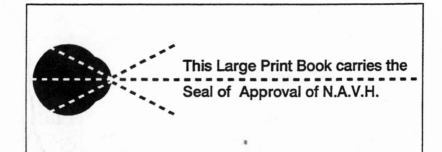

This Large Print Book carries the
Seal of Approval of N.A.V.H.

The Lost Manuscript
of Martin Taylor Harrison

Stephen Bly

G.K. Hall & Co.
Thorndike, Maine

Published in 1996 by arrangement with
Crossway Books, a division of Good News Publishers.

G.K. Hall Large Print Inspirational Collection.

The text of this Large Print edition is unabridged.
Other aspects of the book may vary from the original edition.

Set in 16 pt. News Plantin.

Printed in the United States on permanent paper.

Library of Congress Cataloging in Publication Data

Bly, Stephen A., 1944–
    The lost manuscript of Martin Taylor Harrison / Stephen Bly.
      p.   cm. — (Austin-Stoner files)
    ISBN 0-7838-1596-4 (lg. print : hc)
    1. Large type books. I. Title. II. Series: Bly, Stephen A.,
1944– Austin-Stoner files.
[PS3552.L93L67 1996]
813'.54—dc20   95-45120

For Janni-Rae

ONE

Lynda Austin refused to glance at her reflection gliding along the window of the 5th Avenue boutique. She knew her dark brown hair was wind-blown, the Autumn Rose blush had faded from her lips, and the crow's-feet peeked out from the corners of her Vuarnet CatEye sunglasses. Her Summer Fling perfume had long ago lost its potency.

It was Friday afternoon. She just didn't care.

It had been a long week . . . a long month . . . a long year.

She held the brass and glass door labeled 222 Madison Avenue open for Kelly and Nina. Their heels tapped across the black marble floor as they entered the elevator. Lynda glanced at her watch.

One o'clock! I'll have to take work home this week-end — again.

Even before the dark wood-paneled elevator doors slid open, Lynda heard someone shouting.

"I'm not leaving here until I talk to an editor. Do you understand?" a man screamed. "Don't you realize what I have in my hands?"

The three women stepped out into the lobby of Atlantic-Hampton Publishing Company to see

Spunky Sasser standing on her receptionist's chair. She was waving one of her five-inch, black patent-leather stiletto heels at a red-faced man whose long, stringy, light brown hair hung down from a bald spot.

"I've got the letter right here. . . . Read it. Just read it. Ten thousand dollars on the receipt of final manuscript. Here it is!"

"Spunky!" Lynda called. "What's the problem?"

"I'll tell you what," the man shouted. "They're trying to stiff me!"

"Spunky, call building security," Kelly yelled. "Mister, you've got about sixty seconds to get out of this office."

"You threatening me? I'm not leavin'. I've got the authentic manuscript here!" he shouted.

"Sassy, where's Mr. Gossman?" Lynda called.

"He went home!"

"Already? How about Stan?"

"He said he was too busy to come out."

"I'm not leaving! Do you hear me?" the man shrieked.

"Too busy? How about Frank?"

"He's not answering his phone this week, re-member? He told me he'd yank out my fingernails if I buzzed him again."

Lynda Austin moved closer. "Look, mister, eh . . . what's your name?"

"Fondue."

"What?"

"Felix Fondue."

"Right, right, and I'm Sarah Souffle," Kelly

broke in. "Did you get security, Spunky?"

"They'll be here in a minute. They're tied up on 19 again."

"Mr. Fondue," Lynda boomed, "I'm an editor here. You leave the manuscript, and I'll look at it. Just leave it here and get out of the building. I'll take a look, and then you can come back in three or four weeks, and I'll — "

"You're not ripping me off! I'm not leaving until I get the money!"

"That's not the way the system works, Fondue!" Kelly shouted.

"Lynda! Eh, Ms. Austin," Nina called, tugging at her arm.

"What is it?"

"Come here," Nina whispered.

"What do you want?" Lynda snapped.

"Do you need to borrow my .38?"

Lynda ran her hands through her hair. "Your what?"

"I've got a .38 special in my purse. You're welcome to use it."

"In your purse?" Lynda blurted out.

"Daddy said if I'd carry it, he wouldn't worry so much."

"Well . . . well, it may not worry him, but it sure worries me! Please don't pull that thing out of your purse — ever!"

Lynda turned to the pacing man. "Maybe you'd like to try another publishing house because we don't give advances until we've seen and accepted the manuscript."

"What do you think I am — some hick from the country?"

"You smell like you — "

"Kelly!" Lynda stopped her co-worker. "Mr. Fondue, just what important manuscript do you have there anyway?"

"I have in my hands none other than the authentic, genuine, complete, lost manuscript of Martin Taylor Harrison! This is 'With the Wind in My Face'!"

"Oh, man . . . we should have known!" Kelly sighed. "Have security haul him out of here! Get out of here, buddy!"

"You don't believe me?" he shouted.

"Mr. Fondue, we receive anywhere from twelve to fifty phony Martin Taylor Harrison manuscripts every year. Each one claims to be the famous missing third novel. Look, it's Friday — we're all tired and want to get the week finished. So take your manuscript and go home. We won't call the cops on you. Just leave."

"I'm not leaving! Hayakawa couldn't throw me out of San Francisco State; the sheriff couldn't throw me out of Mendocino; and the BLM couldn't throw me out of the canyons! You aren't getting me out of here until I get my money!"

"Lynda, he's wacko! Hey, here's security. Tony, you and Percy usher this guy to the street," Kelly ordered.

"You're not tossing me out!" The man shouted and ran around behind the receptionist's counter. Spunky Sasser jumped off her chair and ran out toward the lobby carrying a high heel in each hand, her waist-long black hair flying behind her.

"What are you doin'?" one of the guards called out, chasing after the man. "Where'd you get those? Don't do that, man! You're in big trouble now!"

"What did he do?" Lynda called.

"Oh, man! He handcuffed himself to Ms. Sasser's desk."

"He what?"

"Go get the police," Kelly called to the other guard. "This is getting too weird even for Manhattan."

"If you don't believe this letter's authentic, check with G. L. Ramsey. He'll know. Does he still work here?"

A cold chill hit Lynda Austin in the back of her head and shot down her back. "Who did you say?"

"G. L. Ramsey. That's the name on the letter."

"Let me see that letter!"

"We don't have any Ramseys here," Kelly barked.

"Don't let him ruin my phones!" Spunky called out from the far side of the room.

"Lynda?" Nina stepped to her side. "Wasn't G. L. Ramsey editor for Martin Taylor Harrison? I mean, my English lit. prof. said that if it hadn't been for Ramsey, *Alone at the Edge of the Universe* and *When the Last Rock Crumbled* would never have turned out to be classics."

Straightening the collar of her off-white blouse,

Lynda Austin stared at the letter. "It's dated July 12, 1930."

"1930?" Nina looked over her shoulder at the yellowing letter. "That's the year Harrison disappeared, isn't it?"

"Yeah . . . and it's also the year G. L. Ramsey quit the business and moved to that tin-roofed conch house on Driftwood Road in Key Largo."

Nina glanced up at Lynda. "How do you know so much about Ramsey?"

"It's a long story."

"Lynda grew up in the Keys," Kelly interjected.

"Only until the third grade. After that it was just during vacations. Anyway, the signature sure looks like an authentic G. L. Ramsey. Where did you get this cover letter?"

Fondue was busy rifling through a drawer in Spunky Sasser's desk. "I got it from the old man, just like the manuscript. I'm not claiming that I wrote that book. It's not my style."

Spunky jumped up and down in her stocking feet. "Stay out of my desk!"

"I'm hungry. You got anything to eat in here?"

"Stay out of the drawers!" Lynda insisted. "What do you mean, you got this from the old man? What old man?"

"Harrison . . . old man Harrison. He just went by Harry most the time."

"Oh, you're going to claim that Harrison's still alive and you know him? He's been spotted more times than Elvis!" Kelly scoffed.

"He died last June, but, shoot, it was too hot

to hike out of the canyons until the weather changed last week. So here I am, just like he instructed."

"He gave you instructions?"

"Look at the last page . . . a note from Harrison himself. He gave it to me for a Christmas present last year. Wanted me to have half the royalties, and the rest goes to his relatives."

"He doesn't have any relatives! You should have made up a better story," Kelly objected.

"No kiddin'? That means it all goes to me, I guess. He said there might not be anyone left alive."

"He didn't ever have any relatives! I mean, they died before he wrote a thing. That's why the title *Alone at the Edge of the Universe*. I don't know where you got this letter or this manuscript," Lynda continued, "but I'll look at it this weekend and talk to you about it on Monday."

"Lynda . . . this is nuts!" Kelly protested.

"I'm not leavin' it here without the money!"

"I'll give you a receipt. You've got these security guards for witnesses. Your manuscript will be here on Monday — I can guarantee you."

"No money?"

"Not until we decide to accept the manuscript. That's the way it's done with everyone. Those are the rules of the publishing business. Either that or the police will come and cut those handcuffs and take you to jail. What's it going to be?"

"I need some money." The man's voice softened dramatically. "I, eh . . . spent everything just to get here from Arizona . . . and I was — "

"Oh, now it comes out. He's a bum or a dead-beat," Kelly interrupted.

Lynda stared at the letter signed by G. L. Ramsey. "Kelly, I'm telling you, this cover letter and signature are authentic. We've just got to check it out. Where's Gossman when you need him?"

"Eh . . . on the golf course?" Sasser offered.

"Fondue, I'll read it. Spunky, how much you got in petty cash?"

The short receptionist slipped on her high heels and brushed her fingers through her long hair. "One hundred dollars, but I don't think Mr. Goss-man would allow me to use that much for anything but a real emergency."

"Mr. Gossman's not here, and this is an emergency. Mr. Fondue, I can give you a hundred bucks. That's not much for the city. Maybe you can find a cheap place for the weekend and buy something to eat. Now that's all I can do. Have we got a deal?"

"You got an extra room at your place? I could just stay with you and keep my eye on the manu-script."

"No! You are not staying with me!" Lynda barked. "You're on your own. Now will you do that? Or do I turn you over to the NYPD?"

"Let me see the receipt and the cash."

Lynda wrote a receipt on a piece of white typing paper and then took five twenty-dollar bills out of the gray metal box in Spunky's middle desk drawer.

14

"Are you satisfied? Now where's the key to the cuffs?"

"These? Oh, they don't really lock. Not since I chained myself to that tree and they busted them with a splitting mall." Fondue popped the handcuffs off his wrists and scooped up the receipt and the bills.

"What time do you open on Monday?"

"I'll be here by 8:30 A.M.," Lynda promised.

"Okay, I'll go." Felix Fondue walked toward the elevator with a security guard on his arm. Just as the door opened, he turned and called back, "Where's the Dakota House?"

"Upper west side. On 72nd across from Central Park."

"Thanks."

Fondue and the guard disappeared into the elevator, and a collective sigh of relief went up.

"Dakota House?" Nina frowned.

"Yeah, either he's going to spend the weekend with Lauren Bacall, or he's paying homage to John Lennon."

"Probably wants to toss some flowers on Strawberry Field," Sasser suggested. "I did that once. It was awesome. Those guys in the orange robes and shaved heads were there singing some kind of chant. It was almost like a religious experience. Know what I mean?"

Lynda Austin turned and stared at the short, olive-skinned receptionist. Spunky shrugged. "Eh . . . no, I guess you don't. Man, I'm glad to get that creep out of here. Did you smell him? He hadn't had a bath for weeks!"

"Spunky, are you going to be all right?"

"Me? Hey, I was in no danger. One more step and I would have spiked him!"

Kelly Princeton punched the security code, and the three women entered the inner offices of Atlantic-Hampton Publishing. Lynda stuck her head into Stan Silverman's office.

"Thanks for coming out and helping, Stanley!"

"My word, I'm an editor! Get the assistants to handle the walk-in traffic."

"Yeah, and I'm an editor, too . . . or hadn't you heard?"

"Close the door on your way out. If this Margaret Poston mystery is late to the printers, it won't be my fault! With all this confusion, it's almost impossible to work."

Kelly stopped with Lynda at her office door. "Are you really going to take that thing home and read it?"

"Yes."

"I thought you and James were going to a wedding up at Bridgeport."

"Oh . . . you're right! His cousin's getting married again. Oh well, it can't take all that long to read this manuscript."

"You know it's a phony. There's no way Harrison could have been alive all these years. Last June? That would have made Harrison in his nineties."

"I'm telling you, that cover letter is real. He had to get that somewhere. I think by Monday

16

morning I'm going to have a lot of questions for Mr. Felix Fondue."

"Can you believe that name?"

"No, but he's not the only one in this city with a phony name."

"How can you be so sure the cover letter is authentic?" Kelly pressed.

"The signature."

"You mean, you think that's Ramsey's signature."

"I know it is."

"How can you be so certain?"

"I knew G. L. Ramsey pretty well."

"You really knew him?"

"Her."

"Her?"

"Grace Loving Ramsey."

"Ramsey was a woman? I thought . . . I mean, I didn't know there were any women editors until the war."

"Now you know."

"Are you sure about that?"

"Yeah. I'm sure. She was my grandmother."

Lynda Austin left Kelly Princeton standing with her mouth open at the door to her office.

The city was turning the neon rainbow of early evening by the time Lynda Austin hiked from the subway to the entrance of her apartment building. The concrete sidewalk was hard and dirty, and the stale aroma of exhaust fumes hung in the air.

A uniformed man met her at the door. "Evenin', Miss Lynda."

"Good evening, Howard. How have you been?"

"Worried sick all day, that's what. Colleen didn't come home last night."

"Colleen must be about twenty, isn't she?"

"Yes, ma'am. On July 14. But her mama and daddy still worry about her. I pray to God that she's safe."

"I'll pray for her, too, Howard."

"Thank you, Miss Lynda. I surely appreciate it. You need some help with those bundles? You been out shopping, or are you just bringing home work?"

"I'm afraid it's all work, Howard. But I can carry them."

"Well, now . . . if you don't mind me sayin' so — if you keep working every weekend, how in the world are you ever going to have time to find a husband?" The genial guard broke into a wide smile that revealed a perfect set of gleaming white teeth. "Now I know a young attorney up on the ninth floor who used to be a minor league ballplayer. Maybe I could . . ."

Lynda Austin took a deep breath and began to laugh. "Howard, thanks for looking after me."

"An attractive young woman who doesn't have a mama . . . Well, I figure you might miss the naggin'. If I get to be a pest, you say, 'Howard, shut your mouth!' Anyway, thanks for carin' about Colleen. Most folks in this building can't remember my name — let alone my kids."

"Everybody's kind of busy, I suppose."

"No one's busier than you, Miss Lynda. No, ma'am . . . no one's busier than you."

She reached the sixth-floor three-bedroom apartment and punched the doorbell. She hoped Janie was still home so that she wouldn't have to set down her bags and hunt for a key. The door swung open, and a tall blonde in a black slip and bare feet greeted her with a smile.

"Hi, girl! How's New York's finest editor?"

"Tired. Janie, it's been a long, weird day. How about you? When's your flight?"

"Leaving La Guardia at 8:20. I'm out the door as soon as I pull on my uniform."

"You going to Frankfurt?"

"Amsterdam . . . then Frankfurt . . . layover three days and then do the return. I think I'll be back next Friday. You want me to call?"

"No, that's not necessary." Austin dropped her bundles on the leather armchair, reached down, and pulled off her shoes, and then headed for her bedroom. "I didn't get any groceries. Do we have anything in the fridge?"

"I brought home a broccoli and walnut pasta salad. You'll need to finish it up," Janie shouted from the other room.

Changed into her old dark blue University of Michigan sweats, Lynda was rummaging through the kitchen when Janie McCallister buzzed into the room, pecked her on the cheek, and scooted for the front door.

"Adios, kiddo. Be good, you hear? You want

me to bring you something?"

"The same thing as always would be nice."

"Lynda D. Austin, you already own every perfume known to man."

"I bet you can find me something new," Lynda teased. "Let them mix up a European special."

"You've got to be the best-smelling single girl in New York. I'll see you Friday."

Austin opened the living room curtains and glanced out at the lights of the city. She stared down at the street below and waited until she saw Howard help Janie into a yellow cab.

Well, Lord, be with Janie. Bring her home safely. She's like family to me. And Colleen . . . Help Howard and Millie not to worry so much about her. And please help Colleen not to make so many dumb decisions!

She plopped down in the overstuffed green leather chair and took another bite of salad from the plate in her hand. Then she set it on the end table and picked up the big, brown envelope she had labeled " 'With the Wind in My Face,' Martin Taylor Harrison — maybe."

The salad remained unfinished until 11:38 P.M. when she stood up and went to the bathroom to wash her face and pick up a box of tissues. She shuffled back into the living room, turned out the lights, and picked up the salad. With just the city glow illuminating the room, she stepped to the window intending to draw the curtains. Instead, she stared out at the visual noise of New York.

20

This book's phenomenal. It's stunning. It catches you by surprise. Then just when you want to back away, you find yourself racing to see how it ends. You can't stop. . . . It's like running downhill.

Maybe it is the real thing. Won't that make heads turn! Grandma would know! I wish she was still around. I wish she could see me now. It doesn't seem fair that she never even knew I became an editor for Atlantic-Hampton.

I've got to talk to Fondue. His story's too improbable to be true, and this manuscript is too incredible not to be authentic!

She gazed out the window awhile longer and then closed the curtains and padded toward her bedroom. Slipping out of her sweats, she tugged on a long, dark burgundy silk nightgown and parked herself in front of the bathroom sink.

Well, there you are, Lynda Dawn Austin . . . thirty years old, five foot ten, dark brown hair, big green eyes, light skin slightly freckled, smeared eye shadow, long neck, small bust, physically run down, and emotionally drained. Just another week, kid.

"Kelly's right. . . . I need a vacation. I can always go down to Largo . . . maybe in a couple weeks when I get that O'Brian novel done and . . . and this! Good grief, what if this is a Martin Taylor Harrison? That could keep me tied up for a long time!"

When she finished cleaning her face and brushing her teeth, she tugged on some fluffy bunny slippers and scooted back out into the dark living room. Fumbling to find the light switch by the sofa, she plopped herself down and reached for the heavy stack of manuscript paper.

Maybe I'll glance at chapter 3 again. It will knock their socks off! No one ever guessed he'd handle it that way! Talk about a turnaround!

Chapter 3 caused her to reread chapter 4 . . . and 5 . . . and 6 . . . and . . .

A persistent ringing and pounding sound caused Lynda Austin to roll over on the couch and crash to the floor.

"Who's that? What time is it? Morning? Oh . . . no! Nine? It can't be!"

She ran to the front door.

"Who is it?" she called out.

"It's me — James."

"Jimmy? Oh . . . no!"

"Open up, dear. I feel like a jerk standing out here banging on the door. The neighbors are staring."

"Oh . . . just a minute . . . just a minute."

Austin ran for her bedroom and crashed into a magazine stand sending *New Yorker*s and *National Geographic*s sliding across the polished hardwood floor.

"What's going on in there? What's happening?"

"Just a minute!" She grabbed a thick, fluffy burgundy bathrobe and pulled it over her gown as she ran back for the door, leaving her shoes scattered somewhere near the couch.

"Lynda! Open up immediately!" James shouted.

Throwing the deadbolt, she sighed and swung open the white-paneled door.

"Lynda! What's going on? Look at you! You look like you just got up. We've got to leave in ten minutes. Man, I can't believe this!"

"I must have . . . you know . . . worked late. And then I, eh, I think I overslept!"

"What happened to this room? And you . . . you look awful!"

"Eh . . . well . . . you look nice, Jimmy." She glanced up at his short-cropped black hair and his narrow, piercing eyes. "Of course, you always look nice in a tux."

"Lynda . . . good grief, did you stay up all night partying? I can't believe you did this to me! You knew how important this wedding is to me. Do you have a hangover?"

"Jimmy, you know I don't drink," she snapped.

"Are you going to make it to Kristie's wedding or not? I thought last weekend at the concert when you spent the second half in the lobby talking to that Italian author was bad enough . . . but this! Lynda, don't you ever think about us? No one cares that much about work!"

"Oh, Jimmy, you've got to forgive me. I just, eh . . . look, I can't make it to your — "

"This is incredible!" he boomed. "We've been planning this for weeks and weeks. My mother was going to introduce you to everyone. Last night she called me, all excited about having you come along. How am I going to explain this to my mother?"

"Jimmy, I'm really sorry. Apologize to your dear mother. And tell Kristie I'll be at her next wedding — I promise."

"That's not funny."

"I'm tired, Jimmy, really tired. I stayed up all night with a possible Martin Taylor Harrison."

"With whom?"

"With a man-u-script. Remember? I'm an editor."

"Oh, sure, you worked all night dressed like that?"

Lynda glanced down and saw that her bathrobe had slipped open revealing the thin lace bodice of her silk gown, which was obviously turned inside out. She quickly pulled the bathrobe up tight under her chin.

"Yes, I was dressed like this! Something came up at work yesterday afternoon, and it tied me up all night. I didn't know this would happen. I'm on the verge of an incredible literary discovery. I'm sorry, Jimmy. What else can I say?"

Flush-faced and stiff-collared, he looked around the room. "Why didn't you open the door sooner? I don't get it. Is Janie here?"

"She flew to Europe last night."

"No one's here?"

"What are you getting at?" she demanded.

"You don't have some guy here with you, do you? I mean, if there's some other guy, now's the time to say so."

"What did you say?" she yelled.

"I said," he shouted, "have you got some man

in your bedroom?"

Her open right palm caught the side of his face with a resounding slap that caused him to stagger back.

"Don't you ever accuse me of sleeping around, James St. John!" she shouted. "Look in there . . . look in there! That bed is still made. I haven't even been in there, let alone anyone else! The only thing I slept with was that manuscript scattered all over the floor. Now get out of here!"

"Look, Lynda, I didn't really mean . . . I was hurt. I just can't believe you'd put your work before us . . ."

"Get out!"

"I know you're tired and upset," he stammered. "But I think you owe me — "

"Get out, Jimmy, before I call Howard to throw you out!"

"This isn't real! It's a bad dream, right?" James St. John threw his hands in the air and stomped to the door. "Cynthia was right about you! This is exactly what she told me. All you ever intended on doing was stringing me along."

Lynda slammed the door behind him and immediately threw the deadbolt. Then she slumped to the floor and leaned against the wall. She could feel the tears slide down her cheeks.

I'm no good at this. I've been making boys mad at me ever since I was six. I just can't do it. I can't be whatever it is they want me to be! James never gets mad at anyone, and he was screaming at me. It's like I bring out the worst in every man. Cynthia?

Cynthia! He's never let go of her. What does he do — call her after every date?

She spent the next half-hour standing in the shower, allowing the water to mix with the tears. It wasn't until the water started to turn cold that she wrapped herself in the fluffy bathrobe. She pulled back the hunter-green quilted bedspread and slid between the beige sheets.

The clock by her bed showed 3:36 P.M. when she blinked her eyes open. She spent the rest of the afternoon and evening trying to contact L. George Gossman, editorial director for Atlantic-Hampton.

It turned out to be Sunday after church before she reached him and explained the entire situation. They agreed to a Monday morning conference. She spent the rest of the afternoon jogging through Central Park, trying to figure out what to do next with James.

It's over.

How could he say those things? It's like he doesn't know me at all. Three years, and he doesn't know me at all. What's wrong with me, Lord? Why can't I attract a guy who understands?

When she got back to the condo, she put on an exercise video but spent most of the hour lying on her back in front of the television, staring at the living room ceiling.

The first thing Lynda Austin saw when she stepped out of the elevator Monday morning was

Spunky Sasser wearing a tight red leather wrap-around dress and earrings that glittered like disco ballroom light fixtures.

"He's here," Spunky announced.

"Who?"

"Fondue."

"Already? Where is he?"

"In your office."

"My office?"

"You're the one who promised to meet him, right? I didn't want him hanging around out here. You know, we have standards to keep."

"Yeah . . . well, look, Spunky, arrange for some coffee and muffins to be sent to the small conference room in about an hour. We'll be meeting there. Are Nina and Kelly here yet?"

"Nope."

"Well, when they come in, tell them to see me before they get too busy."

Austin turned toward the metal security door that led out of the lobby to the offices. Then she whipped back around. "Spunky! Is that a new dress?"

"Isn't it something?"

"Ah . . . well, it's certainly something. What did Mr. Hampton say about it?"

"Which one?"

"Senior."

"I think he liked it. He just shook his head and mumbled about never in his life had he ever seen anything quite like it. And Junior? Junior said it was absolutely staggering!"

27

Lynda Austin punched in the security codes and entered the office area. T. H. Hampton, IV, better known as Junior behind his back, met her in the hall.

"Ms. Austin, what about this meeting this morning? I got a call at the club yesterday from Gossman. Do you really need someone from the legal department to be there?"

"Yes, sir, there might be a slew of legal questions to go over."

"Do you think Metzer could handle it for us?"

"I'd really like you or Mr. Hampton, Sr., to be there. If this turns out to be authentic, it could be the publishing event of the century."

"Yes . . . yes, I suppose. Say, is Ms. Sasser going to sit in on this one?"

"Spunky? Eh, no, she won't be there. Why?"

"Nothing, nothing . . . that's fine. I'll be there. But I have a lunch appointment at eleven, so I'll probably have to cut out early."

She stepped toward her office and was greeted with a shout. "Have you got it?"

"Mr. Fondue!"

"Have you got the manuscript?"

"Right here." She held up the large envelope.

"I'll carry it. I couldn't sleep worrying about it all weekend. I should have never left it here. It reminds me of the time I lent my Janis Joplin autograph to Kenny Welch. I never saw Kenny again — ever."

She handed Fondue the package. "We're going to meet with you in a few minutes in the conference room on the north side of this floor. Why don't you go down there and have a cup of coffee and some muffins and wait for us?"

"Can I take the manuscript with me?"

"Certainly."

"Do you have decaf?"

"The decanter with the orange handle."

"Is it mechanical or chemical?"

"What?"

"Did they remove the caffeine mechanically or chemically? It makes a difference, you know."

"Eh . . . well, I really couldn't say."

"Are the muffins low-fat? Were they made with brown sugar? You don't use white flour, do you?"

"Mr. Fondue, I really have no idea, but why don't you go check them out?"

"I'll do that." Fondue scuffed his way down the hall in his sandals, shorts, and tie-dyed T-shirt.

A moment later Nina DeJong stuck her head through the doorway. "Did you know that Fondue was down in the conference room?"

"Yes, we're having a meeting at 9:30 with him. Can you be there?"

"You want me there?"

"If this looks authentic, it will take a couple of us to check it out."

"What do you think? Is it for real?"

"It's an extremely haunting book. But there are lots of questions to ask first."

"Vanilla Musk. Right?"

"My perfume? Eh, this one is called Tempestuous Orchid."

29

"Boy, don't give any to Spunky. All the guys are hanging around the lobby drooling as it is. Talk about a power dress. Where do you suppose she buys her clothes?"

"Frederick's of Hollywood?"

Nina tilted her head sideways. "Do you think I ought to get a dress like that?"

"Absolutely not!"

The light from the window revealed a sunny day somewhere above the towers of concrete and glass as eight representatives of Atlantic-Hampton Publishing Company sat watching Felix Fondue consume raisin bran muffins and listening to Lynda Austin's report. Besides Lynda, Nina, and Kelly, there were L. George Gossman from editorial; T. H. Hampton, IV, representing the legal department; Jacob Metzer, vice-president of operations; Wyman Williams, director of marketing; and Julie Quick, Hampton's administrative assistant.

After Lynda presented her detailed evaluation of the manuscript, she turned to Felix Fondue. "We're interested in hearing about your relationship with the author and how you acquired the manuscript. Could you tell us about that?"

"Okay, now look, this has got to be confidential. No tape recorders, video cameras, or anything. Is this room bugged?"

"Mr. Fondue," L. George Gossman assured him, "there are no tape recorders here. Now could you please tell us about your involvement with this manuscript? Is your real name Fondue?"

"Nobody's real name is Fondue. But that's another story. Okay . . . let's see . . . I first moved into the Strip in 1978. I was — "

"The Strip?" Austin quizzed.

"The Arizona Strip. You know — that part of Arizona north of the Colorado River. Anyway, it's called the Arizona Strip."

"Where was your home before that?"

"Oh, I lived here and there . . . wherever I was needed. Anyway, I was sort of . . . needing a remote place to stay."

Metzer pulled off his dark-rimmed glasses. "You mean the police were after you?"

"No, man. Let's just say I needed some space to clear my mind — some inner healing. So I headed out to the canyons. I was looking for a friend of mine named Arkansas Bowie. He had been out there ever since the Manson thing."

"He was part of Charles Manson's 'family'?" Kelly gasped.

"Only in the old days. Anyways, he was afraid some of them would come after him for that incident at Atascadero. Don't you ever think they're all in prison. No way! They're out there." He squeezed a muffin so hard that he ended up with a handful of crumbs.

"Anyway, on my way to find Bowie I got lost just past Mt. Trumbull. There are very few trails down there, so I wandered around in circles for a couple of days. I'm telling you, that is the end of the earth. But good vibes — if you can stay

31

alive. I think it's the karma of the place. You know what I mean?"

"Eh, not really." Lynda shrugged.

"Well . . . anyway, I was just about to starve to death when Harry found me."

"Harry?" Gossman questioned.

"Martin Taylor Harrison. At the time all he told me was that his name was Harry."

Austin laid her pen down and stared at Fondue's nervous, narrow eyes. "You've been living down in Arizona with this man Harry for over sixteen years?"

"Yeah, isn't that something? Anyway, he's got this cool little place half-carved right into the side of a canyon wall — sort of like the Anazasi cliff dwellings, only it's right on the floor of this box canyon with a natural spring not more than fifty feet from the door. He told me he was a prospector. Well, he says I can rest up a few days with him, and I stayed, eh . . . sixteen years."

"That's a lot of rest," Kelly blurted out.

"He was getting older and couldn't tend the garden too well, so I did chores, and we fished and talked, you know."

"For sixteen years?"

"Eh . . . yeah."

"Where did you get your supplies? Did you have a car or something?"

"A car? Get real, man. Oh, if we needed a little salt or flour or coffee, Harry would have me hike out to the highway and hitch a ride."

32

"You mean no one ever drives back into those canyons?"

"Oh, once in a while a BLM rig will scout around, but Harry tried to avoid them. He was always afraid they would toss him out of there."

"BLM?" T. H. Hampton, IV, questioned.

"Bureau, man — the Bureau of Land Management. Most all of it's Bureau land. Anyway, it turned out that Harry didn't prospect very much. Just when we needed supplies, he'd dig up a pinch or two of gold from out of the mine. Then I'd make my way into Rincon and buy supplies from Marlowe."

"Rincon is a town in Arizona?"

"Yeah . . . sort of."

"Sort of?"

Fondue threw up his hands. "Hey, now that's a strange place!"

"Yes, yes," Mr. Hampton pressed, "but when did you discover that this man claimed to be Martin Taylor Harrison?"

"I didn't. I never even thought about it. I didn't ask him if he was Harrison, and he didn't ask me if I was James Dean. I mean, the subject never entered my mind."

"What did he tell you about himself?" Austin asked.

"Well, he just said he'd been down in the canyons since the depression, and that's all I knew. Anyway, he had this old upright typewriter, you know, one of those old-time Royals? For a long time he would peck around most every afternoon,

33

but he never showed me his work. I'd bring him a ream of paper or a ribbon from time to time when I made it out for supplies. But that was about it. Of course, I don't suppose I've seen him type for the past several years or so. I guess he had it finished."

"How did he die?"

"Well, about this time last year he got a cough that just wouldn't go away. He was a rugged old man, I mean to tell you. But this thing was getting him down. I told him we should hike out to the highway and find a doctor. But he insisted he was too old for the hike."

"How long of a walk was it?"

"About three days."

"Three days?" Nina gasped.

"It's a hundred miles, mostly uphill. I told you this was a remote spot."

"Okay, so this . . . Harry was getting sick. Then what?"

"Well, right before Christmas he hauls out this manuscript and some letters and tells me what to do with them after he dies. Now I see the name on the manuscript, and I just about croak. I mean, everybody has read the first two chapters of that book, right? I mean, every college in America uses it as a text, but to think that this really was Martin Taylor Harrison . . . Well, it was a shock.

"Then in January he decided I should hike out to Fredonia and get the whole thing photocopied for him. The original is pretty cracked and yellowed. But the old man was sharp. He made me copy it in two trips. The first time out he gave me every other page. On the second trip I took the rest. I guess he didn't want to tempt me to take off with it."

Lynda Austin ran her fingers through the back of her hair and fanned it up and down. "Mr. Fondue, where is the original of the manuscript?"

"In Harry's cabin down in the canyon. I sure didn't want to hike out of there carrying twice as many pages. Anyway, Harry never did recover from that cough. I doctored him the best I could all spring. I even got some herbs and medicines from Sundown Jack, but it didn't — "

"Who?"

"Sundown Jack — a Kaibab Paiute. Anyway, around the first of June, Harry goes to meet his Maker. He just didn't wake up one morning. So I buried him like I promised."

"You filed a report with the county coroner, I presume?" Hampton quizzed.

"Look, I told you this is all confidential. I buried him — that's all! But June's too hot to hike out of there, and I spent most of the summer trying to squeeze out a little gold from Harry's diggings. I didn't have much luck, just a pinch or two. Anyway, last week I made it to the highway, rode east with some deadheads in a van, and, well, here I am. When do I get the ten thousand dollars?"

Editorial Director L. George Gossman stood and paced the room, rubbing his slightly graying beard. "Mr., eh . . . Fondue, I'm sure you can appreciate the fact that we will have to substantiate the authenticity of this manuscript before any money is paid out. We will have to check the handwriting of the letter. And examine the text itself. Now based on Ms. Austin's review, we will make this a high priority. But, in all honesty, it could take weeks of examining the text before we could come to some decision on publishing it."

"I'm not leaving this with you for weeks. You could have the whole thing printed and sold by then!"

"It is not our intention nor our policy to pirate anyone's manuscript," Gossman huffed. "I can assure you, we will — "

"I'm not leaving it with you!" Fondue's voice raised with each word.

"There is no way we can work with this," Hampton grumped, looking at his watch.

Jumping to his feet, Fondue waved the manuscript above his head. "Yeah, well, maybe I'll just shop it around and see if anyone else is interested."

"Eh . . . Mr. Fondue," Lynda put in quickly, "since Atlantic-Hampton is the publisher of the two known novels by Martin Taylor Harrison, we, of course, would like to print the third. If, indeed, this is the third. Now could we photocopy the handwritten letter, the cover letter, and just chapter 3? I think we could go a long way in evaluation with that much."

"What do I get out of it?"

"In exchange for, say, one thousand dollars expense money."

"One thousand dollars!" Gossman choked. "Ms.

Austin, you do not have the authority to offer — "

"Wait a minute, George," Hampton interrupted. "Hear her out."

"I believe the manuscript is highly publishable, no matter who wrote it. Now if it's not a Harrison, we can still bring it out and recoup the one thousand dollars."

"She's right, Gossman," Hampton insisted. "But don't call it an expense. Call it part of the advance. I've got to scoot to lunch. Cut him a check, George, and let Ms. Austin verify this thing. But I don't want this getting out on the street. I can't begin to describe how valuable this will be if it's proven to be Harrison's. And I can't begin to count how many would lose their jobs if we claim it's authentic and later have to admit it's a forgery. Is that clear to everyone?"

"Yes, sir." Gossman nodded. "Eh, Mr. Fondue, does this sound like a reasonable arrangement?"

"One week. I'll give you one week to verify it. Then I want all the money that's coming to me."

"One week?" Gossman huffed. "We can't possibly — "

"I think we can have some information by then," Austin interrupted. "I know the woman who runs the Martin Taylor Harrison Library down in Key West. Perhaps we'll know enough by Monday whether to continue the investigation. Can Nina and Kelly help me?"

"For one week — that's all," Gossman agreed. "Have we got a deal?"

Fondue sorted through the papers in the thick manila envelope. He pulled out chapter 3 and shoved it at Lynda Austin. "Go make your copies. I'll be back here next Monday. Also, I need the money in cash. There's no one in this city who would cash a check of mine."

"Eh," Gossman stammered, "well, eh . . . I think we could have that by this afternoon. You'll have to sign a limited agreement."

"A what?"

"An agreement that you won't take our one thousand dollars and give the manuscript to some other publisher before next Monday."

"Yeah, well, whatever. Anyway, I'll wait in the lobby."

"Holding the manuscript in his lap, no doubt," Kelly Princeton mumbled under her breath.

At 12:03 Kelly tugged Lynda out of her office and after gathering Nina, the three were on the sidewalk headed for lunch. "Nina, why do you always take those things?" Kelly complained as she and Lynda waited for their blonde co-worker to catch up. "This is New York City. There's a nut on every corner. You don't have to take everything that's shoved at you."

"But he — he handed it to me. How could I refuse?"

"What do you do with them?"

"Well . . . I, you know . . . throw them in the trash in the lobby."

"That's my point. You've got to learn to shine

'em on. Right, Lynda?"

"Kelly's right, Nina. Never smile, never offer a kind word unless you're expecting a tip, and never *ever* take a flier from someone working the streets. It's the New York way! This isn't Wisconsin."

"Sometimes I can't really believe I'm in the city."

Kelly turned and walked backwards as they hurried up Madison Avenue. "You know what I can't believe? I can't believe Lynda hasn't taken her vacation yet. What are you waiting for? Even L. G. had a vacation already."

"I told you, I'm tied up on the latest O'Brian manuscript. It's a mess . . . and the great Terrance O'Brian's sailing to Hawaii in some race. I have to wait for him to call in. I can't leave until I get it cleaned up. And now there's this Fondue thing."

"Ah . . . the exciting life of the New York book editor." Kelly sighed. "Temperamental authors, boring co-workers, demanding bosses — "

"What do you mean, boring co-workers?" Nina complained.

"Oh, present company excluded, of course."

"No, really, be honest. Lynda, is Kelly right? Am I boring? Maybe I should change my hair color. Nobody takes me seriously as a blonde." Nina studied her reflection in a store window.

"Most of the guys in the office take you seriously. In fact . . . ," Kelly started, but Lynda's frown silenced her.

"If I colored it brown, got it cut short, and wore thick-rimmed glasses," Nina continued, "maybe then I would get more respect."

"You'd look just like Barbara Washburn!" Kelly cried. "Talk about bor—ing!"

"You know what I like about walking to Barton's for lunch?" Lynda parked herself at the front of the crowd waiting for the light to change on 37th Street.

"It's not the Reuben sandwich, that's for sure," Kelly teased.

"It's the only time of the day sunlight ever reaches the street. In an hour it will be gone behind the buildings. That's where I've got to go on my vacation — someplace where the sun always shines!"

" 'I got to fly to St. Somewhere. . . .' " Kelly broke into song and danced her way across the intersection, causing several tourists to stop and stare.

"What?"

"You know . . . Jimmy Buffett? 'I've got to go where it's warm!' Hey, L. G. went to Antigua. Why don't you go there?"

"Because I can't afford it. My condo eats up this fabulous New York salary."

"I heard L. G. wrote it off as a business trip," Kelly announced.

"How does he do that? Didn't his wife and kids go with him?" Nina asked.

"Don't ask." Lynda glanced at her gold-banded wristwatch and quickened the pace. "Besides, it sounds pretty boring all by myself. Anyway, I can't go somewhere that the editorial director goes."

"Is there a rule about that?" Nina asked, stopping to collect a sea green flier from a short lady wearing a "Save the Gila Monsters!" sweat shirt.

"Listen, did you two hear that George got his wallet stolen while on vacation?" Lynda quizzed.

"In Antigua?"

"No. Before he left the city. Isn't that a lousy deal?"

"Couldn't happen to a nicer guy!" Kelly held the door of the green and white deli open as the others entered.

"Come on, Kell. George is all right — 'one of the best in the business,' according to *Publisher's Weekly*."

"Well, he knows the business, but I still wouldn't want him for a neighbor."

"Yeah," Nina added, "I don't think I could ever completely trust a man who wears elevator shoes and a cheap toupee."

Lynda scooted into line at the counter where one of the clerks was shouting something in Greek. Jostled by other customers on both sides of her, she turned back to Kelly and Nina. "Maybe you two are right."

"About Mr. Gossman?" Nina asked.

"No . . . about me needing a vacation. I definitely need a break from all this!"

After a hurried half a Reuben sandwich and cup of clam chowder, Lynda found herself leading the troops back up Madison Avenue.

At 2:34 P.M. she stepped out to the lobby to hand Felix Fondue an envelope containing fifty twenty-dollar bills. Several men were leaning against the counter visiting with Spunky Sasser.

"Where's Fondue?"

"In the men's room, I think."

"And the manuscript?"

"He took it with him."

Within ten minutes Felix Fondue walked out onto Madison Avenue carrying one thousand dollars. Austin held a photocopy of the 1930 letter from G. L. Ramsey, all forty-three pages of chapter 3, and a handwritten letter signed "Martin Taylor Harrison."

TWO

At 3:45 P.M. the editorial director of Atlantic-Hampton stuck his head into Lynda Austin's office.

"Sasser said you wanted to see me before I left."

Shoving a stack of papers to the side of her desk, she glanced up and sighed. "Are you leaving now? I needed to go over some plans on this Harrison manuscript verification."

L. George Gossman glanced at his watch. "I've got ten minutes."

"Yeah . . . well, here's what I project. I'll need Kelly to spend the week trying to run down everything we can find out about this guy, Fondue."

"Where are you going to start?"

"California. San Francisco State University. Mendocino County Sheriff, and Mojave County authorities out in Arizona."

"Have you got contacts out there?"

"William Bucknell, the ex-cop who writes those mysteries. I'm hoping he can find something."

George Gossman walked over to a chair by her desk and plopped down. "Have her check with Terry Lavine." He leaned over and meticulously retied each shoelace.

"Terry Lavine — who writes cookbooks?"

"Yeah. He was an SDS radical in the sixties and seventies — arrested at the Democratic Convention and all that. Could be that he's heard of someone named . . . Fondue. I can't believe anyone would purposely want to be called Felix Fondue."

"He's a little strange, but that might happen to anyone living in the desert for that many years. I'll have Kelly contact Lavine. Also, I'll need Nina to pull all the files and search all the records for anything we can find out about Harrison's disappearance. What with the crazy made-for-TV movie about him and everything, it's hard to separate fact from fiction. We still have some old records around, don't we?"

"She'll have to go search the warehouse files."

"I know. That's what I told her."

"She should dig through the newspaper accounts as well. I sort of remember the *Times* doing a fifty-years-ago type of feature back in the early eighties."

"Yes, and I'll have her pull out anything that's been in *Time, Newsweek, The Wall Street Journal, The New Yorker* . . . and the others."

Gossman crossed his legs and leaned back, stretching his hands behind his head. "Have her pull the publishing history of the first two of his books. We need to see how many copies are still selling. Book clubs, collegiate editions, etc."

"I'll have her get the figures."

Sitting up straight, L. George Gossman nonchalantly straightened his toupee and reset his glasses. "So what does that leave you to do?"

"I'll see if the Harrison Library in Key West can fax a copy of Harrison's handwriting. I'll use Lamont D'Angelo to analyze it. His testimony stood up in the serial killer's court trial last summer."

"Why don't you go to Key West and check that third chapter out with the folks down there first-hand? You need a little vacation anyway."

"Mr. Gossman, going to the Harrison Library is not a vacation. But you're right. I should go. In fact, if you'll sign this requisition for expenses, I'll have Spunky find me a flight tomorrow."

"You're leaving tomorrow?"

"I've got to be back Friday so we can put something together for Fondue by Monday. That doesn't leave much time."

"Why don't you scout around south Florida for any old-timers who might have known Harrison. Maybe someone can tell us something about him that might be helpful. Although I would imagine all that can be said has already been published a dozen times." He leaned over the desk and scribbled an illegible signature across the bottom of the printed form. "Is that all you need me to sign?"

"That should do it."

"Okay. Look, Austin . . . do you honestly think this is a genuine Harrison?"

"If it isn't, it's the most incredible imitation ever concocted."

"Well, before you go flying off to Florida, run

45

me a copy of that chapter 3. I want to look at it."

"And be sure you review those first two chapters. I think *The Atlantic Monthly* reprinted them last April."

"Run me copies of that, too. It's been a few years." Gossman strolled toward the window, quoting, " 'I'd rather lose a lover than a principle of faith. A lover can be replaced, but, at best, faith . . .' How does it go?"

" 'Faith only comes back as a weak, ineffective brother-in-law of the original. One you can hardly wait to show the door,' " Austin finished for him. "Every English 1A student in America had to memorize that."

"Yes . . . well, I must scoot. Listen, if this is a Harrison, I want you to know up front that I'll handle the editorial chores. I just couldn't pass this up. You understand, don't you?"

"Mr. Gossman, I'm sure I'll do the same thing when I'm editorial director."

"You really have your eyes set on that, don't you?"

"Yes."

"It might be a long time."

"Or a short time. You land the lost manuscript of Martin Taylor Harrison, and Mr. Hampton, Sr., just might give you your own imprint."

"Now there's an intriguing thought." Gossman walked to the door and then spun back around. "Say, Lynda, give me your opinion . . . as a woman. Is it permissible for us to ask Ms. Sasser not to wear that dress to work? I mean, will we be opening ourselves up for a lawsuit from the National Organization for Women?"

"I don't know about that, but Mr. Hampton, Jr., will be extremely displeased — that's for sure."

"He likes it, no doubt."

"He spent most of the day with his tongue hanging out to his chin."

"Enough said. I'm not about to stand in the way of lust. Will you be coming in tomorrow?"

"Not if I can get Kelly and Nina lined up this afternoon and find a flight early in the morning. I'll call in and let you know how things are going. If that guy Fondue happens to stop by or call during the week, find out where we can reach him. We sent him out the door and have no way of contacting him."

"Yeah, that thought dawned on me, too. I'll tell Spunky to be on the lookout."

Austin laughed. "You'll have to wait in line. The lobby has been strangely crowded all day."

It was 6:18 P.M. before Lynda Austin, Nina DeJong, and Kelly Princeton concluded their planning session.

"You'll call in each day at three?" DeJong asked.

"Right . . . Kelly, if anyone hears from Fondue, tell him the Monday meeting will be at 2:00 P.M. We'll have a staff meeting that morning. Set that for 9:00 — if you can get Mr. Hampton there."

"Senior or Junior?" DeJong asked.

Lynda Austin raised her eyebrows. "Both . . .

47

if Senior feels well enough. They will both want in on it when we announce to the world that we have an authentic Harrison." Lynda gathered up a stack of papers on her desk and slipped them inside the brown leather briefcase. "Is anyone left in the office to close up?"

"I think Mr. Alvarez is still in his office, but I'm not sure," Princeton replied.

"Has anyone seen Frank face to face for the past several weeks?"

"I haven't seen him since June!" Nina DeJong shrugged.

Austin shut down her computer and flipped the surge suppressor switch off with her toe. Then she reached down to pull on her shoes.

"Oh, wow! I forgot to ask. How was the wedding?" Kelly Princeton blurted out.

"Wedding?"

"James's cousin — or something. Didn't you have a — "

"Oh . . . right. That whole thing was a disaster."

"The wedding?"

"No, the relationship!"

Nina DeJong's eyes grew wide. "What happened at the wedding?"

"Who knows? I didn't go."

"But I thought . . ."

"I stayed up all night reading that crazy Harrison manuscript and was sound asleep when Jimmy got there. He blew up and accused me of all sorts of things, and I — "

"James St. John blew up? You mean, he got

mad and raised his voice?"

"Screaming, yelling — the whole works."

Kelly shook her head. "I never ever heard that man get upset over anything."

"What did he accuse you of?" Nina pressed.

"Oh, he asked if the reason I wasn't ready was because I had some guy in my apartment all night."

"James said that?" Kelly exclaimed incredulously.

"Then what happened?" Nina asked.

"He left, I went to sleep, and I've been pushing on this project ever since."

"Did he call?"

"James?"

"Yeah."

"Not yet."

"Are you going to call him?"

"I think I'll just go to Key West and try and sort it out next week. But I'm definitely not going to call him."

It was 11:15 P.M. when Lynda Austin picked up the telephone and slowly dialed the number of James St. John. She was startled when a female voice answered the phone. "Yes?"

"Eh . . . excuse me. I'm calling James St. John. Do I have the correct number?" Austin fumbled.

"Yes."

"Well, may I speak with Mr. St. John?"

There was a giggle on the other end of the line. "Now?"

49

"Yes, I know it's late, but I'm his . . . I'm a friend. Tell him it's Lynda."

"He can't talk to you now. You'll have to call back. Maybe next week. Then again — maybe not."

"What? Who is this? Look, I want to talk to Jimmy . . ."

Slowly she replaced the phone.

She hung up? This is really weird. Jimmy wouldn't . . . He's not the type to . . .

"Maybe I need to take a bath and go to bed," she mumbled, padding off to the back of the condo.

She spent the next thirty minutes soaking in Aurora Mist bubble bath and trying to decide what to do next about James St. John. She thought about him again on Wednesday at 1:15 P.M. while chewing on a cheeseburger and staring at a young man with a leashed iguana on his shoulder at the Margaritaville Cafe in Key West.

He came to mind again when she returned home and found a message on her answering machine from his mother asking if Jimmy was at her house. Janie had phoned in to say she was working a flight to San Francisco and would be home on Tuesday. Lynda got so swamped gathering together a report for the Monday staff meeting that James slipped her mind until 10:30 P.M.

She dialed the number.

Left a curt message on his machine.

And went to bed.

The navy blue tailored skirt had a tendency to

creep up on her thighs, and by the time Austin reached the lobby on the ground floor of 222 Madison Avenue, she regretted having worn it.

I'll be fighting this back down all day. I should just throw it away. Maybe I can give it to Janie. If I ever run out of Rose Mystique! This skirt's the only thing that goes with that perfume.

The book said never to mix scents until you dry-cleaned the clothing. Of course, the book said never have anything dry-cleaned.

She nodded at Spunky Sasser and scooted over to the security doors, but she glanced back at the receptionist as she pushed the code into the lock.

Western miniskirt, teal green boots, lace blouse and bolo — is she going to wear that hat all day? Spunky, you need to get married and settle down.

Yeah, Austin, look who's talking.

She hardly had time to brief Nina and Kelly before they gathered up their reports and hurried into the conference room. Austin placed Princeton and DeJong on each side of her at the round table and sat across from T. H. Hampton, Jr., and his aide, Julie Quick. L. George Gossman filtered in with a scowl and a stack of papers. Stan Silverman had the nerve to show up with a manuscript that he continued to edit throughout the meeting. Also present were Senior Editor Barbara Washburn, Vice-President of Operations Jake Metzer, and finally, about ten minutes late and looking a little pale, T. H. Hampton, Sr.

"Ms. Austin," Hampton, Jr., prompted, "I believe you're in charge of this presentation."

"Yes, sir. Nina will cover the background on Harrison, then Kelly will fill us in on Fondue, and then I'll give you the results of the handwriting tests and what I discovered at the Harrison Library in Key West. Nina."

Nina stood up and peered around the room. She was wearing her dark green power suit.

"To tell you all the truth, I'm a little nervous," Nina admitted. "I'm afraid you might know all of this already. So I'll try to make it brief. If I'm assuming too much, just interrupt me or . . . something. I'll be happy to slow down and give more details. Anyway," she paused, rubbing her nose with the open palm of her hand, "here goes. Martin Taylor Harrison was born on December 12, 1902, to Frank and Maddy Harrison in Butte, Montana. He was an only child, and his mother died in a flu epidemic in 1911. Harrison entered Stanford University at the age of sixteen. His father was killed in a train accident in 1920. Harrison took the insurance money, dropped out of Stanford, and went to Europe." DeJong stopped and looked around the table. "Is this too detailed?"

"No, no. Continue," Gossman urged.

"Okay. While in Europe he mostly lived in and around Paris — seemed to enjoy the company of the left-bank literary crowd and, eh, you know . . . the ladies. In 1926 at the age of twenty-four, he wrote *Alone at the Edge of the Universe.* As you all know, it was published by Atlantic-Hampton in the U.S. and by Hoffman Brothers in Great Britain. It was highly successful on the continent and in Great Britain, but sales were slow in the U.S."

"It was a little too radical for the times, I suppose," Barbara Washburn murmured.

"Yes . . . well, Mr. Harrison (who, so I read, was called Marty by his closest friends) sailed to the Caribbean in 1927 and ended up in Key West. In Paris he had become friends with Ernest Hemingway, who was having success with *The Sun Also Rises*. Hemingway let him stay at his place."

"Didn't Hemingway once say that Harrison was the most influential writer of the 1920s?" Gossman interjected.

Nina glanced over at the editorial director, who used both hands to straighten his wire-frame glasses. "Lots of people use that quote, but frankly I couldn't run it down. However, if Hemingway didn't say it, lots of other people did. Anyway, while in Florida he wrote *When the Last Rock Crumbles*, which, as we know, was a phenomenal success — and the main reason, so I'm told, that we have offices at 222 Madison Avenue. Of course, when *Last Rock* began to sell, *Alone* took off as well."

"Was that when he moved to California?" Austin quizzed.

"Exactly. With the new wealth, he moved to the central California coast and built a fine home overlooking the Pacific. He argued a lot with William Randolph Hearst and spent most of his time in Hollywood chasing actresses."

"When did he write those first two chapters of

'With the Wind in My Face'?" Mr. Hampton, Jr., asked.

Nina turned through several pages of her notebook. "While in California he wrote several short stories, which were critical successes, but they were so pessimistic about the future of the world that the public mainly rejected them."

"Have you ever read those?" Kelly blurted out. "They'll depress you for weeks! We don't still publish them, do we?"

"Only in the collegiate reader series," Gossman replied.

Nina lifted a blue file folder and pulled out several papers. "Now sometime while in California he wrote those famous first two chapters of the third book. That manuscript was to be published in early 1931, but by late summer of '30 he had only finished the first two chapters."

"Authors never change, do they?" Silverman looked up with his blue pencil in hand.

"On September 2, 1930, Harrison called his editor, G. L. Ramsey, here at Atlantic-Hampton and announced that he was taking a short research trip. That was interpreted to mean he was headed to L. A. to visit some starlet. It was the last time anyone ever talked to him.

"In January of 1931, the Boston Brothers Detective Agency of Chicago was hired by this company to track down Harrison. Extensive searching in California yielded no clues whatsoever. In 1937 he was declared legally dead, but no trace of him was ever found."

"Sort of like Jimmy Hoffa," Kelly Princeton interrupted.

"Well, needless to say, Martin Taylor Harrison went on to gain a tremendous following. Each of his books continues to sell close to fifty thousand copies a year, doing especially well with the university and anti-establishment crowd. There was a great resurgence of Harrison sales in the sixties and seventies.

"Although there have been many supposed sightings of Harrison all around the world, there's never been any proof. The first two chapters of book number three are required reading in most college English lit. classes. And all of us have at one time or another tackled the assignment to write the third chapter of Harrison's unfinished book.

"In the last ten years we have logged thirty-one claims of people purporting to have the lost manuscript. All the others were easily disproved and discarded." Nina sighed deeply and then smiled. "That's about it. Any questions?"

"What makes this one different from those other thirty-one?" Hampton, Sr., pressed.

"I think Lynda has the answer to that." Nina clamped her teeth together, grinned, and sat down with an audible sigh of relief.

Lynda Austin stood and motioned with her arms. "We'll get to the evaluations in a few moments. Anyone have any questions for Nina before we go on?"

T. H. Hampton, Jr., cleared his throat. "What kind of income are those two Harrison books providing for the company?"

"Well . . ." Nina dug through her papers. "With no assigns or heirs, most of the royalties are put back into the company."

Mr. Hampton, Sr., unfolded his hands and placed them on top of the table. "We donate to that library down in Florida, don't we?"

"Yes, Mr. Hampton. We give them 7½ percent of retail."

"So what do last year's figures look like?"

Austin pulled out a blue and green spread sheet. "I was going to cover that later, but if we combine book sales, movie rights, and book clubs, the Harrison books generated $420,000 for us last year."

"Profit?"

"Our expenses are minimal, of course. We don't need any changes in the text, and we certainly don't need any publicity. We had a manufacturing cost of about a dollar per book. So we cleared about $320,000."

"How much did the library receive?" Hampton, Sr., quizzed.

"Almost $60,000. But they can probably use more. The building is decaying."

"Well . . . make a note of that Ms. Quick. Let's keep that building in repair. The people who go down there are the ones who buy our books."

"Anything else? Or can we go on to Kelly's report?" Austin prodded.

"Oh . . ." Hampton, Jr., squirmed. "I was just trying to emphasize the point of how important these books are to the house. Proceed. Proceed."

"I had Kelly try to find anything she could on this man Felix Fondue. If this turns out to be an authentic manuscript, the media will have a field day with this guy, and I thought we should try not to have too many surprises. Kelly?"

"All right. Now I want to say I had great help from Billy Bucknell who knows just about everyone in — "

L. George Gossman threw up his hands. "From whom?"

"Eh . . . from William Bucknell — the guy who writes our Barbary Coast Mystery Series."

"Billy?" Austin groaned under her breath.

"Eh . . . we talked quite a bit." Kelly shrugged. "Say, is Billy . . . I mean, do any of you happen to know if Mr. Bucknell's married?"

"Three times!" Barbara Washburn boomed. "And he drinks like a fish."

"Ms. Princeton, please give your report and leave personal matters to the lunch hour," Gossman insisted.

"Oh . . . yeah. Well, thanks to William Bucknell, this is what I found. Fondue was born Hugh Neil in 1952 in Visalia, California."

"Where?"

"Visalia. I don't know if I'm pronouncing that right. Anyway, it's about seventy-five miles north of Bakersfield. He went to San Francisco State in the early seventies where he was arrested several times for campus protests. In March 1971 he was arrested along with three others for attempting to blow up the university's computer center."

"Did Lavine know him?" Gossman asked.

"Mr. Lavine is on a pilgrimage to India, and I couldn't reach him. But I did talk to Fondue's parents in Visalia."

"What did you find out?"

"They haven't heard from 'Hughie' since 1982, but they figure he's doing fine, or else he'd call home."

"Hughie?"

"That's what they said. They sounded a little strange," Princeton admitted. "Anyway, the next report from Felix Fondue — it seems to be the name he got while traveling with some former Manson family members when he was a teenager."

"Manson? Good grief! This thing is getting bizarre!" Jake Metzer grumbled. "Don't tell me he was once married to Elizabeth Taylor!"

"Well, anyway, Fondue was next heard from when he was arrested in 1975 in Philo, California, for growing six acres of marijuana."

"Six acres? That's a plantation!"

"Where's Philo?"

"Was he convicted?"

Kelly held up her left hand for quiet. "Philo is in Mendocino County, one hundred miles or so north of San Francisco."

"Oh, great. Now he's an old hippie and drug dealer!" Gossman added.

"Well, they pegged him as the caretaker of the place, not the owner or dealer. I guess he lived alone out in the hills and irrigated and weeded the crop. But he jumped a $2500 bail bond and hasn't been seen since."

"A criminal, a druggie, a fugitive — this is not good, ladies and gentlemen. This is not good at all," Hampton, Jr., moaned.

"It really doesn't bear on the matter, does it?" Austin insisted. "What we want to do is determine if this is a Harrison novel or not. Go ahead, Kelly."

"Billy . . . Mr. Bucknell found the name of one of Fondue's friends back in the old days."

"You mean they didn't all overdose or end up in prison?"

Kelly shuffled through the papers in front of her. "Oh, no. This man is Harold 'Steely' McKensie. He's a judge down in Tulare County."

"A judge?"

"Yeah, and all he could tell me about Fondue was that he was a very good cook and an exceptionally poor prelaw student. There was no Arizona record of any Felix Fondue. Basically, that's my report on Hughie."

"He didn't have a driver's license or anything?" Gossman asked.

"Well, that information is confidential, but Billy has ways of checking and said Fondue hadn't had a California license since 1975. Say, did you say he was married right now or not?"

"Fondue?" Austin teased.

"No. William Bucknell."

"Who cares?" Nina chided.

Lynda Austin stood to address the group. "Let's all admit it — Fondue is a flake with a very unstable background. But he brought in an unusual manuscript."

"So what did you find out in Florida?" Gossman pressed.

Austin waved her hands as she talked. "Well, I had a handwriting analyst study the note carefully. Here's the good and the bad news. He believes very strongly that the man who wrote this original 1929 letter is the same man who wrote this letter."

"Believes strongly. Does that mean he's not certain?" Metzer questioned.

"Well, he said he could not testify to it in a court of law because, by our own admittance, there are more than sixty years between letters. This letter Fondue brought in is definitely written by a very old person. People change their writing style over the years. But he does feel 80 percent certain that it's Harrison's handwriting."

"How about the library?"

"Well, there was a mixed reaction. The main thing was that chapter 3 was typed on the exact same typewriter as the first two chapters."

"What? But . . . h-how do you know that?" Hampton, Jr., stuttered.

"I took it to an expert in Miami while I was in south Florida. He said it is a Royal upright. There is key damage to five letters and an extra half-space after every *y*. The chances of this happening identically on two Royals is next to impossible. He's ready to testify in court that this is the same typewriter."

"That's marvelous. Hard evidence! Yes, yes, good work, Austin," T. H. Hampton, Sr., lauded.

"What about the Harrison experts down there? What did they say?" Gossman pressed.

"They all reported the same. The style and word usage was almost identical to the earlier novels. The curator was so excited at first that she literally danced around the room."

"At first? What's the trouble?" Gossman insisted.

"Well, she didn't like the content of chapter 3, and when I told her where he went with the rest of the book, she turned testy."

"Testy?"

"Well, you see it's quite different from the other two books. Instead of the existential throwing off of religion, morals, and the political system as in the first two books, the third book shows a man . . . well, frankly, it shows a man coming to grips with faith."

"What?" Silverman woke up out of his editing. He pulled off his horn-rimmed glasses and stared at Austin.

"And that's precisely why I don't like it!" Gossman interrupted. "Now I haven't read the whole manuscript yet, but chapter 3 is definitely inferior to his other work. It must be spurious!"

"Wait a minute. You're saying you think the things a phony because you don't like his conclusions?" Austin challenged.

"Ms. Austin," Gossman chided, "I'm afraid you're letting your personal views interfere with good judgment. This is not the time or place for religious prejudices."

"Nor, Mr. Gossman, is it a place for anti-religious prejudices. As everyone in this room knows, my personal faith affects every single thing I ever do. Of course, it touches my heart when Harrison acknowledges the central place of God in the life of honest men, but that doesn't mean — "

"He does what?" Barbara Washburn choked. "Martin Taylor Harrison — a believer? Why, he's the cause of more atheism and agnosticism among college students than any other single person in the twentieth century! He's the patron saint of the post-Christian era. This . . . this religion thing is preposterous! It's obviously a forgery."

"You are going to sit there and deem this fraudulent without even reading it! That's irresponsible!" Austin raised her voice above the others. "You can't throw it out because you disagree with what you think is in the text. If this is a genuine Harrison, then he deserves to be heard!"

"Wait . . . wait . . . now everyone just calm down," Hampton, Sr., ordered. "Now what do we know for sure here?"

"Okay, okay, here's my opinion." Austin pulled off her reading glasses and rubbed the bridge of her nose. "It is possible that Harrison lived until this year. That would make him ninety-two. Second, the handwriting is an extremely compatible match for a gap of time of over sixty years. Third, the typewriter is the one Harrison used for the previous manuscript. That could not have been faked. He must have carried it with him when he left California. Now some in this room, and I repeat, only some, feel the manuscript is inferior. But that's not the question at this point. The question is, is it authentic?"

"I can't believe . . . Martin Taylor Harrison getting religion. That's . . . that's inconceivable!" Silverman moaned.

"Yes, and so was tearing down the Berlin Wall, the end of communism in the Soviet Union, and the renaming of Leningrad to St. Petersburg," Austin reminded them.

"Not to mention Michael Jackson getting married," Kelly blurted out.

"Well," Austin continued, "we learn to adjust our preconceptions. I am convinced that it's authentic. I believe you'll agree when you read the rest of the manuscript. But I do think there is one more thing we should do."

"And what might that be?" Hampton, Jr., asked.

"We need to go to Arizona, exhume the body, and let forensics prove it is Harrison buried there."

"Can we do that?" Gossman asked.

"The sheriff of Mojave County, Arizona, told me that if we found a grave where someone had been buried without a doctor signing a death certificate, they would exhume the body in order to identify it."

"So what does that mean?"

Austin tried to nonchalantly tug her skirt back down. "I think someone from our legal department should accompany Mr. Fondue to the Arizona desert and get a forensic report on the man Fondue buried down in the canyons. If it's proved to be Harrison, we have to publish the book."

"And I say we can't publish something so controversial as Martin Taylor Harrison's purported conversion!" Gossman huffed. "This house has a solid reputation to uphold."

"Gossman, if it's authentic, we'll publish it," Hampton, Sr., informed him. "Those Harrison books pay the salary for most of the people sitting at this table. We'll publish the book if it's authentic even if the author turns out to be a druid or a sun worshiper."

"Actually, Dad, perhaps we should listen to George about . . . ," Hampton, Jr., began, but one look from his father silenced him.

The elder Hampton spoke. "Ms. Austin's right. We've got to go ahead and get the proof that this is Harrison's work. All we can conclusively say now is that we have discovered what we think is the location of Martin Taylor Harrison's typewriter. What's your plan from here?"

"I think we should meet with Fondue this afternoon at two and lay it out. We will publish the book and pay him a finder's fee of ten thousand dollars if we can exhume the body and confirm Harrison's identity."

"Do you think Fondue will agree to that?" Gossman asked.

"If he hedges, maybe it's a phony," Barbara Washburn said nodding.

"We'll have to have some money for him up

front. For an old anti-establishment, live-off-the-land hippie, he seems to like plenty of cold, hard cash."

"Yes, well, Gossman can negotiate that for us. I have that book show in Europe to prepare for," Hampton, Sr., stated.

"I'd like Nina, Kelly, George, and me to meet with Fondue. Is that all right?"

"Certainly . . . now I think that ends the meeting. Thank you all for being here." Following Senior's lead, they all stood to leave. The gray-haired CEO of Atlantic-Hampton stopped and patted Lynda's shoulder. "Good work, Austin. Don't let the infidels pull you down."

"Thanks, Mr. Hampton."

She stood with Kelly and Nina watching the others file out of the conference room.

"When's Fondue going to be here?"

"At two," Nina reported. "And he's bringing the manuscript."

"What was this raking Gossman gave you about your faith?"

"In the book Harrison artfully destroys some of his earlier assertions about the value of a life without God. I think that scares George."

"And Stan and Barbara and a few others," Kelly added.

"So . . . what do we do now?" Nina asked.

Austin looked at Princeton, and together they shouted, "Barton's!"

"Wait . . . wait for me to change my shoes. I want to wear my tennies this time!" Nina called.

"We'll wait for you out by the cowgirl!" Kelly shouted.

"You know what?" Austin laughed as she grabbed her purse out of her office. "What I hate about Spunky most is that everything she wears looks terrific on her!" She pulled out a tiny opaque bottle of Nicely Naughty and splashed a little on the inner side of her wrists.

"And she knows it. Come on, Lynda D., it's time for the Plain Jane Club to meet for a Reuben sandwich at Barton's."

"Is he here yet?" Nina puffed, lugging a boxful of notes and papers into the conference room.

"Not yet," Austin replied. "Is Kelly headed this way?"

"Yeah, and so is Mr. Gossman. Do you really think Fondue will agree to all this?"

"I think so. But the whole thing is strange, isn't it?"

Nina sat down in a chair next to Lynda. "Well, no matter what happens, it's been kind of fun. I mean, I spend most of my time in that cubbyhole of an office racing up and down lines of print looking for someone's mistakes. It's been a nice diversion."

Kelly Princeton rushed into the room and slung a stack of papers down on the table with a sigh.

"I can't believe it. The jerk's married!" she fumed.

"Married? Fondue is married?"

"Fondue? Who's talking about that creep?

Bucknell. That buffoon gives me a big come-on all week on the phone, and now I find out he got married for the fourth time just two weeks ago."

"How did you discover that?" Nina asked.

"I just read about it! Some Las Vegas showgirl or something. They had an outdoor wedding in front of the volcano at the Mirage. Hey, where's Hughie?"

"He's not here yet. Did you tell him to meet at 2:00 P.M.?"

"Yeah, he phoned in last Friday, then again this morning. Spunky reminded him about the time."

"Where was he staying this week?"

"He wouldn't say. It's all a secret. He wouldn't even leave his phone number."

L. George Gossman barged into the conference room balancing a cup of coffee on top of a thick binder and a Day Planner. "My word, where's Fondue? It's 2:10!"

"He's probably trying to hitch a ride up from the Village," Kelly offered.

"Is that where he's staying?"

"No one knows. It's a mystery," Austin replied.

"Did you ever think that this has the makings for a Geraldo show?" Nina suggested.

"Or a front page on the *National Enquirer*," Kelly said with a laugh. "I'll go out and check with Spunky. Maybe he got lassoed by the cowgirl."

At 2:30 Princeton, DeJong, Austin, and Gossman filed back to their offices. They didn't meet again until 4:45.

"Doesn't look like he's going to show," Gossman said.

"You don't suppose he's talking to another publisher?" Nina worried aloud.

"He wasn't mad or anything, was he? When he called, did he sound ticked off?" Austin asked.

"Not when I talked to him on Friday," Kelly assured her.

"Well, there's one thing for sure — we can't do a thing until he shows up. See you all tomorrow!" Gossman scooted on down the hall.

"What do you really think, Lynda?" Nina asked.

"I think we made a serious mistake in not getting a copy of that complete manuscript. Anyway, I'm going home."

The blue-uniformed security guard greeted her as she entered the building. "Evenin', Miss Lynda. Did I tell you Colleen is doin' good this week?"

"That's great news, Howard! You and Millie might get her raised yet."

"I'm lookin' forward to that day. I surely am. Listen, that little box over on my counter — that's some ginger cookies for you and Miss Janie. My Millie sent them over."

"Thanks, Howard, but why do we rate?"

"You ain't got no mama to make you cookies, and, heaven knows, you're too busy to bake any yourself."

Austin smiled and shook her head. "Do you look

68

after everyone in the building?"

"Those that will let me. I sort of figure that's what I'm paid for."

She picked up the cookies. *Well, whatever they pay you, it's not enough!*

Janie, wrapped in a glittering gold bathrobe, was sitting on the balcony looking at the fading light of the city and drinking a cup of coffee when Austin entered their condo.

"I'm out here, Lynda. Grab a cup of coffee and let's get caught up on the news!"

A few minutes later, Austin, sporting her old Michigan sweats, plopped into a deck chair next to the blonde flight attendant and sighed. "How was Europe? Tell me everything!"

By 10:00 P.M. the two had consumed micro-waved Thin Cuisine Chinese dinners and brought each other up to date. They came back into the living room, closed the sliding glass door, and pulled the peach-colored flowered curtains.

Austin next tackled the nightly chore of selecting something to wear for the next day. After choosing her outfit, she went to the large perfume cupboard in the bathroom and looked at the chart.

With that skirt I normally use Suggestion, but with the blouse I always use Why-O-Why. Perhaps . . . no, I'll stick with Suggestion. I can just hand-wash the blouse afterwards.

At 10:30 she dialed James St. John's number. But she hung up before the first ring was complete.

By 10:45 she was sound asleep.

It was another dream about her mother. This time they were standing by the seashore at Tavernier. The shallow waves of warm water broke and ran over Lynda's feet, and she could feel the sand moosh around her toes.

Her mother floated on an inflatable raft drifting out to sea. She held a book in one hand, a glass of ice tea in the other, and she was wearing a big, floppy straw hat. Lynda waved to her mother, but, engrossed in the book, the older woman never looked up.

As her mother drifted away, Lynda felt no sense of panic or urgency but instead extreme disappointment that she would not even look at Lynda.

"You have to wave!" Lynda shouted. "I'm your daughter!"

But her mother sailed out of sight, never looking toward the shore.

The ring of the telephone caused her to sit right up in the middle of the queen-size bed and stare into the dark. Through the fog of the vanishing dream she could hear Janie answering the phone. After a few muffled words, a light blinked on in the hall, and Janie appeared at the door.

"It's Nina — from work," Janie announced. She plodded back to her bedroom.

Nina?

Fumbling with the light switch by the bed,

Lynda pulled the telephone to her ear.

"Hello?"

"Lynda, are you watching the news?"

"What? What time is it? No . . . I was . . ."

"Oh, you were asleep? Well, look, I was waiting up to see the first part of Letterman. And so I'm sitting here watching the news. Well, there's a story about a couple of tour buses crashing into each other on the upper west side near Central Park West and 72nd."

"The Dakota House?"

"Yeah, and here's the thing. One tourist bus slams into the back of another, but they catch a pedestrian in between. I guess it mashed him up pretty bad."

"You're calling me in the middle of the night to tell me this?" Lynda murmured.

"Well, I hope you're sitting down because the man who was killed was about forty years old, slightly bald on top yet with long hair, and was carrying a big sack of papers that got scattered all over the intersection, making traffic hazardous for quite a while."

"Was it . . . Fondue?"

"There was no identification on the man, and they showed an artist sketch on TV in case someone could help identify him. It was Fondue, Lynda; I know it was Fondue!"

"You've got to be kidding! Oh man, not Fondue! The manuscript . . . It was the manuscript that blew all over the street!"

"That's what I'm thinking. What are we going to do?"

"Did you call anybody else? Did you call Goss-man?"

"No, I don't have his home number. Besides, I wouldn't want to call at this time of the night. I wouldn't call anyone but you."

"Yeah, thanks. Listen, are you sure it was Fon-due?"

"Not completely sure, but it did happen about one o'clock this afternoon."

"What police precinct is that up there? Did they have a number to call in case someone wanted to identify the . . . eh, person?"

"I don't think so, but I'll call the television station and check."

"Good. I'll wake up George and see if he wants to check this out tonight." Austin rubbed her eyes trying to be more alert. "I can't believe this! It's like a bad dream."

"Call me back after you talk to Mr. Gossman."

At 11:39 Lynda Austin reached Editorial Director L. George Gossman. Ten minutes later she was talking to Police Captain Frank Woods. At 12:18 a police car met her in front of her apartment and drove her to the city morgue where she identified the man as Hugh Neil, a.k.a. Felix Fondue.

She spent an hour in the police station trying to determine the whereabouts of Fondue's belongings and what might have happened to the manuscript. The police escort even drove her over to 72nd and Central Park West. Half a block south of the Dakota House she had the policeman pull

72

over while she got out and retrieved two white sheets of paper that had stuck to the black wrought-iron grating of some basement stairs.

By the time she crawled back into bed, it was 4:21 A.M. She spent the next two hours staring at the ceiling and thinking about the blank expression on the pasty white face of the corpse of Felix Fondue.

The next morning she tried to explain the scene to Janie as she hurried to get ready for work but found herself caught between wanting to cry and needing to vomit. She couldn't remember if she had decided on Suggestion or Why-O-Why and ended up smearing on liberal amounts of both. She numbly went through the motions but knew that at some time in the next twenty-four hours she would crash from tension and tiredness. She hoped she would be at home when that happened.

At the reception desk of Atlantic-Hampton, Spunky Sasser wore a long, black silk Chinese dress slit up to her thigh and dark glasses. Lynda headed straight for the coffee pot and was greeted by Kelly Princeton. For a minute they just looked at each other and shook heads.

"It's weird," Kelly mumbled. "You saw him?"

"Sort of. Do we have a meeting?"

"Yeah. Nine o'clock in the conference room. Mr. Hampton, Sr., will be there, too."

"He hasn't left yet?"

"I think he postponed the trip a day."

Lynda stared blankly at the wall.

"Listen, girl," Kelly said softly, "go drink your coffee and unwind. I'll talk to you later."

By 8:55 the conference room was buzzing with activity. At 9:00 precisely, T. H. Hampton, Sr., entered the room.

"Well, what happened and where do we go from here? Ms. Austin, I understand you've got most of the details."

Lynda stood to her feet, brushed dark brown hair back out of her eyes, and sighed. "If I sound tired, I am. Not only did I not get any sleep last night, but for the first time in my life, I was called upon to go to the morgue and identify a dead body. I don't think I ever want to do that again.

"At approximately 1:10 P.M. yesterday, Hugh Neil, known to us as Felix Fondue, was killed on Central Park West when the brakes failed on Big Apple Tours Bus #4650, and it plowed into the rear of City Sights Tour Bus #988, catching Mr. Fondue between the buses. He had apparently spent the lunch hour in Central Park at Strawberry Fields and was running to catch a midtown bus to come to our offices.

"He was killed instantly. He was carrying the Martin Taylor Harrison manuscript, which subsequently scattered for two blocks on both Central Park West and 72nd Street. For the first time in memory, city workers cleaned up and disposed of the 'trash' so thoroughly that all I could recover at three in the morning were pages 162 and 437."

"My word, can't we retrieve the rest of it somewhere?" T. H. Hampton, Sr., questioned.

"No, sir. The trash is now on a barge with thirty-two tons of compressed garbage headed for a land-fill in South Carolina."

"Have his relatives been notified?"

Austin glanced over at Princeton. "Kelly?"

"I called Captain Woods of NYPD and gave them the name, address, and telephone number of Fondue . . . eh, Neil's parents out in California. They will contact the family."

"A sad and gruesome accident. Ms. Austin, I am terribly sorry you had to be our lead person last night," T. H. Hampton, Sr., apologized. "Gossman, why on earth didn't you come into the city and handle this? At the risk of being called a sexist, I don't believe a lady should have to face such a scene."

L. George Gossman sat straight up and cleared his throat. "Eh . . . well, it was quite late before I became aware of the matter, and living out on Long Island, I didn't think . . . eh, besides, Austin is extremely proficient . . . and, well, to tell you the truth, I surely didn't want to offend her by implying she was, eh, incapable of . . ."

"It's all right, George. Mr. Hampton, I appreciate your sensitivity. Your remarks sounded concerned, not derogatory."

"Well, what do we do now? I think we all need a little time. I suggest everyone get back to work, give this Harrison matter some thought, and I'll check with each of you later."

"Mr. Hampton," Austin put in, "I do believe

this is an authentic Harrison. According to Fondue, the original manuscript is in a cabin in Arizona. I believe we should proceed to find the cabin, the manuscript, and where Harrison is buried."

"Thank you, Ms. Austin, I value your opinion. Now I want you to take the rest of the day off. Go home, get some sleep. If you need to talk this morgue thing out, the company will certainly pay for any counseling."

"Thank you, sir, but I've got some office work that needs looking at. I've postponed several projects, so I'll just — "

"Ms. Austin, may I remind you that I'm still the president of this company. I've ordered you to go home and get some rest. This is not to be considered personal leave, a sick day, or vacation. Is that clear, Gossman?"

"Yes, Mr. Hampton. I couldn't agree with you more."

"Now go home, Ms. Austin. Take care of yourself." Hampton shook his finger at her.

Lynda led the line out of the conference room. She shut down her computer, picked up her briefcase, glanced around one time, and then flipped the light switch.

"Kelly, you and Nina call me if anything comes up on this Harrison thing."

"Go home, girl. Nothing will happen today. Turn off your phone and let the machine catch the calls. You look awful."

"You sure know how to cheer a girl up. I think you're right. Some sleep is bound to help."

Janie had left for Connecticut to visit her parents by the time Lynda got back to the condo. She closed the drapes in her bedroom, turned off the phone, carefully laid her clothes on a chair by the bed, and crawled under the sheets that felt relaxingly cool and wonderfully soft.

When she finally woke up, the lights of the city reflected around the edges of the window, and a red light blinked on the answering machine.

She pulled on her robe and shuffled out to the kitchen, poured herself a glass of orange juice, and downed it. Digging at the back of the refrigerator, she found a raspberry yogurt. Then she grabbed a note pad, a pencil, and a spoon and scooted toward the answering machine. She paused and glanced at her reflection in the hall mirror.

Not bad . . . not bad if you just got run over by a train! Girl, you're wearing yourself down. . . . Your eyes look strained. . . . Your smile is drooping. . . . Your shoulders sag. . . . Your hair looks like you could play lead guitar in a grunge band! You need a break. You need some sun. You need . . . a hug.

She punched the play button on the answering machine and took a big bite of sweet/sour raspberry yogurt.

Bee-eep. "Janie? This is Brian. I know you're in town. Call me. I miss you."

Bee-eep. "Hey, Janie girl, I got the tickets! Row 11, right in the center. Can you believe it? Give me a call, kiddo."

Bee-eep. "Lynda? This is Kelly. I know you turned off the phone, but if you just happen to be wandering around the house and hear this, call me. Eh . . . it's about 3:15. Thanks."

Bee-eep. "I'm calling Lynda D. Austin. This is David DuPage of the Spartan Bank of Delaware. It is my privilege to let you know that you have been preapproved for a Gold Master Card with a credit line of ten thousand dollars. I'll call you back at a more convenient time."

Bee-eep. "Janie? This is Ed McMahon. Look, you're going to have to give me a call so I know where to deliver this bag of money. Heh . . . heh. Not really. It's Brian. Where are you?"

Bee-eep. "Lynda, it's James. I heard you were trying to reach me. I'm in L. A. Something came up at work. I needed to fly out here for a couple weeks. I'll try to call you back in a few days. I have to leave now and go out to Palm Springs, so I don't have a number you can call. You can probably leave a message on my machine if it's anything important. Kristie and her husband are staying at my place while I'm gone. I'm sure you figured that out by now. Sorry I yelled last week. Maybe it was just as well we saw each other that way. I don't usually do things like that. It's just . . . sometimes you really tick me off. Bye."

"I tick you off? Cynthia just happens to have a place in Palm Springs. Isn't that a coincidence? Bye, Jimmy boy, bye-bye."

Bee-eep. "Janie, I love you, I love you, I love you! Let's fly away to the Bahamas! You can still get those free airline passes, can't you? I'm kidding. Remember, tonight at Tony's, 8:30. Wear something black."

Bee-eep. "Lynda? It's Kelly again. Hey, I'm going home now. Well, actually I'm heading for Little Italy and an anniversary party for my brother. What I was going to tell you is Gossman, Metzer, Mr. Hampton, Jr., and some others had some kind of confab this afternoon about that Harrison thing, but I have no idea what was discussed. Anyway, I suppose we'll all find out tomorrow. Sleep tight. See you tomorrow."

Bee-eep. "This is the emergency ward at St. Francis Hospital. We have a man named Brian here who is claiming to have heart trouble. He says that he will die if he doesn't hear from someone named Janie. Could you please call him quickly and get this lunatic off our hands. . . . Hey, not bad, huh? Old Brian could have played Tootsie instead of that walk-on part. Listen, are you trying to avoid me? If so, give me a call."

Austin saved the messages for her roommate and sat on the couch finishing her yogurt.

A meeting about the Harrison thing? Without me? I was the one who did all the work. They wouldn't send someone off to Arizona without getting all the information from me surely. I'll likely have to fax everything. Probably it was Junior. He likes to vacation in Scottsdale.

Maybe Gossman wanted to go out. Poor George. He's caught in a bind. He wants the honor of finding the lost Harrison manuscript, but his sacred agnos-

79

ticism feels threatened. Lord, this might be a good time to convert Mr. L. George Gossman. That Harrison novel could do a lot of spiritual good.

After a bout with Bogart and Bacall in *To Have and Have Not* and a Tupperware tub of popcorn, she plopped back into bed.

Lynda Austin hiked up Madison Avenue wearing a sea green dress and Danish Kiss perfume. She felt more rested than she had in six months. The outer office and reception area were empty except for Spunky Sasser wearing a dingy gray set of Columbia University sweats with holes in the knees and dangling football earrings.

Austin stepped into Kelly Princeton's office and grinned. "What's with Spunky? Did someone complain about her being overdressed?"

Princeton looked up and forced a smile. "I guess . . . Anyway, Mr. Gossman wants to see you."

"I got your call. What happened at that meeting yesterday?"

"Editorial Director L. George Gossman will tell you."

"Is it that bad?"

"You aren't going to like it," Kelly cautioned.

"What is it?"

"Go talk to Georgie."

THREE

"You decided what?" Austin fumed.

"We're going to put the whole Harrison matter on hold for now. It's just getting too complicated," Gossman explained.

"We? Who's we? Why wasn't I asked?"

"I think you stated your opinion yesterday. We didn't want to bother you anymore."

"Bother me? You did this behind my back!"

"Ms. Austin, let me remind you that this decision is not your private property."

"Nor is it yours!" she insisted.

"Metzer, Mr. Hampton, Washburn, and I came to this conclusion based on the figures."

"What figures?"

"Providing that it is an original Harrison, Metzer projected the sales and then figured a drop in sales of the other two books."

"What drop in sales? If we publish a new Harrison, people will run out and buy the other two, and you know it!"

"Only at first. After that, of course, the colleges will discontinue the books. If Harrison takes the counterculture steam out of books one and two, they'll be retired to the library shelf. Oh, we could make some quick bucks, but then it would drop off, and we've come to rely on that Harrison money. I'll show you the figures if you want."

"I don't believe this! That's the worst piece of logic I ever heard in my life! We're not talking dollars and cents. We have a literary obligation to publish an original Harrison. We don't agree with 90 percent of the things we publish. You told me that yourself. But people have a right to hear the whole story. You can't ignore this manuscript."

"Ms. Austin, may I remind you that we have no manuscript. We are not at all sure there is one, and we have no idea where it is. Even then, we cannot be sure of its authenticity. Good heavens, even if we found it and found Harrison's body, how do we know that this Fondue character didn't hammer it out himself? And if we were to publish it, and it turned out later to be a forgery . . . Well, I don't have to spell that out for you. You remember what happened to Hamilton and Ross when they published that spurious Stalin diary."

"Fondue couldn't write three coherent sentences, and you know it. You can't just bury this project!"

"We already did."

"Mr. Hampton, Sr., agreed?"

"He had to leave for that book show in Hamburg. The decision was made this morning. Junior agreed with it."

"Junior agrees with anything that doesn't interrupt his philandering."

"That comment was uncalled for! I'm sure Mr. Hampton, Sr., will review the decision when he returns, of course. But the rest of us totally agreed."

"I didn't!"

"You weren't in the loop."

"You don't have to remind me!"

L. George Gossman stood and stepped toward Lynda. "I believe we've talked about this enough. Perhaps you're still tired — "

"Tired? Yeah, I'm tired. I'm . . . I'm going to lunch!"

"At 8:30 in the morning?"

"You have any objections?" she barked.

Gossman threw up his hands. "Eh . . . well . . . no. When will you be back?"

"When I'm full!"

Within five minutes she was stalking up Madison Avenue.

At 1:16 P.M. she returned to the office.

"Hey, are you doing all right?" Kelly asked.

"I'm pretty discouraged, but I've got a plan. I'm not quitting on it yet."

"What are you going to do?"

"I'm going to find the manuscript myself. Can you get Joaquin Estában on the line for me?"

"The one who writes all those westerns?"

"How many Joaquin Estábans do you know? His Idaho number should be in the Rolodex. Ring him through to me if you can reach him. Sometimes he won't answer his phone."

Kelly scooted toward her office, then whipped back around. "Does he really know Tom Selleck?"

Ignoring the question, Austin plopped down at her desk and grabbed the phone, pushing one of the intercom buttons.

"George? This is Lynda. I'll be taking my vacation starting Friday. I won't be back until October third. You said that if I worked through that August mess, I could take it anytime. Well, this is the time."

Nina DeJong appeared just as she cradled the phone. "I heard that you ran into a brick wall with the Harrison manuscript . . . sorry. You finally going to get away?"

"Yeah."

"Where are you going?"

"Arizona, I think."

"Are you going to look for the manuscript?"

"Yes."

Kelly barged into the office. "Hey, all I got at Estában's was his machine. I left word to call you, but I think you ought to listen to his recorded message."

Austin took off her reading glasses and rubbed the bridge of her nose. "What's it say?"

"You'd better call it and listen."

She punched the speaker phone button so they all could listen and dialed the number Kelly had handed to her on a small yellow note pad.

"Hey, partner, this is Joaquin. Just leave a message at the beep, and, dad gum it, if I ever get home, more than likely I'll try to get back to ya. Oh . . . if this is my editor, Miss Lynda, I'm workin' on that new book as fast as I can. I'll have it ready in two weeks. You can trust me." Bee-eep.

Austin looked up at DeJong and Princeton and grimaced. "Real funny. When he goes off like that, I can't reach him for a month sometimes. Nina, check with Metzer and see if Estában's got a royalty check coming. If so, bring it to me. Tell Metzer I'll mail it out."

"You really think you can find Harrison's cabin?" Kelly grilled.

"I've got to try. It would eat at me the rest of my life if I didn't. I can't believe they would freeze this whole thing. It's preposterous. It's like they're afraid to find it."

"They are."

"Have you got a U.S. map, an atlas, in your office?"

"Sure. You want me to get it?"

"Please."

Moments later Nina DeJong slid back into the office with a brown company envelope.

"Metzer did have a check for Estában. What are you going to do with it?"

"Watch me."

Austin dialed Joaquin Estában's number and waited for the beep. "¿Joaquin, qué pasa? This is Lynda Austin at Atlantic-Hampton. I need to hear from you immediately. I have a royalty check setting on my desk. But when you're traveling, I

85

never know where to send it. So give me a call and tell me where to mail this $34,564.20. Hope to hear from you soon because I'll be going out of town for a couple of weeks and hate to leave this lying on my desk. Bye-bye, amigo."

Princeton laughed and handed Austin a map. "So that's how you handle temperamental authors. No wonder you're an editor, and I'm just an associate."

Within forty-five minutes Spunky Sasser buzzed her with a call. "Some guy with a Texas drawl wants to talk to his 'sweet Miss Lynda.'"

"That's Joaquin." She nodded at Nina who was stacking a pile of papers into a cardboard file box. Clearing her throat, she turned on the speaker phone and punched the flashing #2 button.

"Lynda Austin speaking."

"Miss Lynda, how's the editor with the sweetest voice in all of New York City?"

"Impatiently waiting for 'Ambush on the Apache Trail.' You haven't seen a completed manuscript lying around the old bunkhouse, have you?"

"That's my gal — quick and right to the point. Now, darlin', I'll have 'Apache' to you by October first or so."

"Joaquin, it was due August first!"

"August? You're joshin' me, right? I'm sure we said October."

"Check with your agent."

"Eh . . . I fired her. Anyway, what's this about holding on to a royalty check? You just stick that sucker in the mail to the old home corral, and

I'll see that it's put to proper use."

"Joaquin, are you home right now? I've got a favor to ask."

"Miss Lynda is askin' a favor from an old broken-down drover like me? Now that's a first. Actually I'm about . . . oh, say, thirty miles west of Pomeroy on Highway 12 talkin' to you on the cellular. I just happened to check my messages at home."

"Where's Pomeroy?"

"On the way to Pendleton, Oregon. Thought I'd mosey down to the Roundup for a few days."

"Pendleton. Like in the wool skirts and blankets?"

"Yep. But it's also home of the Pendleton Roundup, one of the nation's premier rodeos."

"You're late on a manuscript, and you're off at some sideshow?"

"Austin, you're gettin' real close to havin' me hang up on that darlin' voice of yours. Rodeo is the all-American sport. It's not the circus. If you really want a favor, you'd better — get out of the road! . . . I should have hit the stupid thing!"

"What are you talking about?"

"A llama. The ugliest creature ever brought west. Someone left a gate open, no doubt. Now what's that favor?"

"Joaquin, I'm on my way to Arizona, and I need someone who knows the countryside to help me locate a cabin. You know some Arizona ranchers, don't you?"

"Arizona's a big state. Where are you headed?"

"Eh . . . it's called the Arizona Strip. You know

— north of the Colorado River."

"Whoa, Miss Lynda. You're headed for the ends of the earth."

"Your voice is starting to fade, so I'll make it quick. I need someone to give me advice . . . or someone I could reasonably hire to help locate a cabin that contains an important manuscript."

"You need a Strip cowboy. I know a couple."

"Can you give me a name and phone number? I'll call them."

"Cain't do it, Sweetheart. There aren't any telephones down there."

"No telephones?"

"Once you leave the pavement, there's no electricity and no phones. 'Course there aren't hardly any people either."

"So you can't give me any help?" she asked.

"Well, now, I didn't say that. Sweetheart, for you I'd ride a Brahmer all the way to Cheyenne."

"A what?"

"A buckin' bull. Look, I'll check at the rodeo. A couple of the boys goin' down the road hail from the Strip. I'll see if I can get you hooked up with them. I'm dropping down in a coulee now, so I'll call you from Pendleton."

"You have my home phone number, don't you?"

"Sweetness, I keep it close to my heart at all times."

"Thanks, Joaquin. I'll expect to hear from you tonight."

"Miss Lynda, I'll count the hours until we speak once again. What are you wearin' today?"

"Eh . . . my sea green dress. Why?"

"Short sleeves and a shallow scoop neck?"

"Yes. How can you remember that?"

"That means you're wearin' Danish Kiss. Right?"

"Go rope a bull or something. Call me if you line someone up."

"You got it, Miss Lynda. Bye-bye. And give my regards to whoever else is listenin' on the speaker phone. Those things sound like a tin can from this end. Did you know that?"

"Goodbye, Joaquin."

Kelly had stepped to the door and was listening to the conversation.

"That's the great Joaquin Estában?" asked Nina.

"That's him. Quite a character, huh?"

Nina pierced Lynda with a direct look. "How did he know about your dress and your perfume?"

"He never forgets anything. Never outlines a book, never takes any notes. It's like he can file every scrap of information he ever learned in his mind and retrieve it anytime he wants. Anyway, he always teases me about my perfumes."

"You really leaving Friday?" Nina asked. "Where will you go first?"

"That depends on who I can find to help me locate that cabin. Someone must know that region."

"Tramping through the desert doesn't seem like that great a vacation," Kelly noted.

"Maybe not, but I've got to try."

"You're going to call us and tell us how things are going, right?"

"Yeah, if there's anything to report. Kelly, could you bring all your notes on Fondue? I'm taking a copy of everything worthwhile with me. I really intend to find that cabin manuscript. If anyone is looking for me, I'll be in the copy room most of the afternoon."

At 10:00 P.M. Joaquin Estában called.

"Miss Lynda? You know, if you were with me right now, we could be dancin' right here on the main street of Pendleton, Oregon."

"Be still, my heart. How will I withstand the disappointment? Did you find me an Arizona expert?"

"Here's what I got. I ran across a buddy from the Kaibab Plateau who's cowboyed down in the Strip for years."

"That's great! Thanks, Joaquin! I knew you could find someone. If you were here, I would kiss you!"

"Hold that thought, darlin'. I'm bookin' a flight tonight."

"Not yet, cowboy. You haven't given me the guy's name."

"You got a pen?"

"Yes. Go ahead."

"His name is Brady Stoner."

"Brady Stoner?"

"Right."

"How can I reach him? What's the phone number?"

"Well, now . . . that's a problem. You see, Brady's goin down the road full-bore. What with him sittin' on the bubble, you won't really be able to phone him."

"What did you say? Down the road? Sitting on what?"

"Let me explain rodeo life a little. On the bubble means he's sittin' in about seventeenth place in bareback ridin'. Now at the end of the year the top fifteen go to the National Finals Rodeo in Las Vegas. It's kind of like the world series of rodeo, and the boys can make a pile of money there. So everyone works real hard to make it. That means that Brady's entered in about every rodeo he can sign up for."

"So I can't talk to him?"

"I didn't say that. I said you can't phone him. He just scored a 77 in the short round, and he hopped into his truck and headed south to another rodeo. He said your best bet would be to catch him at the Dixie Roundup on Friday night."

"Dixie? You mean like in Georgia or something?"

"No, no, darlin'. The Dixie Roundup's in St. George, Utah."

"Why do they call it Dixie?"

"Old Brigham Young and the Saints thought it was so warm down there they would grow Mormon cotton, so they called it their Dixie. It's down near the Arizona Strip. Brady'll be too busy to quit rodeoin' and take you down there personal, but he promised to give you some names and directions that will help."

"So I'm supposed to show up at a rodeo in St. George, Utah, and ask for Brady Stoner?"

"Yep. He'll come through for ya. Brady's that way. He's not the kind to jerk you around. You'll see. You'll like him. Of course, you did promise to save yourself for me!"

"Joaquin, did you ever notice that you write fiction even when you talk? Listen, how will I spot him? What does he look like?"

"Can't miss him — lean, rugged, black beaver Resistol cowboy hat, Wrangler jeans, and Justin boots."

"Right. Go over that again. You said . . . wait . . . Won't all the rodeo cowboys look like that?"

"Yep. Just ask any of the gals which one's Brady. I can guarantee they will — "

"Can I fly into St. George? Or do I go to Salt Lake or what?"

"Fly to Vegas."

"Really?"

"Yep. It's only a couple hours to St. George. The rodeo starts about seven, and he'll probably be drivin' off to New Mexico when he's done, so don't be late. He won't wait for you to show."

"Thanks again, Joaquin."

"You got it, babe. Hope it all works out. Hey . . . I Fed Exed 'Apache Trail' this morning. You should have it tomorrow."

"Really? You already sent it?"

"Sure. I was just stringin' you along. Yeah, and it'll knock your socks off. Tell the boys to kick a little more advertising money this way. It will pay off. Wait and see. Oops . . . they're playin' Brooks & Dunn. It's boot-scootin' time. Bye, Miss Lynda."

By midnight Wednesday Austin had a ticket on a 7:45 A.M. Friday flight to Las Vegas by way of St. Louis. She spent most of Thursday finishing correspondence and avoiding L. George Gossman. On Thursday night she called her sister Megan in Muskegon and told her of the trip to Arizona, packed her suitcase, and selected her traveling perfumes.

Early Friday morning she loaded one suitcase and a heavily taped cardboard file box into a taxi headed to Grand Central Station where she caught a shuttle to La Guardia.

It wasn't until she was at 34,000 feet somewhere over Tennessee that it dawned on her.

Lord, what in the world am I doing? I don't know anyone out there. I'm a city girl.

This is weird.

This is really weird.

At McCarran International Airport in Las Vegas, a thin man with a bushy mustache helped her load the heavy cardboard file box and suitcase into the back of the white subcompact rental car.

"Can you give me some directions?"

"Are you staying on the Strip or downtown?"

93

"The Strip . . . you mean, like the Arizona Strip?"

"Nah. Las Vegas Boulevard. Which hotel are you staying at?"

"Oh, no, I'm driving to St. George, Utah, tonight."

"Why on earth would you want to go there?"

"I happen to be headed to a rodeo," she snapped.

"Oh, a buckle bunny."

"A what?"

"Never mind." He shrugged. "Turn left on Tropicanna and stay on it until you get to I-15. Then head east. The signs will probably say Salt Lake City, but it will take you right into St. George. It's a couple hours or so down the road."

"Yeah, well, thanks."

"Hope you get your buckle!" He grinned.

Within minutes she had left the palm-studded parking lots and architectural clutter of Las Vegas behind and was driving across the desert toward the barren mountains in the east. The interstate traffic was sparse, the land vast and parched. Scraggly plants and sagebrush starkly contrasted with the New York City landscape of just a few hours before.

She rolled the window halfway down and took a deep breath of fresh air. Glancing at her reflection in the rearview mirror, she thought she could see fewer wrinkles around her eyes.

"I needed this, Lord. I needed a break. I need some rest. But I don't want this to turn out like Kathleen Turner in *Romancing the Stone*. I surely don't need any thrills and breathtaking adventures. Just quiet, rewarding days . . . peaceful, comfortable nights . . . and a little color in my face."

She unbuttoned the sleeves of her green silk dress and carefully rolled them up her forearms. Then she sniffed her left wrist.

Maybe I should splash on a little more. Almost Heaven wears off so fast I should carry it around in my purse.

During the second hour she checked her watch as it got closer and closer to 7:00 P.M. A service station cashier in St. George pointed her up the hill to the rodeo arena, which already had lights on even though it was still an hour before dark.

She followed the directions of a man in a Lion's Club hat as he ushered her into an uneven grassy field that served as overflow parking. The pickup trucks dwarfed her rental. She watched as family after family unloaded and flooded into the rodeo grounds.

Why didn't I ask Joaquin what I should wear to a rodeo? I'll be the only one in a dress! Heels? No telling what I'll step in out there. I can at least pull out some more comfortable shoes.

The warm September air felt comfortable, with the aroma of fresh grass and fine dust. Without looking at those around her, she stepped to the back of the car and opened the trunk hoping to dig out a pair of tennies. The large suitcase and file box of papers were jammed so tight that she couldn't get either out of the vehicle.

95

"I don't believe this. It's insane! What kind of car is this? You can't get a suitcase out of it," she muttered.

Giving up on the luggage, she pulled her sunglasses down from the top of her head, locked the car, and stepped gingerly toward a line at a small, rustic ticket booth, feeling totally out of place in a teal green dress and heels.

A woman wearing a large silver and turquoise squash-blossom necklace greeted her. "How many tickets ya need, honey?"

"Eh . . . just one, I guess. Listen, what I really need is to talk to — "

"You want general admission or grandstand?"

"I guess . . . eh, grandstand."

"You want to sit behind the buckin' chutes or down by the ropin' boxes?"

"What? Eh, actually all I wanted to do is talk to Brady Stoner."

The woman's face broke into a wide grin. "Don't we all, honey, don't we all? Well, I'll put you behind the buckin' chutes. Barebacks will come close to the beginning of the evenin' right after the Grand Entry and the wild cow milkin'."

"Thank you. Say . . . which one is Stoner?"

"You mean you don't know him?"

"Eh . . . no . . . not yet."

"Well, let me check the program. He'll be third out tonight riding a horse called No Return. He ought to have a number 16 pinned to his back. But with Brady, you can't be sure."

"Thanks. . . . By the way, I didn't have time

96

to stop for dinner. Can I get a bite to eat around here?"

"Try the Ketch Pen back behind those bleachers. The buffalo burgers seem to be a hit with everyone."

Lynda Austin scooted through a crowd of men, women, senior citizens, boys, girls, and teens clothed almost exclusively in boots, jeans, Western shirts, and cowboy hats.

I feel like the only tourist here! Why didn't I wear my tennies? At least I could have worn pants!

With a genuine buffalo burger in one hand and a small diet Coke in the other, she snaked her way into the grandstands on the far side of the arena. She hiked up three rows and turned and sat down next to an older woman with big, round eyes and a man whose face looked leather-tough and wrinkled. They were sitting behind some small metal pens, each containing a horse about as anxious for the rodeo to begin as the people in the crowded stands.

Three junior-high-age girls, each with long braids and a big numbered poster pinned to her back, squeezed in on the other side of Lynda. Holding her purse in her lap, she tried to keep the buffalo burger from dripping on her as she balanced the drink on her knee.

As long as we don't have to stand up, I'll be all right. How in the world will I find this guy Stoner in this crowd?

The Dixie Darlings Riding Club entered the arena horseback from all directions at once. Each woman rider carried an American flag, and the spectators immediately rose to their feet. The men placed their hats over their hearts.

"Can I hold that for you, dear?" The woman next to her pointed at the drink.

"Yes . . . thank you. I ended up with more than I can carry, I guess. This is nice. So what event is this?"

"Oh, this is the Grand Entry. Then they'll have the flag salute and introduce the royalty. After that the events begin. It's your first rodeo?"

Handing the woman her buffalo burger as well, Lynda brushed back her thick, dark hair and fumbled in her purse to put away her sunglasses. "That's kind of obvious, isn't it?"

"Say, you wouldn't be Irene's sister, would you?" Her soft, sweet voice belied the difficulties of living in a harsh land.

Retrieving her dinner, Austin smiled. "Irene? Oh, no. I'm afraid I'm not related to anyone here."

"Well, Irene Carlson said her sister was coming down from Salt Lake City to see a rodeo for the first time, so I naturally wondered. But you are from out of town, aren't you?"

"You may not believe this," Austin sighed as they all sat back down, "but I'm from New York City."

"Well, my, oh my! You don't say. You know, our son Howard went to New York City once." She turned to the man next to her. "Clarence, when was it that Howard went to New York City?"

"He ain't never been to New York. He went

98

to Baltimore, remember? Yes, ma'am, he was in Baltimore for ten days in 1985. Purt near got run over three times. He ain't been back since."

Austin nodded and turned back to stare at the arena.

This is a foreign country! I feel like a sheep at a wolves' convention. What am I doing here?

"There's Brady," one of the girls crooned. "He's totally awesome! Look at that smile." All three began to giggle and poke each other.

Ah . . . teenagers. Well, some things are the same no matter where you live.

"Excuse me, girls," Austin blurted out. "Did you say you spotted Brady Stoner?"

The blonde with braces glanced at Austin and studied her clothing. "Yeah. He's down there in chute number three."

"With the turquoise shirt?"

"Turquoise shirt, chaps, hatband. That's him. Are you like a friend of his mother or something?" the girl inquired.

A friend of his mother? Cute, honey . . . real cute.

She glared back at the girls and calmly announced, "You know, Brady's right on the bubble. He won some money up at Pendleton on Wednesday, and if he does well tonight and at Albuquerque this weekend, he could be on his way to the National Finals. I hear he drawed up pretty good tonight. We'll have to see what kind of mark he gets."

I hope I said that right! Please don't ask me to explain!

The girls' mouths dropped open.

"Oh . . . yeah. That's what we heard. Eh . . . what are you doing all dressed up like that? You been to a funeral or something?"

"Maybe she works in a bank and just got off work," one of the other girls suggested.

"Sort of like that." Austin nodded.

"We're all entered in the barrel racin'!" the third girl offered.

What in the world is barrel racing?

"Oh . . . that's nice. I'll look forward to watching you."

"You a friend of Brady's? My oldest sister dated him once."

The other two girls giggled and almost in unison said, "Everybody's sister used to date Brady!"

"Well, I'm a friend of a friend of his. But I hope to talk to him this evening."

"I don't think you're his type," the blonde cautioned.

Just then the crowd roared for their favorite wild cow milking team. The confusion of having fifteen cowboys horseback and fifteen muggers on the ground chasing twenty wild cows around the arena left Austin in total confusion. She felt relieved when they cleared the arena and announced the beginning of the bareback riding.

She tried to keep one eye on the man in the turquoise shirt as he strapped something on the back of the brown horse. It kept rearing its head and trying to lift its front feet out of the steel enclosure.

But her eyes were deflected to chute number one. The gate flew open, and a bucking horse boiled out trying its best to throw the rider to the ground.

A loud buzzer went off, and the crowd cheered. The rider bounced on the bucking horse until another cowboy rode alongside and helped him to the ground. The number 72 flashed on the scoreboard at the far end of the arena.

"What's the 72 mean? Is that good?" Austin asked the woman fanning herself with a program next to her.

"Well, it's not too bad. Probably won't win him any money though. You see, the horse gets judged on how well it bucks — up to 50 points. And the rider gets judged on how well he rides — up to 50 points. So there's a possibility of 100 points. But no one gets that high. Usually a high 70 or low 80 will win the money in the bareback riding."

"What I really need to do is talk to Brady Stoner. How would I go about doing that?"

"Well, if he stays for the whole rodeo, you could catch him out back in the contestant parking area."

The next cowboy bounced off the back of his horse after a couple of jumps.

"He gets no score," the elderly woman informed her. "Oh . . . here comes your friend Brady!"

Lynda sipped her Coke and leaned forward to watch. She wished she could kick off her heels and wiggle her toes.

Stoner nodded his head, and the big steel gate flew open. The brown horse took a wild leap to the right, then back to the left, then kicked its heels almost straight up to the bright lights that lit the arena.

Stoner leaned way back, his head almost banging against the horse's rump. Dragging his spurs along the horse's neck, he waved his free right hand. About the fourth jump out, he lost his hat. Then the buzzer sounded, and the crowd roared.

"Was that good?" Lynda asked.

"Should be an 80-point ride at least!" the old man reported.

The man on the saddle horse rode around to help the rider to the ground, but just as Stoner leaned over to grab the man, the bucking horse jumped and kicked once more. The snap of the hoof catching Stoner's leg sounded to Austin like a fast ball hitting a wooden bat in Shea Stadium.

Stoner dropped straight to the ground, and the audience moaned. He tried to stand to his feet, but his right leg collapsed, and he signaled for help. Several cowboys sitting on the arena railing jumped to the dirt, raced to his side, and half-carried him out of the arena.

"Where are they taking him?" Austin asked.

"Back behind the stands. There's a hospitality tent set up for contestants. They'll probably have a doc check it out. Old Brady's tough. He'll be all right. And he won some money with that ride."

"Excuse me, I think I'll slip around and see if I can talk to him now." As she walked in front of the rodeo crowd, she felt as if every eye was watching her.

At the back of the arena a man with a deputy sheriff badge and a big, black felt cowboy hat sat on the fence next to a gate that seemed to lead to a large tent.

"Sorry, ma'am, this area is for contestants only."

"I need to talk to Brady Stoner."

"He ain't up to much talkin' right now. Are you family?"

"No."

"Well, this area is for family and press only."

"Press?"

"Yeah, are you a reporter?"

Austin quickly dug into her purse and pulled out a business card. "I work for Atlantic-Hampton Publishing Company. Do I need to get a press pass, or is this sufficient?"

"Atlantic-Hampton? Are you the outfit that publishes Joaquin Estában's books?"

"Yes, we are! Do you like them?"

"Yep. I sure do. 'Course they ain't as good as Louis L'Amour . . . but then who is?"

"May I go through?"

"Yes, ma'am. Say, do you suppose you could get me an autograph from old Joaquin?"

"Sure. Just keep that card and write to me. I'll see that you get an autographed copy of his next book."

"Hot dang! That would be swell! Thank ya, ma'am!"

"No problem. Where did they take Brady Stoner?"

"Into the tent, I think."

Inside Austin found several cowboys milling around and a couple of kids about six or seven trying to rope a chair. Over in a corner on a cot, the turquoise-shirted cowboy lay stretched out. She walked up to the men around the cot and waited for an opening.

"You got to get that thing x-rayed," one man insisted.

"It'll be all right. Just a bruise." Stoner grimaced.

"All right? We heard it break clear across the arena."

"I've got to get to Albuquerque. I drawed good there, too!"

"Come on, Stoner, get that thing looked at. You can't ride broncs with a broken leg."

"Since when? I've been hurt worse than this. Besides, it's not broken! Anyway, you got to keep that ambulance here in case someone gets really hurt."

One of the men spotted her. Then all of the men stopped talking and looked her up and down.

You have seen a lady in a dress before . . . right?

"Excuse me, gentlemen. Mr. Stoner, I'm Lynda Austin from Atlantic-Hampton Publishing Company. I believe Joaquin Estában told you I would be meeting you here."

"Pardon me, Mrs. Austin, if I don't stand, but

I happen to be hurtin' just a tad."

"That's quite all right. And it's Ms. Austin — Ms."

"Yes, Miss Austin. Joaquin said you wanted to talk to me about the Strip."

"Yes, but I don't suppose this is a good time."

"Lady, I'll tell you what," one of the men interrupted. "Why don't you drive this bullheaded Idahoan to get x-rayed. You can talk on the way. Will you do that for us?" Then turning to Stoner, he continued, "How about it, Brady? I got you a ride to the hospital with a purdy lady."

"Well, these boys won't get off my case until I get it checked. Miss Austin, if you can drive me down there, we'll talk."

"I'll go get my car and bring it around."

When she had plowed through to the other side of the arena, she found that all the vehicles were packed into the parking area so tight that she could barely open the door and crawl in. There was no way to drive out. Twisting her right ankle on the uneven ground, she rushed back to the tent amidst the noise of the crowd roaring over some event in the arena.

"My car's blocked; I can't get it out."

"You can drive my rig."

"Rig?"

Stoner winced as he tried to stand. He looked to be about six foot, kind of thin, with narrow, dancing brown eyes. His hat was crammed down on his brown hair.

"Help me out there. We'll gather up Capt. Patch

105

and pull for the hospital."

"Capt. Patch?"

"My travel partner. He'll want to ride along. Grab my chaps and hand me my riggin' bag, would you?" He pointed to turquoise leather chaps and a dusty leather duffel bag.

She grabbed one in each hand.

"Now come over here," he commanded.

He threw his right arm around her shoulder and hobbled along beside her.

"What did you say your name was, darlin'?"

"Lynda Austin. And please don't call me anything so condescending as darlin'," she flared.

"Condescending? I guess that means it's pretty bad, huh? Have you got a middle name?"

"Eh . . . yes, it's Dawn. But Lynda will be fine, Mr. Stoner."

"No, no, Lynda Dawn sounds better. Call me Brady. I don't have a middle name. Are you doin' all right? Hope I'm not too heavy."

"I'm fine. Which pickup is your rig?"

"That black and silver Dodge over there!"

They struggled to the truck, and she tossed the chaps and the rigging bag in back. "Give me the keys, and I'll open up."

"Keys? They're in the ignition, of course. This isn't New York City. It ain't locked."

Opening the door, she stood back and watched him struggle to pull the battered leg into the cab of the pickup.

"Where's this captain guy? Maybe he should drive."

"The captain isn't much of a driver."

Stoner let fly with a loud, shrill whistle. From out of the dark shadows a black and white dog flew through the night, jumped to Stoner's lap, and positioned himself in the middle of the seat. Its tongue lolled out to the right, and it began to sniff at Austin.

"A dog?"

"Yeah, but don't tell him that. He thinks he's human."

"What's on his eye?"

"A black leather patch."

"What happened?"

"A mule kicked him in the head when he was a pup. He lost his right eye."

"But why the patch?"

"He thinks it's cool. It seems to impress the lady dogs. That dog will never bark unless you take the patch off. Then he goes ballistic."

Austin crawled into the driver's seat and strapped on a seat belt. "Can we scoot this seat forward?"

"I don't think I'd better. I need plenty of room with this leg."

"Is that the shifter down there? Why isn't it up here on the steering column? Where's the P–R–N–D?"

"It's a standard transmission with a clutch. You do know how to shift, don't you?"

"Eh . . . yeah . . . sure. It's just that in New York everyone takes a . . . It's been a long time."

A really, really long time!

They jumped, bounced, and lurched their way out of the parking lot and onto the street.

"Which way?"

"Just keep following this road to the left. Hey, I think Capt. Patch likes you."

"How can you tell?"

"He didn't bite you. And he seems really interested in your perfume. That is strong stuff, lady."

"Oh . . . well, maybe I overdid it."

"No, no, I think it's great!"

A doctor and several nurses ran through the lobby toward an elevator as Austin helped Stoner through the emergency entrance of the hospital and into the waiting room.

"I'll go park your pickup. What do I do with Capt. Patch?"

"Leave the sliding window in the back open. Then he can come and go when he wants. I appreciate your driving me down here," Stoner added. "I promise I'll sit down and talk to you about the Arizona Strip after they fix me up."

Lynda Austin didn't try getting the pickup out of first gear as she cruised the parking lot searching for a place large enough. Leaving a sleeping Capt. Patch in the front seat, she stepped inside the hospital and settled down in the waiting room.

Forty-five minutes later a nurse rolled Stoner out with a bulky plastic splint from his shin to just above his knee. His jeans leg was slit to his thigh, but he still wore his boots. The blonde young woman with a white blouse that was too tight parked him in front of Austin.

"Here he is," she announced. "Is this your wife?"

"Eh . . . no," Stoner admitted.

"Girlfriend?"

"No, I wouldn't say that."

"Oh," the girl said beaming, "well, if this begins to bother you, Brady, just call me, and I'll come loosen that brace. You have my home phone number, don't you? You can call anytime!" She smiled, raised her eyebrows, and glared slightly at Austin.

"I sure do, sugar, and I can't thank you enough," Stoner replied.

Lynda Austin pointed at the leg. "That looks pretty serious."

"Doc said three months, but I figure I'll give it two weeks."

"You're joking."

"Why would I do that? I've been hurt a whole lot worse than this. Say, do you mind pushing me out to the truck? I haven't learned to navigate this too well."

"Are you keeping the wheelchair?"

"Nope. You'll have to bring it back here."

After helping Stoner into the truck beside a still-sleeping Capt. Patch, she returned the wheelchair, and then climbed back into the 1990 pickup. "How about me buying you some dinner, and we can talk?" she suggested.

"Sounds good to me. I know a great place. Head 'er back toward town. Say, do you always dress like that at a rodeo?"

"Eh . . . it was my first rodeo."

"Well, what did you think? Isn't it great!"

"I didn't see much, remember? You were the third one out."

"Oh, yeah . . . well, listen, we could go back and catch the tail end if you'd like."

"Why? I only came here to talk to you. Anyway, I apologize for dressing so inappropriately."

"Oh, no . . . I like it. I think a dress is great! You know, this is just between you and me, but I think most women look better in dresses. You know what I mean? Most gals just don't . . . well, jeans often . . . You know, dresses cover a multitude of sins. Only those little barrel racers ought to wear tight-fittin' jeans. That's my theory. Oh, I wasn't talkin' about you, of course. I mean, I have no idea what sins your dress is coverin' — if any! Slow down! Turn in here. Here it is!"

"Eduardo's Burger Barn? This is that good place to eat?"

"Oh, yeah, man, wait 'til you see the food! It's great! Say, I guess I'll need your help to get out."

Austin parked the big pickup next to two others. As she slid her foot down to the asphalt, her left heel gave out and twisted at the ankle before she corrected herself. She staggered around to Stoner.

He threw his arm over her shoulder and limped along to the hamburger joint.

"Don't you need some crutches or something?" she asked.

"Nah. I can get along just fine. They're just

a nuisance — you know what I mean?"

She held the door open, and he stumbled in.

"Hey, Eduardo! How you been, partner?"

"Stoner, you dog! Where do you always find these gorgeous señoritas?"

"Lynda Dawn, darlin' . . ."

She shot a frowning glance his way.

". . . this is Eduardo. Watch out for him. If he starts applying that Latin charm, you'll be dancing the flamenco out in the street before the night's over."

"What can I grill for you?" the wide-smiling Mexican asked.

"Two Eduardo burgers with jalapeños, bacon and cheese, two jumbo curly fries with gravy, and a couple of cans of Coke."

"Oh, no, I can't eat that much. I ate something called a buffalo burger at the rodeo," she protested.

"What?" Stoner glanced over at her. "Oh, no, that was just for me. You can order whatever you want."

"I'll-I'll have a cup of coffee," she stammered.

They had just slid into a booth when two cowboys burst through the front door.

"Hey, Brady!" one called. "Did you break that sucker?"

"Yeah, but I've been hurt worse."

The tall blond cowboy in the black hat sauntered over. "Does this mean you aren't goin' to Albuquerque?"

"I guess not, and I drew good, too. Give my

regards to the boys."

"We'll do that." Then the cowboy looked over at Lynda. "Didn't I see you at the rodeo tonight?"

"Yes, I was there for a while."

"Well, ma'am, we'd be happy to take you to Albuquerque!"

She laughed and shook her head.

The mass quantity of food arrived and filled the entire table. The hamburgers were the size of dinner plates.

"So," Stoner mumbled between bites, "go ahead and tell me what you're lookin' for down in the Strip."

For the next thirty minutes she explained the situation with Fondue and the Harrison manuscript as he wiped the fried potatoes through a river of gravy and occasionally looked up at her.

"What I need is someone who can drive down there with me and help me find that cabin," she concluded.

"Well, two hours ago I'd have had to dig up some names, but it looks like my rodeo career just took a turn. I think I'm going to have a couple weeks to spare after all. I know that country as well as any man, so I might as well hire on to be the outfitter."

"Outfitter?"

"You know . . . the guide. You did say you'd pay for it, right?"

"Yes. Uhm . . . just what do you think it's worth? I did mention that this is coming out of *my* pocketbook, not the company's, didn't I?"

Stoner picked his teeth and wiped his hands on his jeans. "Well, here's what I was figurin'. You pay for the room, board, and gasoline and one hundred dollars a week. If we find that valuable manuscript, you give me a thousand. How's that sound?"

"You've got a deal, Mr. Stoner." She reached out and shook his slightly greasy but strong and callused right hand. "What do we do first?"

"Go to bed," he offered.

"What!" she gasped.

"Come on, Lynda Dawn, I meant we turn in for the night and get an early start in the morning. We'll have to buy some supplies, of course. We can't go down into those canyons without food and water and stuff."

"Actually I was thinking the same thing. Now I need to get a room. Where can I find a good motel?"

Stoner crammed a forkful of curly fries and gravy into his mouth and chewed quickly. "You don't have a room for the night yet? There isn't anything in town left. This is roundup week. They've been booked for months!"

"Well . . . I guess I could drive back to Vegas."

"No, no, you don't have to do that. I'll work something out."

"Where are you staying?" she asked him.

"I planned on sleeping in my rig over at a rest stop near Shiprock, but with the broken leg, I guess I'll just park it out at the roundup grounds with the others. But then maybe I'll . . . bingo! I got it! Hang on. I'll see if I can roust out some rooms."

Brady Stoner stumbled his way to the pay phone at the front of the Burger Barn. In a few moments he returned with a wide grin.

"Hey, it's all set. Heather Martin's girls are sleeping over at a friend's tonight. She's got two spare rooms. What do you say?"

"Is it sort of like a bed and breakfast?"

"Well, not exactly. It's more like double-wide on the outskirts of town. Heather's a friend of mine. Goes way back. There's no charge, and she'll throw in some ham and eggs for breakfast."

"You mean she just agreed to let some stranger from New York move in?"

"Well, of course, I didn't know you were strange, and you don't get to move in — just spend the night. Really, you'll like Heather. She's the school librarian now. You two can talk about books."

Lynda took a sip of cold coffee. "What does her, eh, . . . husband think about this?"

"Now that's a clever way to pump me. Richard died about six years ago. She's a widow. About your age, I suppose."

"How old are her daughters?" She stared as he shoved about a quarter of the hamburger into his mouth at once.

He swallowed hard. "About fifteen and sixteen, I would guess. They're gettin' as pretty as their mama. I didn't think I had time to stop by for a visit this time through, so this old broken leg

114

came in handy for one thing anyway."

"Just how old do you think I am?" she pressed.

Without a moment's hesitation he shot back, "Twenty-nine?"

"Close. I'm thirty. Now you don't mean to tell me Heather's twenty-nine?"

"Well, no, she would be thirty-three on her next birthday, but I still think of her as twenty-nine."

"Are you sure she doesn't mind company?"

"Come on. She's a sweetheart."

Austin drove them down two side streets, under the interstate, and out to where the street lights ended at a double-wide mobile home set back in tall cottonwood trees.

Capt. Patch jumped out the back window, across the pickup bed, and tore off down the street.

"Where's he going?"

"He's checking on an old girlfriend, I reckon."

"How about Brady Stoner? Is that what he's doing?" she teased.

"Nope. Heather's . . . well . . . like a sister, but that's a long story."

She helped Brady up the stairs. A black-haired woman in jeans welcomed them. She had stunning blue eyes and wore an ample supply of what Austin identified as Queen of the Prairie perfume. Barefoot, but wearing a ruffled white blouse and dangling feather earrings, she ushered them into the country blue kitchen.

They visited for several minutes around the oak

table, drinking coffee and eating fresh oatmeal cookies.

"Oh . . . I just remembered!" Austin moaned. "All my things are in my rental car back at the rodeo."

"I'll run you down there, Lynda," Heather offered. "Looks like Brady won't be driving for a while. Let me grab my boots, keys, and put on some lipstick. Brady, show Lynda the girls' rooms. You two can decide who gets which."

Reaching the end of the hallway, Austin said softly, "I like her."

"Yeah, she's great. How's this one look? I don't think I could sleep in a pink room."

"That's fine. What happened to her husband?"

"Got killed on the job several years ago."

"And she hasn't remarried?"

"Nope. Says she won't even date until the girls are grown. She's a stander. You know what I mean?"

"I think so."

"Lynda," Heather called. "I'm ready if you are."

The two women left Brady Stoner heading for the shower and walked out to Heather's pickup truck.

"Have you known Brady long?" Austin finally thought of something to say.

"About ten years, I suppose. He's a good man. Solid as a rock."

"He has nice things to say about you, too."

"Well, that's the way Brady is — always finds

116

the best in every situation."

"Heather, you don't have to talk about this if you don't want to, but how did your husband die?"

"Brady didn't tell you?"

"No, he just said he died at work or something."

"Well, if you have the time, I'll tell you a story you could write a book about."

FOUR

Heather Martin and Lynda Dawn Austin bounced in the pickup across the darkened cow-pasture-turned-parking-lot and pulled up next to the small, white car sitting alone like a lost calf in the moonlight.

"This yours?"

"Yeah. Kind of pitiful-looking out here, isn't it?"

Heather turned off the lights and killed the engine. She locked her tanned arms against the steering wheel and stared out into the night.

"About six years ago Brady and my Richard were working late in the fall for the Quarter Circle W Ranch down on the Strip. We all lived around the ranch headquarters about twenty-five miles south of the highway. Well, the boys finished the fall gather up on the Kaibab."

"Fall gather?"

"The roundup and branding in the high country."

"They still have roundups?" Austin quizzed.

"Yeah . . . where did you think that New York City filet mignon came from? Anyway, in the fall

118

they drive the cattle down across the Hurricane Cliffs to Wolf Hole Valley to winter out. It's not so severe down there. After the cattle's moved down, they have to go back and ride points."

"Points?"

"High mesas up in the timber country that jut out into the valley. They're so steep that the cattle that wander up there can get snowed in and can't get down. Many a lost cow has frozen out on the points. So the cowboys ride up there after the main roundup and clean up the points.

"Well, that particular year Richard was up on Wildcat Point, and Brady was working Sublime Point when a horrible blizzard hit."

"In the desert?"

"It's above seven thousand feet up there. The wind was blowing from the high country back out to the point, and the snow was so bad the horses refused to ride into it. A horse won't ride long straight into a storm, you know. They'll either turn around and go the other way or just give up. So Brady actually led his yellow gelding down the side of Sublime Point. Until that time no one knew it could be done."

"Sort of like the movie *Snowy River*?"

"That's what I figure. But Richard never made it back to camp that night. Well, the storm was so bad the next morning that none of the boys wanted to go out. You can't blame them. Chances of makin' it back alive weren't very good. The powder was drifting so bad they couldn't even use a snowmobile. It was a killer storm. But Brady took two fresh horses and started out to Wildcat Point on his own. He knew he could make it in because the storm would be at his back, but there was no guarantee he could ride out of there. And not even Brady could get a horse to ride off the cliffs at Wildcat Point. It drops straight off for a couple thousand feet.

"I stood by the cabin window day and night for forty-eight hours staring into that blizzard and praying for Richard and Brady.

"About daylight the third day, Brady came troopin' through the snow leading a horse. The one he had been riding died in the storm, but he loaded Richard on the other and walked him out of there."

"Was Richard — dead?"

"No, but he was delirious. In fact, he never regained his senses. We helicoptered him up here to St. George, but he died after three painful days. It was a blessing to see him go. He was hurting so bad I couldn't stand it." Heather reached for a tissue box on the dash, pulled out a couple, and then continued in the same soft, pained voice.

"I was in a daze for a while trying to arrange the funeral and take care of the girls. We didn't have much more than a pickup and a couple of boxes of clothing to our name. Anyway, on the day of the funeral, Brady was one of the pallbearers, of course. And after the words at the grave site, he came over to me, and we hugged a long time and cried a lot. Then Brady handed me an envelope and said, 'Heather, this is Richard's. I

120

owe it to him, so I want you and the girls to get a place in town.' "

"What was in the envelope?"

"A cashier's check for twenty thousand dollars."

"Twenty thousand dollars? Why did he owe that to Richard?"

"He didn't. It's just Brady's way of making sure I had to take it."

"Where did he get that kind of money?"

"Rodeo money, I figure. He had a pretty good summer that year. He's always talking about buying a ranch of his own. Anyway, at the time I was too stunned and disoriented to figure it out, so I put a down payment on this trailer and doled out the money for a while, living on that and what I could make as a teacher's aide. Then I landed the librarian's job, and things have been better since.

"That's the way Brady is. My girls think 'Uncle Brady' can walk on water. And you know what? So do I!"

Lynda wiped back a tear. "Thanks for telling me. I feel better about hiring this total stranger now." She glanced over at Heather in the darkness. "If I'm not out of line, why haven't you and Brady . . . you know . . . gotten together? You seem so compatible."

"I thought about it a few years back, but it won't ever be. You see, a man like Brady has a pretty strict code that he lives by. In his eyes I am now, and I will continue to be forever, Richard's wife.

121

Brady will look after me and the girls to the day he dies. That's his bond to Richard. Nothing on this earth will break that."

"I think I like that code."

"Some of the ladies never see past the gold buckles, flash of the chaps, and the dimples in his smile. He deserves better than that. Be good to him, Lynda."

"Well, actually, I'm just hiring him for a few days to help me locate a cabin down in the Strip, that's all."

"Yeah . . . sure. I guess I forgot. Well, that's the story of Heather Martin."

Lynda followed Heather back to the double-wide. But her mind was up in a blizzard on Wildcat Point. With Heather's help she freed the heavy suitcase and box of papers from incarceration in the trunk of the rental.

When they reentered the house, Brady was asleep in his borrowed bedroom. Lynda dug out her University of Michigan sweats and tennis shoes to wear the next day, selected Hot Desert Night #4 from her perfume box, and went to bed.

The sound of giggling woke her up the next morning. She slipped out from the desert print sheets and pushed open the pink and white gingham curtains. In the bright light of sunrise, Brady stood propped against an old redwood picnic table with a rope in his hand talking to two laughing teenage girls who looked up at him with wide eyes.

Austin scooped up her clothes, a cosmetic bag,

and poked her head out the door. Finding no one in the hall, she scampered toward one of the bathrooms. On the way she passed Heather Martin dressed in jeans and a long-sleeve blue denim shirt rolled up to the elbows.

"Mornin', Lynda. How was your night in the pink room?"

"Oh, fine. Thanks again, Heather. Say, are those your two girls out in the back with Brady?"

"Yes. I called them last night to say he had stopped by, and they decided to come home at five this morning. Hope they didn't wake you up too soon."

"Oh, no. Which is the older?"

"Heidi is the blonde. She's sixteen. Wendy has dark hair, and she's fifteen going on twenty-five. They . . . well, they miss their dad a lot. Brady still treats them like little girls. He'll bring them a doll and spend time playin' with them. If anyone else did that, they'd be insulted. But Uncle Brady can do no wrong. You hungry for breakfast?"

"Oh, please don't do anything fancy. Just some coffee and toast will be fine."

"No problem. Brady has to have his bacon and eggs every morning. I'll fix plenty."

Lynda Austin spent most of the breakfast sitting quietly as Brady and the girls teased each other. Heidi and Wendy shot an occasional icy glance toward her.

Girls, I'm not interested in anything but a reliable guide in the desert. Don't worry, I'm not going to steal your beloved Brady off to New York City. Brady Stoner, I don't really understand why you don't marry their mother.

Suddenly he stood up, shoved a toothpick into his mouth, and announced, "Time for me to go to work. Right, boss?"

Austin tried to smile.

"Heather, we'll be taking my rig, so we'll leave that pitiful little white thing in your drive if it's not too embarrassin'. Now, Heidi, how about you findin' Capt. Patch, and Wendy can help Miss Austin load her things."

"I'll help Heidi," Wendy insisted as both girls started toward the front door.

"I'll help Lynda," Heather offered. "What about you? Can you get your gear together, cowboy?"

"I'll manage," he assured her, reaching for his black hat.

Heather carried the file box out to Brady's pickup as Austin toted the suitcase. "Hope you'll forgive the girls for being so possessive of Brady. They don't ever seem to want to share him."

"It's all right. They're both turning into beautiful women."

"Yeah. Kind of scary, isn't it? Especially when I remember what I was like at their age. When I think of what the next few years will bring, I get to missin' Richard even more."

"The Lord can help you get through it."

"Well," Heather said with a sigh, "I sure do hope so. But to tell you the truth, I just about prayed myself dry during those two days of looking at the snow and waiting to hear about Richard."

Lynda searched her heart for a good reply and found none. They heard Brady shout, "Come on, Patch, you old Romeo!" The black and white dog broke from his trot beside the girls and jumped into the back of the pickup, diving through the half-open sliding window and into the cab.

"You girls watch out for the boys. If they don't behave, you tell 'em your Uncle Brady will teach 'em a lesson or two. Now take good care of your mama," Brady lectured. He grabbed Heidi and Wendy around the shoulders and gave them each a quick peck on the cheek. Then he stepped over to Heather and wrapped his arms around her. They hugged for what seemed like a long time. Finally he tossed the keys to Lynda and hobbled to the passenger side.

"You're the driver, boss. It's about time I earned my money."

Within seconds they were bouncing and grinding gears down the driveway and onto the streets of St. George.

"Heather's really nice. Which way we turning?" she asked.

"Turn right. Yeah, Richard was a lucky guy."

"Lucky? He froze to death."

"No, I mean," Brady muttered, "lucky to have Heather for a wife."

"She's not married now," Lynda continued. "Where are we headed?"

"The Corral. See it down there? Well, maybe

125

she'll find a nice city guy sometime."

"What is this? A feed store? It looked to me like you were hugging her an awful long time."

"Yeah, but it's got Western wear and supplies, too. I figure a widow just might miss those hugs most of all. So I try to oblige."

"What a nice fellow. Why are we stopping here?"

"Supplies."

"What kind of supplies?"

"Clothes, for one."

"What do you mean, clothes?"

"Obviously, you need some good jeans and boots, a decent shirt, and a hat. This is the desert — not Central Park on a Sunday afternoon."

"What's wrong with my clothes?"

"They aren't tough enough."

"Tough?"

"Yeah, the prickly pear cactus will stab through sweat pants, not to mention what a rattler can do to tennis shoes."

"Snakes? I hate snakes worse than Indiana Jones!" she moaned.

One hour later she emerged from the store carrying several large heavy sacks and wearing new clothes and a frown.

"What am I doing? $320! I don't have that kind of money," she mumbled.

Capt. Patch stood on the top of the cab like a canine sentinel. Shoving the packages behind the seat, she piled in.

"Now you're lookin' sharp," Brady complimented her. "I won't be nearly so embarrassed being seen with you."

"Embarrassed? That's why you had me buy this stuff — because you felt embarrassed?" she fumed.

"Sure. Besides, you had to have something to match the intensity of the perfume. What are you wearing anyway?"

"Eh . . . it's not important."

I'm not about to tell him that it's Hot Desert Night #4.

"Take a left here," he pointed.

"Where?"

"Right there! Where are you goin'? You've got to turn when I say turn!" he huffed.

"That's a supermarket. What on earth do we need to go to a supermarket for?" she complained.

"For lunch."

"We just ate breakfast."

"This is the last store we'll see for at least ten, twelve hours. We better take some lunch supplies."

Austin turned left into the driveway of a small stucco home, ground her way into reverse, and backed out into the street to go back to the market.

Two weeks? I'm not about to drive this thing for two weeks. We'll just have to find that cabin today. Then I can call Gossman and . . .

She bounced into the parking lot and stopped near a pay phone. She dug a twenty-dollar bill from her purse. "You go buy lunch supplies. I need to make a call. How's your leg feeling?"

"Oh, I been hurt a lot worse than this. Did I ever tell you about the time I was ridin' saddle broncs, and my foot got caught in the stirrup, and I got drug around the arena with my head bouncin' in and out of that horse's hooves?"

"No! What happened?"

"I lived." He grinned. "What do you want for lunch?"

"Anything will do. I don't think I'll be hungry after all that breakfast."

Brady limped away while Capt. Patch perched back up on top of the cab. Austin waited impatiently at the telephone for the connection to go through.

"Kell? Hey, this is Lynda. . . . No, we're in Utah, but we're driving down to the canyon right now. Me and Brady Stoner. The cowboy who knows the area. Remember? The one Joaquin Estában recommended? . . . I guess . . . sort of. In a cowboy kind of way. Anyway, I just wanted to . . . No, I haven't even . . . Of course not! Come on, Kelly. You know I'm out here for research! . . . No, but . . . well, dark brown. They're sort of a dreamy brown, I guess. . . . About six feet, thirtyish. Look, I just hired the guy to show me the canyon. I didn't hire an escort! Quit giggling or I'm going to hang up! Look, we're going down into the Arizona Strip south of St. George, Utah. We'll be gone all day. At least ten hours or so, and I was calling so that someone would know where I am."

She moved the telephone receiver to the other

ear and rubbed the lobe that now sported a silver feather earring.

"How would I know if he can dance the two-step? He's got a broken leg. . . . He was kicked getting off a horse at the rodeo, and it happened to be a good ride! He scored an 84 and won the go-round. Well, I'll tell you someday. Anyway, I've got to go. Look, think about me. I'm the one driving that big rig — pickup . . . I've got to drive it; he has a broken leg, remember? . . . Don't worry, I will. . . . You behave *yourself!* It doesn't concern me one bit. The only thing I'm worried about is snakes. . . . Yeah, that's what he said. *Hasta la vista,* Kell. I'll call you in a day or two. . . . Yeah, yeah, dream on. Bye."

Austin lounged beside the pickup looking at the gear tossed in the back when she saw a shopping cart headed her way. A girl who looked about eighteen and had her hair in a ponytail was pushing the cart. Brady had his arm slung over the girl's shoulder hobbling along.

"Toby, this is Lynda," he said introducing her.

Chomping on several sticks of gum, the girl looked her over. "Hi! Are you with Brady?"

"Yes, I'm his mother."

"No, really — are you his girl?"

"No, I'm his boss. He works for me."

"What? Really? Are you kidding me? Oh, wow! I didn't know you could . . . How much would it cost if I . . . Oh, here! Here's your groceries." She turned and winked in his direction. "Goodbye, Braaa-dy!"

"Goodbye, darlin'! Remember what I told you about gettin' a different saddle. Thanks for helpin' me out."

He set the bags of groceries behind the passenger seat, and they climbed in.

"That's a lot of groceries for twenty dollars," she observed.

"I'm a good shopper . . . and I kicked in a few bucks myself."

"Goodbye, darlin'," she mimicked. "Do you use that for every woman?"

"Yep. Isn't she a sweetheart? But if it makes you jealous, I'll stop."

"Jealous?" she boomed. "What on earth do I have to be jealous about? Good grief, I don't care who you flirt with."

"I wasn't flirtin'."

"You were too!"

"Was not. It so happens that I roped one July with her brother, and she tagged along, that's all."

"Brady Stoner, you were flirting! Forget it. Look, let's get going. Where's our road?"

"Out there and to the left."

"It looks like it just leads back to those houses."

"Trust me." Brady reached over and scratched Patch on the head. "This is called Price City Hills, but it will lead us to Arizona."

About three miles south of St. George the houses ended. Five miles south of the town, the pavement suddenly disappeared.

"Oh, great!" she moaned. "This is the end of the road!"

"It doesn't end." He laughed. "Just keep drivin'. Oh, the pavement ends. That's 'cause we're in Arizona now. But just keep drivin'. There isn't any blacktop down in the Strip except the state highway."

"You mean we're going to be driving on roads like this all day?"

"Not hardly. They get a whole lot worse." Brady pushed his cowboy hat back revealing the less-tanned part of his forehead.

The first twenty miles was fairly level across the high desert plateaus spattered with creosote, yucca, and sage. A plume of dust rose up behind the pickup and drifted to the east. The slight wind blew in a few scattered clouds that seemed to be stacking up against the mountains on the eastern horizon.

Austin could see another mountain to the south.

"Is Mt. Trumbull up there? Fondue said the cabin was beyond Mt. Trumbull."

"That's Seegmuller Mountain. Trumbull's a long ways away," Brady reported.

Austin kept her window rolled up to prevent the dust from fogging in, but Stoner kept his rolled down. Finally to reduce the heat reflecting through the window, she rolled down her window as well.

They came to a fork in the road. "Do I go right?"

"No, left!" he hollered, and she swerved to the left.

"What's over there?"

"Just a corral."

"But the road seems nicer than this one."

"Well, watch out. This thing gets pretty narrow in the pass."

The gravel road turned to a dirt road at the beginning of the chaparral country leading up toward Mt. Seegmuller. Austin found herself shifting into second and driving carefully as the one-lane road wound its way to the pass. They drove through junipers and piñon pines, none of which seemed over twelve feet tall. The dust was not as bad at the slower pace, and Austin caught a hint of coolness in the air.

Coming down the mountain grade, she noticed a dry lake bed to the west and what looked like a cabin tucked back against the hills on the right.

"Could that be it?" She pointed. "Is that a cabin?"

"Oh, it's a cabin, but it's been abandoned since 1964. The floor is ripped out, and the inside is about a foot deep in dried manure. We can ride over and take a look if you like."

"Eh . . . no, that's all right. Does this road get any better?"

"Nope."

Austin straightened the rearview mirror. "Did you know this mirror keeps slipping down?"

Stoner looked back at the road behind them. "Yeah, but there's no one back there."

"There hasn't been one single car on this road since we left St. George," she added. "No wonder Harrison came down here. A person could go for a long time and never even see anyone."

"You really think it was Harrison?"

"Well, the more remote we get, the more promising it looks. Doesn't anyone ever come down here?"

Stoner reached behind the seat and began to rummage through the groceries. "Oh, a BLM guy will be along during the week, but this being Saturday, I don't expect we'll see anyone."

"This valley looks different from that one south of St. George," she commented.

"There's a little more rain and snow in here. That means more grass can grow. 'Course it's all dried up now, but there are still plenty of nutrients in it. The Rockin' K will bring some cattle in here next month, and then there'll be a little traffic when huntin' season cranks up."

"What do they hunt for?" Austin quizzed.

Bringing out a thick deli package, he sliced it open with his pocket knife. "You want a hot wing?"

"Well, I don't think . . . I have to drive."

"Ah, you can drive with one hand. Come on, these are really good. Give one a try." He handed her a barbequed chicken wing and then proceeded to stick a whole one in his mouth, pulling the bone, stripped clean, back out.

Austin nibbled at the edge of a wing, trying to hold it away from her new clothes. The first taste was sweet. Then it blazed on her lip like a lit match.

"Oh! Give me something to drink. Give me some water! Quick!"

Stoner fished out a clear plastic container of

133

water and pulled the spout up on the squeeze bottle. "Good, aren't they? Here. As I was saying, the hunters will come in and look for deer and antelope."

Propping the steering wheel against her knees, Austin held the hot chicken wing in her right hand and the water bottle in her left. After a couple of gulps, she took a deep breath.

"Oh, is this the place where the deer and the antelope play?" she managed to tease.

The words had just escaped her scorched mouth when a tan and white animal with black horns darted right in front of the pickup.

"Oh, no!" she cried, dropping the chicken wing and clutching the steering wheel with a sauce-covered right hand. She swerved abruptly to the right.

"Keep on the road!" Brady yelled.

Trying to correct the error, Austin cranked the steering wheel violently to the left, and the vehicle flew back across the road, crashing into a sage about the size of an orange tree. They slid down into a rocky ravine about eight feet lower than the valley floor.

"Turn off the engine!" Brady yelled as his braced leg slammed into the front dash. Capt. Patch bounced off the windshield. Dust fogged around them as the vehicle halted.

"You should have hit it!" he yelled.

"What was it?" she hollered.

"An antelope . . . a pronghorn. You should have stayed on the road and hit the animal!" he shouted.

"Quit yelling at me! I did the best I could!" she cried, reaching up to brush a nervous tear from her eye.

"Ahhhh!" She let out with such a piercing scream that Capt. Patch picked himself off the floorboard and dove out the window on Brady's side.

"What's the matter?"

"Get me something quick!" she screamed. "The hot sauce . . . I just rubbed it in my eye! Quick!"

Stoner struggled to move his leg around so he could reach over her and grab the water bottle that had dropped to the floor. He couldn't brace himself and suddenly fell into her lap.

"What are you doing?" she screamed with her eyes clamped shut. "What are you doing?" She swung at him and cracked her left hand into the steering wheel.

"I'm gettin' the water you dropped! Hold still!"

"Get out of there. Get away from me!" she cried.

Stoner sat straight up and pushed her head back on the seat. "Open your eye! I have to flush it out," he hollered.

"I can't! It hurts!"

"Open it up!"

Brady began to pour the water over Austin's right eye. "Hold still!" he called.

"You're getting me soaking wet," she complained.

"Of course I am."

"Get me a towel," she bawled.

Stoner poured half the bottle over her eye and

then looked around the rig. He yanked the snaps on his shirt and pulled it off, placing it in her hands.

Lynda wiped her eyes and tried to control her sobs. Finally she opened her left eye and glanced over at Brady Stoner.

"What do you think you're doing?" she yelled. "Where's your shirt?"

"In your hand."

Finding the ravine too narrow to open the door, he struggled to pull himself out of the pickup window. His broken leg dragged along like a sack of potatoes.

"Where are you going?"

"To see how much damage you did to my rig."

"You make it sound like my fault."

"Whatever."

"It's not my fault," she protested. "I didn't even want to be driving, remember?"

Dragging the bum leg over the rocks of the ravine, Brady Stoner knelt down and surveyed the damage. Capt. Patch darted in and out among the sage while Lynda Austin looked in the rearview mirror and tried to do something with her soaking wet hair.

She pushed open her door and slipped out to the boulders. Her Western shirt was soaking wet and clung to her. She noticed red-hot barbeque sauce smeared on her new jeans.

"What's the damage report?" she asked, puffing as she climbed out of the ravine.

"The gas tank, oil pan, and radiator are still

fine, so we should be able to drive it — *if* we can get it out of that gully, replace the busted front left tire, and straighten the tie rod. Of course, it will have a horrible shimmy."

"It doesn't look like we hit anything with the body. There aren't any dents."

"Not yet." Stoner took a deep breath and sighed.

"Look . . . I'm sorry. I did the best I could. I panicked. What else can I say?"

A slight smile cracked across his face.

"You're right. I shouldn't have yelled at you. Hey, we'll get it out. It was kind of excitin', wasn't it? Kind of like riding a bull. You aren't sure you're goin' to live through it, but it's a buzz for a few seconds."

"Did we make the bell?" she kidded, starting to grin.

"Yeah, and we scored pretty well, I assume. Probably picked up a few dollars anyway."

Stoner laughed and looked her over.

"I'm a mess," she confessed.

"I've seen worse."

"I need to change my shirt."

"Why?"

"It's soaking wet and it . . . you know, clings." She started to blush.

"Don't worry about that, ma'am. I can assure you it reveals absolutely nothing!"

"Stoner, I don't know whether you meant that as a compliment or an insult."

"Let's see if the rig will drive out of there first. Then you can change into anything you want."

"What do we need to do?"

"You need to get in there and put it in low four-wheel drive and back it — "

"Me?"

"It's a cinch I can't drag this leg down there."

Lynda Austin crawled down the boulders and back into the front seat of the pickup.

"Put it in neutral and start the engine," Stoner ordered.

The motor caught on quickly.

"Now you see that short gearshift down there on the floor?"

"Yes."

"Step on the clutch. Then shove that down to the right and down again."

"It won't go."

"Pump the clutch."

"What?"

"Step up and down on the clutch and try it again."

"There! I did it!"

"Good . . . Now put it in reverse and see if you can back it out of there."

"Back?"

"It's our only chance. Now let out the clutch nice and slow."

The truck started to climb out and then stalled against a rock.

"It's stuck," she yelled above the engine noise.

"Give it a little more gas!" he shouted.

She slammed the accelerator to the floor, and the pickup bounced over the rocks and then shot out of the ravine like it was launched.

"Stop!" Stoner screamed, waving his arms and trying to run after her as she ripped up the valley floor, spinning the wheels back out into the dirt roadway.

She slammed on the brakes. The rig skidded to an abrupt stop, killing the engine and bouncing her against the back of the seat.

Stoner puffed his way through the dust and up to the side of the pickup. "Nice drivin', darlin'," he chided.

She stuck her tongue out at him. "Oh, I bet you say that to all the girls! Should I move it off the road?"

"Nope. I'll change the tire right here."

"But what if someone comes along? We'll be blocking the road."

"Yeah. Then they'll have to stop and help us." He stopped and stared at her for a minute. "Man, that perfume you're wearin' is really potent. I like it."

"Oh, well, maybe I went a little overboard when I . . . perfume? Oh no!" Austin reached back for her suitcase and pulled it up to the front seat. "Oh, no!" she moaned again.

When she opened the case, the aroma of perfume flooded the pickup. She pulled out the leather pouch that had held twelve neatly packed perfume bottles. All had been crushed on the impact of the journey into the ravine.

"Wheweee!" Brady choked and moved back away from the cab.

The slippery bag slid through her hand, and the perfume and bottle fragments spilled across the Indian blanket seat covers.

"I can't believe this!" she shouted, jumping out of the pickup and dragging her suitcase behind her. Several personal items tumbled to the dirt road.

"I think you're losin' it," Brady cautioned.

"Losing it? Losing it! I'm as calm as I can be," she yelled.

"No, I meant your goods there. Clothes and . . . They're fallin' on the ground."

"What? Oh, no! Close your eyes!" she yelled. "Turn around and close your eyes!"

Brady hobbled around facing away.

"It's not exactly like I never seen those items before," he teased.

"Well, you've never seen mine!" she hissed. "I can't believe this — my underwear in the dirt and my perfume spilled all over the seat of your truck."

"It what?"

"Don't you turn around yet!"

"You poured that perfume into my truck?"

"I didn't pour it. . . . That must be four hundred dollars worth of perfume in there!"

"Great! Now my rig will smell like the parlor at a . . ."

"At a what?"

Brady limped around to the back of the rig and began to crank down the spare tire. "Never mind. Look, I've got to change that tire. How about you

cleaning up the cab the best you can and haulin'
us out some lunch?"

He yanked a black T-shirt out of his duffel bag
and pulled it on. Then he changed the flat and
beat on the bent tie-rod with the tire iron.

Lynda had the front seat picked clean of broken
glass and had spread a loaf of bread and several
packages of meat and cheese out on the tailgate
by the time Brady let the jack back down. His
jeans and T-shirt were covered with dust and dirt.

"Now you're a mess," she teased.

"Does this mean you ain't goin' to the prom
with me tonight?"

She shrugged. "I've never been to a prom in
my life."

"Sounds like a good story."

"I'll tell you about it if we're ever locked in
jail and run out of things to talk about. Clean up
your hands, cowboy, and eat some lunch. How's
that leg feeling?"

"Oh, it doesn't hurt, but it's sure getting to be
a bother. How are you doing? You about ready
to go back to New York?"

"Not me, buckaroo. Oh, I'll admit that I had
that thought for a split second."

"When you lost control of the truck?"

"No . . . when I broke all my perfume!" She
laughed. "Here have a sandwich. What kind did
you buy?"

"One Jalapeño Supreme and an All-American.
Which do you want?" He handed her the All-
American before she could answer. "Now tell me,

141

what is there about this Harrison thing that keeps drivin' you?"

She sat on the pickup tailgate, swinging her legs and munching on her sandwich. "Brady, did you go to college?"

"Well, the first two years I went to the College of Southern Idaho at Twin Falls."

"What did you major in?"

"Rodeo mainly. Oh, I was officially labeled an ag major. You know, basic animal production, metal shop, a class called fertilizers. But most days we were out at the practice pen. They've got a good rodeo team there, you know."

"Rodeo's a college sport?"

"Sure. I even had a scholarship. How about you? Where was college?"

"I went to Michigan and majored in journalism and communications with a minor in philosophy." She stopped long enough to chomp down on another big bite of sandwich. Looking around for a napkin, she finally wiped her mouth with the back of her hand and continued.

"I liked the major, but philosophy's a drag. I spent four years taking classes where all they did was sit around and ridicule my Christian faith. From day one, the professors tried to make sure that no person would leave the class a believer in God."

"Did they succeed?" Stoner asked.

"No. They didn't change me, but they sure made me discouraged. And do you know what their best weapon was?"

"Was it Bishop Berkeley's *Principles of Human Knowledge?* Or Hobbes's *Leviathan?* John Stuart Mill's *Utilitarianism?* Or Kant's *Critique of Pure Reason?* Friedrich Schleiermacher's *On Religion,* Jean-Paul Sartre and his existentialism, David Hume and his phenomenalism, or perhaps the neo-realism of George Santayana?"

"Whoa!" Austin whistled. "This isn't your ordinary cowboy! I thought you were an ag major."

"The first two years. Then I started to rodeo professionally, and I needed classes that I could take on Tuesdays and Thursdays and still have the weekends free. By then I was attending Northern Arizona in Flagstaff. So I ended up graduating *summa cum laude* in philosophy. A more worthless degree has never been given. I haven't had a philosophical thought since 1985."

Austin stared at Stoner. "I don't believe this. You're not the type to take philosophy classes."

"That's what the professors kept sayin', but they had to give me good grades because they all graded on a curve, and I was usually the only guy in class who did all my assignments. Now here's the answer to your original question. The most effective tools in most classrooms to destroy faith are Harrison's *Alone at the Edge of the Universe* and *When the Last Rock Crumbles.* Right?"

"I still don't believe this. You graduated in philosophy, and you're out riding wild horses for a living?"

"Not wild horses. Those are the mustangs running around the Great Basin. I ride bucking horses. But how does all this explain why it's so important to find another Harrison? I'd think you'd want to leave his other book buried."

"That's just the point. In this third book — and I'm the only one who's read it — Harrison refutes all those earlier claims. He claims to believe in God!"

"No kidding? Well, isn't that a pop?"

"That's why I've got to find it and see that it's published. I owe it to all those other students who had their faith shot down by those wonderful philosophy classes."

"Sounds good to me. And I thought you were in it because it would make you world famous and fabulously rich," he teased.

"Yeah, that too. Sometimes a gal's got to take the bad with the good." She laughed.

"You ready to roll on?"

"Soon as I have a drink. You still want me to drive?"

"Sure," Stoner encouraged her. "Nothing else can go wrong now. Right?"

Both of them stared at each other and then broke into wide grins.

"Don't think about it too much." She laughed.

Lynda decided not to change her shirt since it was now mostly dry. They repacked the cab and kept the windows rolled down to try to defuse the perfume.

Capt. Patch refused to ride up front and now roamed in the pickup bed. Just as Lynda began driving down the road, the front wheels started to wobble.

"What's wrong?"

"It's out of alignment."

"What am I supposed to do? I'm only going fifteen miles an hour."

"Drive faster."

"Are you serious?"

"Yeah. Sometimes it doesn't wobble when you go faster."

At thirty-five the wobbling decreased, and at fifty it almost disappeared.

"Is it safe to go this fast out on this road?" she asked.

He laughed. "Well, I guarantee you won't get a ticket. Don't worry about it. I know a guy over in Fredonia who can fix the truck. He owes me a favor, too."

Austin pointed to a dust cloud fogging up the far side of the valley. "We have company."

"Yep, it looks like it's on the way to Pipe Springs or maybe Rincon."

"Rincon? Fondue mentioned someone in Rincon. I could dig out the notebooks and find his name. Marland . . . or Milton or . . ."

"Marlowe?" Stoner suggested.

"Yes, that's it! Do you know him?"

"Maybe. Half the people in Rincon are named Marlowe."

"Really? That's odd."

"Not really. It's a strange little town. I'll tell you about it sometime. Let's see if we can meet this old boy at the crossroad. Looks like he's coming in from Poverty Mountain."

"Why do we want to meet him?"

"Maybe he's an old-timer who knows something about an old man livin' in a canyon. Or perhaps he's a tourist that needs directions. Maybe just a local hankerin' to sit and talk a spell."

As they inched closer to the other column of dust, Lynda turned to Brady and blurted out, "How about you, cowboy — do you believe in God?"

"Shoot, yeah. Doesn't everybody?"

"You know what I mean. Do you really? Do you pray and read the Bible and worship and — "

"To tell you the truth, I'm kind of all prayed out, if you know what I mean. Blink your lights."

"What?"

"Blink your lights, and they'll know to stop at the crossroad."

She turned the lights on and off several times. "What do you mean, you're all prayed out?"

"It's kind of a long, boring story. I think they're slowing down. Hey, look, they stopped!"

"Do you always avoid the subject when it's about your personal faith?"

"Yep. Say, that pickup looks just like Eddy St. John's."

"St. John? My boyfriend . . . I mean, this guy I'm dating . . . well, I used to date . . . his name is St. John."

"Is he Paiute?"

"What?"

"Is he a Paiute Indian?"

"Heavens no!"

"Then he's not related to Eddy."

"I think they're backing up."

"That will keep them out of our dust."

"It looks like a bunch of children!"

"All right! It's Amanda and the kids."

"Who?"

"Eddy's wife."

"She's a . . . large lady."

"And a sweetheart!" Brady added. "Slow down, and we'll shimmy to a stop."

Before the rig halted, Capt. Patch flew out of the back of the pickup and began leaping into the giggling, playful arms of the St. John children.

A girl who looked about twelve ran to their rig before either could open a door. Her long, black hair hung in two pigtails, and she wore a red T-shirt with "Paiute Nation Pow-Wow" emblazoned on it.

"Hi, Brady. Did you come to see me?" She smiled.

"I sure did, Jamie. And you're lookin' more beautiful every day."

The young girl scowled. "Brady, you aren't married, are you?" She wrinkled her wide, brown nose and shook her dangling beaded earrings at Lynda.

"Nope. This is my boss, Lynda Dawn Austin, from New York City."

"Does she smell bad? Is that why she uses so much perfume?"

"Well, I'm afraid some got spilled. Jamie, you aren't married yet, are you?"

Jamie giggled, then assumed a serious expression. "Now I told you, Brady Stoner, you'll just have to go on and live your life without me. I'll probably just break your heart, and then you've wasted all the good years of your life waitin' for me!"

"But, Jamie, you'll always be my first love," Brady teased.

"I know," she said matter-of-factly. Then she ran off to the other children to play with Capt. Patch.

"What was that all about?" Lynda asked.

"Just a game we started playin' the day Jamie came home from school cryin' because some boy at school called her ugly."

"But she's a beautiful girl."

"That's what I keep tellin' her. Come on, I'll introduce you to Amanda."

Brady slid out of the pickup and hobbled to the Indian woman who stood about five and a half feet and looked to Lynda like she weighed close to two hundred pounds.

"Amanda, darlin', I should have stole you away from Eddy twenty years ago!" He threw his arms around her and gave her a tight squeeze.

"Brady, you lie just like all those other whites, but I sure like your lies better." She laughed. "Eddy's going to be jealous when I tell him I talked to you out here. Now what happened to your leg? And what's a big rodeo star doing out on the

148

Strip?" She glanced over at Lynda Austin. "You out here on business or pleasure or health? She does look a little sickly."

"Strictly business. Amanda, this is Lynda Dawn Austin. She's a New York City book editor doin' a little research out here, and I'm showing her around."

Raising her coal black eyebrows, Amanda nodded. "Well, I bet you are!" Then she asked again, "What about the leg?"

"Oh, that old bucking horse at the Dixie Roundup decided to crack a bone as I was piling off. It'll probably keep me out of Las Vegas come December. What about Eddy? I thought I'd see him in St. George."

"He took a horn up in Cedar City. Punctured a lung. So he's recuperating at the house. I guess he won't be back on the circuit until January in Denver — if we can afford the entry fees."

"Well, maybe it's time for me and Eddy to find some real work," Brady commented. "The kids look healthy."

"The kids? They're indestructible. Always playing, always laughing. But they haven't learned much about working yet."

"What are all of you doing out here anyway?" Brady quizzed.

"Playing Indian," she replied. "With Eddy laid up, things are getting tight. You know how rodeo life is, Brady. So me and the kids have been out harvesting some piñon nuts."

"How'd you do?"

"Oh, we probably have enough for a couple bags of groceries, so I can't complain." Her round face seemed incapable of any expression other than a smile.

Brady stepped over and put his arm around Amanda's shoulder, walking her away from Austin and the children. Lynda noticed that he reached into his back pocket, pulled out his wallet, and shoved some bills into Amanda's reluctant hand. Finally they turned and walked back toward the others.

"What kind of research are you doing?" Amanda asked Lynda.

"We're looking for a cabin where an old man has been living like a hermit down in this area."

"Yeah," Brady joined in. "All we know is that it's south of Mt. Trumbull toward the canyon."

"Did you ever hear of Shotgun Canyon?" Amanda asked Brady.

"Eh . . . yeah, I heard rumors about it. But we never ran any cattle that close to the rim. Is there really such a place?"

"My father says that it got its name because an old white man lived in there and would shoot his shotgun at anyone who tried to enter."

"Do you know how to find it?" Brady asked.

"All I know is that there's a trail to it somewhere east of Paw's Pocket. But no one goes down there. For all I know that story might be from fifty years ago. Father doesn't have a good sense of chronological order."

"Well, it gives us something to check out."

"I wouldn't spend much time up here," Amanda continued, waving her silver-ringed fingers toward the sky. "These clouds are bringing in rain. If it gets slick, you know what it's like."

Austin shifted her weight to her right boot and tilted her head. "What's it like?"

"It gets so muddy and slippery that you can't drive out for several days. But we're coming out tonight, so we should do all right," Brady assured her.

"We better get home and buy some groceries for supper," Amanda called. "Come on, *niños*. Leave Capt. Patch and jump in the truck!"

Then she squeezed Brady and kissed him on the cheek. "Thanks. We'll square up after Denver."

"Or Ft. Worth or San Angelo or Houston. You know it doesn't matter."

Brady and Lynda walked her to the rig. "Yeah, I know. Listen, stop by if you're up at Pipe Springs. You and your lady friend are welcome to stay with us. Mother would be delighted. She still clips the newspaper whenever your name is listed."

"Give my regards to all of them. Bye, kids," he shouted.

"Bye, Braaa-dy!" they intoned in unison.

"Get a life, Brady Stoner," Jamie yelled. "You can't sit around pinin' for me forever!"

"You're breakin' my heart, Jamie!" he hollered back with a smile.

A tall column of dust rolled to the east marking

the direction of Amanda's exit.

"She seems like a nice lady — and a good mother," Lynda commented as they stood watching the departing pickup.

"Yep."

"You gave her some money?"

"Oh, not much. I only had sixty dollars in my wallet."

"And how much did you give her?"

"Sixty dollars. But I don't need any money on this trip. You're buying groceries, right?"

"Eh . . . yeah, that was our deal. But doesn't it bother you to be broke?"

"In the winter of 1988 me and Eddy were makin' some Christmas money breakin' wild horses for the BLM to sell at auction, and I got a bad chest cold that turned into pneumonia. I spent four weeks in bed, and it was Amanda's mother who nursed me day and night for most of that time. She treated me like a son, wouldn't let me pay her a thing. I couldn't even buy the soup or pay for loads of wash at the laundry. Someone like Eddy and Amanda . . . Well, you just help them out. That's all."

Austin climbed back into the pickup and waited for Brady to pull himself up.

"This rig really does smell bad!" he complained. "Maybe I can park down by the stockyards and get it to smellin' normal."

She lifted her sunglasses and stuck out her tongue.

"What about this Shotgun Canyon?" she asked.

"Does it really sound like the kind of place a man could hide out in for sixty years?"

"As long as he had enough shotgun shells to keep others away, I guess. I'm not so sure it's a real place. There's always a lot of stretchers about a place like this."

"How will we find out if it's real?"

"We'll head for the rim southeast of Paw's Pocket."

"What about the storm?"

"If there's a trail, maybe we can locate it and then race over to Fredonia. I think we'll have time."

"And what happens if we get stuck?" she pressed.

He dug through the grocery sacks and pulled out a large bag of Oreos. "Well, then we'll have another adventure for you to call home about. Now rev her up, boss, and let's get on down the road."

"You really don't have to call me boss."

"Well, darlin' is too condescendin'; boss is too formal; and I'd gag havin' to say Ms. Austin, so I'll just call you Lynda Dawn."

"I told you Lynda is fine."

"Nope. Lynda Dawn. I think *linda* is Spanish for beautiful, so your name must mean beautiful sunrise. . . . I like that."

The road narrowed and grew rocky as they wound around the base of Mt. Trumbull. Lynda was surprised to find an ample supply of pines and firs scattered on the mountain. The only trace of civilization was a large wire-fenced corral covered with No Trespassing signs.

"What's that all about?" she asked.

"Oh, I suppose it's an outfitter who brings hunters in during the season. They're afraid someone is going to use their pasture . . . or somethin'. Kind of refreshing to know that no matter how remote you think you are, there's always someone there to tell you to get off their property."

As they descended the mountain, the road flattened out across the Tuweep Valley. As far as Lynda could see, there was absolutely no sign of life.

"The road looks better up there." She pointed.

"Yeah, but we aren't going that way. The road will fork right up here past that pile of lava rocks. Take a right."

She raced along, keeping the shimmying at a minimum, and then slammed on the brakes. Several Oreos tumbled from the bag and rolled on the floorboard.

"Why didn't you turn?" he shouted.

"Turn? Turn where? Where's the road?"

"Right there!"

"Right where?"

"There — the bent grass. See how it's bent over to make two tracks across the valley?"

"That's a road?"

"It will take us up to Paw's Pocket. Trust me."

"I can't drive down that! I can't even see where to steer."

"I'll tell you if you get goin' wrong."

"I'm not driving fifty miles an hour."

"No . . . no, you'll have to take it easy. The rig will shake pretty bad, so you'll have to hold on tight. Say, you want an Oreo?"

"No!" She hit a pothole that almost bounced them into the roof of the cab. "I can't believe I'm doing this!"

"You're doin' fine, Lynda Dawn. But you really ought to have an Oreo. Here. I've fixed this one up with double fillin'. Come on. It tastes as good as a Moon Pie."

Bouncing along with the front end in a constant shimmy, she glanced at Brady. "I can't take my hand off the wheel."

"Open your mouth."

Like a baby bird begging for a worm, she dropped her jaw. He slid over in the seat and reached up with a fat cookie. The rig hit a rock and lurched forward, causing him to cram the entire cookie into her mouth.

Austin slammed on the brakes. Stoner banged against the dashboard. The engine died, and she tried to get a breath of air. The result was a cough that sent black crumbs and white filling spraying across the cab of the truck.

He pulled himself back onto the seat. "If you don't like Oreos, just say so."

"Like them? I was about to be the only person on earth to die of an Oreo overdose! Have you got some water?"

"Yep . . . there's still some in here." He handed

her the new squeeze bottle. "And there's some out there."

"Where?"

"Look. On the windshield. It's starting to rain."

FIVE

The occasional drops of rain turned into a steady mist by the time they parked the truck somewhere southeast of Paw's Pocket and hiked toward the canyon rim. Capt. Patch scampered over the granite rocks ahead of them, his black tail signaling them to follow.

"Look, I don't mean to be forward, boss . . . I mean, Lynda Dawn, but if we're going to take a peek over the edge, we'd better hold hands or somethin' because it's mighty steep out there. Some folks have been known to panic at the height."

"Brother! That's the same dumb line I get from the geeks on the observatory at the Empire State Building. You afraid of heights, cowboy?"

"No, ma'am." Brady led the way over the wide granite slab. "I was just worried about you."

"Well, thanks for worrying, but I'll manage on my own. You're the one with the broken leg. Now if you need help, just admit it."

Stoner shoved down his black cowboy hat and limped along. "It's a little slick with this drizzle, so be careful. But it will be worth it. The sight will knock your socks off."

157

She took a deep breath. The storm clouds smelled slightly of sulphur. "Look, I'll let you in on something," she boasted. "I live and work in high rises every day. My office is on the twelfth floor. It's this flat, barren land that seems strange, not heights."

Brady shoved his hands into the back pockets of his Wranglers and turned toward her. "And I'll let you in on something. The Empire State Building is about 1,250 feet high — "

"I know that."

"And, Lynda Dawn Austin, we're now standing about three times that height above the Colorado River!" He swooped his arm to the east. Lightning cracked on the distant rim, and yet flickers of daylight illuminated the muddy river coursing far below them.

Staring down at the incredible expanse of the canyon, she felt every muscle in her body freeze. "Oh!" she yelped. "Oh my . . . I . . . no! Don't go out there! Wait! I mean . . . Where's the guard rail? What are they doing leaving this open? A person could get hurt. Come back here! Brady!" Her voice cracked. She sat down and clutched at a granite rock beneath her.

"Lynda Dawn, quit ramblin'. It's unbefitting an editor. Now would you like to take my hand and walk over and get a good look at the edge?" She could see the dimples in his cheeks when he spoke.

"Absolutely not!"

"I think there may be a little trail down there on the side of this thing. It just might lead to Shotgun Canyon. I'll take a peek. You can't see it unless you go right out to the edge."

"Brady Stoner," she cried, "you are going to take my hand and lead me back to the pickup . . . right now!"

"What?"

"Right now, Stoner!" She was almost in tears. Her hands began to shake. Suddenly the rough, wet granite felt amazingly slick. Any moment she expected to plunge over the edge that was still nearly twelve feet away.

"We just got here!"

"I'm the boss, and you'll do as I say! Get yourself over here and help me back to the pickup . . . right now!" Her voice rested somewhere between begging and absolute terror.

"Hold on, darlin', I'll be right there."

"Don't call me . . . oh . . . hurry . . . please!" she sobbed.

Stoner lifted her shaking frame to her feet. His right arm gripped her shoulder and pulled her away from the edge of the sheer rock canyon and back to where Capt. Patch now stood guard on top of the pickup.

"It's okay. . . . We made it. Lots of folks freeze up at that sight. It's one of the canyon's little-known vistas, and maybe that's why."

"You can turn loose of me now," she instructed.

"Surely, Lynda Dawn. You just sit here." He held the door open for her. "But I need to go back out there just for a minute."

"Why on earth?"

"I've got to check that trail. I still want to know if we could take horses down it."

"We? Are you kidding? I'm not going down that! No way. Harrison wouldn't be stupid enough . . . He would have fallen off and died fifty years ago. He couldn't be — "

"I'll be right back."

"Brady!" she cried out as he disappeared behind some rocks. "If you fall over, don't expect me to come looking for you! Brady, do you hear me?" It wasn't that cold, but she could feel her teeth chatter as she pleaded.

Stoner returned to the pickup in about five minutes as the mist turned into a rainy drizzle. The clouds had dropped lower, and the sky grew dark. Lynda came walking toward him from the west, over a granite scarp. A slight roar of wind whipped over the canyon rim.

"What were you doin' up in the juniper?" he asked.

"I was visiting the ladies' room — if you must know." She glared at him and climbed back into the driver's seat. "Now if you're through humiliating me in this place, don't you think we should get off this plateau?"

"Yeah . . . look, I thought . . . well, you said heights didn't bother you."

"Normal heights don't bother me. There's nothing normal about that place!" She jerked the pickup forward before he had his door completely closed.

"This is obviously a dead-end lead," she continued. "But I didn't expect to find the cabin on the first day anyway. I think we should go to Rincon and find this guy Marlowe. Maybe he can point us in the general direction of Harrison's cabin." She could feel her wet hair mat to her forehead. "I think the tires are starting to slip a little."

"Slow it down and put it in four-wheel drive."

"Will it shake a lot?"

"Yep."

They plunged along the grassy ruts for several minutes without talking. Lynda glanced over at him and noticed a smug look on his tanned, chiseled face.

"Is that the road over there?" she asked.

"Yeah, you're getting a little to the left."

"Well, at least we're not slipping."

"That's because we're still on the grass. Once we make it out to the dirt road, it will get real slimy."

"We are not coming back to that cliff again," she insisted.

"We'll talk about it when we get to a motel in Fredonia."

"No, we won't." She brushed back her damp, dark hair and then gripped the steering wheel tight. There was a knot in her stomach. "We are not coming back. I have no intention of spending my vacation and my savings account wetting my pants." She refused to acknowledge Brady Stoner's response.

"What if Harrison really had his cabin down that trail?"

"He wouldn't dare! In fact, I'm going to write to the Bureau of Land Management demanding they do something about that cliff. It's . . . it's reckless endangerment, to say the least."

"Yeah," Brady teased, "maybe they'll fill in that hole."

"I'm serious, Stoner. Besides, Harrison was an old man. A ninety-year-old man doesn't hike in and out of a canyon like that."

"Who said he had to? Didn't you tell me this Fondue guy was packin' in the supplies?"

"I don't want to talk about it," she barked.

By the time they reached the dirt road, it was dark enough to flip on the headlights. Lightning streaked the top of Hurricane Ridge.

"This will take forever at ten miles per hour," she complained.

"Nope. It will take about eight hours. We're about eighty-five miles from Fredonia. But once we hit the highway, there'll be pavement."

"How far is that?"

"Around seventy miles from here."

"Oh, great. If we're lucky, we can get there by two or three in the morning!"

"Maybe the rain will stop."

"What if it doesn't?"

"Then we spend the night on the Kanab Plateau."

"Where?"

"Up the road a piece."

"Have you got any friends out here we can stay with?" she asked.

Stoner took both hands and tried to move his cast around to a more comfortable position. "No one lives this deep on the plateau whether they be friend or foe."

"Does Brady Stoner have some foes?"

"Oh, you'd better believe it. 'He makes no friend who never made a foe.'"

"Tennyson?" Clutching the steering wheel, she jerked the rig back into the center of the narrow dirt road. "Did you feel that?" she blurted out.

"It's startin' to get slippery all right."

"And dark," she complained. "When those heavy torrents hit, I can barely see out — at any speed."

"Well, boss, here's the options as I see it. We can keep creepin' along, but there are some washes across here that fill up fast in flash-flood weather like this. If we happen to get stranded in one of those, we're talkin' about life-threatenin' danger. And even if we can keep goin', it will be three or four in the mornin' when we get back out to the highway."

"What's the alternative?"

"We could just look for some high ground and park the rig . . . try to sleep in the cab and see what it looks like in the morning. We'll stay dry but not too comfortable. I've got to find some way to keep this leg propped up for a while."

"Are there any other choices?"

"There's the old Tuweep church building."

"Where?"

"About three miles up the road."

"I didn't see any church when we drove in here."

"That's because we came by the St. George road. This is the Fredonia road."

"What's a church doing out here?"

"Well, it was built back in the thirties when folks tried to homestead here."

"Homestead? In the thirties? I thought that homesteading thing was a hundred years ago."

"During the Depression, a couple dozen families tried to come out here and raise a few crops. They even built the little one-room church. But by the time the war came along, everyone was broke, starvin', and moved off. In fact, the church is about the only building still standing. It's been vacant for over fifty years now. But it will be dry and out of the wind."

"Is the floor filled with manure?"

"Nope. The boys fenced it off years ago."

"Is it all right if we use the building? Isn't that trespassing?"

"Not out here in a storm. The Bar 88 leases the ground, and I know all those cowhands pretty well. Besides, no one will be coming by tonight — that's for sure."

"Well, let's try the church. What with you and your broken leg and Capt. Patch, the pickup looks a little crowded."

A few minutes later Brady motioned for her to

164

turn the rig to the right and out into the sage-brush. Just ahead stood an unpainted building overgrown with grass and sage. The wind had stacked tumbleweeds against the sagging wire fence.

She stared into the headlight-illuminated night. "Is this it?"

"Yeah. Do you still want to go in?"

"Eh . . . are you sure something Stephen King-ish won't happen?"

"Trust me."

"I don't suppose it has electricity, heat, or plumbing?"

"Nope. And that brings up a small problem. Do you have a bedroll in all that gear of yours?"

"A bedroll? Oh, sure, this is the time in the story where you announce that you only have one sleeping bag, and we'll have to share it, right?" She could feel her damp face start to flush. It hit her all at once how very alone they were.

"Now, boss, I'm disappointed in your opinion of me. I guess you believe most of those novels you publish and have a pretty low opinion of all men."

"Okay, okay, you're right. I didn't give you a chance to explain yourself."

"Thank you. As a matter of fact, I do only have one sleepin' bag with me. But why on earth should I carry two? Capt. Patch surely doesn't need one. But you may have the sleeping bag. I do have a nice throw quilt that Doc Myer's last wife made for me, and it'll do me just fine. We won't have a fire, but we can eat chili beans out of a can and little sausages . . . and drink lukewarm Cokes. Now if you don't like that, you can lock yourself in the pickup, and I'll stay in the church . . . or lock yourself in the church, and I'll stay in the car. You decide what you're comfortable with."

"Eh . . . actually . . . I'd kind of like for both of us to go into the building, but I'm not sure I'll be able to fall asleep."

"That's fair enough. Leave the engine running and the lights on 'til I find us a way inside."

After about six trips through the mud, Brady Stoner had Austin, Capt. Patch, suitcases, and a bag of groceries inside the one-room church. With flashlight in hand they inspected the building.

"It's all empty!"

"You expectin' pews and hymnbooks?"

"I guess."

The room was dry. Only a faint breeze whistled through the walls and windows. The floor felt slightly gritty to Lynda's hand, but Brady had swept most of the dust and dirt to the side with an old broken broom he found. The odor in the room reminded her of her grandmother's house in Key Largo where all the little nicknacks were covered with dust after years of neglect.

She sat cross-legged with Brady's sleeping bag zipped open and wrapped around her like a comforter. With a small star quilt wrapped around his shoulders, Brady opened a can of chili beans with his stockman's knife. His legs seemed even longer sprawled out across the floor in the shadows.

"I think there are some spoons in that sack." He motioned. "Now, darlin', this isn't — "

"Don't call me darlin'."

"Well, eh . . . Lynda Dawn, darlin', this isn't exactly an elegant New York restaurant. Say, can you eat in the dark?"

"I suppose. Why?"

"That flashlight will only be good for about half an hour more, and I don't want to use it up."

"Sure. Let's give it a try."

"Here you are. You need a knife?"

"For canned beans?"

"No, for protection. I want you to feel safe."

"Brady Stoner, do you promise before God and these witnesses you won't try any funny business with the lights out?"

"What witnesses?"

"Eh . . . Capt. Patch."

"I so promise. Hey, that's the first time I ever gave a woman a vow in a church."

"You may turn out the light."

Lynda held the can close to her mouth and fed herself a spoonful of beans. The room was totally dark.

"There's one thing you ought to know," she added.

"What's that?"

"I bite."

A deserted building in the absolute middle of nowhere! This is about as removed from midtown Manhattan as it's possible to get in the States. This is

167

*crazy. Lord, I've spent the past twenty-four hours
doing things that I would have sworn I'd never do.*

"Are you still there?" he asked.

"Am I going somewhere? Of course I'm still
here."

"Kind of weird sitting in the dark with someone
smacking their lips."

"I don't smack my lips . . . Do I?"

"Yep."

"That's what Janie always says."

"Who's Janie?"

"My roommate. She's a flight attendant."

"I didn't know you had a roommate."

"Of course she's gone a lot. How about you?
Do you have a roommate?"

"Nope. But I do have a room."

"Where? Where is home to a travelin' cowboy?"

"Is it that time?"

"What time?"

"When we tell life histories?"

"I guess. It's going to be a long, dark night."

"Who goes first?" he asked.

"You."

"Why?"

" 'Cause I'm the boss."

She heard him scoot his broken leg around on
the floor. "Okay, here goes, but I'll make it short.
I was born in February of 1964 in — "

"February! So was I," she interrupted.

"What day?" he asked.

"The twelfth," she replied.

"All right! I knew you were an older woman.

I was born on the fourteenth."

"Valentine's Day? Well, isn't that charming!"

"No jokes."

"Why, certainly not . . . my little cupid." She giggled.

"I'd pour a bowl of beans over your pretty hair if it wasn't for the fact that I respect my elders," he returned.

"Okay . . . go on."

Pretty hair? He thinks this mess is pretty?

"As I was saying, I was born on a ranch in the Reynolds Creek, Idaho, area — which is in the boonies of the Owyhee Mountains about an hour and a half southwest of Boise. My parents still live in the family house and run the ranch with my second oldest brother Brock. He's about thirty-six.

"My oldest brother Butch was killed in a deer-hunting accident in 1981. My family started ranching in that area in 1892. I told you about college. I came down to the Strip and started cowboyin' during the off season about ten years ago. I lived down here and worked on most every ranch in the area.

"I've rodeoed for about ten years . . . been to the National Finals twice. My best year was '89 when I finished ninth. Four of the past seven years I've injured myself in a fall. I guess I'm sort of accident prone. I seem to spend more time re-cuperating than competing.

"I've never been married, and I don't have any children. The closest I ever came to getting married was when I was nineteen and dated a girl named Kathy. She dumped me for a computer whiz after my sophomore year in college. She married him, and they have a huge home just north of Boise and another in Sun Valley. He invented some sort of computer chip and runs a big company. Leaving me was the smartest thing that girl ever did.

"I'm savin' my money to buy my own place. There's a little valley on Red Water Creek just south of Beulah in eastern Wyoming — a great place to raise registered cows and calves. I aim to buy a ranch there.

"I don't plan on getting married until I have that ranch 'cause a woman deserves to have a little something when she gets started. So I keep rodeoin' and cowboyin', hopin' to see something come together. If it doesn't, I'll probably end up runnin' a feedlot or somethin'."

She heard Stoner take a deep breath. "Okay, your turn. You want some more beans?"

"Eh, no thanks." It was quiet and peaceful except for the sound of their voices and a steady patter of rain on the roof. Her hands and toes felt warm. The cold beans tasted amazingly good. The sleeping bag around her shoulders began to feel heavy, and she let it slip to the floor. Even with her eyesight adjusted to the darkness, she couldn't distinguish anything in the room.

It's like being blind. And kind of like prayer. You know Someone's there, but you can't see Him.

"Well, Lynda Dawn Austin was born in Key

Largo, Florida. Moved to Grand Rapids, Michigan, in the third grade. Graduated from the University of Michigan in Ann Arbor. I told you that, remember?

"My grandmother on my mother's side was Grace Loving Ramsey who was the editor for Martin Taylor Harrison's first two books."

"So that's what's drivin' you!"

"It's part of it. My grandfather on my mom's side — well, he was really my stepgrandfather — was named Lloyd. I never knew my other grandparents. Anyway, I have a brother named William who lives in Miami and imports Italian fountain pens and — "

"You can make a living doing that?"

"He's extremely wealthy. And an older sister Megan who's a school teacher and volleyball coach at a high school in Muskegon, Michigan. My father and mother divorced in 1972 when I was about eight. He's a building contractor in Alaska somewhere. He remarried a woman with six kids, and I haven't heard from him in several years.

"My mother died of cancer in 1988. Bitterness consumed her final years. She felt she had been cheated out of the good things in life. I should have spent more time with her, but it was always so depressing. Right out of college I worked in Chicago as a receptionist for Trademill Publications and worked weekends at a restaurant called Beef & Buns. Don't laugh!"

"I'm not laughing. I think it was Capt. Patch that was laughing."

171

"Anyway, I got on as a copy editor at Trademill. In 1989 I moved to New York City and became an assistant editor at Atlantic-Hampton. In '91 I became an associate editor, and in '92 I moved up to editor."

"And here you are."

"Here I am. I play a mediocre trumpet, like to shoot skeet, and wanted to be a spy when I was young but could never do chin-ups."

"You have to do chin-ups to be a spy?"

"That's what I thought. My favorite possession is a baseball autographed by Ryan Sandberg during his rookie year. I was hit by a foul ball and lost a lower front tooth. He came around and signed the ball after the game.

"I collect perfumes, am over-organized, and have used Autumn Rose Blush lipstick ever since the homecoming dance in my junior year in high school. Okay . . . that's about it. You now know everything about Lynda Dawn Austin."

"Oh, no, I don't. I didn't hear one word about loves and lovers."

"Well, that isn't very interesting. I enjoy dating, but I have had only three serious boyfriends."

"Were *you* serious, or were *they?*"

"A little of both. Robert Elliston was a poly-sci major at Michigan. We dated off and on for several years. But he worked on the governor's campaign and ended up in Lansing as press secretary. Then there was Patrick Lancaster."

"The hockey player?"

"That's the one. I was really serious about him.

We dated for six months, he proposed, and I accepted. Two nights before our wedding he went out with some blonde waitress at the Sheraton. When I found out, I called off the wedding and haven't seen or heard from him since."

"Whoa, that's pretty dramatic. A last-minute reprieve. How about this St. John fellow you mentioned?"

"Jimmy's a stockbroker. Works hard. Saves his money. Treated me very nice . . . most of the time . . . I mean, until last week. And he's as boring as mud. I think it's all over with him."

"Why?"

"Well, I've been too busy the last week to call him and see if it's all over. But the last I knew, he went out to Palm Springs to visit a former flame."

She could sense him snicker. "Well, darlin', I can assure you, it's definitely all over. . . . How about the future? What do you want to do — move down to the Keys and write novels, right?"

"Nope. I like being an editor. There's a secret satisfaction in taking raw meat and anonymously making it into a tasty morsel."

"That reminds me . . ." Stoner flipped on the flashlight. It seemed to give off more light than she remembered. "Speaking of raw meat, where are those little sausages?"

The light clicked off, and the conversation drifted from weather to old movies. The voices became softer until Lynda realized she was nodding off.

Later, lying on the hard wooden floor fully clothed with the sleeping bag pulled up to her neck, Lynda Austin thought about the review of her life she had given Brady.

Sometimes when I edit a book by or about someone famous, I am amazed at how much they were able to do, achieve, see, spend, love, cram into life. But my life . . . it can be completely scrutinized in three minutes, complete with detail and commentary in six minutes, tops. Lord, there has to be more than that! There's got to be something for me to do in life that will stretch beyond the self-written vanity blurb in Who's Who.

In the pitch-dark, musty room with the storm raging outside, Austin found it easy to imagine she was somewhere else. Warm, dry and comfortable, she let her drowsy mind begin to wander.

I could be in the hold of a ship sailing to the Orient, carried off by white slavers to serve a vicious Mongolian master. Or is it a surprisingly compassionate Mongolian master? Or I could be in a hovel in the jungles of Central America on the trail of notorious drug smugglers. . . . No, it's too cold outside for the jungle.

Ah, hah! I could be locked in the Gulag. Imprisoned for my faith in Stalinist Russia . . . "Long live the czar!" Or perhaps a Chiricahua Apache girl captured by a handsome but desperate American outlaw who is fleeing to the canyons and plans on taking me with him. Or I could be . . .

"Lynda Dawn?"

"Yes?"

"Did I wake you up?"

"No, not really."

"I couldn't get to sleep," he told her. "What were you thinkin' about?"

"Oh . . . nothing. Well, sort of . . . I mean, when I told you about my life, there wasn't much, was there? Thirty's still pretty young, but I really don't think I'll ever have to worry about someone publishing an illegal biography about me."

"Does that bother you? Do you want to accomplish something important?"

"Yes . . . I guess that's part of the reason I'm down here. It seems like something important to do."

"For yourself or for God?" he asked.

"Both, I guess. How about you, Brady? Are you going to do something important?"

"Yep."

"What's that?"

"Win the World Championship."

"When did you decide to do that?"

"When I was sixteen. I watched Bruce Ford beat out Mickey Young and J. C. Trujillo at the finals in Oklahoma City. I said, 'I'm goin' to win the World just like Bruce Ford!' "

"What about after that? What happens if next year you get that gold buckle? What then?"

"Then I'll find me that good ol' gal who will settle down with me on my Wyoming ranch and raise a pack of towheaded stock riders, ropers, and barrel racers . . . and leave all the important things in life to be done by busy folks in New York City."

"Yeah, well, we're getting pretty tired of having to carry the whole load," she teased. "How about you doing your share?"

"I thought about findin' a cure for cancer or child abuse, but I just couldn't think of any. So I guess I was meant to put a little protein on the table for those brilliant Ivy League minds to do their thing. It's okay. I can be happy with that."

"Did you ever want to do anything important for God?"

"I guess I never thought about it. Me and God don't interfere with each other too much, if you catch my meanin'."

"No. Tell me about it. Tell me about how you can be all prayed out. You said you'd tell me when we had lots of time."

"Are you sure you aren't busy? I mean, if you have other things to do . . ."

She grabbed up the flashlight and shined it in his blinking eyes. "Stop stalling, Stoner, and tell me the truth, the whole truth, and nothing but the truth." Then she flipped the light off.

"Did anybody ever compliment you on being subtle?"

"No. Never."

"I can see why."

"Stoner . . ."

"Yes, your honor. Well, this is the honest story why Brady Stoner doesn't pray as much as he used to. I think Heather told you about me bringin' Richard off Wildcat Point?"

"She told me all about it."

"Well, chances are she left out a few of the details. At the time I was attendin' a little Bible church up next to the highway whenever I got a chance. It was just a little rural church with simple folks like me. It reminded me of my home church up in Reynolds Creek. Well, that year before the fall gather, the preacher had been speakin' on prayer. I figured this was one subject I knew something about.

"Well, going out that day in the blizzard, I had one prayer. Over and over and over again I prayed, 'Lord, let me bring Richard in alive to Heather and the girls.' From the minute I rode off into that storm, I knew that prayer was going to be answered. That thought sustained me for two days and even kept me warm at night.

"Well . . . dad gum it, I did it. I brought him in alive, and it's haunted me ever since. Some nights I wake up in a cold sweat hearing him scream."

"What do you mean, scream?"

"Richard was alive, all right. But he was delirious — out of his mind in pain the whole time he was in the hospital. I don't know what the cold does to a body or a brain. I don't understand anything medically that went on. But he would scream in pain so loud that you could hear him out in the hospital parking lot. Hour upon hour Heather sat by his bedside and watched him suffer. I don't know how she did it. I would just hike up there on the rim behind the hospital and cry."

"Couldn't they give him any painkillers?"

"Oh, the first few hours they pumped him full of morphine and quieted him down a little. But after that he would rant and rave. He would say vicious, horrible things about Heather. He would call her names, put her down, even cuss at her. That wasn't Richard. You never met a kinder man in your life. It was . . . it was like he was being forced to view a horrible nightmare, and he told us every scene in shameless, gruesome detail. Dementia, I guess you call it. I never really understood.

"Lynda, I laughed and cried for eight hours the day he died. I couldn't tell if I was happy or sad. But I figure I was through prayin'. You see the Lord gave me exactly what I asked for. It would have been better for Richard, Heather, and the girls if he had died out on Wildcat Point.

"I don't want my prayers answered anymore. I figure God can just do things His way, and I'll accept it no matter what. So don't ask me to pray. I don't understand it at all. And I'm no good at it."

Both lay silently in the dark for a long time. The floor had begun to feel very hard. She longed for a hot bath and clean sheets.

"Lynda Dawn?"

"Yes."

"I'm sorry I said all that. I've . . . never told anyone all that garbage before. You shouldn't have to listen to stuff like that."

"It's okay."

"I promise I won't carry on like that again. I

had no business talkin' negative."

"No, really. It's all right."

"Thanks."

"Sure. Are you going to try to get some sleep?"

"Yeah, my leg's feelin' better now that it's propped up. How about you? Will you be able to sleep?"

"Oh, sure."

A good two hours later she finally dozed off.

It was the icky, slimy feeling of a rough, warm, wet tongue lapping between her fingers that brought her out of a deep, uncomfortable sleep.

Just enough daylight was breaking through the poorly boarded windows of the old church to allow her to see Capt. Patch, with his constant smile and a tongue that seemed to be permanently slung out the side of his mouth, standing above her hand. She could also see that Brady Stoner was not in the building.

Draping the sleeping bag across her shoulders and dragging it like a grand rustic train behind her, she opened the door and looked out across the valley floor. There was a bright campfire burning between the church and the pickup. Brady Stoner sat beside it in the morning shadows.

"Hey, Clint, what you doin' out there?"

"Who?"

"Clint Eastwood. You know, in *The Good, the Bad, and the Ugly*."

"Which one am I?"

"I haven't decided yet."

"Pull on your boots and come join me. The wind's died down, and it's goin' to be a beautiful mornin'. It will be a *linda* dawn."

Every bone in her body felt stiff and sore as she returned to her suitcase. Wearing the same clothes all night made her feel extra grimy. Her hair proved to be terribly tangled. She changed her shirt and socks and pulled on an insulated purple and teal nylon jacket and combed her hair.

It seemed strange not selecting a perfume, but she could smell the strong aroma of spilled fragrances on everything she wore. She found a wide purple ribbon and tied her hair back with it. Then she ventured out the door.

"Mornin'."

Moving closer, she could see that he had the little quilt padding a rock and had propped his bum leg on top of that near the fire. "Morning. How long have you been out here?"

"Maybe an hour. I hate missin' a sunrise . . . know what I mean?"

"Eh . . . not really."

"Sit down. That rock is dry by now. I found some shingles that had blown off the roof. Those and some dry sage make a nice little fire."

"It's beautiful out here."

"Yep. The wind blew the clouds up to the mountains and probably dried out the road some. The air is real clean, and the sun will be peekin' up over the Kaibab any minute now. Look at those pink clouds over there in that blue-gray mornin' sky."

For several moments Lynda Dawn Austin stared at the morning sunrise. The air was slightly cold, but the fire warmed her face. Every breath brought a freshness to her lungs and her mind.

The sage was still greenish gray, the grass still brown from the previous summer's sun, and the valley still completely devoid of any evidence of human life. Yet it all seemed in much clearer focus than before . . . as if yesterday had been in a flat perspective, but this was three-dimensional. In the far distance the mountains looked black on top, but she knew that was just the trees. Orange bolts of light heralded the coming sun.

She gazed in amazement at the orange, pink, blue, and black shadows in the eastern sky. Finally the sun peeked over the edge of the mountains as if checking to see if all was ready for its ascent. A quarter of it was up . . . and then a half . . . then the whole glorious sphere. For a moment it sat on the shadows of the horizon like a fifty-cent piece balanced on a counter. Then it shoved off and started its daily voyage across the light blue sea called sky.

"Well, thank ya, Lord. That was quite a display," Stoner mumbled almost, but not quite, to himself.

"Wow! That was something. Are the sunrises down here always like this?"

"No, ma'am. Sometimes they are awesome, but that's the best we can do this mornin'," he teased.

"No wonder you like working out here. Most days I hardly see the sun until I go to lunch. Can you imagine living in a place where they erect buildings so tall they block the sun? It's insane."

"Yeah . . . the sunrise is always sweet. But it also gets 100 or more degrees in the summer for sixty, ninety days at a time. And the wind chill can stay below freezing for weeks in the winter. That's when you decide if you really like livin' down here."

"How about you, Brady? You've been through it all."

"Yeah, I love it, but not just the weather. It's the quiet . . . the grandeur . . . the lonesomeness. This land doesn't crowd a man — in body or in spirit."

"Why not buy a ranch down here then?"

"It's all government lease land. I want to buy a place the radical environmentalists can't take away from me. You want some breakfast?"

"What are we having?"

"Fruit Loops without milk, leftover beans, bananas, and fairly cold Diet Cokes."

They sat for several hours at the little fire, talking mainly about the cattle business and the advantages of having irrigated hay fields and the absurdity of the *New York Times* bestseller list. The sun was a quarter of the way across the sky when they packed the pickup and scooped up Capt. Patch. Soon they were creeping along the muddy road back to Highway 389.

About 2:00 P.M. they reached the blacktop eight miles below Pipe Springs National Monument.

Stoner had Austin shimmy into Fredonia and straight to a mechanic's house. The man greeted Brady like a long-lost brother.

"I'm going across the street and rent us a couple of rooms at that motel," she informed him. "It will be morning before we go anywhere, right?"

"Yeah. Tony probably won't have it fixed up until this evenin'."

Lynda managed to get a shower, wash her hair, change clothes, have lunch, buy some perfume, and have a long talk with Talbet Turner of the Bureau of Land Management.

Just before six Brady Stoner strode unevenly out of his room, clean-shaven and wearing a red, white, and blue long-sleeve Western shirt. His black beaver felt cowboy hat was pushed to the back of his head as he held the guard rail and slowly came down the cement steps from the second story of the motel.

"You should have taken a ground-floor room!" she greeted him. "Is your truck fixed?"

"Well, Tony said he repaired the tie rod and the tire, but he couldn't do a thing about the horrible smell in the cab!"

"I'm sure you'll be pleased to know that I've bought more perfume. Are you ready for dinner?"

"Boss, let's get our terms square. Dinner is what you eat at noon. What we want is supper. And I just happen to know a great place."

"Somehow I figured you would."

County Line Pizza was really an old two-story farmhouse several miles west of Fredonia. Its upper floor was only accessible by outside stairs, which had been sealed off for years. The bottom of the house was converted into a pizza place complete with red-checkered tablecloths and a jukebox that seemed to Lynda to be incapable of playing any song written after 1962.

She enjoyed watching Brady limp from table to table visiting and kidding with everyone in the room. He finally limped back to her about the time a girl everyone called K. G. brought a huge barbequed chicken pizza.

"If you cain't eat it all, I get off at nine, Brady," she suggested.

"Why, thank ya, K. G., darlin'. I'll keep you on my mind all evenin'."

As soon as the waitress left, Brady looked at Lynda and grinned from ear to ear. His eyes seemed to sparkle. "I just can't help it."

"Stoner, I'm going to start carrying around a barf bag when I go someplace with you. Look, I don't care what you do tonight or who you want to eat pizza with."

"That's mighty considerate of you."

"But here's what I want to do in the morning. Mr. Turner at the BLM said he didn't think there was any way to make it down that ledge of the canyon. They won't let any of their personnel down there. Besides, he figures it's either part of the Grand Canyon National Park or Lake Mead Recreational Area. He said our best bet was to go straight west from the old Mt. Trumbull school. Do you know where that is? He said there was

184

a rumor of several old prospector types living out there."

Lynda followed Stoner's eyes to a man who had just walked into the restaurant and was talking to K. G.

"Brady, are you listening to me?" she insisted.

Suddenly, Brady Stoner stood to his feet, hobbled straight over to the man, and tapped him on the shoulder. The thin-faced man with weak eyes and sideburns turned in surprise.

Stoner let fly with a right cross to the man's chin and then a violent left uppercut that cracked like a whip. The man staggered back, trying to keep his balance.

She heard her own voice scream, "Brady!"

Stoner hit the man twice more in the midsection and then tackled him to the ground. Lynda joined the crowd forming around the two men.

Stoner pounded the man's head into the wooden floor of the restaurant over and over. Someone tried to pull him off but was violently shoved back.

"Brady! Stop it!" she cried. "Stop it! You're going to kill that man! Stoner, are you listening to me? Stop it!"

Surprising herself, Lynda Dawn Austin jumped on his back and tried to pull his hands away from the man.

"Brady, stop it!" she screamed in his ear. "Stop it, or you're fired!"

An icy glare met her eyes. "I quit," he growled, "so stay out of this!" Shoving her aside, he turned to throw another punch into the man's already bleeding face when a man with a badge and a gun suddenly appeared in the shadows of the cafe.

"Stoner! Stand up, turn around, and put your hands behind your head. Right now!"

Brady took several deep breaths and rubbed his bleeding knuckles. Then he stood to his feet and put his hands behind his head.

"Okay, folks, I'll take care of things," the deputy assured the onlookers. "Someone take care of Joe Trent."

No one stooped to help the injured man.

"Well, call the EMTs, for Pete's sake!" the deputy shouted.

After frisking Stoner, the deputy pulled his hands behind his back and snapped on plastic wristband handcuffs. "I told you, Brady, that if you beat up on Joe Trent again, I'd haul you off to jail!"

Again? Lord, what's happening? Who is this guy Trent? Who is Brady Stoner really?

"Brady," she called, "what's going on?"

He didn't respond.

"I don't know who you are, lady, but this cafe's in Mojave County. So I'm taking Stoner to jail in Kingman."

"Brady?"

Finally he looked back at her. "Listen, I'm sorry I can't help you find that cabin. There are some things a man's got to do — that's all. I don't figure you'll understand. Do me a favor, Lynda Dawn Austin. Leave my truck and Capt. Patch at Heather's. Tell her I'll pick it up when I get out

186

of jail. Could you do that for me?"

"Yes . . . but . . . what's this all — "

"There's no good explanation. Pray for me, Lynda Dawn Austin. Pray for me."

He sounded like a helpless child who was falling out of a tree.

She prayed for him.

She prayed for him when she checked out of the motel that she had hardly used.

She prayed for him when she loaded his things and hers into the pickup.

She prayed for him as she and Capt. Patch drove the hour and thirty minutes to St. George. Not remembering how to find Heather Martin's house in the dark, she called ahead and got directions at the minimart. When she pulled into the driveway, Heather was out in the yard to meet her.

"You said Brady was in trouble. Can we talk out here? I don't want the girls to hear. What happened?"

"Heather, he went crazy. I don't know what to say. I've never seen anything like this even in the city. This guy walks into the pizza place west of Fredonia, and Brady jumped up and started beating the guy senseless without ever saying a word."

"Was it Joe Trent?"

"Yes! What's this all about?"

"Did they haul him off to Kingman or Flagstaff?"

"Kingman. The deputy said it had happened before. What kind of a man is Brady? I thought

187

I knew him. He seemed so kind and gentle."

"He is," Heather assured her. "I'll get the girls situated. Then I'll drive down to Kingman with you and bail him out. It's three and a half hours from here."

"Eh . . . I'm not going, Heather. I fired him. I just came by to drop off his rig and Capt. Patch and pick up my rental. I can't work with a guy who goes wacko like that."

"Lynda, there's nothing unreasonable about Brady's actions. At least not in his eyes."

"I don't understand."

"Well, I'll give you the three-minute story, but then I'm leavin' for Kingman. I suppose bail will be about $350. It's a good thing they take a credit card."

"Who is this guy Joe Trent?"

"About five years ago, Brady was real sweet on a girl named Cindy LaCoste. She worked for the BLM down on the Strip and loved barrel racing, so the two of them went to a lot of rodeos and things together. Well, I guess the feelings weren't exactly mutual. They must have had a fight or something, because when Brady invited Cindy to the big New Year's Dance over at Mesquite, Nevada, she turned him down flat. The Casino has a big whoop-te-do on New Year's.

"So he showed up here the day before New Year's askin' me if I would go with him to the dance. Well, I had already agreed to let some of the girls' friends sleep over here, so I had to refuse. And Brady went off to the party on his own.

188

"According to police reports in the paper, Cindy had gone to the party with Joe Trent. Trent was married at the time, and rumor had it he was running illegal aliens across the border in southern Arizona. For a fat fee, of course. And lots of the illegals were gettin' ripped off by Mr. Trent once they got here."

"A nice guy."

"A real scumbag. But it gets worse. Instead of bringing Cindy straight home, Trent decided to pull off the interstate and see how far she would go. Well, they were parked in the desert when a dozen bikers came roaring up and dragged them out of the car.

"These guys were all doped up and started getting rough with both Trent and Cindy. I guess Joe fought free and jumped in his car and took off."

"Leaving Cindy with the bikers?"

"Yeah. He claimed to be going for help, but he was in Las Vegas before he thought to mention it to any troopers. It was almost daylight when they found her."

"Alive?"

"Barely. She had been beaten and raped repeatedly. She never did really recover. Took to drinking. Lives in some mental hospital in Carson City, so I hear. Anyway, when Brady heard about it, he sort of went berserk. Boys out at the bunkhouse had to sit on him to keep him from tearing the place apart.

"He called up Trent and told him if he ever

came to the Strip, he would pound his head into the ground. Brady keeps his word."

"How many times has this happened?"

"Just once before, about three years ago. Trent's divorced now and runs a porno shop over in Vegas. He shows up from time to time but only when Brady's out on the circuit. He obviously didn't know about Brady breaking his leg. Look, I don't know what you think about him, but there are some things Brady won't tolerate. And the one thing he hates worse than men who beat on ladies are men who fail to protect ladies.

"As far as I know, those are the only two fights he has ever been in. Not many folks around here blame him. If he wanted to go to trial over the assault charge, any jury in this county would acquit him. Anyway, I've got to make some kind of arrangement for the girls so I can drive to Kingman." She turned and started to walk back toward the house.

"Heather, I, eh . . . I think maybe I overreacted a little," Lynda admitted. "Look, can I drive to Kingman for you? You stay here with your girls. I'll go get him out."

"I thought you fired him."

"I did. But I still need to talk to him."

"How do I know you'll follow through?"

"Trust me."

"If I don't get a call from Brady by noon, I'm driving down myself," Heather insisted. "Do you want me to go with you?"

"I can do it. Really."

"It's a long drive."

"I need the time to think."

At 1:30 A.M. Lynda pulled into Kingman, Arizona, and turned down Andy Devine Boulevard.

Lord, I've been out here one weekend, and I've just driven a stick shift pickup truck almost four hours through the middle of the night to bail out a cowboy I've only known for forty-eight hours. It's like I'm living out the novels that I edit. I have no idea if what I'm doing is noble and brave — or just dangerous and dumb.

The night guard at the Mojave County Jail was reading *Trouble on the Rim Rock* by Joaquin Estában when Austin approached.

"Can I help you, ma'am?"

"I believe you have a Mr. Stoner just brought in from up on the Strip near Fredonia? I'd like to post his bail, but I'm not sure how to go about it."

The pencil-thin deputy with bushy dark eyebrows and mustache looked her over from head to toe.

"Yep . . . I imagine you would. Well, ma'am, I'll tell you what. I'd post bail myself for Brady for what he did. But he's gone and decided to plead guilty to the assault charges. He'll come before Judge Harper this mornin' between ten and noon. Our procedure is to just hold a man until he meets with the judge when it's only a matter of hours."

"Can I see him?"

191

"Not until after 8:30."

"Could you give him a message? It's really important to me."

"Sure, ma'am. Brady's pretty tired, and I let him sleep back there in the guards' room. The cot's a lot more comfortable. What do you want to tell him?"

"Tell him I want to hire him back. I didn't mean it when I fired him. And tell him I'll be in the courtroom this morning with bail money or whatever."

"And what's your name, ma'am?"

"Ms. Austin. No, just tell him it's Lynda Dawn."

He looked her over once more. "You one of them barrel racers, are you?"

"No, sir, but that's one of the highest compliments I've had in a week."

"Well, I'll tell him . . . Miss Lynda Dawn."

Leaving Capt. Patch in the pickup with the sliding back window slightly open, she warned him neither to run away or make a mess. Then she checked into the Holiday Inn a little after 2:30 A.M. and asked a blurry-eyed clerk to give her a nine o'clock wake-up call. After calling Heather and giving her a report, she crawled under the covers and immediately fell asleep.

Austin wore a dress, heels, and a new fragrance called Desperate Kiss as she sat in an almost empty courthouse and listened to the baldheaded judge pass sentence.

"Three days in jail, $350 fine, and a one-year

192

probation. Jail sentence suspended to time already served. So ordered."

Then the judge turned to Stoner. "For Pete's sake, Brady, stay away from that jerk Joe Trent. Son, the Good Book says vengeance belongs to the Lord, and you're going to have to leave it to the Almighty."

"Yes, sir, you're right about that. I don't aim to be botherin' you again, Judge."

"Good. Do you have a way to pay your fine?"

Stoner glanced around at Austin, and she nodded. "Yes, sir, I do."

"Settle up with the clerk."

Glancing up at the judge, Brady smiled and said softly, "Give my regards to Leslie, sir."

"She's still waiting for you to stop by and go water-skiing again. But I suppose that broken leg keeps you out of the water."

Brady Stoner limped over to Lynda, and the two stepped to the clerk's office and paid the fine. He called Heather and explained everything. Then they walked out into the bright sunlight of Kingman, Arizona. Austin shaded her eyes with her hand and dug into her purse for her sunglasses. Jamming them on, she shook her head at him.

"Does this mean I'm rehired?"

"Oh, you're hired. But I'm shaking my head because you seem to know every young lady west of the Mississippi."

"That's not true at all. I hardly know anyone in . . . say, Kansas or Nebraska."

"Who's Leslie?"

193

"The judge's daughter. She's blind."

"Blind? And she water-skis?"

"Water-skis, rides fast horses, and plays a mean electric guitar. She's a real — "

"I know, I know. She's a real sweetheart, right?"

"Yeah."

Climbing into the pickup, Brady tousled an eager Capt. Patch by the ears and hugged his neck. "Now did you take good care of Miss Austin like I told you to?"

She turned out of the parking lot to the west. "Where are you going?"

"Back to the Strip. We have work to do, remember."

"Don't you want to get some lunch?"

"Yeah. Yeah, I know — there's this great place that serves spicy food that would melt most people's stomachs, and they just happen to have a waitress that bats her eyes at Brady Stoner."

"You really think you know me? Well, turn right up here. Now . . . on the left. See the Drovers' Cafe? Turn in there. It happens to have the best chicken-fried steak west of Ft. Worth."

The waitress was also the cook and proprietor of the little cafe that sported four tables and six stools at the counter. She was a gray-haired woman with a smile as wide as her ample hips. Her white apron was less than sparkling clean, and she had a pencil shoved behind her ear.

"Brady Stoner! Honey, where have you been? I swear if we didn't get you in for the rodeo, we'd never see you at all!"

194

"Daisy, this is my boss, Miss Lynda Dawn Austin."

"Pleased to meet you. Don't you look pretty! Whew, that Desperate Kiss perfume is mighty strong stuff, ain't it?" Then she held up her hand and shaded her mouth so Brady couldn't hear. "I use the same thing myself every Saturday night!"

"Desperate?" Stoner whispered. "It's a sad thing . . . and such a young and attractive woman, too!"

"Shut up, Stoner!"

They finished eating about the time the noon crowd boiled in. Soon they were leaving Kingman behind, heading for the long trip back to the Arizona Strip.

Stoner scrunched down in the seat and lifted his broken leg to the dashboard. "Why did you change your mind?"

"Well, I acted without thinking, and Heather . . . she gave me some things to think about."

"Like what?"

"Like telling about what happened to Cindy LaCoste."

"That's what I figured. Anyway, I got to learn to control my actions."

"Well, it's understandable anger."

They sat in silence for a long time.

"Heather didn't tell you everything about that night. There's some parts she doesn't know. There's one part only two people on earth know about, and one of them's in a mental home in Carson City."

"What's that?"

"I sure did some thinkin' last night in jail. I know I've got to tell someone, and you're about as neutral a person as I can tell."

"Eh . . . I think that's a compliment."

"Well, the one part nobody knows is that when I got to that dance, Joe Trent was pretty drunk and already draped all over Cindy. She was gettin' stoned, too, but was obviously embarrassed and maybe a little scared. She got away from Joe while he was in the men's room and asked me if I would take her home.

"I was feelin' purdy rejected, so I sarcastically told her I'd call her a cab. After cussin' me out real good, she wandered off with Trent again. Later on I noticed that she and Joe were gone, so I checked out of the party and drove back to the bunkhouse.

"Shorty Smith had stayed at Mesquite all night playing poker and heard the account of Cindy's rape the next morning. He drove all the way to the ranch to tell me. I guess I kind of went crazy. They say I just about tore up the entire bunk-house."

They drove almost half an hour without either saying another word.

"So who did you bash last night — Joe Trent or Brady Stoner?" she finally asked.

He opened his eyes and repositioned his broken leg. "Some of both, I reckon. I keep trying to set that in the past. Do you think the Lord can ever forgive me for not helpin' Cindy when I had a chance?"

"Oh, yeah, He'll forgive you. But can you forgive yourself?"

He stared out the window for a long time without answering. For the next three hours, Lynda Dawn Austin drove back toward St. George, Utah, while Stoner and Capt. Patch slept.

SIX

Contrasts.

Absolute, almost disorienting contradictions.

Lynda Dawn Austin didn't bother to stop in Las Vegas as she sailed along the interstate headed for St. George, Utah. But she did stare at the casinos — and at the desert to the north.

Out of the purity . . . and freshness . . . and the sublime loneliness of the desert, look what we've built, Lord. A tawdry, ostentatious, and gaudy world that exists on false promises of money, fame, and sex. A voracious appetite that feeds itself on destroyed lives.

What are we doing to this world, Lord?

What are we doing to each other?

She drove the black and silver rig straight east toward the distant, barren mountains for another hour without any noise except the hum of the tires on the road and the rush of wind that swirled through Brady's open window.

I've been out here about five days, and I don't know if I want to go back. Maybe I could move out here and do free-lance editing. I could hook up a fax and modem and then —

"You look good today."

Brady Stoner was slumped down in the seat, his black hat still pulled down over his eyes. She brushed her hair back off her eyes.

"What? Really? Are you awake?"

"Yeah . . . I'm awake." He sat up and pushed his hat back. Unsnapping the cuffs on his green shirt, he began rolling up the long sleeves. She thought she could see a slight smile creeping across his face, but she didn't want to turn and stare. "When I turned around in court and saw you sitting there all dressed up, I said to myself, 'Brady, that is one classy lady.' "

"Well . . . thanks. You sound to me like a lonesome cowboy trying to line up a date for the rodeo dance."

"You think I'm makin' a pass at you?"

"Well, aren't you?"

"You've got to be kidding! You call that a pass? Where do you live — in a convent in New York City or what? Aren't you used to having someone compliment you?"

"Oh, just forget it," she pouted.

"Look, all I meant was that when I woke up and glanced over at you drivin', you were thinkin' about somethin' . . . just staring out at the desert. You weren't trying to be some important New York editor. You weren't tryin' to be boss. You weren't trying to be a nineties lady. Your expression was kind of like . . . kind of . . ."

"What?"

"Well, kind of like a little girl riding a pony for the first time. Anyway, it's an expression that

199

wears well on you. It was a nice, relaxed, natural look. I imagine you don't get to be yourself very often, do you?"

She set her jaw firm. "I don't know what you mean."

"Sure you do. 'Course, now you've slipped back into your take-charge-lady mode. Take this next exit. There's a little market back in those cottonwoods. I'll buy you a . . . Well, you can buy me a Coke or something."

Brady Stoner, how dare you figure me out so quickly! It's been so long since I was brave enough to be myself, I hardly remember who I am. I'm certainly not going to be myself in front of a total . . . well, an almost total stranger!

Capt. Patch was in a fight with a big black dog before she even had the truck completely stopped at the little market.

"Aren't you going to help him?" she asked.

"Nope. It's his fight. And he didn't ask for help."

"He's getting chewed up pretty good."

"Come on, this place will whip us up a couple of great sandwiches."

In ten minutes they were back on the road. A brown paper sack between them held two giant meatloaf sandwiches, a bag of chips, two red apples, and a six-pack of cold diet Cokes.

Capt. Patch cowered in the back of the pickup nursing a nasty wound on his left foreleg.

"When are we going to eat this wonderful lunch?" she asked.

"In a minute. . . . I'll show you."

In the rearview mirror she could see his brown eyes shine. His lanky frame sprawled over most of the cab.

Watch him, girl. He's going to sweet-talk you just like the others.

They entered the mountains and canyons of southeastern Nevada, winding their way past steep cliffs and a quietly flowing stream. Deep in the canyons, he signaled for her to take the next exit.

"Ranch exit?" she questioned. "What does that mean?"

"It means they only put in this exit so they could get to the ranch. It's kind of like a private freeway ramp."

"Why are we turning here?"

"For lunch. Now turn left back under the freeway."

"It's a dirt road."

"You've got experience on dirt roads."

They bounced along the one-lane road rocketing a trail of dust as they wound their way up the river and into a deep red rock canyon. The road faded out near an old brush corral.

"Pull over there by the river." He pointed.

She turned the rig into the sage and grass that was still a little green along the river.

"I can't believe I'm doin' this."

"What?"

"Driving to where no woman has ever gone before!" She laughed.

"Not bad for a city girl. Park it here. I'll grab

the lunch. Get that quilt in the back."

"Quilt?"

"For a tablecloth! Dad gum it, you're suspicious today."

He hobbled out across the grass toward one lone, stubby cottonwood tree.

"Maybe I should change shoes," she called.

"Come on . . . the snakes will be busy sleepin'."

Lounging on the quilt, with half a sandwich in one hand and a soft drink in the other, she glanced up at the red cliffs of the little canyon.

"Beautiful, isn't it?" he asked.

"Indescribable. I wish I had a camera."

"Of course, you always have lunch down in a canyon, right? A concrete and steel canyon."

She thought about Barton's during the noon rush, about Nina and Kelly and a million other people in midtown Manhattan trying to get back to work by 1:00 P.M.

"Brady, there is nothing about this scene that in any way reminds me of New York. People back there don't even know how to dream this good. This is a different world. Look at the color of the sky against those cliffs! And it's so quiet! What's the name of this place?"

"Oh, it's nothin' special. Part of the Virgin River Canyon, I guess."

"The Virgin River? You're kidding me."

"Eh . . . no, why?"

"Oh . . . nothing." She brushed back her hair and slid her sunglasses to the top of her head. "Listen, this would be a good time to go over the game plan for the next several days."

"Wait, I'm still tryin' to figure out why you were so startled by the name of — "

"Look," she interrupted, "it's already two, so we won't get anything done today. First thing in the morning, I think we should check with the guy named Marlowe at Rincon. Fondue mentioned him, remember? Then we'll follow through on the leads that the BLM man gave me yesterday. He marked the topo map where he thought a couple of old prospectors were holed up. We can do all of that in one day, can't we? I mean, if it doesn't rain, and if the road doesn't get slick, and we have to run for a cabin . . . and if nobody gets jailed . . ."

"You sure do talk a lot when you get nervous."

She was biting her lower lip and immediately stopped. "What makes you think I'm nervous?"

"Oh, I make one shirt-tail compliment, and you — "

"This is a ridiculous conversation." She looked back toward the brush corral. "We might as well stay in St. George tonight. I didn't get much sleep last night."

"We can probably bunk out at Heather's. The girls can double up, and I'll sleep on the couch," he suggested.

"Oh, I couldn't impose again. But I . . . eh," she stammered.

"Look, you paid for two motel rooms last night that, thanks to me, were hardly used. You can't afford that too often."

"Well, I'm not sure the girls will be too happy to see me."

"Since when are you pushed around by a couple of teenagers?"

"If Heather doesn't mind." She kicked off her left heel and rubbed her right leg with the stocking-covered foot.

"It's a done deal."

"Then we'll go down to Rincon in the morning?"

"You're the boss. What I want to know is when will we be goin' down that steep little trail on the granite cliff?"

"Never."

"Come, Lynda Dawn, that's the best lead we have, and you know it."

High above the canyon she watched a hawk drift as he circled in a thermal. She had the urge to dig into her purse for more perfume. "Why are you in such a hurry to get me to fall off that cliff?"

"Why are you avoiding the most obvious trail we have?" Stoner dug into his jeans, pulled out his pocket knife, and began to clean his fingernails.

"Look, while I was waiting for court to open this morning, I went over to the assessor's office and checked out the Mojave County maps," she continued. "There is no Shotgun Canyon listed on those maps, and the place where you think you found a trail is probably on government property. There couldn't be a cabin down there. It would be illegal."

Stoner folded the knife and jammed it back into his pocket. "Who owns that place — the Park Service, the Recreational Area, or the BLM?"

"They didn't know," she admitted.

"And do you know why they don't know? Because no one has ever been in there. There are still side canyons down there that no one has ever explored. What better place for a guy like Harrison to spend his life? No one is going to go looking for him."

"Brady, I'm not going in there . . . I can't go in there. A person knows the limits of what they can do and what they can't do."

"Then I'll go in, look around, and bring you out a complete report," he offered.

"I'm not about to send a . . . a crippled man down the face of that canyon."

"You'll change your mind."

"I will not."

"Oh, no, you'll change all right. Sooner or later you know we'll have to go down there."

"Not me. You don't know me very well," she huffed.

"I know you a lot better than you think. You're a bulldog."

"You mean I'm stubborn?"

"I mean, once you get your teeth into something, you can't let go if you tried. You want to find that cabin and manuscript. Not even a fear of heights is going to stop you."

"You're goin' to be surprised then. Because I won't go down in that canyon."

He lifted his hands and shrugged. "Well, you've surprised me before."

"Like when?"

"Showing up in court this mornin'. I figured after last night I'd never see you again."

"I told you I had a long talk with Heather."

"But you and I both know that's no excuse for my actions. I go along pretty good most of the time . . . sailing along, everything under control. Then I do somethin' totally dumb. I can't figure it. Does that ever happen to Lynda Dawn Austin? When was the last time you did something totally dumb?"

"I think it probably was last Friday . . . or maybe this morning." She laughed.

Brady Stoner stood up and pulled the split jeans back down over his braced leg. "Well, I did a lot of thinkin' on the way to jail last night. I've been tellin' myself I can get along just fine pushin' God way to the back of my life."

"And now?"

"And now . . ." He refused to look at her, choosing to stare up the canyon. "I'm gettin' way too serious with all this talk. I'll race you down to that red boulder and back. The winner gets the other half of your sandwich!"

"Cowboy, you're changing the subject! Besides, you can't race. You have a broken leg."

"You afraid of losin', are ya? You aren't goin' to be all that fast in heels and a dress."

"I don't even want that half sandwich. You can have it."

"Oh, sure. Worried about being bested by a cripple."

"Stoner, you're crazy!" While still sitting on the blanket, she wiggled her toes out of her other shoe without letting him see her.

"Are you runnin' or not?"

"Help me up." She reached out her hand. As he pulled her up, she yanked him toward her and flew past him yelling, "On our mark, get set, go!"

"Hey, you can't . . ."

Holding her dress above her knees, Austin sprinted in her stocking feet toward the big rock. She could hear Stoner huffing and puffing behind her. Spinning around the marker, she ignored the pain of the pebbles and sticks of the valley floor and bolted toward the finish. She dove onto the little star quilt.

"Ta da!" she yelled.

Turning around, she watched Stoner stumble around the rock with Capt. Patch prancing at his side.

"Come, Brady, you're not expecting sympathy, are you?"

He slowed his pace but was still breathing hard when he reached the blanket.

"I won!" she triumphed. "I ruined a good pair of hose, but I won!"

"So did I."

"What do you mean?"

"I said you were a bulldog. You just proved it."

"You made me mad."

"I know." He pulled off his hat and wiped his forehead. Then he placed the hat on her head. The black beaver felt hat slipped over her ears.

She pushed it back. "Do you think I could pass for a barrel racer?"

"Not in that dress you couldn't. But the hat looks good. Maybe you ought to buy one."

"Sure, Spunky Sasser and I could have cowgirl day at the office!"

"Who?"

"Our well-dressed receptionist. I'll tell you about her sometime. Come to think of it, I won't tell you!" She picked up the other half of her meatloaf sandwich and took a big bite.

"I thought you didn't want that."

"I don't."

"Then why are you eatin' it?"

"Because I won it. You lost, Stoner. When you lose, you don't get the prize, boy."

"I'm not a good loser."

She raised her eyebrows and nodded. "Neither am I."

It was after four when they drove out of the canyon and hit the interstate. By five they were at Heather's house, and by six Austin was on the phone.

"Nina? This is Lynda."

"Where are you? We've been worried."

"Why? I'm on vacation, remember?"

"Well, sure, but the last we heard you were riding off into the sunset with some cowboy."

"Eh . . . that's not exactly true."

"Is everything all right?"

"Yeah. Oh, we got stuck all night out on the desert and had to stay in an abandoned church. I almost fell three thousand feet to my death. I had to drive a four-wheel-drive truck all night and spend $350 of my money to bail him out of jail. And now we just had a picnic in the Virgin River Canyon. Other than that it's been routine."

"All right, lady, that's enough. Who are you really?"

"Huh?"

"Don't you be calling me up impersonating Lynda Dawn Austin, straight-laced New York City book editor!"

"Crazy, isn't it?"

"Sounds like a great vacation. By the way, are you still looking for that lost manuscript?"

"Of course I am!"

"Does he have a friend?"

"Everyone in the county is his friend . . . except one guy."

"Listen, have you talked to Kell?"

"No, what's happening?"

"Didn't you read the papers? It was even in *USA Today*."

"What was?"

"Mr. Hampton's stroke."

"Stroke?"

"Yeah. Mr. Hampton, Sr., had a serious stroke in Hamburg. Junior took off this morning to fly him back to the States if they can."

"No!"

"It was pretty tense around the office today."

"Have you heard anything more?"

"Nope. Maybe you ought to check in at the office tomorrow."

"We're going down to Rincon and then back out on the desert. Look, Nina, I've got to run. I promised Heather I'd help rustle up some supper."

"Rustle up some supper? In five days you're starting to talk like that already?"

"Yep."

"Yep? What will happen after two weeks?"

"Why, shucks, missy, it ain't nothin' to worry your pretty little head over!"

"That did it." Nina laughed. "You come home right now!"

"I'll call you tomorrow and find out about Mr. Hampton."

"One last thing. Is he really cute?"

"Compared to whom?"

"Compared to James St. John. You do remember him, don't you?"

"James! Oh, I should try to call him, I guess."

"You didn't answer my question."

"Yes, he's cute. You know, in a boots-and-cowboy-hat kind of way."

"What does that mean?"

"Got to run!"

"Lynda Dawn Austin!"

"Adios, amigo!"

Tomorrow came a lot sooner than she figured. Clear, cool, and windy.

After a predawn breakfast of bacon and eggs and fried mashed potatoes, Lynda, Brady, and Capt. Patch watched the pink and blue sunrise as they drove east through Hurricane, Utah. She wore her boots, jeans, and a plaid flannel shirt she had borrowed from Heather, and a new fragrance called Elegant Enchantment.

"Now who's the guy we have to go see so early in the morning?"

"Gabby Snyder."

"Gabby? Oh, sure, a little old man with greasy, gray beard and a hat turned up in the front, right?"

"Nope. Slow down a little, or you'll miss the turn."

Austin hit the brakes but couldn't see any turnoff. "Where? Turn where?" The black leather-wrapped grip of the steering wheel felt comfortable and familiar.

"I'll tell you when." Stoner unsnapped his shirt sleeves and began rolling them up.

"Who is this guy?"

"Gabby was the mailman out here from about 1940 to 1990."

"Fifty years?"

"Yeah, they made him retire, or he'd still be delivering mail, I suppose. He's got to be eighty by now."

"And you think he might remember if any mail

was sent to Harrison?"

"Not exactly. If Harrison was out here for all this time collecting mail, your publishing house would have found him years ago. If he ever got mail, it would have been under some other name." He pointed out into the glaring orange morning sunlight. "There! I think that's it!"

"It says, 'No Motorized Vehicles Allowed.' Is this a wilderness area?"

"Nah. It's Gabby's place. He's sort of . . . well, you'll see. He's kind of gone back to nature, you might say."

She turned to stare at him. "Good grief, he's not a nudist, is he?"

"No . . . at least I don't think so. Park it over there. We'll have to walk back to see him." Stoner grabbed the black and white dog as Austin stepped out of the pickup. "Sorry, Capt. Patch, you have to stay here."

"Why's that?" she asked.

"Well, you'll see. Anyway, Gabby is sort of losin' his memory, but if you catch him on a clear day . . . well, maybe he might remember someone who used to live down in the canyons."

"Don't tell me he delivered mail out there."

"Nope, but he can . . . well, you'll just have to wait."

"Why didn't you come out here and ask him the other day?"

"I thought he moved up to Salt Lake or something, but on the way to Kingman the other night the deputy told me that Gabby had come back to his place on the border and was crazier than ever."

"Are we in Utah or Arizona?"

"We parked the car in Utah, but we'll walk into Arizona. Let me do the talking, and don't give your opinion on any political or social issue. Promise?"

"What?"

"Trust me!"

Stoner's phrase was almost drowned out by a shout from the top of the incline. "Halt! Do not proceed!"

Austin grabbed Stoner's arm, and her eyes searched the horizon. "Where is he?"

Brady stopped walking and cupped his hands. "We would like permission to talk to Gabby Snyder!" he shouted.

"He doesn't know you! Go home and take your chemically polluted bodies with you!"

"Let's get out of here!" Austin tugged at his arm.

Brady turned to the old man. "You know me, Gabby — Brady Stoner . . . Stoner . . . out at the Running R!"

"*Pro Rodeo Sports News*, June 14, 1988 — postage due, twenty-eight cents?"

"That's me!"

"You got my money?"

"Yep."

"All twenty-eight cents?"

"Yep."

"Cash only. You have it in cash?"

"Yep."

"Who's with you? Is that your darlin'?"

"Yep."

"Becky darlin', 1221 Palomino Drive, Santa Maria, California, 93454, no forwarding address?"

"You've got a great memory, Gabby!"

"Proceed through the screening area."

Lynda leaned closer to Brady and whispered, "What does he mean, the screening area?"

"You'll see."

She walked arm and arm with him as the split-rail fence narrowed to a thick arch of deer antlers. Scooting down off the hill came a thin, almost gaunt-looking man wearing buckskins and sporting a shock of untamed gray hair. An animal was leashed by his side.

"Is that a . . . a panther?"

"Panther, cougar, mountain lion — it's all the same. He calls her Eleanor Roosevelt. Just follow my lead."

"Form a line at the gate," the old man ordered. He reeked of garlic. "You two will be first. You carrying any concealed weapons?"

"Nope."

"Any pesticides, insecticides, or poisons?"

"Nope."

"Any aerosol sprays known to be harmful to the ozone layer?"

"Nope."

"Any red meat or artificial sweeteners?"

"Nope."

"Have either of you tested positive to carrying

214

known viruses or diseases?"

"Eh . . . no."

"Are either of you now, or have you been in the past, employed as an agent of biological warfare for any foreign or domestic government or agency?"

"No, sir."

"Where's the twenty-eight cents?"

Stoner handed him some change.

"Put on the surgical masks and rubber gloves, and you may proceed."

"Is he kidding?" she murmured.

"Nope."

They picked the items out of a box and suited up, stepped through the archway of antlers, and followed the frail, little man back to a house dug out of the side of a red limestone cliff. A large garden, mostly spaded under, spread out away from the home toward a spring of water that puddled into a small pond.

Looking right at Austin, the old man blurted out, "You're as fat as a pig, girl. Are you pregnant?"

"Am I what?" she gasped, unconsciously sucking in her stomach.

"Breast-feed them, I say. Artificial formula is killing the babies of the world."

"Let's get out of here," she mumbled to Brady.

"Gabby, I thought you moved to Salt Lake," he remarked to the old man.

"I did! Evil! The whole place is evil. They're killin' each other. The air is so contaminated the birds are dropping out of the sky dead. The water is contaminated, and filth is piled up in the gutters. You mark my words, there won't be one person alive in that city in three years! The desert is our last chance, Mr. Brady Stoner, *Pro Rodeo Sports News*, 101 Pro Rodeo Drive, Colorado Springs, Colorado 80919."

"I feel funny wearing this mask," she whispered.

"You look funny."

Brady turned to the old man. "Gabby, I'm lookin' for someone. Thought maybe you had heard of this old boy."

"Roy? Roy McNeilly, Pipe Springs, C.O.D. from El Paso, Texas, $14.99."

"No, not Roy. His name was Martin Taylor Harrison. Did you ever deliver mail to Martin Taylor Harrison?"

"Harrison? Burton L.? Edward E.? Elmer H.? Ernie E.? Lyle L.? Mildred K.? Morris H.? Norma? Roland?"

"Martin Taylor Harrison."

"Martin? Otis? P. J.? Patricia F.? Raymond E.? Richard and Shirley? Ted?"

"No." Austin waved her hands for emphasis. "Martin Taylor Harrison — that's his name!"

The old man reached down and patted the cougar on the head. "Never heard of him."

"Gabby, did you ever hear of a place called Shotgun Canyon?"

"Shotgun Mountain, Shotgun Creek, Shotgun Mesa, Shotgun Spring, Shotgun Butte . . ."

"No Shotgun Canyon?"

"Nope."

Austin looked the old man in the eyes, and he stared right back. "How about Harry?" she asked. "Fondue called him Harry."

Stoner pulled off his hat and held it in his hand. "An old man called Harry? Do you remember him?"

"Harry Copeland, Harry Grasser, Harry Viola, Harry Schmidt . . ."

"How about Fondue? Mr. Felix Fondue?" she asked.

"Nope." The old man's face was expressionless.

Stoner turned to Austin. "Well, it was worth a try." Then he turned back to Snyder. "Thanks anyway, Gabby. I've got to run."

"Do you want to take some artichokes?"

"Eh . . . no, no thanks," Brady replied.

"They make wonderful pies!"

"Did he say pie?" Lynda gasped.

"You goin' without dinner?" he asked.

"We've got to get out to Toroweap Valley," Brady informed him.

"Don't stay out late."

"We won't." Lynda tugged Brady back toward the arch of antlers.

"Have fun, kids. Be careful."

"We will. Thanks, Gabby," Brady added.

"Say, don't I know you?" the old man asked.

Brady paused and stared at the man for a moment. "I . . . I live down in Shotgun Canyon.

My name's Harrison. You got any mail for me?"
Brady stuttered.

"Harry? Shotgun Canyon Harry?"

Stoner glanced at Austin and then back at the old man. "Eh . . . yeah . . . Shotgun Canyon Harry!"

"Three letters, 1943. No return address. Two cents postage due. Where's my money?"

Brady Stoner reached into his pocket and started to pull out some change.

"Make it cash. I don't accept checks."

Brady handed him two pennies. "Thanks, Gabby."

"You leavin'?"

"Yep."

"Is she leavin', too?"

"Yes."

"Good. There ain't enough food here to feed a woman of that size."

Brady and Lynda hiked back out the long dirt path through the low-lying hills to the pickup. Neither said a word until they were seated in the rig.

"Fat? He called me fat! No one has called me fat since Lance Lowe in the second grade in the Keys, and I bloodied his nose!"

"Whoa — the aggressive Miss Austin!"

"Am I fat?"

"Are you kidding? You are in no way fat. Why, you could use a little beefin' up in some places, especially — "

"Don't you say it, Stoner! I'm really irritable

about that subject. You say one more word, and it will be the last thing you ever say on earth," she threatened. "Anyway, I say that old man's weird!"

"Gabby lives in his own world . . . but don't we all? He'll probably outlive every one of us."

"Just the same, that place gives me the creeps."

"He's an example of one of the reasons I love this country down here. You're free to be yourself. You can't bother other folks, but you can be yourself."

"You think Shotgun Canyon Harry could be Harrison?"

"It sounds possible, doesn't it? You said that Fondue guy called him Harry. And Amanda said some old man had been living down in a place called Shotgun Canyon. See, I knew we should go down that granite trail. I think it leads to Shotgun Canyon."

"And I think it leads to a heart attack. Harry's a common name. He might be confused. Everything he said was confusing! I'm not going down in that canyon."

"Maybe there's another way in."

"I told you, nothing shows on the topo map." She started the engine and pulled back onto the highway. "Are we still going south?"

"To Rincon."

"How far is that?"

"Five miles or so. Look, we could take some horses into the canyon and ride over the rimrock and see if we can spot the canyon from some other angle. How's that?"

"I don't do horses. I'll hike, thank you."

"You can't hike that country; it's too dangerous."

"I told you, I don't ride horses!"

"You don't do canyons, and you don't do horses! I don't know if you really want to find that manuscript."

She fumed for a few minutes. "You're right. I've got to do one or the other. Well, if we must, let's try the horses. . . . Only there's one thing you ought to know. I've never ridden a horse before."

"Hey, no problem. I'll help you. If there's anything you need to know, just ask."

She grinned and reached over to jab him in the arm. "There's one thing I do need to know."

"What's that?"

"Who's Becky darlin', 1221 Palomino Drive, Santa Maria, California, no forwarding address? I gave you the history of Lynda Dawn Austin, but you held out on me."

"Becky Powell. She's the one ridin' English in those Grangemont Dog Food commercials — you know, with that pack of dogs running in front? I met her at a rodeo at the Forum in Inglewood."

"Where the Lakers play?"

"Yep. They fill the arena with dirt and have a rodeo. She asked me to go with her to a party in Malibu. Afterward she gave me her address and made me promise to write."

"Well?"

"I did. She didn't. She moved. End of story."

Austin slowed the pickup as they reached a crossroad. "Is this it already?"

"Yeah, turn left." He motioned. "Now you want to talk about a different kind of place — this is it. What do you know about Rincon?"

"Nothing except you said lots of people are named Marlowe."

"Well, this will be your second lesson of the day about life in the high desert. Drive slow and tell me what you see."

"Hmm . . . red cliffs in the background, peaceful, lots of gardens, houses or . . . apartments spread out."

"Those aren't apartments. They're homes."

"But each one has three or four cars, and it looks . . . They're all being built onto. Look at that one. It's already huge. How many kids do they have around here?"

"Oh, every guy has from twelve to thirty kids, I guess."

"Thirty! What are you saying? No woman can have thirty kids!"

"I didn't say every woman had thirty. I said every guy. Turn to the left."

She ground a couple of gears and turned the pickup. "Are you telling me they have more than one wife?"

"Yep. Polygamists."

"Brady, don't lead me on."

"Lady, I'm telling you the truth. This is a fundamentalist Mormon community. They practice polygamy."

"I don't believe you. It's . . . it's against the law. We don't have that kind of thing in the United States . . . do we?"

"Yep. Believe, kid. I don't know a whole bunch about the movement, but as I understand it, back in 1890 the LDS church leaders came out against plural marriages. This became official doctrine of the church. They needed that change in order to have Utah accepted into statehood. Well, some of the Saints didn't like the change. Thought it violated the earlier teaching of Joseph Smith, Brigham Young, and all those. But the church pressed their case and enforced the edict.

"So sometime around the turn of the century or a little thereafter, a few of those so-called fundamentalists moved just across the border to Arizona and set up an isolated community. That paved highway wasn't always there, you know."

"Well, isn't it illegal to have polygamy in Arizona? They arrest guys in New York for things like this."

"No, they don't. They arrest a man for bigamy — that is, legally marrying more than one woman. But out here they just have a marriage license for the first wife. The others live there out of choice."

"And the authorities let it slide?"

"What can they do? Arrest the lady for living with a man without a marriage license? If you did that, half the folks in New York City would be imprisoned, right?"

"Can't the government do *anything* about it?"

"Well, for years this was so isolated it was mostly ignored. You found out how far it is to the county courthouse the other night. In 1953 they had a big raid up here and jailed the men and hauled off the women and kids. But the case fell through, and they all moved back." Brady motioned for her to pull into a paved parking lot in front of a fairly large market.

"I notice the kids all dress alike."

"I guess most of them still do — girls in dresses, hair pinned up . . . boys in black pants, long-sleeve shirts. They're always neat and scrubbed up clean."

"Is this Marlowe's grocery store?"

"Nope. They sort of hold everything in a religious trust, so this is a cooperative market owned by the village families, I think. But the Marlowes are one of the original founding families. There's bound to be some Marlowes working here."

They parked the rig next to a fifteen-passenger van and left Capt. Patch inside the cab.

"Do you know some of the people here?" she asked.

"Not really. I never felt right comin' in here. I don't believe in this stuff, and I didn't want to bother them."

Austin didn't notice anything unusual about the market except that the patrons and clerks dressed in a similar fashion and a half-dozen children between six and ten years old looked remarkably alike.

Stoner limped over to a young woman in a long

dress stacking groceries on a shelf. Lynda noticed she wore no makeup or earrings.

"Excuse me, ma'am, we're searching for a man who used to live down in the canyons. We were told he knew a Mr. Marlowe here at the store. Do you know which Mr. Marlowe that might have been?"

"Well, I'm a Marlowe, but I'm not sure. . . . Maybe it's my husband. I'll ask Sister Anne." She stepped over to the produce section and spoke with a tall, middle-aged woman stacking grapefruit. Then the young woman returned.

"Sister Anne said you should really talk to our husband. Mr. Marlowe and the boys are in that big field down by the creek digging potatoes today."

"And his first name is?" Brady questioned.

"Wendell." She smiled. "Wendell, Sr."

"Thank you, ma'am." Stoner tipped his hat and turned toward the door. Austin tried to force a smile and then hurried after him. Once inside the cab of the truck, she stared at him for a moment. Then she started the rig and began to drive to the north.

"Did she say 'our husband'? You mean that girl and that older woman are 'married' to the same man?"

"I reckon so."

"I thought she said they were sisters."

"Well, sisters can marry the same man. But she probably meant sister-wife. I think that's a term they use."

"Brady Stoner, the Arizona Strip has some strange people."

"Fiercely independent maybe, but not strange. I was in Times Square one time . . . now *there* are some strange people! Stop here." He pointed. "This looks like it."

She pulled off the pavement onto the edge of a plowed field. "You want to come with me or wait here?"

"Oh, I'm coming with you. This is like walking through a novel!"

They hiked toward men working on some tractor-towed farm machinery in the middle of the field. A man who looked about sixty walked toward them. He wore a San Francisco Giants baseball cap pushed back on his gray hair. His face was darkly tanned and leathery, with a slightly graying beard.

"You folks lookin' to buy some potatoes?" he asked.

"No, sir. I wanted to speak to Mr. Wendell Marlowe, Sr."

"Well, you're lookin' at him. You aren't from the newspaper or TV, are you?"

"No, sir. We are tryin' to locate a cabin down in the Strip where a man named Martin Taylor Harrison lived."

"The infidel writer?"

"Yes, he was a writer!" Austin nodded. "Did you know him?"

"Absolutely not! And his books aren't allowed in this town, you know."

225

"No, I didn't know that," Stoner replied. "Sir, we don't think much of those two books either. But we have some evidence that he might have come down into the canyons back in the thirties and lived like a hermit. We were told he might have done some shopping . . . you know, for staples and stuff up here at Rincon."

"I'll tell you folks something. We keep to ourselves back here. And those that come in to trade, well . . . we don't ask 'em any questions, and we sure won't tell nobody where they are. That's just the way we are. Sorry we couldn't help. Are you sure you don't want some potatoes?"

"No thanks." Austin stepped closer to the man. "Mr. Marlowe, I'm from Atlantic-Hampton Publishing Company in New York City."

"I don't talk to reporters!"

"I'm not a reporter. But we have reason to believe that the manuscript for Mr. Harrison's third novel is laying in a cabin down in that canyon country somewhere. I read a copy of it recently, and in it he refutes all of those arguments against the existence of God in those earlier works."

"You don't say."

"But I was also told that Mr. Harrison died last spring or summer. So we need to find his cabin, locate the grave, and retrieve the manuscript. We don't wish to exploit him or you, sir."

"Well, that does make a difference . . . but to tell you the truth, I'm sure Martin Taylor Harrison has never been to Rincon. I've worked the co-op since I was fourteen, and I would certainly remember if he had come in."

Stoner reached down, picked up a dirt clod, smelled it, crushed it in his hand, and let the dirt roll through his fingers. "Nice sandy loam. Have you tried a little ammonium-nitrate?"

Marlowe's eyes lit up. "I've been thinking of dripping a little in with the irrigation water."

"It boosted production over at some Fredonia gardens by 15 to 25 percent."

"You don't say!"

"You might want to give it a try. . . . It could be that Harrison was known as Shotgun Canyon Harry," Stoner added.

"Shotgun Harry? Well, now you're talking! That's a different matter."

"You knew the man?" Austin pressed.

"He always paid in gold. Back in the old days several of the prospectors came out of the canyons paying in gold. But since the raid, I think Harry and The Hippie have been the only ones. Shotgun Harry . . . was he really Martin Taylor Harrison? Who would have known? It's surprising the people who live in this country, isn't it? I think I have an old picture of him."

Austin nearly jumped out of her boots. "You what? Really?"

"Follow me up to the old schoolhouse. That's where some of the old photos are kept these days."

They drove behind his pickup to a one-room schoolhouse sitting by itself on a knoll in the middle of town. They slid out of the pickup and followed him into the building.

"This is where they rounded us up in '53. All the men were herded into the yard before they hauled us off to jail. . . . Now over here in this file are the pictures. In the old store, we used to have a number of pictures on the wall. Well, when we opened that new market, we piled all those old photos in a box and stored them up here. Seems to me I remember a snapshot of Shotgun Harry."

"You look in that box, young lady, and if this cowboy will check that one, I'll look here."

"Will it be labeled?" she asked him.

"On the back, I think. Look for a man dressed like in 1930, riding a horse, and leading a string of pack mules."

Most of the photos were of dirt streets and small children standing in front of simple cabins and houses.

"What are these pictures with numbers?" she asked him.

"Those are government photos of the '53 raid. They lined up our wives and children and made them hold numbers like they were criminals or something."

In the photos women in long gingham dresses and aprons holding frightened, well-scrubbed children stared with confusion and anxiety at the camera.

"Well . . . here it is!" Marlowe shouted. "Yes, sir, this is the one I was thinking of!"

"It's Harrison!" Lynda cried out. "It's him! There were all sorts of pictures at the museum down in Key West! I know it's him!"

"What's it say on the back?" Stoner asked.

Wendell Marlowe, Sr., turned the photo over. "Well . . . there's two notations. The first says, 'Prospector, September 1930.' "

"And the other?" she asked.

"It's in pencil . . . I think it says, 'Shotgun Canyon Harry, when he first came into the Strip.' Must have been written later on."

"Are you sure that's Harrison?" Brady asked.

"I'm sure. This is great! I can't believe it! It's really him! Mr. Marlowe, is there any way you can sell me that picture or let me take it out and make a copy of it?" she asked.

"That picture? Why, you just haul it on out of here. If I'd known it was Harrison, I might have ripped it up years ago."

"Are you sure?"

"Positive. I don't want it here."

"Thank you very much, Mr. Marlowe. You've really helped us a lot."

"You sure you don't want any potatoes? I've got a fifty-pound sack in the pickup."

"Sir, you might be right. I think we'll buy those potatoes." Stoner nodded. "You pay the man, darlin', and I'll load them into our rig."

They sat in the front seat of the pickup and watched Wendell Marlowe, Sr., drive back toward the creek.

"Brady, can you believe it? Harrison was here! He really was in the Strip during the thirties. This isn't a wild goose chase. This is incredible!"

"I thought you knew that already."

"But I didn't have any proof. It's worth the whole trip just to get this picture. Oh, man, I've got to get to a phone and call Kelly and Nina!"

"Are they your sister-wives?" he teased.

"In your wildest dreams, Stoner!" she shot back. "Where are we going for lunch?"

"The Kaibab Indian Reservation cafe, I suppose."

"Is there a pay phone there?"

"I reckon so. Just drive back out to the highway and turn left."

The cab of the pickup was hot and stuffy. Both Austin and Stoner rolled their windows down, and the wind whipped through her shoulder-length hair.

"Yes! Yes . . . yes!" she squealed. "Pinch me, Brady. We have proof that Harrison was down here!"

"Man, you are one happy lady. You do know what this means, don't you?"

"What?"

"It means now you have to go down into Shotgun Canyon."

The smile fell off her face. "No! No . . . no . . . no!"

He pushed his hat back and grinned. "Yes."

Taking a deep breath, she sighed. "It's just not fair. I'm making one of the most important literary discoveries in the past fifty years, and I'll never live to enjoy it."

"It will look good in your obit.," he joked.

"Thanks, Stoner. Hey, how long till we get to the reservation?"

"Fifteen, maybe twenty miles."

"What's the deal on those potatoes? We can't use that many. And why did you make me pay for them — darlin'?"

"Because he did us a favor, and we ought to do something in return. You can just take it out of my wages. I'm broke, remember?"

"Your wages? Counting the fine, you're already in the hole."

"Yeah, this job is just like cowboyin'." He grinned. "Always goin' in the hole."

"What are we going to do with fifty pounds of potatoes?"

"I was figurin' on stoppin' by and seein' Eddy St. John and leavin' the potatoes for Amanda and the kids. Is that all right?"

"Well, it's either that or feed them to Capt. Patch."

"Nah. The Captain likes his potatoes fried."

"With chicken gravy over the top, right?"

"Beef gravy. He doesn't like chicken gravy."

After delivering the sack of potatoes to a grateful Amanda and Eddy St. John with the line, "Can you do me a favor and take these off my hands? What am I going to do with fifty pounds of raw potatoes?" Brady Stoner pointed Austin to the Broken Arrow Cafe.

"I'll order for you while you make that New York call," he offered.

"I haven't seen a menu yet."

"You don't need one. You're having a taco salad on Indian fry-bread and a diet Coke with a twist of lemon."

"Indian fry-bread?"

"You'll love it."

"Does it have salsa?"

"Sure."

"Put the salsa in a side dish," she instructed and scooted out to the lobby and the pay phone. She hiked up her jeans and tried to tuck her flannel shirt back in. Yanking off her sunglasses, she dialed the number and punched in the calling card number.

"Spunky? It's me, Lynda. I need to speak to Kelly or Nina. . . . It doesn't matter. Nina's fine. Sounds noisy in the reception area. You don't happen to be wearing that red leather outfit? . . . Hey, just a lucky guess."

The phone rang several times.

"Nina, it's Lynda. You'll never guess what we . . . What's wrong? Are you all right? What's happening? . . . Oh, no! Really? Oh, man . . . When?"

Twenty-five minutes later she rejoined Brady Stoner. At her place waited a huge taco salad with lettuce, tomatoes, onions, two different kinds of cheese, olives, spicy ground meat, and refried beans piled on top of what looked like a puffy, pregnant tortilla.

"I started without you. I didn't know it would take so long. Are you all right? You look like the dog died."

"Worse than that. Mr. Hampton, Sr., died."

"Over in Germany?"

"Yeah . . . complications from that stroke. He was a good man — a really good man. Kind of like a father to all of us, Brady."

"I'm sorry, Lynda Dawn. I'm truly sorry."

She sat down and ran her fork around in the salad, just staring but not taking a bite.

"Mr. Hampton was the one most enthused about publishing another Harrison. He was about the only decision-maker in that company who wasn't completely controlled by the bottom line. I'm goin' to really, really miss him."

"Were they excited about your finding the picture?"

"I didn't tell them."

"What?"

"They were all broken up about Mr. Hampton. I'll tell them some other time."

"How old a man was he?"

"In his mid-seventies, I guess. That's not all that old, really." She gazed across the cafe and could feel a tear slipping out of the corner of her eye. "It won't be the same house without Mr. Hampton, Sr."

"Kind of like gettin' kicked in the belly by a horse, ain't it?" he observed.

She stuffed her mouth with lettuce and nodded.

SEVEN

Lynda Austin stuck her head out the pickup window and studied the John Ford-esque landscape. Sage. Red cliffs. Tall distant pillars of semi-eroded sandstone. "Are you sure it's all right to take this trailer?" she called.

"When I signal, back up about a foot. Remember, you've got to come straight back," Brady Stoner hollered.

What am I doing? Hooking onto a trailer at somebody's ranch, and they didn't even give us permission! Seems like stealing.

"Hold it!" Brady yelled.

She slammed on the brakes and killed the engine. Then she turned off the key and slid out of the silver and black Dodge.

"Will that work?" she asked, hiking back to the trailer hitch.

His long sleeves were rolled up above his elbows revealing tan, muscular arms. "Give me a hand. Let's rock the truck back just a tad. I didn't know you were going to stop so quickly."

"Neither did I." She pulled on the tailgate and helped roll the truck back an inch. Stoner let down the trailer over the steel ball hitch. She glanced down at her tattered, torn, and dirty fingernails. "Tell me again how it is we can just drive up to a ranch and hook up a trailer."

"I told you, I used to work for the Double 8. They won't be needing it for a couple of weeks. Old Salvador won't mind."

"Well, shouldn't we leave a note or something?" She brushed her brown hair back with her fingers but knew it wasn't doing much good.

"Leave a note with who?"

"We could nail it to that old barn door or something."

"Nah. He knows no one would take it unless they really needed it."

"But how can you tell the difference between that and stealing?"

"Stealing? Who in the world would steal a horse trailer?"

Austin jammed her hands into her front jeans pockets and felt several folded one-dollar bills in one and a small piece of paper in the other. "But what if this man Salvador doesn't work at the ranch anymore? What if it's been sold? What if they forget who you are? What if we get arrested for stealing a trailer?" She pulled out the little scrap of paper that read "Inspected by #12" and jammed it back into her pocket.

Brady Stoner's brown eyes peered at her.

"Lynda Dawn Austin, you worry too much. You've got to learn to think Western. This isn't New York City."

235

She stepped up on the back bumper so that she could be as tall as he. "How much does a horse trailer like this cost?"

"About five thousand dollars."

"Oh, man . . . I can't believe I'm doin' this!" she moaned.

"I can't believe a big-city book editor is startin' to drop her *g*'s."

"My what?"

"You just said you couldn't believe you were doin' this. Did you hear that? Doin' — not doing."

"It's contagious, I reckon," she teased.

"That's all right if it goes one way. But if I start soundin' supercilious and have an urge to wear Italian loafers, that's when I'm pullin' out. Now get up there and test the brake lights and turn signals. I want to see if I have the wirin' hooked up right."

He waved at her after she completed the tests.

"You know, I've never pulled a trailer before," she announced as Stoner and Capt. Patch crawled back into the cab.

"A week ago you hadn't driven a pickup. You'll learn. Just take it easy until you get used to it. Besides, we'll be on dirt roads anyway. Make slow wide turns and don't plan on passin' anyone."

The driveway of the summer headquarters of the Double 8 Ranch was about three miles long. The high desert was flanked by the Vermillion Cliffs to the northeast and the Kaibab Forest to the southeast. Austin stared out across the vacant

236

landscape as a warm breeze whipped in through the open window. She knew her hair would now be blasted to an unmanageable state, but at the moment she didn't even bother looking in the mirror.

"It's so empty."

"The gas tank?"

"No . . . this land. It continually overwhelms me that there are places in our country that are so — so barren. There's nothing out there. No houses. No people. No power poles. No fences. No roads. No nothing!"

"Ain't it great?"

"Yeah. A person needs this every once in a while. Life's so confusing in the city. Take my office . . ." Her voice faded out, and she stared blankly straight ahead.

After several minutes he finally asked, "You thinkin' about Mr. Hampton?"

She sighed, brushed a tear out of the corner of her eye, and nodded her head. "He cared about every person who worked for that company. You don't find that in many people. It makes everyone work a little harder when they know the boss really cares."

"Kind of like the Lord, isn't it?"

Startled, she turned to look at the serious expression on his face.

He continued, "The more you understand that He loves you, the more you want to please Him. Is that what you mean?"

"Eh . . . sure. I didn't think you . . ."

"You didn't think what?"

"Never mind."

"You thought I was some sort of heathen?" He wiped the sweat from the side of his neck and smeared a streak of dirt clear to his collar.

"No . . . it's just . . . Well, you seemed to be mad at God." Lynda wanted to reach over with a rag and clean him up, but she resisted the urge.

"Not mad but at times confused — that's for sure. But I just — "

A loud explosion from the top of the hill interrupted him. Lynda stopped at a gravel road at the end of the ranch drive.

"Is someone shooting at us?"

"Hey, that looks like Salvador!"

"Oh, no, we're going to get arrested! They'll pack us off to Kingman."

"Nope. We're in Coconino County now. They'll have to haul us to Flagstaff."

A white flat-bed truck churned the dust toward them. Another loud explosion blasted their ears.

"He's shooting at us!"

"Nah, it's just that old service rig backfirin'. Just hold your horses." Brady Stoner stepped out of the pickup and ambled forward, leaning his desert-tough frame against the front of the rig.

Austin slipped the pickup into neutral and turned the engine off. *Lord, I don't think I want to be here!*

The white truck slid to a stop in the middle of the road. Lynda had to look around Brady to see the driver. A grim-faced, dark-complected, middle-aged man jerked a rifle from the gun rack and jumped out of the truck. He was wearing jeans, a long-sleeve dirty white shirt, and a greasy-looking straw cowboy hat.

"Stoner, you miserable excuse for a cowboy, what in blazes do you think you're doin' stealin' my trailer?" the man shouted and waved his rifle wildly. "Say your prayers, boy. You ain't walkin' away from this one!"

"Salvador, you overweight, ugly Apache half-breed, I'm takin' this trailer, and you can't stop me. Now go back and hide in your wickiup with the women!"

He's going to get into another fight! The guy has a gun. Lord, please help!

"You've insulted the Apache Nation for the last time!" He whipped the rifle to his shoulder. "Don't bother beggin' for mercy!"

"Now you've got me really mad," Stoner shouted. Then he stepped out of the way of the pickup and gave her a full view of Salvador. "Go ahead, Lynda. Drive the rig over the top of this blight on civilization!"

Lord! What shall I do?

Suddenly a wide grin broke across Salvador's face. He pushed his sweat-stained hat to the back of his head and squinted to see her in the cab.

"You got some barrel racer in there?" He flopped the rifle across his shoulder and walked around to the open window of the pickup. "Excuse me, miss, I didn't know . . . I hope I didn't scare you."

Then he turned and strolled over to Stoner and slapped him on the back. "*¡Compadre! ¿Qué pasa?* What's this broken leg?"

"Would you believe I placed on the horse, and he kicked me when I was climbin' down?"

"Excuse me! Time out here!" Austin huffed as she slipped out of the truck.

"Oh." Brady glanced back. "Salvador, this is Miss Lynda Dawn Austin from New York City. She's hired me to — "

"Wait a minute!" she barked. "You mean to tell me all those threats and shouts were just a game?"

"Well . . . sure. I told you me and Salvador were long-time friends!"

"You thought we were goin' to . . . ," Salvador began. "Oh, shoot, miss, me and Brady . . . Why, he came into this country ten years ago as a fairly good rough string rider, but that was about it. I had to teach him to cowboy and rope."

"Rope? You taught me to rope?"

"Well, he still can't rope worth spit, but heaven knows, I tried."

"Can't rope? I can out-rope a half-brained old man like you!"

"Them's fightin' words, Stoner. What do you want, guns or knives?"

"Do you guys keep this up all day?" Lynda interrupted.

"All day?" Salvador laughed. "Didn't he tell you? We kept it up all one winter!"

Shaking her head, she started to walk away toward a clump of Joshua trees.

"Where you goin'?" Brady asked.

"For a walk with Capt. Patch. All this male bonding is having a negative effect on me."

"Male bonding? What in the world is that?" Salvador asked.

"It must be something they do in New York. They're pretty weird up there," Brady interjected.

"Hey, Little Vic's drawn good in Winslow. Did you hear about . . ."

The voices faded as she hiked over the hill and into the trees. When she returned, Stoner was handing a canvas duffel bag to Salvador. The dark-skinned man tossed a saddle into the back of the pickup.

"Are we ready to get back to work?" she asked.

"What'd I tell you? She's a slave driver."

"Ma'am, if you ever want to be foreman of the ranch, just let me know! If you can get your money's worth out of this bum, you're a better man than I am."

"I was the top hand, and you know it."

"That proves my point about the sorry state of the cowboy business."

"I choose knives!"

"Don't start this again," she griped and pulled herself back into the pickup. Within minutes they were bouncing their way down the gravel and dirt road to the southwest. In the mirror she watched Salvador turn around and drive back up the hill.

"Brady, that wasn't funny. Wavin' that gun and

all — it scared me to death."

"Sorry about that, Lynda Dawn. I guess I wasn't thinkin'. Besides, I thought you were a shooter."

"Clay pigeons are the only thing I ever aim at. I don't even like shooting birds. What did you give him in that bag?"

"I loaned his son my bareback riggin'. He's drawn good in Winslow but left his gear with a friend in Walla Walla."

"So where are we going now?"

"To pick up Punkin."

"Who?"

"The smoothest-gaited mule you ever straddled."

"We're ridin' mules?"

"I'm not. You are."

"Why did you decide on a mule for me? Aren't they . . . stubborn?"

"Not any worse than New York City editors. Besides, Punkin never spooks on the trails — no matter how narrow or steep."

"Oh, no!" She waved her finger at him. "I'm not riding off the side of that cliff!"

"Now, Lynda Dawn, relax. I told you we're going to try and find the back side of the canyon. But anyway you look at it, there will be some downhill ridin'. Punkin will get you there, and all you have to do is hang on."

"Where is this wonder mule?"

"Up there in the pines!" He pointed to the trees that crested a distant mountain range.

"How do we get there?"

How in the world can a guy covered with dirt and grime still have a sparkle in his eyes?

"Just follow this highway."

"This one-lane gravel road?"

Lynda Dawn, you're a professional editor on a research trip. Get a grip!

"It is — compared to the one we're goin' to be on."

By 4:00 P.M. they had the mule loaded in the trailer and were headed into the setting sun — back out on the Kanab Plateau.

"What do you mean — no one owns Punkin?" she demanded.

"Well, he lives up near those broken-down corrals, and the cowboys see that he has some extra hay for winter food. A mule won't overeat like a horse. The boys from the Double 8 give him shots and dewormer, and the Bar RT hands will shoe him if they need to. Folks just take him out to work and then bring him back. He's sort of a free-lance mule, I guess."

"Where to now?"

"The Bar RT has a roundup cabin back in here. We'll camp there for the night. I'll throw a loop on Barstow and pick up another saddle."

"Barstow?"

"A strawberry roan. Slowest horse in the Strip."

"Why would you want him?"

" 'Cause he's never stumbled in his life. And nothin' scares him, short of bobcats and bears."

Lynda Dawn Austin found that if she drove twenty-five miles an hour and never met anyone else on the road, pulling a horse trailer was no big deal.

She flipped on the radio. "How about finding us some news? I feel like the whole world is passing us by. I haven't read a newspaper or watched television for over a week."

"Well . . . you aren't goin' to get any radio out here," he informed her.

"Come on. Are you telling me there are places in the U.S. where there's no radio reception?"

"Paul Harvey and Rush Limbaugh don't reach everyone. The only radio out here is in the dead of night. KFI out of L.A. or maybe KSL out of Salt Lake — if they're bouncin' right. Darlin', you're sitting on the edge of the earth. When you grow up, you tend to think that the center of the world is your own house. When you grow up on the Strip, you know that you are on the fringe of everything."

"Okay . . . no radio."

"Well, I don't have a CD, but you can listen to some cassette tapes . . . or I can sing."

"You never told me you could sing."

If he plays the guitar and sings, I'll know this is all a dream!

"Every cowboy in the West can sing," he announced. "Most of us can't carry a tune though. There's a lot of difference between singin' and hittin' the notes."

"What kind of tapes do you have? Or should

I ask? Country Western, no doubt."

"Nope."

"What then?"

"Well, out here there's a difference between country and Western music. I'm afraid all of my tapes are Western."

"What do you mean, Western?"

"Cowboy music."

"You mean . . . Roy Rogers and Gene Autry?"

"Sure, I might be able to dig up a little Roy and Gene. . . . But what I had in mind was Ian Tyson, The Sons of the San Joaquin, or Riders in the Sky."

"Now I know I'm in a different world." She laughed. "All right, let's hear this Western music."

For almost an hour neither said much as they tooled across the Kanab Plateau. The songs were about deserts and prairies, cows and cowboys, riding tall and getting thrown hard, losing a lady and gaining a good horse, lonesome trails and even more lonesome old drovers.

Coming over a rise, she thought she saw a glimmer of something against the distant mountain.

"Is that a cabin over there?"

"Yep. And that reflection is good news. It means they repaired the windows this year. Is this your first time at sleepin' in a bunkhouse?"

"Obviously." She turned off the tape player and gaped across the desert at the cabin in the cottonwoods. "Is it much different from sleeping in an abandoned church?"

"Depends on how many hands are bunking out."

Her eyes blazed. "What? I thought you said it was vacant! There are going to be men staying there? Look, I'm not about — "

"Relax. I was joshin'. There'll only be one guy there, and he's practically harmless."

"Who? What's his name? How old is he?"

"Me."

"Stoner, you don't count."

"Now just why do you think you're safe out here with me?"

"Because if you were the type to do something stupid, you would have tried it before now. And, second, I watched you around Heather and Amanda and the others. You're pretty easy to read."

"You ever been surprised by a man?"

"Nope," she said with more certainty than she meant. "Now is there going to be anyone else at this cabin or not?"

"Shouldn't be. But you can sleep in the pickup if it's a worry."

"What? And pass up my only opportunity to spend a night in the ol' bunkhouse? Where should I park this rig?"

"Rig? All right! Now you're buckin', Lynda Dawn! Park over by the windmill pump."

They stopped in the middle of a dirt yard near a wood-slatted building with white paint peeling off the walls and new glass in the windows. Off to the side stood a corral where each fence post was propped up with a pile of big rocks.

Brady slid out of the pickup and looked back in at her. "If you want to, you could sweep the spiders out of the bunkhouse."

"What are you going to do?"

"Saddle up Punkin and go find Barstow. There's a spring at the base of that bluff. At this time of the day the whole string will come in to water."

"Should I fix something to eat?"

"Sure."

"What are you hungry for?"

"Pork and beans."

"Sounds delightful. You want me to warm them up?"

"It's up to you."

"Is there a stove or anything?"

"Nope."

"Then we'll have them cold."

"I'm takin' Capt. Patch with me." He stepped to the back of the trailer and began to unload the mule.

The bunkhouse had a screen door, and both it and the main door were unlocked. Inside, the room was dusty but fairly neat. Lynda found a broom in the corner behind one of four sets of bunk beds. The rustic wood-frame beds were all pushed against the walls. In the center of the room stood a round wooden table surrounded by broken chairs, crates, and tree stumps — all of which looked as if they were used as chairs. Wooden pegs lined the walls with assorted unfamiliar horsey-looking gear hanging from them.

A faded handwritten sign on one door read: Restroom. Carefully pushing open the door, she found herself staring outside at the dirt back yard and the grove of cottonwoods.

Real cute! Lord, in case I never thanked You for indoor plumbing before — thanks.

Stepping back out front, she walked over to where Brady sat in the saddle on the mule. His broken right leg stuck out to the side. Still, she noticed how straight he sat.

"You look like you're at home."

"I'd rather be on a horse. I'll be back in about thirty minutes."

She looked up at him and shaded the setting sun out of her eyes with her hands.

"Well, darlin'," she drawled, "don't you stay late. You be home for supper, ya hear? The children and I will be hankerin' somethin' fierce for your company."

He glanced down at her for a minute.

"You're startin' to enjoy this, aren't you?"

"Yeah. Is that crazy or what?"

"It wears good on you, Lynda Dawn. Maybe you ought to be more worried than you are."

"About what?"

He turned Punkin toward the cliffs and kicked him with the heel of his good foot. The mule started to trot away.

"About me!" he shouted back.

You be the daddy, and I'll be the mommy, and we'll play house. . . . Lord, it's almost like a kid's game. I can't believe I'm standing in the absolute boonies watching a guy ride off into the sunset. Maybe this is just a virtual reality diversion, and I'll find myself in an arcade in Rockefeller Center.

She opened the windows and swept the room, scrubbed the table, and carried in the sleeping bags and food. Unable to find a can opener, she decided to wait for Stoner's return to prepare the pork and beans.

She dragged out the only chair that had all its original parts and put it on the front porch, which was a warped wooden boardwalk. Digging through her cardboard file box in the pickup, she yanked out her Day Planner.

Back inside the rustic cabin, she sorted through her suitcase, pulled out a wide green ribbon, and then tied her hair back with it. A broken piece of mirror was wedged into the casing next to the door, and she stopped to look at herself.

Well, you're not exactly Miss Penny Pioneer . . . but you aren't Jackie from the upper east side either.

She dug through her taupe leather purse, dabbed her lips with Autumn Rose Blush, and blotted them on the corner of a brown paper sack. The small glass bottle was labeled Evening Rhapsody, and she sprinkled it behind her ears and on her wrists. On the wall was a fairly beat-up gray felt cowboy hat. She pulled the green ribbon out of her hair and tied it on the hat as a hatband, with the tail of the ribbon trailing off the brim.

She carefully placed the hat on her head and then she glanced in the mirror again.

That's better. Although I'm not sure why I feel I need to get dolled up.

She plopped down in the chair out front. The

evening sun seemed sprawled on the western mountains — according to her guess, near Mt. Trumbull. She began to write in her Day Planner.

To Do Tomorrow After the Ride:
1. **Call Kelly & Nina, find out about services for Mr. Hampton. Tell them about the picture of Harrison (& about Rincon!).**
2. **Call Megan — let her know what little sister is up to.**
3. **Call James — tell him?**
4. **Do some laundry (at Heather's if we get back there. Buy her a gift!).**
5. **Check on canyon helicopter services. How much per hour to explore the north rim?**
6. **Have a good talk with Brady.**

Glancing into the sun, she thought she saw a couple of horses coming up the drive. She could see some dust and two animals, but the reflecting sun prevented her from recognizing the rider — or riders.

Brady's probably leading that horse he went after . . . but he went to the east, not the west! Two riders? Oh, man, it's some Bar RT cowboys coming to use their cabin. Where's that rodeo bum, Stoner, when a girl needs him?

For almost ten minutes she watched them ride up the drive. Finally the two middle-aged men wearing T-shirts and jeans entered the dirt yard.

"Howdy, boys," she called. "Are you looking

for Brady? Brady Stoner? He'll be back any moment now."

"Well . . . we were — we were surprised to see anyone over here."

Is that the cowboy way to tell us to leave? How come they don't have on cowboy hats?

"Brady's picking up a horse, and we figured to . . . Well, I'll let him explain it when he gets home — I mean, when he gets back."

What am I supposed to say? What kind of buckaroos wear tennies?

"It's about supper time, boys! Would you, eh . . . like to . . . eat with us?"

"What did I tell you, Gerald? These Western people know what hospitality is all about! Well, thank you, Mrs. Stoner, we'd like to, but — "

"We're having cold pork and beans, but there's plenty of them!" she offered.

Oh, man, that was dumb. Really dumb.

"Don't that beat all, Stan? These folks livin' out here with nothing but cold beans, and they offer to share it with us. Now you don't see someone from New York City treating a person that way, do you?"

Lynda gawked at their Nikes. "Just where did you boys come from?"

"Oh, we rented these horses from a wrangler at the Bar RT. He's goin' to meet us about dark down at the crossing. We'd love to stop for dinner, but it's a package deal that includes a big steak tonight. We better eat there. It's costing $125 apiece for this ride."

The short one pulled off his NY Mets cap and wiped the sweat off his forehead. "Sorry to barge in on you like this. We just had a little time to kill."

"Say, I'd appreciate your recommendation. Stan and I are bankers in the Big Apple. We don't get to ride much. So we are going to be really sore tonight — "

"Tonight? I'm dying already!"

"Anyway, the wrangler said don't worry. He gave us some horse liniment to rub in. Now is he trying to play us for saps, or does that stuff actually work?"

Austin pushed her hat back. "Boys, I can't think of anything that works better than horse liniment!"

"See there, Stan? We got it from an expert. This lady knows what she's talking about! Thanks, Mrs. Stoner."

"Oh, I'm not Mrs. Stoner. . . . Really, it's just a job, and I, eh . . ."

"Well, I'll be! So equality came to the old range? I've got to get a picture. Do you mind standing over here?" He motioned. "Stan, be sure and get me on the horse and this lady . . . say, what's your name?"

"You can call me Lynda Dawn."

"Lynda Dawn? Is that a Western name or what? Man, that beats all the Tiffanies and Allisons and Kimberleys in New York! Do you mind if I take a picture of your house?"

"Go right ahead."

Gerald tipped his cap. "Ms. Dawn, this has been the highlight of the ride for us. Authentic people in an authentic ranch house. Man, this is the part they don't have in the movies. . . . Well, ma'am, we have to be moseyin' back out to the highway." He laughed.

"Say," Stan offered as they were about to leave, "I noticed you writing when we rode up. If you like, we could take any letters out and mail them for you."

"Oh, no, that's not necessary," she protested, trying not to burst out laughing.

"No, really, it wouldn't be any bother. We'll buy the stamps."

She collected herself and looked him in the eye. "What month is this?"

"End of September. Why?"

"Oh, we'll be going to town for winter groceries in October. I can take the letters in then!" She looked down quickly, afraid of cracking a smile.

The two nodded with blank expressions and began to ride back out the driveway.

"Did you hear her? They go to town in October? Wait until I tell Natalie! She thinks waiting until after lunch to go shopping is a major sacrifice."

"You're right, Stan. They just don't make women like that anymore!"

She was still watching them in the distance when she heard hoofbeats behind her. Brady rode a reddish gray horse and led Punkin.

"Is that Barstow?"

"Yep. Who are those two out there?"

"Tourists."

"From the Bar RT?"

"Yeah."

"I thought they only did that tourist ride thing in the spring." Brady carefully swung his cast over Barstow and lowered himself to the ground. "Did you talk to them?"

"Yep. I invited them to supper."

"You what?"

"Isn't that the Western way?"

"Yeah, sure . . . provided you have something to offer them."

"They turned me down. But they wanted to take my picture. A genuine Western cowgirl, they called me."

"They thought you were a cowgirl? What planet were they from?"

"New York. It must be my hat."

"Well, it's a nice hat. I like the ribbon. Say, tomorrow remind me to show you the place where we buried the guy who used to own that hat."

She yanked the hat off her head and held it in her hand.

"Oh, don't worry. It wasn't an infectious disease or anything. Just old age. You can wear it."

"Are you ready for supper?" she asked.

"Yep. Let me corral these animals, and I'll be in. How have the children been?"

She smiled from ear to ear. "Brady Jr.'s been chasing sissy around with a rattlesnake, and I told him that his daddy's going to whup him good when he gets home."

"Send that boy out to the barn, Mother. There's no reason for you to have to put up with that."

"Oh . . . yeah . . . have you got a can opener?"

Stoner reached into his jeans and pulled out a stockman's knife and tossed it to her.

"That's it?"

"Trust me."

She caught the pocket knife and turned back to the cabin.

Trust me? Why do men use that phrase all the time? Do they teach them that in grade school? I think maybe their dads pull them aside when they are three and say, "Son, this one will always work. Just look at them with puppy-dog eyes and say, 'Trust me.'"

They ate their supper sitting on the boardwalk in front of the cabin, watching the last flicker of daylight blink into darkness. Half the evening Brady explained how to get a 75-point ride even when you've drawn a lousy horse. The rest of the time Lynda illustrated the comic difficulty of publishing an autobiography of a twenty-seven-year-old Hollywood actress who had made a zillion bucks but had absolutely nothing to say.

There was nothing but moonlight to guide them back inside the cabin.

"We're pullin' out before daylight, Lynda Dawn, so it's time to turn in."

"I don't think I've gone to bed at nine since I was ten."

"Well, think of it as midnight eastern time."

"After the ride tomorrow, I need to make some phone calls, do some laundry, maybe pick up a few things. We are planning on being through before dark, aren't we?"

"That all depends on what we find." She could hear him pull off his boots and bang them to the rough wooden floor.

"Well, if that canyon is about where you think it is, it's only about twenty miles from the dirt road. Now if we're there at daylight, it would take . . . what? About an hour to ride back in there? An hour or two to look around and find the manuscript and an hour out. We should be back to the blacktop by early afternoon, and then we — "

"Eh, there's a flaw or two in your logic."

"What's that?"

"First, twenty miles by horseback in the country we're going through will take about seven hours."

"What? But — "

"And if we don't find a back door to that canyon, we'll have to come out and go down that granite cliff."

Lying fully clothed on top of the borrowed sleeping bag on one of the bunks, Austin proclaimed, "I'm not going down that trail."

"You're going if I have to blindfold you and tie you to the saddle."

"Brady, I'm not making this up. I'm just too scared to go down that trail. I can't help it. Aren't there some things you just can't do? I mean . . . like sing a solo at Carnegie Hall in front of thousands of people . . . or something?"

"It would scare me spitless," he admitted.

"Well, that's exactly the way I feel about that trail on the cliff."

"But," he went on, "I'd do it if it was the only way to win the World Championship."

"What?"

"If singing that solo was what was standing between me and a life-long goal, I think I'd do it."

"Even if the action would kill you?"

"Would or could? There's always a risk. I don't want to be a dead champ. . . . But I'm tellin' you, you won't die ridin' down that canyon."

The moonlight filtered into the cabin just enough to see the dark gray shadow of the bunk above her. "I don't want to talk about it anymore."

"Okay, let's talk about your perfume."

"My perfume?"

"Yeah, I can smell it way over here."

"Sorry."

"Oh, no, it smells wonderful. I love it. It's just that . . . Well, I'm still tryin' to figure you out."

"What do you mean?"

"Well, I thought the reason women poured on the perfume was to, you know . . . get a man's attention."

"Or it could be because she has to sleep out in the bunkhouse with no place to shower and clean up."

"Yeah, I guess you're right. Never mind then."

"What do you mean, never mind?" she demanded.

"Nothin.' "

She lay quiet for several minutes staring in the darkened cabin.

"You mean you think I put on this perfume just to give you a come-on?"

"I didn't say that."

"That's what you were thinking, wasn't it, Stoner? You think I'm some flirt who's trying to get you to pay attention to me? Well, you don't know me very well. I happen to enjoy my perfume, and I'd be doing the same thing whether you were here or not!"

"As old Ben Jonson would say, 'The dignity of truth is lost with much protesting.' "

"Are you going to start quoting seventeenth-century pundits now? Look, I like to wear perfume. You like to wear cowboy hats. Let's leave it at that. You keep on your side of the room, and everything will be fine."

"Me come over there? The thought never crossed my mind."

Even though neither said another word the rest of the night, Lynda Dawn Austin lay awake for a long time.

Girl, how do you do that? You have a delightful evening of small talk, then go inside, and ruin everything! At this rate you'll end up like Barbara Washburn — walking your dog and reading manuscripts every night when you're fifty.

She rolled over on her right side and tried scrunching up the nylon jacket she used for a pillow.

"The thought never crossed my mind." The liar!

A cramp in her lower back caused her to scoot around in the bed and find a more comfortable position.

Why didn't the thought cross your mind, Brady Stoner? You only go for the bimbo waitress types?

She had a strong urge to get up, make herself a cup of tea, and go out on the balcony of her condo to watch the lights of the city. Lying in a bunkhouse in one of the most remote parts of the United States, she thought about Janie, James, Nina, Kelly, George Gossman, Mr. Hampton, and Spunky Sasser.

I know it's a rut — a routine, but it's my routine, Lord. Maybe I miss it. Maybe one week out here is about all I'm good for. This is Brady's world . . . not mine. There is a cultural barrier.

Listening to him snore, she thought about getting up and going for a walk in the moonlight.

I wonder if snakes come out in the night?

She made no attempt to get out of bed.

Lord . . . forgive me. Brady doesn't chase after bimbos. That wasn't fair. He's right. I put on this perfume to get his attention. How come I seem to want men to be crazy about me but keep their distance? I'm thirty years old. I should have figured this all out years ago.

Sometime after midnight she fell asleep. And it was still pitch dark when she felt a hand on her shoulder.

"Come on, boss. Time to rise and shine!" the obnoxiously cheery voice boomed.

In the dim light of the flashlight, Austin packed up as Stoner loaded the horse and mule into the trailer so smoothly that it seemed easy.

"I thought we'd eat in the rig," he announced. "You have everything loaded?"

"I hope so. It's still kind of dark in there." She nodded toward the bunkhouse.

He cleared his throat, then looked away from her. "Uh . . . I left things a tad unpleasant last night, and it's been churnin' my stomach most of the mornin'. If you and me ever get a chance to talk personal, maybe I can explain why I acted the way I did."

"Oh, don't worry about it. It didn't bother me at all. . . . Well . . . I mean, I figure I deserved it."

"Lynda Dawn, did you ever think that we're really a lot alike? In a New York/Idaho sort of way?"

"Are you goin' to quote another philosopher?"

"Yep. This comes from old Willie Nelson. It's time to get 'on the road again.' "

Pulling a loaded horse trailer down a narrow dirt road in the blackness before daylight made Austin nervous — for about fifteen minutes. After that it was just the rumble of the rig, a song about an Alberta moon from Ian Tyson, and little powdered-sugar doughnuts that puffed crumbs across her lap. An hour later the eastern sky softened into a dull charcoal gray.

"How are we going to find the place to begin? You called it a trail head, but there really isn't any trail, is there?"

"Nope. But we'll turn east at the old church building where we stayed the other night."

"I don't remember a road going east."

"I didn't say there was a road. I just said we'd turn there. We'll drive across the valley until we hit the hills. Then we'll park the rig and saddle up the animals."

When they reached the church, it was breaking daylight. By the time they bounced their way to a little box canyon, Lynda could see everything clearly.

She sat on the back of the pickup and watched him saddle up the animals. "What's that huge pile of orange and yellow dirt?"

"Tailings. At one time they tried to mine out here."

"Gold?"

"I suppose. I'm not sure about this pile."

"This is a remote spot for a mine."

"All those old mines were started in remote places. Roll up a change of clothes in that red sleeping bag and bring it over. I'll tie it on Punkin."

"Sleeping bag? We aren't going to be out here tonight, are we? I need to make some calls. I need a shower!"

"Can't guarantee what will happen this far back in. It's better to be prepared. Hand me my bedroll and that green duffel. I stuck a couple bottles of water and some food in there. You can probably stick a few things in the duffel. Anything else you need cram down in the sleeping bag."

She stuffed a change of clothes and her purse in the duffel and then jammed her Day Planner and several notebooks into the center of the sleeping bag. "Seriously, we really are going to try to get out before dark, right?"

"Yep. You ready to ride?"

"I guess. What do I do first?"

"If you've said your prayers, you can climb up on Punkin. Come over here and put your left foot in the stirrup. I'll hold the reins until you climb aboard."

She stabbed at the stirrup with her foot. Then with one hand pulling on the horn and the other on the cantle, she swung up into the saddle.

"It's high up here!"

"You can see better."

"I can fall further."

She watched him put all his weight on his broken leg and jam his left foot into the stirrup. Then with some effort he brought the broken leg up over the horse and settled down into the saddle.

"Doesn't that hurt?"

"Like a hot knife punched through my knee."

"Why do you do it?"

"Because there's only one way to mount a horse."

She held the soft leather reins in the right hand, and her left rested on the saddle horn. "How do I make him go?"

"Here's all you need to know about Punkin. Touch both heels to his tummy, and he'll move forward. The harder you punch him, the faster he will run. If you want to turn him right, pull the reins to the right. Don't pull on the bit though. Just the weight of the leather strap on his neck will tell him which way you want to go."

"What if I want to stop him?"

"A real gentle tug straight back will do it. Holler 'whoa,' and he'll stop."

Lynda Dawn Austin kept expecting the mule to stumble, buck, kick, bite, lunge, or gallop off into the sunrise. Instead, Punkin plodded behind the rear end of the roan horse. Capt. Patch raced from one rock and sage to the next chasing imaginary rabbits and other villains.

"This isn't so bad," she finally admitted.

"It will make you sore. But it's a great way to see the country."

Rolling, barren hills with sagebrush and tufts of dead grass spread under the clear desert sky. A slightly warm breeze blew from the west.

"What are we looking for?"

"We'll ride up on that bluff, then cut back to the west and look for the tail end of a north-south canyon — somethin' that leads toward the Colorado River. It won't be too easy to spot, or they would never have made that trail down that sheer rock cliff."

They rode for two hours, took a break, then mounted up, and rode straight west. Brady sat tall — back erect, yet at ease. Lynda felt tired, dirty, sore, and stretched wide.

"I think I need a narrower animal," she finally said.

"Yeah. Maybe that's why those old-time ladies rode sidesaddle. If you get to hurtin' too much, pull your right foot out of the stirrup and swing it over Punkin's head. You can just sit sideways for a while."

"I think I'll stay right here."

When they reached some stubby junipers, Brady signaled for time to rest the horses. He helped her off, then loosened the cinches on the saddles, and buckled leather hobbles on the forelegs of each animal.

He pulled off the green duffel with the food and water. Then he turned to see Lynda standing in the exact same spot where she had dismounted. Her feet were spread wide apart, and she was doubled over at the waist.

"You doin' okay?" he asked.

"I don't think I can move!" she moaned.

"Kind of rough on your first try. In a week or two, you'll get toughened up."

"A week or two of this, and I'd be ready to jump off that cliff."

"Come on over here into the shade of this piñon pine. . . . You want me to help you?"

"I'll make it. . . . I can do it." She staggered, stiff-legged and back bent. He pulled the quilt out of the center of his bedroll and spread it out on the dead grass.

"I don't want to, eh . . . If this sounds wrong, you tell me, but if you'd like . . . I could, you know, rub your back if you wanted me to."

"I'd love for you to."

"You would?"

"Cowboy, my backside hurts so much you could drive a truck over me, and it would feel better."

"Are you hungry?" he asked.

"Starved."

"You want cold canned ravioli or cold canned fettuccine?"

"Oh, we're having Italian! I'll have the fettuccine."

They ate out of the cans with plastic spoons. Then Lynda lay down on the blanket on her stomach, and Brady rubbed her back, starting with the shoulder blades. His strong hands poked, gouged, kneaded, and rubbed all the sore spots clear to the base of her spine. Then he started back at the top and repeated the process.

"How you doin' now?"

"Much better." She sighed. "Where did you learn to give a back rub like that?"

"Debbi's a barrel racer from Texas who was always needin' her back rubbed. I guess she sort of taught me how to do it."

"I'll bet she did! Anyway, thank you, Debbi."

"Is that enough?"

"How about one more pass down my back?"

"You got it, boss."

By the time he reached her lower back, she felt

so relaxed she could sleep all day.

"Well, that's where I stop. I don't go further than that." He laughed.

"Neither do I."

"I know . . . I know about you, Lynda Dawn Austin. You're as predictable as a Joaquin Estában novel."

She rolled over and sat up. "Does that bother you, cowboy?"

"Nope. I like a gal to be predictable."

"Well, I'm going to take that for a compliment. Are we really going to get back on those animals?"

"From here on should be the good part."

"What do you mean?"

"Level ground around the rim. Somewhere between here and the dirt road may be the tail end of Shotgun Canyon. You ready to ride?"

"Of course not! Come on, Stoner, help me up."

For over two hours they rode with the sun straight above them. The ground was rocky but fairly level. They seemed to be zigzagging around clumps of junipers, pines, and cedars. She could hear absolutely no sounds other than the ones they made. She felt a numbness in her backside that she knew would fade into severe pain at some future time.

Stoner and Capt. Patch were about thirty yards ahead of her when he started waving his arms.

"What is it?" she called.

"Stay there!" he hollered.

"Is something wrong?"

He turned the roan horse around and rode back to her. "Well, the good news is, I think I found the northern edge of Shotgun Canyon."

"What's the bad news?"

"It's worse than that trail out at the Colorado."

"What do you mean, worse?"

"Drops off about two hundred feet, then nothing but boulders and loose rock for another thousand feet. No way to ride down into it."

"It can't be worse than that other way."

"Climb off your mount and come take a look."

"Can't I just stay up here?"

"Sure, hand me the reins."

"Why?"

"So you won't panic and do something dumb."

The view was spectacular. The drop wasn't as deep as the one near the river, and the sloping boulders gave a more gentle feel to the vista. Yet she clutched the saddle horn with both hands.

"That's close enough! Really, I can see. You're right. We can't go down this way!"

Riding back away from the edge, she began to relax. "So what are we going to do? Maybe this isn't really Shotgun Canyon."

"We're going to do what we should have done all along. We'll swing around to the west and reach the top of the lookout point. Then we'll ride down that cliff and into history."

"We'll be history, you mean!"

"I promise to get you to Shotgun Canyon alive. You do trust me, don't you?"

She stared expressionless into his eyes for a moment.

" 'Thou wilt not utter what thou dost not know; and so far will I trust thee, gentle . . .' Brady Stoner." She tried to grin as she finished the quote.

"Well, at least you didn't call me Kate. *Henry the IV*, right?"

"Yes, but don't tell me you majored in Shakespeare, too?"

"Nope. But me and Tad Laudry spent one winter up in the Kaibab with nothin' in the cabin to read but a one-volume complete works of Shakespeare. So we read out loud every night after the chores were done. We must have gone through that sucker ten times."

"I'm impressed."

He shrugged. "There was nothing else to do. Come on, I think we can get to the trail by three."

"I take it we will be spending the night in the canyon."

"One way or another."

"Stoner, that wasn't funny!"

"No, darlin' . . . it wasn't."

"Don't call me . . ."

"What?" He glanced over at her with brown-eyed innocence.

"Nothing," she sighed.

It was almost four in the afternoon when they reached the isolated granite overlook at the Colorado River. They dismounted, and Austin staggered around trying to find a comfortable rock to stretch her back across. Finally, draped over one the size of a washing machine, she looked around for Stoner.

"I don't think I can do this, Brady. I'm not kidding. I really don't think I can."

"Look, we'll let Capt. Patch lead the way. Then I'll go ahead of you. Punkin can make it down anything this horse can. All you have to do is hold on to the horn and close your eyes, or look at the granite side of the trail. It won't be that narrow all the way."

"I still don't think I can."

"As sore as you are . . . you have the rhythm now. You and Punkin have gotten used to each other. As far as he's concerned, it's no different than walking up here on top. He hasn't stumbled on you once today, has he?"

"No, but it's been . . . Well, we haven't had . . . Are you sure he isn't scared of heights?"

"Positive."

"Well . . . Lord, help . . . Let's get it over with. Listen, if I get scared, you've got to promise we'll turn around and come back. Will you promise me?"

"Nope."

"Why not?"

"There won't be any way to turn an animal around on that trail. We're goin' all the way to the bottom."

"Yeah," she mumbled. "That's what I'm afraid of."

Every muscle in her body was shaking as she followed Brady Stoner off the top of the cliff and down the trail that was no more than eighteen inches at its widest.

"Braaa-dy!" her voice quivered.

"I'm here, darlin'. Just keep your eyes closed. You're doin' fine."

"I can't do it, Brady." She began to cry. "I tried . . . really. But I can't do it."

"We can't turn back now, darlin'. Horses and mules don't back up a trail this steep. Sing a song or somethin'."

"You're joking! I'm lucky to breathe."

"Are you peeking?"

"I'm not looking . . . 'Oh, Lamb of God, who taketh away the sins of the world, have mercy upon us!' " she groaned.

"Do you know the song, 'Goodbye Ol' Paint?' "

"No!" she sobbed.

"Well, I'll teach it to you."

It took several times through all five verses, but finally she began to whimper, "I'm ridin' Old Paint; I'm leadin' Old Dan; I'm off to Montana for to throw the hoolihan — "

"Your eyes are open," he interrupted.

"I'm just lookin' at the cliff. I think I'd like going uphill better than this downhill stuff," she managed to gasp.

"You're right about that. I think we're off the worst part. Capt. Patch ran on down the trail lookin' for critters. It must widen up there. You're doin' great, darlin'. I bet there aren't six women in the country who have ever seen this sight."

"That's because their eyes were closed," she tried to kid, but it sounded to her more like a pathetic whine. "Why are we stopping?"

"It's a little wider here. Take a big deep breath and look out to the right."

"I . . . really, I . . ." She gently lifted her right hand off the saddle horn. Her fingers were so stiff she could barely open them. Her backside felt as if she were sitting on one big blister. Her legs were cramped. Her neck was so stiff she could hardly turn it.

In one split second all thoughts of pain disappeared from her mind. Stretched out before her was the most spectacular sight she had ever witnessed. A brilliant, cloudless blue sky hovered above a vast canyon that left her breathless. Twenty miles away, the south wall of the canyon reflected oranges, yellows, violets, purples, tans, and whites in a design that burst out, yet had a soothing calming effect.

Up the canyon to the east, she could see the dark greens of the pines and firs that crested the north rim. Every view was so immense that she felt small . . . small enough to rest easy on a ledge high above the river.

She took a deep breath and felt the clean, fresh air swirl into her lungs. Deep beneath them the Colorado — mighty and muddy — danced from one side of the canyon to the other.

"Oh . . . Brady," she gasped.

"You're not goin' to faint, are you?" he hollered.

"It's . . . it's the most wonderful thing I've ever seen in my life!"

He pushed his black hat back and called out, " 'When I consider the work of Your fingers . . . which You have set in place . . . what is man that You are mindful of him, the son of man that You care for him?' "

She chimed in, " 'O Lord, our Lord, how majestic is Your name in all the earth!' " Then she loosened her right hand from the saddle horn and took another deep breath, relaxing for the first time on the descent.

"You like Psalm 8, too?" she asked.

"Yeah, it was written by a man who spent most of his early life out on a hillside tendin' livestock. I can relate to that. You ready to go on down?"

"Will we go clear down to the river?"

"I'm thinking maybe not. If Shotgun Canyon is that low, the rafters would have discovered it years ago. I've got a feelin' there must be a box canyon about halfway down with a spring runnin' out of it or somethin'." Then he turned in the saddle and looked at her. "Hold on, Lynda Dawn, and close your eyes."

"I think I'll keep my eyes open now. I don't imagine in my lifetime I'll ever again have an opportunity to see a sight like this."

"Are you glad we came down here?"

"I have never been so sore, never been so scared, never been so thrilled in my whole life."

"You didn't answer my question."

"Yes, Brady Stoner, I'm glad we came down here. You were right. . . . I was wrong! Is that what you were waiting for?"

He laughed long and hard. "Yeah! I love it when I'm right."

"Is that Capt. Patch? That's the first time I've ever heard him bark."

Brady sobered up fast. "Stay here! I'll check it out."

The words were hardly out of his mouth when Capt. Patch ran straight at them on the narrow trail with what looked to Austin like a yellow fur-ball chasing him.

Instantly, Brady leaped off the back of the roan horse and screamed, "Get off that mule!"

"What?"

The roan horse reared up on its hind feet.

"Jump off!" Brady screamed again.

Frozen to the saddle, she could see the horse make a wild desperate leap over the top of Capt. Patch and the yellow cat and then gallop wildly down the trail. At the same moment Punkin spun to the right to try to flee back up the trail. But his front feet slipped over the edge of the granite cliff.

"Lynda, jump!"

The mule began to plunge over the edge. Lynda turned loose of the saddle horn and tried to shove herself back over the sleeping bag rolled up on the cantle. She tumbled across the mule's rump. It felt like a truck crashed into her shoulder. She slammed against something as solid as a brick wall.

The flesh on her hands rubbed on rough granite until they bled.

"Oh, Lord Jesus . . . Lord Jesus, please! Just this once! You've got to help this time! . . . Right now, Lord!"

The cry sounded desperate, pleading, distressed —and much too deep-voiced to be her own. Right before she passed out, Lynda realized that the voice she heard praying belonged to Brady Stoner.

EIGHT

Lynda Dawn Austin had no fear of death.

But she dreaded the process of dying.

From the moment she had accepted Jesus Christ as Savior at summer camp on Lake Michigan when she was sixteen, she had known that she would spend eternity with her Lord.

It was the pain of dying that terrified her.

She had sat by the bedside in the tin-roofed house in Key Largo when her grandmother peacefully died in her sleep. She had stood among the life-support systems of a crowded ICU hospital room and watched in shock as her pain-racked mother died.

And now, she knew, it was her turn.

But more terrifying than the pain she felt were the scenes that rolled on in her tormented and frightened mind. It wasn't her past life that flashed before her but rather the future — all of those unreached goals, a husband she would never caress, children she would never bear, books she would never bring into publication, friendships that would never flower, and that ambiguous God-given task that was always just around the corner.

It dawned on her that it wasn't fear, but dis-appointment and gloom that haunted her. In the deep blackness of semiconsciousness she struggled to gain control of her mind.

I never thought I'd go to heaven so depressed! Lord, I can't go feeling this way. Jesus has prepared a place for me — a place of joy and wonder. Something's wrong here!

Then the shocking thought came to her.

I'm not going to heaven!

Followed by another revelation.

I'm not going to die!

She blinked her eyes open and listened to her own uncontrollable sobs. It took several moments before she could tell what was happening. Some-one was there. . . . Someone was talking to her, but she couldn't understand. She fought to get a breath of air. There were two people crying. She could see tears cut muddy lines across the cheeks of Brady Stoner as he cradled her in his arms. The pain was unrelenting in her face, her hands, and especially her right shoulder.

The voice gained a little clarity, if not coherence. "I'm goin' to take care of you, Lynda Dawn. . . . You're goin' to make it. . . . It was a bad one. Darlin', I'll take care of you like I promised."

He was lifting her up. Pain shot through her right shoulder as if it were being sliced by a red-hot knife. She heard her own piercing, horrified scream, and then she slipped into a soft, dark world.

One without torture.

Or fear.

Everything was a blur . . . out of focus . . . distant . . . almost as if she were watching herself.

There was a long time in Brady's arms. She remembered the hardness of his muscles and yet the tenderness of his touch. He stopped at least once to set her on a boulder. There was a flat space — a cold stream where he washed her face and hands. The constant pain in her shoulder . . . and then some type of house . . . cabin . . . a bed. The most comfortable bed in the world!

He made her drink some water and swallow something . . . pills . . . Then he hugged her so tight she screamed with pain. It was a horrible pain. She remembered shrieking out horrible things, vicious words, unspeakable phrases. He was killing her, and all he did was stand there and cry.

Then came one of God's greatest blessings.

Sleep.

When she woke up, candlelight flickered in the room. Two men sat in the shadows by her side.

Twins.

Identical twins.

Then the two floated together and were only one.

"Brady?" Her voice sounded weak and shaken.

"I'm right here, darlin'." He reached out his hand and laid it on hers. She could feel a raw soreness in her fingertips. "How you doin'?"

"My shoulder really hurts. Did I break some bones?"

"I don't think so . . . but we'll get you to a doc as soon as we can."

"What happened?"

"Would you like a drink of water?"

"Yes. I'm really thirsty."

"Just roll your head this way. I don't think you ought to raise up yet."

The water tasted cool and fresh.

"How about a wet rag on your forehead?"

"Yes, doctor." She thought of smiling but couldn't make her face do it. "What happened? Where are we?"

"Well, let me give you the bad news first."

"Is there some good news?"

"Yep."

"Are we in Shotgun Canyon?"

"Yep."

"Did you find the manuscript?"

"We found it, darlin'. But you're getting ahead of the story."

"No kidding . . . it's really here?"

"Lynda Dawn Austin, are you goin' to let me tell you what happened or not?" he scolded.

"I knew I could find it! Go on, go on. I'm feeling better already."

"Well, that was a cougar chasing Capt. Patch. Barstow and Punkin were righteously spooked."

"I thought you said they were the calmest mounts on the trail."

"They are. Well, with me on the ground,

Barstow leapt over the cat and ran all the way down here to Shotgun Canyon. He's back at the spring, and if the reins hadn't got tangled in the brush, I'd never have gotten the saddle off him. The horse and mule scared the cougar, and he scampered right up that canyon wall, leaving Capt. Patch cowering at my side."

"How about Punkin? What happened? I thought I was going over the edge. I thought I was dying, Brady!" She started to sob.

He took the wet rag from her forehead and gently wiped her cheeks. "It's okay, darlin'. It's all my fault. I was the one who made you ride down that trail."

"You prayed for me, didn't you? I thought you never asked anything from God."

"I changed my mind." His brown eyes softened.

"I'm glad." She glanced away from his piercing gaze. "It seemed strange that you and Him weren't on speaking terms."

"Well, I think that's changed now. Anyway, Punkin wanted to turn around and run back up the trail, but his front feet slipped over the edge. As he was tumblin', you finally turned loose of the horn and bounced back on his rump. In one last act of desperation, Punkin kicked wildly as he fell. His hoofs caught your right shoulder and flipped you up against the granite wall above the trail. It scraped up your face a bit . . . and your fingers."

She turned her gaze back to him. "And Punkin?"

"He . . . you know . . . went over the edge.

I guess he hit the rocks or the water."

"Did you carry me here — with your bum leg?"

"You weigh less than a big bale of hay."

"I really thought I was dying."

"I know, darlin'. So did I."

She stared up at the exposed rafters.

"What's Shotgun Canyon like?"

"It's beautiful. . . . I'll show you when you're feelin' better."

Lynda reached up with her left hand and rubbed her eyes. Her vision began to get clearer.

"You hugged me, didn't you? And you did something awful that really hurt bad. I said some dreadful things."

"I don't remember a word of it," he mumbled without much conviction. "I was hopin' you wouldn't remember. Punkin's kick dislocated your shoulder. I had to reset it."

"You did what? How . . . I mean, how did you know how to do that?"

"In the rodeo one guy or another gets a separated shoulder about every day or so. I've set many a shoulder — including my own. I know it hurts, but it has to be done."

"Mel Gibson . . . Lethal Weapon, II."

"What?"

"Eh . . . nothing."

"It will take a couple days for you to feel like moving around very much. I know. That's what it takes me after throwing out a shoulder."

"We're goin' to stay here then?"

"Yep. Until we figure what to do next. Don't

worry about it. Get some sleep. You need the rest."

She reached up and felt something sticky on her cheek. "Am I bleeding?"

"Not anymore. That's aloe. Harrison had some growing out front, so I doctored you up a little. It will help you heal quicker."

"We really found the manuscript?"

"You found it — Ms. Lynda Dawn Austin, famous New York City editor."

"My friends just call me . . . darlin'." She tried to grin.

A wide smile broke across Stoner's face.

"Well, darlin', you almost died out there on the trail. And to tell you the truth, I almost died watchin' you go over the edge. If you would have gone down . . . I don't know . . . I couldn't have lived with myself! You get some sleep. I'm goin' to sit right here and read on this manuscript as long as I don't go blind in the candlelight."

"I'll be all right. Go ahead and get some sleep," she murmured.

"No. You might wake up and need something. I found your purse in the green duffel. Good thing I hitched that on old Barstow. Anyway, I pulled ibuprofen out. If you need pain pills, let me know. I've already given you four. Good thing you crammed your purse and clothes in that green duffel with the food. I'm afraid the sleepin' bag we borrowed from Heather and whatever you stuffed in it went down with Punkin."

"I think I'd like to rest a bit."

"Go to sleep and dream about your picture on

the cover of *Publisher's Weekly* . . . or something."

"My Day Planner!" she cried out. "And my notebooks!"

"Your what?"

"In my sleeping bag. I crammed my appointment book in there . . . my schedule . . . my deadlines! Everything!"

"Well, maybe this old manuscript will cause you to change that whole schedule anyway."

"But my phone numbers, addresses, my business cards . . . my perfume chart!"

"Darlin', every one of those things can be replaced. You can't."

She closed her eyes for several moments, trying to collect her thoughts. Dozing in and out of sleep, she felt beads of perspiration on her face. She woke up and brushed her forehead off with the sleeve of her sweat shirt.

Suddenly her eyes flipped wide open.

My sweat shirt?

She reached under the navy blue sweat shirt and felt her bare skin.

"Brady Stoner!" she hollered, causing him to jump straight out of his chair to his feet. "What in the world am I doing wearing my sweats? What did you do to me?"

"Relax, darlin'. I just — "

"Don't call me darlin'," she demanded.

"I thought you just told me to call you — "

"I changed my mind! Who gave you permission to pull off my clothes?"

282

"Look, Lynda Dawn, you can have me arrested when we get out of here, or whatever. When you hit the wall, it ripped the buttons right off the front of your shirt. And your . . . you know . . . underwear . . . eh . . . your bra busted. They're piled right over there in the corner. You can check them out."

"And my jeans? Are you going to tell me my jeans got ripped up, too?"

"No, ma'am. You vomited on your jeans. You can verify that real easy. I'd be happy to hand them to you."

"You really did play doctor with me, didn't you!" she yelled. "You had no right to do that! You . . . you violated my privacy! You ruined everything!"

"Lynda Dawn Austin, so help me, God, I did what I thought was best. I treated you like I'd treat my own sister if I had one."

"Well, I'm not your sister, Brady Stoner!" She began to cry.

He sighed and looked down at his boots. "I know."

For the longest time the only sound she could hear in the room was her own quiet sobs. Brady Stoner walked back into the shadows.

"Where you going?"

"For a walk."

"In the dark?"

"Yep."

"Are you coming back?"

"Yep."

Daylight had broken into the cabin before she saw him again. Black cowboy hat in place, he stuck his head in the doorway of the large one-room cabin.

"Mornin', boss. You want me to bring you some breakfast? Harrison had some chickens down here. They've been runnin' wild, but I managed to find some fresh eggs."

"I thought you were coming back into the cabin last night."

"I slept out here on the porch. I figured it was more proper-like."

"Proper? Since when do you worry about being proper?"

"Since you put me to appropriate shame last night."

"We've been together almost day and night for a week, slept in an old abandoned church and in a bunkhouse. . . . Why all this?"

"Miss Austin, I like being friendly, and some-times . . . I just get too familiar. You had every right to be mad at me last night, and I'll probably regret to the day I die offendin' you like I did. I don't know what made me think I knew you well enough to do that. You just got to believe I did what I thought was right at the time. Thinkin' about it last night, I should have just wrapped you in a blanket or something and left those messed-up clothes on you 'til you came to. But I can't go back and do it over."

He took a deep sigh, and she saw the lines around

his eyes relax. "Now . . . you want some eggs?"

She laid there staring at the ceiling.

"Eggs?" he asked again.

She wiped her eyes on the bedding.

"Yes, thank you. Do you think it would be all right for me to try to get up? I think my rear end hurts worse than my shoulder."

"Well, you take it slow. You'll need to keep wearing that sling I fixed up for you. I'll be out here. If you need something, holler."

"Is the kitchen out there?"

"Well, ma'am, the best I can figure, they just cooked over a campfire."

He closed the door.

Ma'am? Instead of darlin'? Just like that? He's pulling away now.

The cabin had windows only on the front side facing the rising sun. The room housed a large fireplace and a long, narrow homemade table littered with books, papers, and an old upright typewriter. Stacked against the walls were wooden boxes crammed with more papers and books. Another narrow bed at the other end of the room looked like it was used for a sofa. Above the rustic rock mantel hung a cross made from the spine of a small saguaro cactus.

Gingerly swinging her feet out of bed, she sat still for several minutes until her head cleared. Her derrière felt blistered. Her right shoulder ached, but the pain was tolerable as long as she kept on the sling made out of Brady's big burgundy silk bandanna. On the floor next to the chair where

Brady had sat was a yellowing manuscript. Reaching over with her left hand, she retrieved the pages and flipped through them.

This is it! It's the original. Fondue was right.

She laid it on the chair and stood to her feet, wobbling to keep her balance. It felt good to stand up straight. The wooden floor felt a little gritty on her bare feet, but it was smooth and not splintery. Finding the green duffel bag against the wall, she gingerly bent over and dug out her purse and clean underwear.

She examined the stack of clothes on the floor. Heather's flannel shirt was shredded. The fastener on the front-hook bra was ripped out of the material. She didn't bother picking up the jeans. She could smell their condition.

Austin shuffled over to a bowl of water by the bed and picked up a rag. She tried to comb her matted hair and clean up, but she left her right cheek and forehead smeared with aloe. With a shaking left hand she applied some lipstick and forced herself to smile into the small mirror she had retrieved from her purse.

You look like a train ran over you. Your face is bruised, your hair's stringy, your body's a mess. But you just made the literary discovery of a lifetime. How come you don't feel better, girl?

She stuck her head through the doorway. "Can I come out barefooted? I can't put my socks and boots on with one hand."

"Come on out."

"Don't look at me! I look horrible."

He gazed at her intently.

"Seein' you walk out that door is a beautiful sight. But so is this place. Take a look at this little canyon. Isn't it a dandy?"

As wide as a football field, it was at least a mile deep. The floor of the valley at the cabin end was fairly level. Outside the garden area she saw foot-tall sage and clumps of dried grass. Capt. Patch chased a large bird in the distance.

"It's delightful."

"There's a spring of sweet water right out there in the middle. If it's running at this time of the year, it must run year round. They had a big garden out toward the front. I picked a couple of tomatoes and some bell peppers to stir into the eggs."

"A little isolated paradise." She glanced back at the cabin. "No wonder it only has windows in the front. It's dug out of the side of that cliff!"

"Yeah, and look at the way the cottonwoods lean out over it. I bet you can't even spot this place from an airplane. Do you want me to help you pull on your socks and boots?"

"Yes, please."

"Sit down over on this bench, and I'll — "

"I'd rather stand," she groaned.

His strong hands were gentle as he pulled on her socks and slipped her feet into her boots. She put her hand on his shoulder to balance herself.

"Is it funny wearing boots with sweat pants?" she asked. "It's all I have with me down here."

"Who's going to complain? There you go,

ma'am . . . all booted up."

"Is that the outhouse?"

"Yep. Sorry, there's only one."

She started walking toward it, then turned back. "Brady . . . this is going to sound really strange after our conversation last night. But I need your help on something else."

"Yes, ma'am, what can I do?"

She took a deep breath and then turned away from him. "My right arm is useless. Could you please reach up under the back of my sweat shirt and hook my bra for me? I can't do it one-handed."

She waited for a moment, wondering what expression was going across his face. Then she felt his hands fumble with the hooks.

"This is awkward, isn't it?" he mumbled.

"Humbling, to say the least."

"Well, there you go, ma'am. Do you need me for anything else, or shall I go back to cookin'?"

"One more thing. For Pete's sake, stop calling me ma'am. Brady, did you notice how every day we spend trying to make up for our words or actions the night before?"

She refused to look back at him as she ambled toward the little shack with the quarter moon carved in the door.

Sunlight stretched across the canyon from wall to wall. The air was warm but fresh-tasting. The sky was still a deep blue with an occasional white cloud. The sides of the canyon gave Lynda the feeling of being in a big hole, yet she knew that out front the Colorado was still a thousand feet or more below.

"The eggs are great!" She stood up as she ate. "Listen, Brady . . . I'm sorry about some of the things I said last night. I should have thought it through a little more. It was just a scary feeling to know that someone had been doin' things to me that I didn't know about."

"I was the one out of line, Miss Austin."

"Look, if you don't call me darlin' or Lynda Dawn, I'm going to hit you over the head with this frying pan! You wouldn't call your sister ma'am, would you?"

"No, I guess not."

"I looked at my clothes. You were right. They're horrible! I think we ought to bury them."

He set a tin plate of eggs down for Capt. Patch and scratched the tail-thumping, one-eyed dog. "Don't toss all the clothes. Those jeans will clean up okay. I found a wash tub and board over on the porch. You know how to use one?"

"Eh . . . no. Do you?"

"Yep."

She spent the rest of the morning standing up or lying on the soft mattress of the feather bed. Stoner saddled up a reluctant Barstow and explored Shotgun Canyon. The sun was straight above them when he came riding back.

"You ready for lunch, cowboy?"

"Did you cook?"

"Yes, we're having warmed-up canned ravioli

289

and boiled garden vegetables."

"My favorite. Man, what I wouldn't give for a cheeseburger."

"A 'cheeseburger in paradise'?"

"Huh?"

"Never mind."

"How's that shoulder?" he asked as he straddled a chair and began to eat.

"Well, if I lie down every hour or so, it doesn't throb too much."

"You need to take some more pills?"

"I'm trying to save them. Did you find us another way out of Shotgun Canyon?"

"Nope. It's the beauty of this place, I guess. You just can't get here except on that trail."

"Well, what did you find back there?"

"Several wild plum trees . . . some diggin's in the north slope under that red bluff up there."

"Diggin's?"

"That's where he's been scratching out a little gold, I imagine. It looked fairly promising. I suppose he hauled the dirt down here and panned it out near the water. I imagine the tailings were worked into the garden."

"Fondue did say that Harrison used gold dust to buy supplies."

"He had a self-contained world down here. But it must have been awful lonesome."

"That's what made even a flake like Fondue seem like a welcome guest, I suppose. Did you find a grave?"

"Yep. It's back by those wild plums."

"How do you know it's a grave?"

"Fairly fresh mound of dirt and a wooden cross stuck in it. Looks like a grave to me."

"I found the shotgun," she added. "It was braced up in the rafters."

"Shotgun Canyon Harry's original shotgun?"

"Yeah . . . an old model 12 Winchester 'Tournament' gun. It's a beauty. Even a couple boxes of shells."

"Say, I've been meanin' to ask you. Where did you learn to shoot trap and skeet anyway?"

"You ever hear of Lonnie Sutton?"

"The trick shooter? I saw him once at a rodeo in Kissimee, Florida."

"He was a friend of my grandmother's down in Tavernier. He taught me one summer. . . . Anyway, if there's no back way out, what's the plan?"

She glanced up to see him smiling at her.

"What's the matter? What are you staring at? Have I got food on my face?"

"Nothin'. Actually, your face is healin' up mighty good. How's your hands?"

"Raw . . . but I'll manage. Have you got a way to get us out of here with that manuscript?"

He pulled his hat off and laid it, crown down, on the wooden table. Then he leaned back on the bench until he was in the shade of one of the cottonwoods. "Well, sit down, and I'll tell you what I've been figurin'."

"I'd rather stand."

"You know, if you mash up some of them aloe

leaves and apply it right on the tender part, it might help that soreness."

"No. It is my opinion that I will never be able to sit down the rest of my life."

"Well . . . we've got two options. I can ride Barstow out of here as soon as you're able to take care of yourself. We'll mark some kind of big signal out there in the garden area. I'll contact a search-and-rescue helicopter, and we'll try to land out there and pick you up."

"Can they do that?"

"Sure . . . provided we can find the canyon from the air, which no one seems to have done for the past fifty years . . . and provided the wind shears in the canyon will allow them to come in here. The Grand Canyon can be mighty dangerous flyin' at times."

"But," she asked, "what if you go and fall over the edge on your way out or you can't find the canyon again. I'm left down here on my own for-ever!"

"If I don't show up in a week, you'll need to hike out. I'll leave Capt. Patch with you."

"Capt. Patch? He's the one that stirred up that cougar! Just in case I'm not ready to stay down here by myself, what's the other plan?"

"We'll give you a couple more days to rest up. Then we'll double up on Barstow and let him haul us out. You can sit up on top of the bedroll. We'll take the manuscript with us."

"Brady, I've a horrible cramp in my stomach right now just thinking about that trail. How in the world will I go up it again?"

"Kickin' and screamin', I imagine. It can't be much worse than your trip down."

"Oh, yes, it can!"

Austin took a long afternoon nap and woke up smelling food frying out on the campfire. Stiff-legged, her right arm in a sling, she walked out. Stoner was humming a tune while cooking something in a big, black skillet. His sleeves were rolled up, his hat was pushed back, and his right jeans leg flopped around the bulky brace. The smoke seemed to follow him like a puppy.

"Is it supper time?" she asked.

"Probably. I figured on saving this hen from getting eaten by hawks and owls. It beats canned ravioli. Besides, we're all out of packaged food. Sure wish I could offer you a chair."

"I'm doing fine. I think this shoulder is actually feelin' better."

"As long as you don't do anything with it for a while. It will pop back out of there real easy."

"Should we try to ride out of here tomorrow?"

"You mean it? You really feel ready to ride?"

"Brady, when we head up that trail, I plan on yelling, screaming, crying, calling you horrible names, and trying to beat you to a pulp. The rest is up to you."

He rubbed his hand across his face and painted a smudge an inch wide on his chin.

"That sounds like fun. Well, this time I'm goin'

to set Capt. Patch in my lap and tie you on behind. We aren't stopping until we're out on top. If anything happens, we'll all go together."

"That sounds cheery."

"We'll make it. I read some of that manuscript the other night. It's important to get that into print. We've got to get it out."

Her green eyes lit up. "It's great, isn't it? I think it might be the most important piece of Christian apologetic in this century. It could outdistance *Mere Christianity*."

"I'm gettin' kind of excited about it myself. That story about the senseless man on the moon is funny and so powerful it will force evolutionists to counter with something new. Does he keep coming back to that character throughout the book?"

"Oh, yeah. Just about every chapter."

"Does he have any success in building that radio?"

"Not hardly."

"Well, what does a man without sight, hearing, touch, taste, and smell actually build?"

"He spills his canteen and can't find it of course. So the only thing he can contribute is a muddy footprint in the moon soil."

"That about sums up most of our lives . . . doesn't it?"

"Just a muddy footprint?"

"Yeah. Say, does he tackle his old argument about the narrowness of the Cross?"

"Didn't you get that far?" she pressed.

"No. It was gettin' tough to read. My eyes were

sore, or we were fightin', or somethin'."

"How about reading the whole thing out loud this evening?"

"Can we finish it in one night?"

"Maybe. But we could always read it tomorrow on our way out. Then again . . . maybe not." She scooted around to the other side of the fire so that the smoke wouldn't get to her. "It's clouding up."

"Yep. This morning's white puffies are getting a little thicker and darker."

"Is it going to rain?"

"Maybe. If it does, we can't go out that trail. It will be too slippery."

"Do we have enough food in here?"

"As long as we don't get tired of chicken, eggs, and vegetables."

It began to sprinkle right before dark. Brady Stoner was still outside cleaning up camp. Austin stood at the unpainted wooden door and felt the cool breeze.

"Brady, you get in here before you get wet!"

"The porch is covered. I'll be all right out here."

"You aren't sleepin' on the porch. There's another bed in here, you know."

"We settled that last night," he called. He limped over to her. "Here's your jeans. They cleaned up fine. Just a little damp still, but they should be all right by mornin'. You want me to build a fire in there?" He stared into her green eyes. "Eh, in the fireplace?"

"Brady, can we talk serious tonight?"

"About what?"

"About us."

"Have you got it figured?"

"I think so."

"Good, because I sure can't. It's been the craziest thing I've ever been around."

"Well, come on in and get a fire going." She smiled. "In the fireplace."

Just like pioneers . . . a hundred miles to the next neighbor . . . isolated . . . peaceful . . . just him and me . . . exciting . . . reckless . . . and scary!

Entering the room, Stoner pulled off his slightly damp hat, shook it off, and jammed it on a peg by the front door. She walked back toward the bed.

"I hope you don't think me impolite for lying down . . . but I'm a little tired."

"Take a rest." He nodded. "You're the one who has everything all figured out anyway."

"I don't have everything figured out." Lying back, she rested her right arm across her stomach and propped her left hand under her head. "Look, I've known you for only a week, and I've spent more time with you than I have with James in a whole year."

"You know the last time I spent a week with the same girl?"

"How long?"

"Ten years."

"The high school sweetheart who married the computer whiz?"

"Yeah."

296

"Why did she dump you?"

Stoner used a scrap of brown paper sack and got a fire burning in the rough rock fireplace. "Because I was determined to rodeo. She didn't want me goin' down the road. Can't blame her. She told me, 'Brady, I'm not spendin' every night wonderin' whether you're busted up or so sleepy you drove the rig off into a ditch . . . or some buckle bunny's tuggin' on your sleeve tellin' you how good she can make you feel. I've got to have a guy I can count on — one who loves me more than he does gold buckles and buckin' horses. I don't want to spend my life havin' to add up the price of every item in the grocery basket just hopin' I'll have enough money to pay for them.' "

"Sounds like you have the speech memorized."

He walked over and opened the front door to allow a draft to keep the smoke from backing up into the room. "I hear it word for word every time I meet a new lady. That voice haunts me."

"But you still decided on a rodeo life."

"I work the ranches to save up a few dollars and head down the road to the rodeos. Someday when I get that ranch, then I can say to some lady, 'Darlin', we're goin' to build a ranch house and raise some Black Angus, some Corriente ropin' steers, and a pack of babies that will make a grandmother proud.' "

He strolled over and sat down in a homemade chair next to the long, narrow table.

"You know what, Stoner?" Austin said.

"What?"

"I think that's all a big cow pie."

"What? You mean, what I just told you? I poured out my heart, and you don't believe it?"

"Oh, I believe everything you said. You just didn't get around to the basic stuff."

"What do you mean by that?"

"Well, I'd say you try not to get too close to any one lady because you're scared to death of women. You don't understand them. . . . You're afraid they wouldn't really like you if they get past that awesome smile. You're afraid you couldn't deliver whatever it is they really want, so you play this little waiting-game routine. You'll probably keep this up 'til you're fifty. Am I right?"

"How can you say that? You don't know me well enough to shoot down my dreams just like that!" he fumed. She could see the veins tense up on his tanned neck.

"We probably know each other better than we'd choose to admit." She slipped both hands behind her head. "Well, it must be evening because we're arguing again. But you didn't answer my question. Am I right about what really keeps you at a distance from any one woman?"

He stared into the fire in silence.

Great! Lynda Dawn just stabbed another one. Girl, you're better at writing letters. Nina was right. I should just date by computer and never meet the guy.

"Maybe I was wrong," she admitted. "But can I tell you something? I'm scared to get close to men. I never can figure out what they want in a relationship . . . I mean, besides sex. Most days

I'm a neurotic wreck on the inside. I don't like to clean house, don't really like to cook very much, and am absolutely terrified to think that I might one day be a mother. So I tell myself that when I meet the right guy, all these hang-ups and fears are going to vanish. Well, I'm thirty years old, and they haven't. In fact, they've probably grown worse. Now that I've been dumb enough to blurt all of that out, do you really think I was that far off about you?"

He sat idly stirring the fire. She could hear the rain dripping off the roof and splashing to the ground. The front door swung open as Capt. Patch trotted in, shook himself dry, turned around three times, and plopped down next to the fireplace. Stoner stood up and limped back over, shoving the door until it was almost closed.

"How did we ever get into this conversation? Man, we should be talking about manuscripts and Martin Taylor Harrison and how to get out of this canyon and — "

"I'm giving you one more chance, Brady Stoner. Did I pretty well sum up your life or not?"

"Lynda Dawn Austin, I don't know what to do with you. If we were at the cafe in town, I'd tip my hat, wish you well, and go on down the road. But that would only prove your point, wouldn't it?"

"Yes, it would."

"Well, I guess you're right about some things . . . sort of. I never stop and think about it much. It just seems like the closer I get to someone, the more I realize they deserve somethin' better than me."

He stepped over to where she was gingerly propped up on the bed. Shoving his hands into his back pockets, he smiled a wide, toothy, little-boy grin. "Can we stop talkin' about this? I'm breakin' out in a sweat, and it's not the fire that's doin' it."

"We're an awful lot alike, aren't we?"

"Yeah . . . pig-headed, self-centered, goal-driven, tease but don't touch . . . should I go on?"

"No!" She laughed. "Let's talk about something else. What if this rain keeps up, and it's too slick on the trail tomorrow?"

"Then we stay in Shotgun Canyon and read a good book."

Austin swung her feet out of the bed and sat up.

"Are you feeling better?" he asked.

"In places." She grimaced. "My arm is starting to ache. Can I take it out of the sling and stretch it?"

"Be careful."

"Yes, doctor." She flashed a fake smile. "Besides, I feel like a character out of a Victorian novel . . . lying on my bed while a handsome young man stirs the fire."

"Well, thank you for both lies."

She slowly stretched out her arm and held it straight out to her side. "Did you read that part where Harrison talks about a morality vacuum?"

"A what?"

"He makes a strong case that when you remove moral absolutes from a culture, you create not an emptiness, but a vacuum that begins to suck out all positive moral values and produce a destructive society of anarchy, greed, and violence. It will destroy the culture unless something is quickly crammed into the gaping hole."

"Something like communism?"

"Yeah, or socialism, fascism, or tribalism. But he claims each of those are temporary solutions that will eventually be sucked out as well."

"So what does he suggest?"

"Only by returning to an absolute moral standard, one provided by a heart that has combined absolute power with absolute love."

"Christianity, in other words?"

"Yes. But he says no culture has ever had the moral strength of soul to enact that solution once the hole is punched in faith. According to him, no society in history has ever rebuilt its moral fiber."

"Sounds pretty pessimistic."

"What did you expect from a man who checked out of society sixty-four years ago? Anyway, do you see how this can affect those first two books?"

Stoner scooted to the door, swung it completely open, and stared out at the rain. "Thousands of college professors will have to change their lesson plans."

"That's why it's got to be published." She brought the manuscript over nearer the fire so she could read it in the dim light.

"Does he make mention directly of his earlier works?"

"Listen to this. 'No man under fifty should ever attempt to write serious works. Let him stick to mysteries, science fiction, and westerns if he must write. Let him be satisfied with poetry, journals, and reviews. Only the mature mind, one that has tasted the rapture of success and the ignominy of failure and has had years to contemplate both, should write books of mental challenge and debate.'"

She glanced up. "Shall I go on?"

"Let's save some for tomorrow. I'm afraid I'll doze off and miss something." Brady leaned his head back and closed his eyes. "You know, just in case it keeps raining."

It rained without ceasing for two days.

They read the lost manuscript three times.

Then the wind blew all night, and by daylight on their fourth morning in Shotgun Canyon it was sunny and warm. Without any discussion, they both began to pack up.

Lynda wore blue jeans, the Michigan sweat shirt pushed up to the elbows, her cowboy boots, and a fragrance she had bought in Fredonia called Starlite Enchantment. She toted Brady's bedroll and the green duffel bag out of Harrison's cabin.

Stoner was jerking the latigo tight on the rested and recovered roan horse when she approached.

"Hey, you shouldn't be carrying anything with your right arm!"

"It's feeling good — really! It's kind of nice to straighten it out." She watched him carefully pack the horse.

"You know what, Stoner? You've just been selected to be at the top of my list of cowboys I'd like to get stuck in a remote desert canyon with."

His brown eyes sparkled. "Yeah? Who's in second place?"

"Troy Aikman."

"Aikman? What does a football player know about desert survival?"

"Who cares?"

"You want any breakfast?" he asked.

"Chicken and veggies again?"

"Yeah. It sounds gruesome, doesn't it?"

"I'd really like a hamburger," she admitted.

"Or a steak! I know a great place to eat just north of St. George. How about tonight? To celebrate?"

"Not until I get a shower, wash my hair, and put on something clean!"

He grabbed the bedroll and tied it on behind the cantle.

"Where's that million-dollar manuscript?"

"It's in the duffel bag. But I didn't say it was worth a million . . . for sure."

"But I'll get my thousand, right?"

"You got it, cowboy."

"If I were you, I wouldn't let that manuscript out of sight until you've got it in print. Strange things seem to happen to that book."

"That's purdy good advice, partner, for an ol'

boy who's spent all his life goin' down the road!"
she drawled. "Hey, did I say it right? Am I getting
the accent?"

"Well, like Mark Twain would say, 'You have
all the right words, but you don't know the
tune.' "

"Thanks! I suppose I'm doomed to sound like
a New York editor."

"Yep."

She looked more closely at the saddled horse.
"Well, how in the world are we going to load up?"

"I've got it all figured out. Get up there on top
of the table with Capt. Patch. . . . Look at the
three of us — the lame, the injured, and the blind!"
He laughed. "We need all the help we can get."

He led the horse over.

"Okay, you crawl up on top of the bedroll, but
don't strain that right arm or shoulder. Are you
sure you don't want the sling?"

"It's fine — really." She straddled the horse and
scooted back onto the bedroll.

"Hold the duffel bag for a moment."

Capt. Patch cocked his head and whined.

"Yeah, yeah, it will be your turn in a minute."
Brady Stoner carefully swung his braced leg over
the horse and slid down into the saddle, jamming
his left foot into the stirrup. "Now hand me the
duffel!"

He looped the handle of the green bag over the
saddle horn and then began to uncoil the rope that
had been hanging from a leather strap on the right
side of the saddle.

"What are you going to rope?" she asked.

"You."

"What?"

"You don't have a good grip, and I don't have good mobility . . . so I'm going to rope us together."

"And Capt. Patch?"

"Nope, he's on his own. But you, me, and that duffel bag will be tied together. We'll all make it . . . or . . . well, you know."

"Yeah . . . I know," she murmured. "This rope is hard and stiff. What's it made of?"

"Three-eighths inch scant, medium-soft nylon."

"Sorry I asked."

"Put your arms around me."

"I beg your pardon?"

"Come on, boss. You've got to hold on to something. It might as well be me."

"Brother, do you think I'll fall for that old line?"

"Yep."

She slipped her arms around his midsection and tried not to think about how nice it felt.

"Since you won't wear this sling, I'm going to tie your hands together so your grip won't get tired. Tell me if this is too tight."

"It's fine."

"You ready to ride?"

"One way or another I'm planning on this being the last horseback ride in my life."

"Come on, Capt." The black and white cow dog leaped into Brady's lap and rested on his left hand.

The journey out of Shotgun Canyon was smooth and quick. Austin was relieved to be sitting on the soft bedroll. When they came to the narrow trail up the granite cliff, she took a deep breath, closed her eyes, turned her head away from the river, and whispered, "Talk to me, Brady. Talk to me quick."

"Well, darlin', just daydream about how all those New York literary types are going to drool with envy when you bring out the third Harrison. This thing is so startlin', it's bound to get a lot of media attention. How are you at television interviews?"

"I've never done one. I won't get too much coverage. Gossman's already told me he's going to be the one to edit the book if it's authentic."

"He's what? I thought you said he doesn't even want it published. What kind of business is this? You do all the work, purt near get yourself killed, and he gets the honors."

"That's the way the system works."

"It's a lousy system. That's what I like about rodeo. You only earn what you personally worked for."

"Well, I know what part I've had in this. That's what really matters."

"That's a crock!" he insisted. "You should get what you deserve. That's what justice is all about. Unless, of course, you deserve something horrible. . . . Then we don't want justice, but mercy."

She leaned against his blue and white striped shirt and laid her head on his back. "Don't take this hugging personal," she explained, "but I'm scared to death!"

"Boy, that's the sorriest excuse I ever heard. If you can't keep your hands off me, just admit it."

"Stoner, if you don't shut up, I'll barf all over your back!"

A few minutes later she quipped, "I've got my eyes closed, but I know it's morning."

"What gives you the clue?"

"We're laughing and getting along. It's only at night that we argue. Why do you think that is?"

"Maybe we feel safer in the daytime."

"Safer?"

"Yeah. At night neither one of us knows what to expect next . . . nor what's required of us, right?"

"That makes us sound like a couple of kids."

"Well, Lynda Dawn, if you only got one saddle, that's the one you have to ride in."

"Are we getting around to cowboy philosophy now?"

"You want cowboy philosophy?"

"Sure."

"Okay, here's one: 'You cain't never tell which way a pickle will squirt.' "

"Eh . . . all right. Just exactly how does that apply to anything?"

"About a week, ten days ago . . . I was a rodeo cowboy on the bubble, trying to make it to the finals. That was the only thing on my mind. A couple weeks ago before this guy Fondue showed up, you were the big city editor with no clue that

307

soon you'd be busted up and ridin' up one of the most remote and spectacular canyons in the United States, clingin' to the back of a buckaroo wearing a dirty, sweaty old shirt. You see, 'you cain't never tell which way a pickle will squirt.' "

"It does blow my mind when I think about it. I'm sure glad we don't know what's going to happen in the future."

"Admit it — you would've avoided ol' Stoner all together, wouldn't you?"

"Nope. And you aren't all that dirty and sweaty either."

"That's because that perfume of yours can be smelled at one thousand yards!"

"It's kind of strong, isn't it?"

"Yeah . . . but I really love it. I've never been around a gal that uses so much perfume."

"It's kind of my thing. My trademark, I guess. What's your trademark?"

"Broken bones. About every time I make a real good run at the finals, something gets busted. 'Whatever happened to Brady Stoner?' they ask. 'He used to have lots of potential.' "

"You're still young. You can win the World next year."

"Sure, that's what I've been sayin' for ten years. Truth is . . . I only got a few more years at best. So it better be — wow! Would you look at that!"

"What? You aren't getting me to open my eyes, Stoner."

"The sun off that far canyon wall. Sort of reminds me of a Van Gogh. You know how the colors just burst off the canvas?"

"A cowboy art critic? You are full of surprises. I like French Impressionists myself."

"You mean old Manet, Degas, Monet, Renoir, and the boys?"

"Yes, the brightness, the reflected light, the informality, the spontaneity, the colors — I love them."

"Oh, sure, they're okay if you want to look at the world through a pair of bad glasses. Everything's out of focus."

"You call Renoir out of focus?" she huffed.

"Sure. Now if you want to talk art . . . let's talk about Charles M. Russell. Why, the way Charlie painted the moonlight reflecting off the mane of a horse was just about the most beautiful sight a man — "

"Charles M. Russell? I thought we were talking about art!" she interrupted.

"That did it!"

"What are you doing? Why are we stopping?"

Suddenly she felt Stoner kick the horse, and Barstow began to plod on up the narrow incline.

"Why did you stop?" she demanded.

"I was thinkin' about tossin' you off and makin' you walk."

"Well . . . you're getting a little touchy when I mention your favorite artist."

"It's just that . . . I don't suppose I've ever been around anyone who didn't like Charley Russell paintings."

"Well, we've just blown my theory."

"Which one is that?"

"The one that says you and I only argue at night. It's nice to see that we can tick each other off anytime, night or day. How much farther?"

"You sound like a little kid in the back of the family station wagon. We still have a long trip. Maybe we should sing."

"I've heard you sing," she teased.

"Well, let's make some plans. I mean, after we get out of here and you call your publisher and we clean up and all that. What's the next step for you?"

"I'll need to get back to New York. I suppose they've already had funeral services for Mr. Hampton. Anyway, I've got to bulldog this manuscript through all the right doors. I don't think Mr. L. George Gossman and a few others will want to publish it unless they can prove it's Harrison's body buried out there."

"I guess you could have that body exhumed. I would suppose they have some way of identifying it."

The warmth of the day and the rhythm of the ride were causing her to get sleepy. "You know what else I need to do?"

"Call this James fellow and tell him *adios?*"

"Eh . . . no. I mean, I do need to call him. Why were you thinking of James?"

"What was the other thing you needed to do?"

"You didn't answer my question."

"Well, I was just thinkin' about things I needed

to do when we get out."

"Oh? Don't tell me you have some girl to call up and tell *adios?*"

"Nope. But if there was one, I think I'd have to tell her that."

"Why?" she pressed.

He didn't answer.

"What was the other thing you needed to do?" he finally asked.

Stoner, you clutz! This would have been a really good time to say something nice and personal!

"Well, I think the Harrison museum in Key West will want to have all the artifacts, books, papers, typewriter — "

"And an old shotgun?" Stoner added.

"Yeah. Of course I'd really like to have that myself. Anyway . . . I'm not too sure how to get that stuff to Florida."

"If you've got the money, honey, I've got the time."

"You're not going to start singing ol' Hank Williams, are you?"

"Whoa . . . this lady knows Hank! What I was suggesting . . . if someone wants to finance the venture, I'd hire a helicopter and fly in there and find that canyon and lift the stuff out. Besides, the Mojave County coroner will have to go back there also."

"Would you do that? Really, Brady? I'm not kidding — that would be terrific!" She gave him a tight hug.

"Look, I'm out of the runnin' for the finals now.

So if I can make a few dollars while I'm mendin' and then line myself up some winter work that will get me by until Denver — "

"Denver?"

"One of the first of the big indoor winter rodeos."

"How much money would you need?"

"If the company is paying, one thousand dollars plus expenses."

"What if it's Lynda Dawn Austin that's paying?"

"For you, darlin', it's one hundred dollars plus expenses. Don't you think the mighty Atlantic-Hampton will cover the costs?"

"I hope so. Are we getting close to the top?"

"Not hardly. . . . You want to sing?"

"Not . . . really. But you can. It won't insult you if I doze off back here, will it? The sun feels so warm I think I could actually go to sleep."

"I might take a snooze myself. I'm surprised that Barstow hasn't balked. Now old Barstow is a strawberry roan, and it's only fitting that I sing a little of Curley Fletcher's classic about the strawberry roan. I think he wrote it around 1914 up at 'the daddy of 'em all' — Cheyenne."

The tone was not pure.

The notes were not distinct.

Nor the lyrics particularly haunting.

But it was restful. And somewhere right after "He was a sun-fishin' son of a gun," she fell asleep.

"You all set for a little action?" Brady's voice

seemed to boom up the canyon.

She opened her eyes, saw the wall of the granite canyon, and instantly shut them again.

"Why did we stop?"

"Well, I think Barstow just remembered what happened on this trail. He froze up."

"What do we do now?"

"I'm going to punch him real good, and he just might hightail it right to the top. But you better hang on."

"Hang on? You've got my hands tied around you. I couldn't turn loose if I wanted to."

"Well, let's ride, cowgirl!"

Brady kicked the horse hard in the belly with the heel of his left boot. Suddenly Barstow sprinted up the narrow trail. Jolted by the severe bouncing, she opened her eyes and viewed the canyon. She could remember Punkin trying to turn back and hear the mule's frantic bellow. Her shoulder ached, her head hurt, and a deep scary feeling hit the pit of her stomach. She couldn't help crying. She closed her eyes and buried her face in Brady's back.

After what seemed like an hour, Stoner reined up the horse and hollered, "We're out! We did it, Lynda Dawn Austin!"

She blinked open her eyes and tried to adjust to the daylight. Capt. Patch jumped to the ground and dashed ahead of Barstow.

"We're really out of there! Praise the Lord! I guess I won't die in some lonesome canyon after all!"

"Hey, don't count it out. You have several good

years left. You can still munch it in a canyon."

"I'd slug you, Stoner, if you hadn't tied me up."

"You want to get down and stretch, or shall we head to the rig?"

"Do we have to ride clear back around that north rim?"

"Nope. We can just follow this trail out to those hills. The truck's over there."

"Let's keep going."

"You want me to untie you?"

"Oh, sure, so I can fall off on level ground? Just leave it like it is."

"I knew it." He laughed.

"Stoner, shut up! No more wisecracks about not being able to keep my hands off . . . Hey, is that a helicopter up there?"

"Where?"

"To the left?"

"Oh . . . yeah. It doesn't look like BLM. Maybe it's one of those Grand Canyon tours, but I've never seen them up here. Wave to them."

"Wave? My hands are tied up."

"They're comin' in to land. That's strange! They must be havin' some engine problems if they had to fly up here to land. The old-timers said an army jet landed out here one time back in the fifties. Folks thought it was from outer space — "

"Up there, Brady . . . It looks like a couple of cars headed this way."

"Those are state patrol rigs! They never come out here. What's going on?"

"Maybe they have something to do with the

helicopter. It seems to be hovering and landing behind us."

"Must be drug dealers or something."

"Out here?"

"I don't know. Let's get off the road and let them do their thing." He reined Barstow to the right and trotted off the trail. "Come on, Capt. Come on, we'll go over here."

"They're coming right out here into the sage! Brady, what's going on?"

"They're nuts! Hang on tight, darlin'. Maybe they think they're playin' a game or something. I just don't want old Barstow to bolt."

With the wind and the noise of the helicopter behind them and two state four-wheeled vehicles racing a trail of dust right at them, Barstow froze. He refused to move another step. Austin and Stoner stared in amazement as the state vehicles spun to a stop and several men armed with shotguns piled out of each rig.

Suddenly a voice boomed from a loudspeaker behind them. "Put your hands in the air and slowly dismount. Do not make any sudden movements. Any failure to comply with this order will be interpreted as an act of aggression."

"Are they talking to us?" Her voice quivered.

His hands up in the air, Brady shouted, "I can't get down. We're tied together, and I can't dismount without untying."

"Keep those hands in plain sight."

"Ma'am, can you pull away from him?" someone shouted.

"No, we're tied!"

"Well, don't worry. We're moving in. We'll have you free in no time!"

"What do they mean — free?" she asked Stoner.

Six armed officers surrounded the horse and began to move in on them, guns drawn and pointed. When they got within twenty feet, Austin called out, "What's going on here?"

"Don't worry none. We've got him now."

Austin glanced around at all the gun barrels. The men holding them looked determined. "I don't know who you're looking for, but you have the wrong people. Do you know who we are?"

"He's Brady Stoner, and I presume you're Ms. Lynda Austin of New York City. Good grief, lady, the whole country knows who you are!"

NINE

"What are you talkin' about?" Stoner called out.

"You lower those hands an inch, mister, and you're dead!" a man with a badge shouted at him. "Officer, go cut her down!"

"Come on. Don't do that! It's my good rope!"

A group of people now stood south of the ring of police, taking pictures and videotaping. She thought she heard another helicopter landing behind them.

"Why did you have to cut my rope?" Brady Stoner complained. "Take it easy with her!" he yelled. "She's got a dislocated shoulder!"

"He did that to you, miss?" one of the men hollered. "We ought to shoot the — "

"No!" she cried out. "He didn't do this!"

"Lynda!" a woman's voice cried out.

"Kelly? What are you doing here?"

Kelly Princeton ran to her side and threw her arms around her. "Lynda, girl . . ." Kelly began to sob. "We thought . . . we thought you were dead!"

"Why on earth would you think that?"

"The dead mule by Lava Falls, your Day Planner . . . the rafters reported . . . They've been searching the river for two days."

"What are you talkin' about?"

"But he's such a violent man!"

"Who?"

"Brady Stoner?"

"Violent? Who told you that?"

"You said you had to bail him out of jail for getting in a fight. Then there was that TV interview two nights ago."

She turned around in time to see two officers slam Brady to the ground and yank his hands behind him. She pushed away from Kelly and ran stiff-legged over to the officers.

"What are you doing to him?"

"Arresting him."

"On what charges?"

"Kidnap, assault, violation of the Mann Act."

"Mann Act?"

"Transporting a woman across state lines for immoral purposes."

"Who's pressing these charges?" she demanded.

"We'll get the paperwork together, and you can sign it when you're feelin' better."

"Me? What are you saying? You're doing this for me? Brady, what's goin' on?"

"I don't have any idea . . . but could you get that jerk to take his boot off my broken leg?" Stoner groaned.

"Get away from him!" Austin shouted. "Get away!" She began to shove the officers back in wild and blind fury. Within a moment all the men had backed up, several with guns still drawn.

Tears rolled down her cheeks. Her head felt light. She was afraid she was about to faint. Like a mother bear defending her cubs, she circled Brady as he lay face down in the dirt. She glared into the line of police officers and reporters.

"Mr. Gossman? What are you doing here?" she choked out as she spotted the editorial director of Atlantic-Hampton.

"The company is concerned for your welfare, of course," Gossman weakly explained, nervously shifting his weight from one foot to the other.

A couple of burly officers began to move forward toward Stoner.

"Wait! Before you do one more thing you'll regret, let me explain," she screamed. Stopping long enough to get her breath, she felt as if she might throw up.

"Relax, Lynda Dawn." Brady's voice sounded amazingly calm. "I'm okay. You just tell them what really happened."

His face was in the dirt. He tried to lift his head up and see the people standing around.

"You got a crowd, girl. Tell them about what we found in the canyon."

"Look . . . I'm Lynda Dawn Austin from New York City, and I happen to be on vacation . . . as my boss, Mr. Gossman, can tell you. I hired this man, Brady Stoner, to guide me down into these canyons to look for a manuscript that I thought might be in a cabin down here somewhere.

"Mr. Stoner, even though his leg was broken, consented to help me explore the canyons. On our journey down, my mule got spooked and went over the edge. In the process I got kicked in the shoulder, and it was dislocated. Brady carried me for several miles to a cabin where he reset my shoulder and cared for my injuries. We couldn't come back out earlier because the narrow trail was too slick after the rains!"

Most of the crowd surrounding her now stood with cameras, notebooks, or guns at their sides.

There're only twenty-five people within a hundred miles, and they're all crowded on the same little patch of desert. Well, we've circled the wagons, and we won't give up without a fight.

She bent low and scooped up a small stick no more than a foot long, waving it in front of her like a weapon.

"The only charges I'll press are ones of use of excessive force and police harassment unless he is instantly released. Do I make myself clear?"

"That a girl," Brady cheered. "Oh, how I love that New York editor talk!"

"You aren't pressing charges?" one officer asked, scratching the back of his neck with the barrel of his revolver.

"For what? For saving my life, looking after me, cooking my meals? Don't you all have something better to do? I can't believe you actually thought Brady was a threat to me. I've never been with a kinder man in my life!"

"But the interview," a female reporter in a tailored suit called out. "What about the interview?"

"What interview?"

"Joe Trent. He was on 'The Real Story' and told of Stoner's violent past."

"He what?" Brady Stoner hollered. "I'll . . ."

Austin shouted over the top of Stoner's words, "Joe Trent is a liar! Are you going to release Brady, or do I bring charges against Mojave County and the entire state of Arizona?"

A man wearing a dark suit and tie nodded to a uniformed officer. "Release him."

"You brought us all the way out from Vegas for this?" one of the reporters grumbled.

"I'll give you a story as soon as Brady's released and the police have pulled out!"

"What kind of story?"

"I'll tell you what we discovered in the canyon."

"Ms. Austin!" L. George Gossman called out. "You might want to consult with the firm before you make any premature announcements."

"I'm on vacation, George. I'll say whatever I want."

One of the officers cut the plastic binding off Brady Stoner's wrists.

"You tell 'em, Lynda Dawn." Stoner rolled over and sat up on the ground, brushing dirt off his face and rubbing his wrists.

Within five minutes all the police officers were gone, leaving only the helicopter of reporters and the Atlantic-Hampton staff.

Taking Brady's arm, Austin escorted him over

to a large boulder along the road. The two of them leaned back as the crowd gathered.

Gossman tried to push his way to the front. "Ms. Austin, are you sure you want to — "

"Mister, would you shut up!" Stoner insisted. "The lady wants to speak. Can one of you at the back go over to that horse and pull that green duffel bag down off the saddle horn? All right, Lynda Dawn, tell them what you discovered."

For the next thirty minutes in the bright, high-desert sunlight of Toroweap Valley, with sagebrush and barren hills for a backdrop, New York City book editor Lynda Dawn Austin explained the discovery of Martin Taylor Harrison's lost manuscript.

Cameras clicked.

Videos whined.

Reporters questioned.

Austin answered.

And Gossman groused.

From time to time she consulted with Stoner as to the sequence of events and the geographical details. As she concluded, several of the reporters turned to Gossman.

"I presume your publishing house shares Ms. Austin's enthusiasm for this discovery?"

"Why didn't Atlantic-Hampton follow up rather than letting an editor spend her own time and money pursuing this?"

"When can the public expect to see the book in print?"

"Just a minute," Gossman protested. "One at a time! Yes, indeed, Atlantic-Hampton is excited about publishing the third Harrison book. We've been waiting for sixty-four years for this manuscript. That should be some kind of record. But I want to make it clear that what you have just heard are the words of a very excited and obviously somewhat, eh . . . pained editor. But she does not exactly represent the publishing house."

"What do you mean by that?" Stoner demanded.

"Well . . . we will examine this manuscript for authenticity and quality. If it meets those criteria we will, of course, be overjoyed to publish the book. We do own the rights to it, and since Martin Taylor Harrison had no heirs or assigns, the future of this manuscript lies with our publishing house. Ms. Austin understands this."

"Can we have a picture of you and her holding the manuscript?" someone asked.

"Certainly."

"Eh," Austin protested, "I need to clean up and change clothes and put some makeup over the bruises on my face and . . ."

"You look fine, darlin'," Stoner encouraged her.

He moved aside to let Gossman and Austin brave the dry desert wind for a picture-taking session with a stack of almost five hundred yellowing typed pages in their hands.

"In fact," Gossman said, pulling the manuscript from her weak right hand, "I'll be taking this back with me to New York now."

Stoner's grip, strengthened by years of clutching

bareback rigging, slapped down on Gossman's shoulder, causing the editorial director to wince and jump.

"Give it back to the lady!" Brady insisted.

"What? This belongs to the publishing house! Tell your . . . eh, cowboy friend it's time for him to ride into the sunset," he blurted to Austin.

Brady Stoner stepped closer but didn't loosen his grip on the trembling and perspiring L. George Gossman. "You reporters tell me if I'm wrong, but didn't this man just say that the authentic Harrison belongs to the publishing house, and he isn't totally convinced yet this is Harrison's work?"

"Yeah. What's your point?" asked a reporter.

"This manuscript remains the property of Miss Austin until such time as they can prove it's authentic."

"That's true!" one of the reporters chimed in.

"Well . . . well, of course, technically . . . but Ms. Austin is a professional editor, one of our best. I'm sure she trusts us to keep the manuscript safe until such time as we have verified its authenticity."

"I'm sure she trusts you." Stoner released his grip, yanked the pages out of Gossman's hand, shoved them back into the duffel bag, and handed it to Austin. "But I don't. I believe this belongs to you, ma'am."

"Thank you, Mr. Stoner. If there are no more questions, we need to get on the road. It's been a few days since I've had a bath or change of clothes," Austin reported.

Kelly came up to her side. "Fly back with us, Lynda. There's room for you in the helicopter."

"For both of us?" Austin asked.

Stoner pushed his hat back and rubbed his wrists. "Whoa, boss! I've got to take care of Barstow and run the horse trailer back and drive my rig out of here."

"Oh, yes . . . I forgot, Kelly. You go on," Austin urged. "I'll be in Las Vegas by this evening and then — "

"You go with 'em, darlin'," Stoner interrupted. "You've got work to do. I'll meet up with you later."

"No, no, I wouldn't think — "

"Come on with us, Lynda. We have a lot to talk about." Kelly tugged at her arm.

"But . . . but you can't drive that rig," she protested to Stoner.

"I'll make it. Capt. Patch can drive."

"I thought you said he didn't know how."

"I'll teach him. It's about time he did something helpful!"

"Really? You don't mind? I would like to get cleaned up."

"Go on."

She turned to the reporters. "I'll fly back with you, but give me three minutes to talk to Brady alone . . . okay?"

"You got it. It will take us that long to get loaded up," one of the men replied.

Brady Stoner limped over toward the saddled

horse. Austin walked at his side carrying the green duffel bag.

"Well, kid . . . that was quite an adventure." He turned to meet her gaze.

"This is bizarre! I never thought losing a mule would cause so much commotion."

"I do think I owe Joe Trent a little visit."

"Remember what the judge said? Next time you'll stay in jail."

"That was in Arizona. How about if I go to Nevada?"

"Brady, it's not worth it. Guys like that are not worth the effort."

"If he insulted me . . . well, I'll let it slide. If he's dishonored you, he'll pay for it. Listen, I'm not the only combative one. You put on quite a performance to get me off the hook."

Her wide grin revealed straight white teeth, an orthodontist's good work. "Yeah, I did, didn't I? I was really ticked off. I can't believe anyone would believe such a story about you."

"Don't worry about it. It's all over now. Personally, I'm just glad they didn't get around to asking me a couple of questions."

"What questions?"

"Questions like, Did you ever hurt this lady? and Were your actions toward her ever improper?"

"Were you improper, Mr. Stoner?" she teased.

"No, ma'am."

Don't say, "Trust me."

"Trust me."

She shook her head in amused disgust. "Can

you really drive the rig?"

"I'll manage."

"Where will you go? To Heather's?"

"Yeah, I'll clean up there, and then in the morning I'll try to find someone to drive your rental car into Vegas. I'm sure I can't drive that small a car with a broken leg."

"My car! Oh, yeah . . ."

"Where are you going to be staying in Las Vegas?"

She turned and yelled to those by the helicopter. "Kell, what hotel are we staying in?"

"The Tropicanna!"

"I'll see that the car gets there."

"Will you be coming into Vegas later?"

"Probably not. I better call my folks and let them know the kid's all right. Good thing they don't have television. Then I need to evaluate this leg and figure out if I can rodeo anymore this year. If not, I'll need to go lookin' for a day job. I'll probably stay out at Heather's for a day or two waiting to hear if you want me to go down and pack that stuff of Harrison's out of the canyon for the library."

"Good. I'll call you tonight."

Stoner nodded. "Now, Lynda Dawn, Gossman wants to take that manuscript away from you. You keep your hands on it. Don't give it up until you got a guarantee they'll publish it just like it is. Listen, if you need anything at the Tropicanna, just go down to the group reservations office and ask for LeeAnne. Tell her you're a friend of mine and — "

"And she'll bat her eyes and say, 'Oh, how I miss that Brady!' "

"Probably not. But she does owe me a few favors. You better get over there. They're waitin' for you. You might want to have a doc take some x-rays to make sure everything's all right in your shoulder."

"Yes, Daddy." She winked.

His brown eyes looked startled. "Am I talkin' down to you?"

"No, you're talking like you care about me. I like that, really."

"You're goin' to call me tonight?"

"Yep!"

"It would break my heart if you don't. Well . . . bye, Lynda Dawn . . . it was quite some adventure."

She turned to the helicopter, took two steps, then whirled back around. Austin tilted her head slightly and then scooted back to Stoner.

"I need a hug," she sheepishly admitted.

He threw his strong arms around her, but she felt a gentle touch on her right shoulder.

"Is this it, girl? Are we sayin' goodbye?" he whispered.

"Maybe." She gave him one last squeeze and stepped back.

"Well . . . I've got a mind full of memories to keep me warm all winter. Thank ya, ma'am!" He tipped his black felt cowboy hat.

"I'm going to leave before I cry or say something absolutely stupid. I'll call you tonight. You can count on that."

"You take care of yourself, big city editor."

"And you take care of yourself, cowboy."

He stood beside Barstow and Capt. Patch all the time the helicopter was taking off and heading north of Mt. Trumbull. Lynda looked back as long as she could, holding the green duffel bag in her lap. Then she ignored the scolding words of L. George Gossman all the way back to Mc-Carran International Airport.

I really don't want this to be the way it ends, Lord — me flying off into the western sunset leaving the cowboy standing there. I'll call him tonight, and he can come into the city. I've still got a few days left of vacation. We can have dinner and go see a show or something.

And then . . . well, then . . . then I can fly off into the eastern horizon.

She brushed back a tear that puddled in the corner of her left eye.

From the elevators at the Tropicanna, Austin gazed across the floor of the casino. With frantic urgency, gamblers were shoving coins into noisy machines and lining up at green-felt-covered tables.

"What time is that conference this afternoon with Gossman?" she asked.

Kelly Princeton ran her fingers through her curly hair and glanced at her gold wristwatch. "At four. What do you think it's all about?"

"My dramatics out in the canyon, I suppose. He was pretty ticked."

"I can't believe he stood there in front of the cameras and tried to pull the manuscript out of your hands," Kelly fumed. "He really wants the honors on that one, doesn't he?"

"Yeah. I'm not sure what disturbs him most — me finding the book or the contents of the book itself. Hey, is there a dress shop in here? All my clothes are back in Brady's rig."

"His rig?"

"Yeah . . . his pickup."

"I was wondering about your sweat shirt, jeans, and boots outfit," Kelly remarked. "I did see one store on the other side of the casino. I think it's sort of a Western-wear place, if you know what I mean."

"Do they have perfume?"

"Eh . . . I think so."

"Perfect. Go look for a dress for me that will look good with these boots."

"You're kidding."

"Nope. Something cowgirl-looking. I'll be there in a minute."

Kelly started walking down a row of slot machines manned mainly by gray-haired women. Then she turned back. "Where are you going?"

"To see a girl named LeeAnne."

"Who?"

"I'll tell you later."

Austin purchased a blue denim dress with white

fringe on the yoke and a bottle of something called Buckaroo's Delight, took a shower, and by 2:00 P.M. was sitting on one of the queen-size beds in room 906. She wore one white towel wrapped around her body and another around her wet hair.

"I can't believe that one mule falling over the edge of the canyon made national news!"

Kelly flopped down on the other bed. "It was a slow news day. Nina was the first to see it. She's been a nervous wreck ever since. Her father wants her to go home to Wisconsin."

"Coast-to-coast coverage?"

"Yeah, but it may have worked out well to launch the book. I talked to Nina while you were in the shower, and she said the office buzzed all afternoon when they heard what really happened out there. Spunky is jealous and is threatening to wear something really wild tomorrow."

"That would be different. Look," Austin requested, "you've got to tell me about the service for Mr. Hampton. I really wanted to be there."

"It was up at St. John's, of course . . . so many people there they wouldn't have missed you. I'll tell you all about it, but you have to fill me in on what happened to you for four days. The last we heard, you bailed out the cowboy and were going back to find a place called Shotgun Canyon."

"Did I tell you about an old man named Gabby Snyder? Or about the town of Rincon?"

"No, but you can't leave out anything! Nina made me promise to call her back no matter what time it was and tell her everything."

For the next two hours and fifteen minutes Lynda Dawn Austin talked nonstop. She was still talking and fully dressed when the phone rang in the room.

"It's Gossman." Kelly grimaced. "He wants us to hurry up. I guess he's got Mr. Hampton, Jr., on a conference call."

The meeting room was set up to accommodate about fifty people. L. George Gossman looked small and lonely sitting by himself with a telephone and a briefcase in front of him.

"You're late, Ms. Austin. I said we'd meet at four."

"It's my vacation, remember? Unless, of course, you want to count this as work time, in which case I still have vacation coming."

"No . . . you're, eh . . . right. It's just that Mr. Hampton is on the speaker phone."

"Hi, Mr. Hampton. I sure am sorry I couldn't be back for your father's service. You know how much I loved and respected that man."

"Your condolences are gratefully accepted. But we should get on with the business at hand."

"Yes, sir. And what is that business?"

"The manuscript you brought out of the canyon."

"Yes, sir. It's exciting, isn't it?"

"Do you have the text with you?"

"Yes," Gossman replied, "but she doesn't seem to want to surrender it."

"I have it in my room."

"I'd appreciate it if you would give it to George. It belongs to the house, of course."

"I was counseled to keep it until authenticity is proven."

"Who told you to do that? Did you hire an attorney?"

"Not exactly."

Gossman turned to Austin. "I don't know what you're scheming, Austin, but with no assigns or heirs of Harrison, that manuscript is the property of Atlantic-Hampton Publishing Company."

"Mr. Hampton, this is Kelly Princeton. Do you know the projected publication date for this book? The reporters have been asking me."

"Tell them it will take a year or more."

"What?" Lynda gasped. "What do you mean, a year or more? It's a good clean text. With high priority it could be edited by Christmas and out in the spring. Why would we wait?"

"Tell her, George."

"Mr. Hampton and I agree that the manuscript still lacks authenticity and is certainly not of the high quality of the first two books."

"Are you kidding me? You haven't read anything but chapter 3!"

"Yes, and chapter 3 will have to be completely rewritten."

"Why?"

"Well . . . well . . . we can't use his vicious attack on his own material. We talked this out ten days ago. We have a Harrison image to uphold."

"For what purpose? Let Harrison say whatever he wanted to say."

"We still don't have proof that it was Harrison's work."

"You can go out there and dig up his body!"

"I'm afraid we've had all the negative publicity we need for a while. We are not about to go around digging up bodies. Your actions would have made my father sick. It's a blessing he didn't have to live and hear all this trash."

"What?" she choked. "What are you talking about?"

"Watch that disgusting television show 'The Real Story' tonight and you'll see."

"What do they say?"

"I wouldn't repeat it in mixed company. If you want the text proven, you'll have to give us the manuscript so we can date the paper and the ink."

"You will only need one sheet for that. Besides, who cares when during the last sixty years it was written?"

Gossman fidgeted with the ballpoint pen in his hand. "We need to know not only who wrote chapter 3, but also who wrote the final pages. This chap Fondue was quite an opportunist. He could have scratched together the last part."

"I think I'll hold onto it until I get to New York myself."

"Ms. Austin, you are stealing company property. . . . Now I know you've been through quite an ordeal. We'll talk again tomorrow. If Mr. Gossman does not have the manuscript in his hands at that time, I'll have to turn it over to the legal department to begin proceedings to recover stolen property."

"I can't believe you'd say that, Mr. Hampton!" Lynda fumed.

"Might I remind you, Ms. Austin," Gossman interjected, "insubordination is cause for dismissal."

"You mean you'll fire Lynda if she doesn't give you the manuscript?" Kelly gasped.

"That's a possibility."

"I can't believe this!" Kelly shouted. "I can't believe what I'm hearing!"

"Ms. Princeton, your position is not all that secure, so you had better believe it."

"I'll take it to another publisher. They'll print it if you don't have the guts to," Lynda threatened.

"No, they won't. That would be a violation of the copyright laws. With no heirs and assigns, we have exclusive rights to the book. It does not get printed unless we say so."

"You're stonewalling this project because you're afraid of what a Christian Harrison will do to the sales of atheist Harrison's first two books!"

"Absolutely not!" Gossman retorted.

"If I see that charge in print, Ms. Austin, you will be immediately fired. Do you understand?"

"Yes. We all understand that," Kelly groaned.

"You watch that television program tonight. You'll see why we need to let this whole matter cool off before we even begin to consider publishing the book. Now we're all a little edgy about this matter. I suggest we get some rest and discuss it in the morning. George, when are you flying back?"

"I've got tickets to leave after lunch tomorrow."

"Call me in the morning, and we'll figure out something. I've got to scoot along."

"Yes, sir, I'll do that."

"And give the ladies one hundred dollars and tell them to go to a dinner show or something. Company treat. I'm afraid I've sounded rather — dogmatic."

"That's not necessary, Mr. — "

Kelly poked Lynda in the ribs. "Thank you, Mr. Hampton," Princeton responded.

Lynda and Kelly didn't talk much in the elevator, which they shared with six other people, a bass fiddle, and a three-foot, pink-ribboned poodle. But they fumed plenty when they got back to the room.

"Do you believe this?" Lynda stormed. "If I push on this hard to get it published, they'll fire me!"

"Or sue you if you take it to another publisher."

"I'm so mad I could . . . spit! Who does he think he is?"

"He thinks he owns 56 percent of the company, I suppose."

"We're talking history here! We're talking literary discovery! We're talking business ethics! I can't believe what I've heard. They're paranoid about this lost manuscript. It's like it attacks their mother or something!"

Kelly unfolded the hundred-dollar bill and waved it at Lynda. "Listen, kid, it's the girls' night out. You've got your new party dress. Let's go use this up."

"I can't believe you were so easily bribed," Austin chided.

"Bribe? I just figured it was severance pay. The way things were going for a while, I thought we would be unemployed by now. So where are we going?"

"There's a good steak place just north of St. George, Utah!"

"You missing your cowboy already?"

"He's not my cowboy. But I did promise to call him. I'll make a phone call, and you pick out the place."

"Kenny Rogers is just down the street. You want to do the early show with him? That's about as country as I think I can take."

"I don't suppose Ian Tyson is playing?"

"Who?"

"Kenny will be fine . . . whatever. I just want a good dinner. Let me call Brady. Then we'd better watch 'The Real Story.' I can't believe Mr. Hampton watches such a sleazy show! What time is it on out here?"

"Six o'clock. Channel 7. I've looked it up already. How can you say the show is sleazy? Just the other night they showed a video of a cat and

337

dog getting into a fight. Then without warning, the cat blew up killing them both! There were animal parts splattered everywhere!"

"A stunning piece of video art, no doubt."

Lynda called Heather Martin in St. George, Utah, at 5:30 P.M. PDT.

There was no answer.

Then she sat on the edge of the bed in stunned silence when the teaser for "The Real Story" began with the words, "Bound and battered, cowboy's love-slave refuses to press charges." Accompanying the narration was a videotape of her and Brady riding Barstow. The camera zoomed in on the rope tied around her and then faded out with a close-up of the bruises on her cheek.

The segment on her was only three minutes long and made no mention of the lost manuscript. At the end of that portion, Kelly Princeton turned off the TV.

Tears burned as they rolled across a raw portion of Austin's cheek. "Love-slave? How can they say that? That's slanderous. They can be sued for slander, right?"

"If you have enough money to pay the attorney's fees, I suppose. Don't let it drag you down. Nobody believes that stuff anyway. Besides, this is cool. I've never known a real, live love-slave before. Can I be the editor of your best-selling autobiography, *I Was a Cowboy's Love-Slave*?"

Austin started to grin, then stood up and glared.

"How can you joke at a time like this?"

"Well," Kelly said with a shrug, "I'm either going to laugh, or I'm going to cry. Laughing doesn't smear my mascara."

"I need to talk to Brady about that show. He can go off the handle when he gets mad."

"But we're going out on the town, right?"

"Yeah . . . I guess. You know, for thirty years I've been in total control of everything in my life. Now my whole world's spinning wildly. I feel like a steel marble in a pin ball machine."

"Well, I can tell you one thing — it's not boring. Think about it. We can talk about this for the next ten years over lunch at Barton's."

"Provided I don't get fired."

"Hey, there are other houses in New York. You're a good editor," Kelly insisted. "Come on, we're getting depressed. Are you going to wear that new dress, or do you need to start wearing black leather and chains?"

"What?"

"You know . . . the love-slave attire."

Austin sailed a pillow into the side of Princeton's head.

"It's absolutely absurd, isn't it?" Lynda chuckled.

"Can you imagine this in your high school annual: 'Lynda Dawn Austin — most likely to be a love-slave'?" Kelly teased.

"You know what really makes me mad? I get labeled a cowboy's love-slave, and I never even kissed the guy!"

"You lived with him for ten days, and you didn't kiss?"

"I didn't live with him! I hired him to help me find — "

"Oh, come on, girl, save that for the media. You spent several nights with the guy — alone at the edge of the universe."

Lynda Austin's head jerked around. "Did you hear what you just said?"

"Hey . . . I'm just teasing you."

"No . . . no . . . you said being down in the canyons is like being alone at the edge of the universe. That's why Harrison went down there. He was living out his first book!"

"*Alone at the Edge of the Universe*. Wow! I can be so profound sometimes. Now give me five minutes to make my face beautiful, and we're going out!" Kelly buzzed into the bathroom.

"I'll try calling Brady again."

She sat on the edge of the bed and punched in Heather Martin's number. She was just hanging up the phone ten minutes later when Kelly came back into the room.

"How's the cowboy?"

Austin took a deep breath and sighed. "I didn't talk to him. Heather said he called in an hour ago on a short wave phone from Salvador's house."

"What's a short wave phone?"

"I have no idea. Anyway, I guess he had some sort of trouble with his rig, so he and Salvador went out to fix it or something. He said he'd call me later."

"So he didn't get to see 'The True Story'?"

"No, but Heather told him about it."

"How could she see it an hour ago when it was just on?"

"That's Mountain Time over there, and they receive it on a Salt Lake station."

"Well, what'd the cowboy say about it?"

"He said he'd kill Joe Trent if he had anything to do with it."

"He was joking, right?"

"I hope." She stood up, picked up her purse, and walked over to the mirror by the door. "Come on, let's get this wild night over with. I told Heather to have Brady call back after eleven."

They returned at 11:15 P.M. Lynda sat up eating complimentary crackers in the shape of miniature playing cards and chocolates wrapped like poker chips until midnight.

At 12:04 she and Kelly went to bed.

At 3:31 A.M. a loud ringing interrupted a dream. Then she heard a muted voice mutter something. A bright light flipped on, and Kelly shoved the phone her way.

"It's a lonesome cowboy," she mumbled.

Lynda stared at the phone in her hand.

"Brady?"

"Hi, darlin'."

"What time is it?"

"Over here it's about an hour shy of daylight."

"Is something wrong?"

"Eh . . . no, it's all right now."

She longed to hang up the phone and go back to sleep. "Why did you call?"

"You called me, right? And Heather said — "

"Oh . . . Brady! Wait a minute. . . . Let me wake up." She sat up on the edge of the bed and saw Kelly roll over and pull pillows over her ears. "What happened to you?"

"Well, darlin', I hate to admit this, but I got the rig stuck right off the bat and had to ride Barstow all the way out to Salvador's. I guess I missed my good driver. Anyway, I called Heather. Then we went out to dig the thing out."

"And you just got to St. George?"

"Well, I got in around three hours ago."

"And you waited until now to call?"

"I called when I got in, but they didn't have your name listed as a registered guest."

"I'm staying in Kelly's room."

"Yeah, I figured that. But I didn't have a clue to what Kelly's last name is."

"So what did you do?"

"I gave up and went to sleep. Then a few minutes ago I woke up with a name on my mind. It was sort of like the Lord's leading."

"Princeton? You remembered Kelly's last name is Princeton?"

"Nope. But I did remember that your boss's name is Gossman."

"You called George at 3:30 in the morning and asked for my room number?"

"Yep. 'Course, he didn't sound real pleased."

"I'll bet. You didn't see the television tonight, did you?"

"No, but Heather told me some about it. Did Joe Trent have anything to do with that program?"

"No. It was just some footage that someone shot out in the desert when we came out of the canyon."

"Did they show me flat on the ground with my face in the dirt?"

"Not really. They seemed to be fascinated with my being tied up and looking battered."

"Yeah, Heather's girls asked me if you were really a love-slave." He laughed.

"What did you tell them?"

"I said you were a slave driver. So how is everything else going? Did you get anything worked out for your company to send me back in there for Harrison's goods?"

"I think they're trying to stonewall it, Brady. They're going to keep it out of print as long as they can. That's not fair! They're pushing me to turn over the manuscript and imply that if I don't, I'll be fired."

"Take it to some other publisher."

"They said they would sue me if I did."

"Can they do that?"

"I think so."

"Don't let them push you around, Lynda Dawn. I think that just might be your God-given task."

"My what?"

"Remember down in the canyon when you thought you were going to die? You said you regretted not having completed your God-given task. Well, maybe this is one of yours."

She stared at the teal hotel carpet.

"Lynda Dawn, are you still there?"

"Yeah, I was thinking about what you said. Thanks for encouraging me. I'm glad you called. I was sort of missing our evening conversations."

"I thought you said we got into a fight every night! Maybe what you miss is my fine cooking."

"Get real, Stoner!"

"Now you're soundin' better. Get some sleep, and you've got to promise to call me before you go home."

"We've got another big meeting this morning. I should know something after that."

"What time's the meeting?"

"At nine. Will you be at Heather's?"

"Yeah, she's having trouble with her rig, and I said I'd look at it in the mornin'."

"I'll call you later."

"Night, darlin'!"

"Yeah . . . good night, darlin', to you too."

She hung up the phone and slumped back into bed.

A teasing voice came filtering up out of the pillows. "Good night, darlin', to you too!"

"One more crack from you, Princeton, and I'll toss you out the window!"

"Maybe this is why they call it the Wild West!" Kelly giggled and reached up to turn out the light.

Lynda washed one small stain off the sleeve of her new blue Western dress and pulled it back on the next morning. Grabbing bagels and coffee, she and Kelly met L. George Gossman at nine in the hotel conference room.

"Good morning, ladies. . . . Hope you slept well. I had a lousy night — no thanks to someone looking for his darlin' Lynda Dawn. No doubt some crazy who saw you on television."

"Sorry about that, George. Are we conferencing with Mr. Hampton?"

"No, I've already talked to him."

"Oh . . . but I thought we were — "

"Sit down, sit down. I'll explain everything."

She and Kelly sat across from Gossman as she sipped her lukewarm coffee.

"Mr. Hampton and I are beginning to realize just how much personal effort you have put in — at your own expense . . . to this project. When the rest of us were dragging our heels a little, and then with the loss of Mr. Hampton, Sr. . . . well, you pushed right out here and recovered the manuscript.

"We think — and truly this was Mr. Hampton's idea — that you have compensation coming. The company would like to pick up your expenses for this whole trip, and you can have the next two weeks off for your personal vacation."

"All right!" Kelly applauded.

"Plus, we feel . . . well . . . decided that when the time's right to release the book, you should be the editor."

"Thanks, George. I know you wanted to do the honors."

"Well, I'll assist you in whatever way I can. Of course I'll be listed as giving editorial oversight to the project."

Austin flipped open her notebook and reviewed her notes. "In that case, we need to get a coroner back into that canyon and confirm that the body in the grave is Harrison's. Then there are his personal belongings to bring out for the library and — "

"Yes . . . yes, but not until spring or summer."

"What?"

"Right now we just want to get all of us back to New York and catch up on some current projects. We can do all that in the spring and summer after this 'love-slave thing' dies down."

"Excuse me? You mean you're still stalling about bringing it out?"

"We're not stalling at all!" Gossman's voice sounded high-pitched and tight as he shoved his glasses back up his narrow nose. "We need to research the matter and bring it out at the best possible time. This project is much too important to rush."

She glanced over at Kelly, who shielded her mouth from Gossman's view and silently mouthed the words, "No way!"

"Atlantic-Hampton has utmost confidence in your ability to work with us on this matter. Ms. Princeton and I will be flying back this afternoon. I'm not sure when you were scheduled to depart. As I said, if you'd like to take a couple of weeks of vacation at this time, that's up to you. We will need a list of itemized expenses — with as many receipts as you might have. But don't worry if you're missing some. Oh, and I'll take the manuscript with me so that we can keep it in a safe place."

Both women raised their eyebrows.

"It's in a safe place. I'll just keep it with me for now."

"What?" Gossman choked. "Haven't you heard a word I've been saying?"

"I heard it all. You wanted to bribe me out of the lost Harrison manuscript."

"Bribe? There you go again! The manuscript is legally ours to begin with. It is only out of generosity that all of these concessions have been offered."

"Is this meeting over?" Austin demanded.

"Well . . . well . . . as soon as you hand it over."

Lynda Dawn Austin stood to her feet.

"Where are you going?" he shouted.

"I'm still on my vacation. I'll be in the office on Monday morning, and we can discuss the matter then."

"Wait a minute! You can't just walk out of here! You don't know what you're doing!"

Leaving a cold cup of coffee and a rock-hard bagel on the table, she hiked toward the door. She could hear Gossman and Princeton scurrying behind her. Just as she stepped through the door into the hotel lobby, Gossman grabbed her right arm and held tight.

"Oh! Don't!" she yelped. "That's my sore arm."

"You aren't walking out on me. I want that manuscript, and I want it before I leave for New York. Is that — "

She whirled around to see why Gossman had released his grip.

"Brady!"

"Howdy, boss."

The tall, tanned cowboy had grabbed Gossman by the back of the suit coat collar and almost lifted him off the ground.

"Mister, you need to learn a lesson in Western etiquette. You don't touch a lady unless she has invited you to do so!"

With a look of sheer panic in his eyes, Gossman squeaked, "I'm warning you, I'll call security. I'll have you arrested for assault."

"Good, let's go talk to security right now. I want to mention to them how you made improper advances at this lady."

"I did nothing of the kind."

"That's what it looked like to me. I did hear Lynda Dawn cry out in pain. Did you hear that, miss?" He nodded at Kelly.

"Well . . . yes, actually, she did seem hurt."

Gossman yanked himself free from Stoner's relaxed grip.

"Ms. Austin, I will see you in the office at 9:00 A.M. Monday . . . or don't bother coming back at all."

He stormed off toward the elevators.

"Brady, what are you doing here?"

"Looks like it's a good thing I showed up."

"This is a mess. Hey . . . you know Kelly, don't you?"

Stoner tipped his hat. "Miss Kelly, nice to officially meet you. I've heard a lot about you. Say, are all the women editors in New York beautiful?"

"That's the dumbest line I've ever heard." Kelly laughed. "Say, do you have a friend?"

"You didn't tell me why you're here," Austin insisted.

"I brought your rental car back myself."

"How could you drive it with that big brace on your leg?"

"I pulled it off. The brace, not the leg! I had a short plastic splint left at Heather's, so I put that on and can pull my Wranglers on this way without slitting them to the thigh."

"Do you two need to be alone?" Kelly asked.

"Why?" Stoner responded.

"Oh, I . . . I thought . . ."

"Have you two girls had breakfast?"

"Not really," Austin replied.

"Okay, let's go across the street to the MGM Grand. They have a great breakfast buffet."

"Chicken and veggies?"

"Come on, we can walk over there." He grabbed their arms and began to lead them to the door.

"Say . . ." His eyes began to sparkle. "Which one of you two wants to pay for breakfast?"

They had just sat down with their food when a twentyish-looking woman with waist-length straight, brown hair, dragging a reluctant young man, came to their table.

"Say . . ." The girl giggled, shoving her hands in her jeans pockets. "Eh . . . didn't I see you on television last night?" She looked right at Lynda Austin.

"Well . . . it's possible if you had the right channel, I guess."

"I knew it as soon as I saw the bruises on your face. I knew it! Troy, I told you it was her!" She giggled again. "Can I have your autograph?"

Raising his eyebrows, Brady intoned, "Looks like you're a star."

"She sure is!" the girl continued. "Could you sign it for my dad? His name is Roy."

"Your father?" Austin coughed.

"He says you're the best. And when we saw how you guys beat the Rumblers last night . . . I mean, taking that elbow in the face and then being able to come back and score five points right at the buzzer, that was something! Your face really took it, didn't it? Look at that bruise, Troy. You don't fake a bruise like that. I told Troy that might have been the best Roller Derby match I ever watched!"

"Roller Derby!" Brady exclaimed. "She isn't in Roller Derby."

"She isn't?" the girl gulped.

"Lynda Dawn here is a professional mud wrestler!"

"She is?" Her companion in the Denver Bronco's T-shirt perked up and smiled, revealing a silver front tooth.

"Uh . . . yuck! Come on, Troy . . . Troy?" The girl tugged on the shirt of the six-foot young man, who stared with wild, excited eyes at Lynda Dawn Austin.

The three watched as the young couple receded across the restaurant.

"Mud wrestler? Why did you tell her that?"

"I had to think fast."

"And lady mud wrestling comes to your mind quickly, does it?" She glared.

"Well, what did you want me to call you — a love-slave?"

"Shut up!" she barked. "Stoner, so help me if you ever use that term again, I'll . . . I'll push you off a cliff!"

"Yes, boss." Then he turned to Kelly. "You see how we get along? That's why I needed you to accompany us, Miss Kelly — to protect me from this she-cat."

"She-cat?" Kelly leaned forward and rested her chin on her hands.

"Unpredictable and vicious to the core."

"Lynda Dawn Austin — the one woman in New York City who has every minute of every hour completely organized?"

"Really?" he asked.

"Have you ever seen inside her closets?"

"No, but I would certainly like to."

"Kell! Don't start in on that!" Austin protested.

"Kind of touchy this mornin', isn't she?" Brady replied.

Kelly took a sip of grapefruit juice and nodded her head. "When are you two going to get serious?"

"Right now," Brady answered, stabbing a green melon ball with his fork. "What are we going to do now, boss? I figure that I don't get my thousand dollars."

"My plane doesn't leave until Saturday. I think I better retrieve all I can from that cabin."

"Okay, that makes sense. Then let's go back in there as soon as possible. I'll check out the helicopter services. I think I can guide them into Shotgun Canyon. Are you coming with us, Miss Kelly?"

"No, she's not coming!" Austin insisted.

Kelly and Brady both turned and looked at her.

"Oh . . . I mean . . . your flight leaves this afternoon. She has to go back to New York."

"Well, now that's a shame. I was hopin' my boss would give me a little time off before you had to fly back. Miss Kelly, did you ever line dance?"

"No, why?"

"Well, you have the look of a natural line dancer. If it weren't for my broke leg, I would be more than happy to show you how."

"Really?"

"Listen, Stoner, quit flirting with Kelly and pay attention," Austin intruded.

"Yes, ma'am."

"You line up the helicopter. Have them take us into the canyon in the morning and come back for us right before dark. Whatever we can box up during that time will be all we haul out of there."

"I think we ought to get the Mojave County coroner over there to identify the body buried in that grave," Stoner suggested.

"I'll call the coroner's office. I talked to someone there the other day. But how will they find Shotgun Canyon? It's sort of been hiding for sixty-four years."

"Find out when they'll be coming in. Tell them it will be about ten miles east of Toroweap Valley, close to the Colorado River. I'll build a smoky fire. They can follow it in."

"You think they'll actually do that?" Kelly asked.

"Oh, yeah," Brady assured her. "If you build a fire . . . they'll come. I think Kevin Costner said something like that."

The rest of the day flew by for Lynda Dawn Austin. Brady borrowed her car and arranged for an early morning flight for them into the canyon. She and Kelly shopped for one more pair of jeans and two Western shirts. Then she took Kelly to the airport.

L. George Gossman sulked behind *The Wall Street Journal* and refused even to speak to her.

After a thirty-five minute phone call to Kingman, Arizona, Austin talked the coroner of Mojave

County into meeting them in Shotgun Canyon on one condition — that if they could not find a body, she would have to reimburse the county for the flight.

She called the Harrison Library in Key West and broke the news about the possibility of artifacts. They agreed to pay for storage of the items until the museum curator could fly out and inspect everything. She asked Austin to sort the material and toss out the obviously unrelated items in order to cut down on the storage bill.

Then Lynda soaked in the tub for over an hour.

Waiting for Brady to return, she fell asleep on top of the bed. When she woke up, the room was getting dark.

Brady should be back by now. Where did he go? I've got two days before everything collapses. The entire legal team of Atlantic-Hampton Publishing Company will be sitting on my desk Monday morning. It all seems so weird, Lord. If Fondue hadn't stormed into the office, everything would just be rolling along smoothly. In the same boring, smooth rut.

Where is he? I don't think I've ever had to wait so long for the same guy. I waited all night for him to call. I waited all afternoon for him to come back. I'm mad because he's not hanging around all the time.

Lord . . . this is getting serious, isn't it? I've known this guy ten days, and I'm already trying to direct every hour of his life.

A knock at the door startled her. She flipped on the light before she called out, "Who is it?"

"It's me, darlin'. Who are you expectin'?"

She fumbled with the latch. "Brady, where have you been? I've been sitting here . . ." Swinging the door open, she caught sight of Brady, and her mouth dropped. His left eye was almost swollen shut. Blood trickled down the side of his face.

"What happened? Did you get in a wreck?"

"Can I wash up a bit?"

"Yes . . . but I . . . What happened?"

"Oh, this? I've been hurt worse than this. A couple of fellows decided to rearrange my looks."

"Who? You didn't get in a fight with Joe Trent, did you?"

"Not exactly. Let me explain while I wash up."

He limped over to the bathroom and pulled off his red and white Western shirt. She could see a slight trickle of blood on his back.

"Did you get cut?"

Turning his back to the mirror, he looked over his shoulder.

"Well, I'll be dad gum . . . I guess I did. One of those boys was flashing a knife around, but I didn't think he was serious. You got any Mercurochrome?"

"Eh . . . no."

"It's okay. I've cut myself worse on an envelope. I got everything lined up for Desert Tours to take us out to Shotgun Canyon."

"But what happened to you?"

"I'm coming to that. . . . Relax, darlin', it's nothin'. Anyway, they can only fly out to the canyon once a day. So we'll have to fly back the next

355

day. Is that all right with you?"

"Well, we've been out there all night before."

"It will cost $750 for the flight."

"Do they take a credit card?"

"Yep."

"Well, that's not too bad. I thought it might be a thousand."

"That's $750 each day."

"You're kidding!" she gasped.

"We can always ride Barstow in there. Then you just fly the stuff out," he suggested. "Or I'll just go in by myself."

"Forget it. I'm going in. I'll borrow the money from my brother to pay off my credit card if I have to. How come you don't tell me what happened to you?"

"Just wait . . . just wait. Hey, does this look better?" He popped around the corner and smiled.

Seeing him without his shirt reminded her of the long horse ride out of the canyon when she had her arms around him for so long.

"I said, do I look better?"

"Well, at least you're cleaner. Your eye is horrible."

"Yeah. Maybe this time they'll accuse *me* of being a love, eh . . . you know what."

"You want that other eye shut, Mister Stoner?"

He started to pull on his shirt. "Anyway, after lining up the air flight, I went over to the newspaper."

"What for?"

"Well, I know this lady reporter who — "

"Don't tell me. She's been chasin' you for years!"

"Nope. Stacy's a fifty-year-old grandma who is about the best rodeo photographer in the business. But she also writes a column for the local paper. I wanted to set things square and balance things off with Joe Trent's story. She talked with me for over two hours. She was real interested in the manuscript. I think it will be some good coverage. She said I should have you stop by after we come out of the canyon, and she'd like to do your story."

"Really? No kidding! You got an interview just like that?"

"Yep. Stacy and me go way back. When her daughter Cody was at UNLV, she used to do a lot of barrel racin', and we'd . . . you know, go out to her house for pizza after a rodeo."

"Ah-hah! There is a cute barrel racer with long, braided hair behind every story, isn't there?"

"Not every story. *You* don't race the barrels, and your hair isn't braided . . . yet."

"Don't sweet-talk me, Stoner. I'm not a buckle bunny. How did you get hurt?"

"I decided to drive over to have a little chat with Joe Trent. I was not exactly likin' his comments about me on television. But he runs this porno video and book store on a road behind Caesar's Palace. I drove by the place and decided it was just too raunchy for me. So I stopped at a pay phone and gave him a call. I couldn't get through to him, but I told them to tell him to meet me for a little friendly discussion at Carl Jr's over on the Strip."

"You mean you called him out?"

"Just to talk. Anyway, I waited for about an hour, but he didn't show, and just as I was leaving, this guy dressed in black leather said Joe was out back and wanted to see me."

"And you went around there? I can't believe this! Are you that naive? I suppose Joe Trent wasn't there, but a couple of strong guys jumped you and beat you to a pulp."

"Yeah . . . how'd you know? Anyway, I held my own, and some folks from the fast-food place called the cops, and it was over pretty quick. I guess Joe isn't in a talkin' mood."

"What were you going to talk to him about? You just went over there for a fight, right? And he beat you to it."

"I guess I just wanted to hear it from him. I don't like having to count on what someone thinks he heard someone else say on television."

"Look, promise me you won't go after Joe Trent again — at least until we settle this matter in the canyon."

"Well, I won't take him on in Las Vegas, that's for sure." Stoner grinned and then grimaced and held his side. "I think they gave me a pretty good kick in the ribs."

"Have you got a clean shirt?"

"Down in that little white tin can of a rental car."

"Well, let's get you a shirt and then have supper here at the hotel. We'll get to bed early tonight and get a good start before you get into any more trouble."

"Yes, Mother."

"Stoner, you need a mother! Someone's got to look after you."

He scratched his head and jammed on his black cowboy hat. "You know, you aren't the first woman to say that."

I'm sure I'm not. Every woman you ever met wants to mother you. Or hug you. Or both.

"You haven't gotten a room yet, have you?"

"Is that an invitation to stay with you?"

"Nope."

"Good. 'Cause I would have turned you down."

"I know. Come on." She tugged at his arm. "We'll get you fixed up."

TEN

Everything is easier to see from the air.

Except what you're looking for.

The Desert Tours helicopter flew over the vicinity of Shotgun Canyon four times without Austin, Stoner, or the pilot spotting it. As they expected, the cabin, built into the canyon wall under an overhang and covered by cottonwood trees, was completely hidden from sight.

Brady searched for the garden area, but the soil was the same burnt red as the surrounding canyon, making it indistinguishable from the air. Depth perception was misleading as well. Since the main body of the Grand Canyon, as well as the Colorado River, lay far below, Shotgun Canyon failed to present a dramatic profile in contrast.

Finally Brady had the pilot fly over the river itself. They spotted the rock ledge trail that he and Lynda had traveled. By flying out over the main part of the canyon, they followed the trail until they reached the narrow waterfall opening that led back into Shotgun Canyon.

After several moments of jockeying the helicopter, they landed between the spring and the garden area. They tossed out their bags, and Stoner helped Austin to the ground.

"You can open your eyes, darlin'!" he teased.

"You're really having fun at my expense, aren't you?"

"Yeah. Come on, let's get out of the dust!"

"Build a big, green fire in the morning, or I'll never find ya again," the pilot yelled behind them.

They grabbed their bags and scooted toward the cabin as the helicopter lifted off. Even though Austin wore her sunglasses, she shaded her eyes as she watched the aircraft take off. Even the chopping sound soon disappeared. They were left staring at the canyon.

"Well, darlin' . . . here we are — home again. I guess we might as well settle in for the winter."

"That's not even funny, Stoner. You know, I can't imagine anywhere in the lower forty-eight that's more remote and hidden than this canyon."

"Neither could Harrison, I presume. Did you read Stacy's article?"

She nodded and pointed to the supplies. "Yeah, I put the paper in one of these supply sacks. It's a good article. You did a pretty good interview for a . . ."

"For a dumb, backwards cowboy?"

"No! For a person who doesn't work in the publishing business. You got a lot of things right."

There was just enough breeze to blow away the dust the helicopter had stirred up.

"What'd I get wrong?"

"Well, the headlines were a little shocking."

"You mean, 'Million-Dollar Manuscript Found in Deserted Canyon'?"

"Yes. That makes it sound like a gold mine, and I might not even be able to get it published. If that article gets back to Atlantic-Hampton, they'll . . ."

"Pitch a fit?"

"Something like that."

"I thought you said it was worth a million."

"Well, it is if it were open for bid, but Atlantic-Hampton will see that that doesn't happen."

"So it's really not worth that much?"

"Not at the moment."

"Oh, well . . . it sounds better than the Joe Trent interview anyway. Did you say the coroner would be here at ten?"

"He thought it would be closer to eleven, but if they had another call, he'd have to take care of that first."

She stepped up on the porch and heard the familiar creak of worn wood under her feet.

"Well, you go figure out which of this stuff we need to take back with us. I'll scrape up some firewood. There's nothin' around here close, so I'll hike to the back and see what I can find. I won't start the fire until about 10:30."

After stacking their supplies and extra containers on the porch, Brady limped off toward the back of the canyon. Lynda entered the cabin and shoved open the wooden shutters on the windows. Then she propped the front door open with a chair to allow fresh air to filter in.

Even though it was late in September, the high desert air was warm. The dust in the old cabin hung in the beams of sunlight. Sticking her sunglasses on top of her head, she grabbed up a plastic trash bag and began to comb the cabin for obvious throw-away items.

She found half-used supplies, some petrified in the containers. There were a few newspapers and catalogs that she stacked near the fireplace in case some later occupant would need fire starters. She sacked up clothes, trying to determine which would have been Harrison's and which Fondue's. Coming across two cigar boxes full of shotgun shells, she pulled down the model 12 Winchester from its rafter resting place and held it lightly to her sore shoulder. After shoving a couple of shells into the gun, she stepped out into the yard and followed an imaginary clay pigeon across the sky.

"Lord, I'd really, really like to take this home. But I know the library in Key West will want it. Someday I'm going to buy myself one."

She propped the shotgun against the doorjamb inside the cabin and returned to sorting out the odds and ends. Stacking the typewriter against the wall, she cleared off the table and began to dig through the boxes of paper. The first homemade wooden crate held page after page of drafts of a manuscript.

How in the world did he get all this paper down here? I wonder if that was part of what was on that original pack train? And what happened to all those mules he led in here? I guess they died of old age.

Mules don't . . . reproduce . . . do they?

She sniffed the inside of both her wrists to make sure the perfume was holding up.

It was.

Hearing noise out in the garden area, she stepped outside. Brady Stoner was dragging a piece of canvas loaded with firewood.

"Where did that wood come from?" she asked. "There can't be many trees left in this canyon after sixty years of cook fires."

"Just those cottonwoods at the cabin and the wild plums. You remember that cliff in the back of the canyon that we looked over the other day?"

"The one that dropped straight down and then slanted for a while?"

"Yeah, that's the one. Well, I think Harrison or Fondue, or both, would go out to the ledge trail, gather wood up on top, and shove it over back there. That way they didn't have to bring it down the trail."

"Didn't it bust up when it hit the rocks?"

"Yeah, that's the point. They probably didn't have to split much wood. Anyway, there's a whole pile back there, and it wasn't grown in this canyon. How's your progress in the cabin?"

"Oh . . . it's kind of hard to throw anything away," she admitted.

"I'll drag up another load and then come in to help you. It's not time to light this sucker, is it?"

"Not for an hour. How's your leg?"

"Feelin' pretty good actually. I'll probably need to raise it up after a while. I just might try enterin' a couple of little rodeos to test it out before the Cow Palace. I think doctors worry too much. Shoot, I've been hurt worse than this from a calf kickin' me."

"I can't believe you, Brady Stoner! What are you trying to prove — that you're the world's toughest man? You're going to go back into that rodeo arena and ruin your leg permanently! Then you'll have to find some woman who doesn't mind taking care of a cripple for the rest of her life. Look, you're not going back to rodeo until that leg's completely healed, and that's final! Sometimes you act like you don't have any brains in your head at all!"

He stared at her a moment. She could tell she was blushing.

Why in the world did I say all that?

"Nag, nag, nag, woman! Git in there and clean the house, and maybe if you're real sweet, I'll buy you a new pair of shoes and a second dress for Christmas."

Great! Girl, keep this up, and with any luck he'll go running and screaming out of the canyon, and you'll never even have to say goodbye.

Several boxes were piled on the table, and pages were scattered around the room when Brady finally came inside the cabin.

"Are you makin' heads or tails of this? It sort of looks like a dorm room right before finals!"

"Well, I think what we have is several revisions of the book until it got to the present stage. It seemed to start out quite different. I suppose all of this ought to be saved. How much room is there on that helicopter? We don't have to worry about overload, do we? Can we take about six of these boxes, those two sacks . . . the typewriter, and the shotgun?"

"If they come out empty like they were this mornin'. Are you takin' out pots and pans and the like?"

"I don't think so. I can't even decide about some of these papers. Harrison didn't always number or label the pages, so I'm only guessing at what it means. Maybe we'll just take all these papers and let the Harrison library figure them out."

"There could be other stories in there to publish."

She reached up and rubbed the wrinkles out of her forehead. "You may be right."

They packed all the loose papers and manuscripts into boxes and stacked them by the front wall.

"How about these journals and things?"

"What journals?" she asked.

Brady took a stack of old, yellowed newspapers off the top of a box and lifted up a hardback ledger about fifteen by twenty inches. "Looks like a diary or something."

"Let me see that!"

"There's more in here. . . . Why don't you sort through them? I think I'll go and start a smoky fire. That coroner could be in any time."

"Yeah . . . okay . . . ," she mumbled as she

flipped open to a page dated 1953.

1953? Did he date them? This could be incredible! Why didn't I find these the last time we were here?

There were a total of twelve ledgers in the box. Some were written in ink and still mostly legible. Those that had been written in pencil were faded almost beyond legibility. Finding the oldest one, she dragged a beat-up chair out to the porch where the bright daylight made easier reading.

"Hey, this one's from 1933!" she hollered. "Listen to this: 'The noise of the wind awoke me from my sleep like a dear friend with secrets to tell. In the winter, she alone comes to call. The coyotes have slunk down to the river, and the little brook, like a tortoise, has withdrawn to the safety of its muddy shell.' Is that good or what?"

"What time is it?"

"After eleven."

"Where's your coroner friend?"

"He said he might be late. Did you hear what I read you?"

"Yeah . . . yeah." He waved his hand. "It was wonderful . . ."

It IS wonderful, Stoner, but you're too busy with your little fire to really listen. That's our problem, isn't it, Lord? We're all too busy to listen . . . to hear . . . to see. But not Harrison. He came down here and listened to the message in the winds. That's it! I'll pull together a collection of writings from his journals and call it The Message of the Winds. *All right!* The Message of the Winds *by Martin Taylor*

Harrison edited by Lynda D. Austin . . . eh, Lynda Dawn Austin. Yes! I won't let Mr. L. George Gossman take this one away. They don't have any legal rights to any other manuscripts.

She stared up at the clear, blue desert sky and thought of the long evening shadows of New York City.

They might ask me to lecture around at the universities . . . teach a short-term class at Columbia. . . . I could do that . . . maybe do a spot on "The Today Show." Wouldn't that be something? Instead of walking by on the sidewalk looking in, I'd sit right there in Rockefeller Center studio —

"I said, darlin', are you gettin' hungry?" Brady shouted.

"What?" She glanced over at him.

"How about you makin' some sandwiches? I think I ought to stay out here and signal in the helicopter."

"Oh . . . sure." She put down the journal and went back into the cabin.

I'm designing my literary future, and he wants to talk about food!

After a few minutes of sorting through the sacks and grumbling to herself, she carried a box of items out to the hand-hewn wooden table in the yard.

"You want to eat over here?"

He pushed back his hat and sauntered toward her. "Yeah . . . that thing should keep signalin' for a while."

"What makes it so smoky?"

"Wet wood. It's noon, isn't it? They're late."

"Oh, well, we've got all day." She shrugged. "Listen, these journals are really good. I think I might take them back to New York so I can finish reading them before I send them to Key West."

"What have you learned?"

"Well . . . in the early thirties all he seems to write about is how hopeless the world is. He predicts a catastrophic war . . . the bankruptcy of bolshevism . . . the failure of fascism, and the demise of democracy," she informed him. "Do you want pickle on your sandwich?"

"Sure."

"Here."

Wiping his hands on his jeans, he took the sandwich. "Thanks."

"There's some apples in the box."

Stoner chomped into the turkey stack sandwich on sourdough bread and mumbled his question. "So what is the cause of all of Harrison's pessimism?"

"Because we in the West have developed our minds to a stage where we know we must behave better than we are capable of controlling ourselves to do."

"What's his solution? Should everyone move to a cave in the desert?"

"No . . . he sees no solution. Western societies will collapse, and emerging nations will pull themselves out of chaos and present the new order."

"So he went down into the canyon to wait for a new world order to form?"

"That's the puzzling thing. It seems that he came down here to avoid some failure. He talks about each man reaching a crossroad where he chooses the wrong path. After a wrong choice he has forfeited his right to take a place in a reorganized society."

"And he's made his mistake?"

"Yeah. That's what it seems. But listen, I'm only on the first journal. Maybe it makes more sense later on."

"And you like readin' this stuff?"

"It's fascinating!"

"I thought you said it was depressing."

"Well, it's fascinating in a depressing sort of way."

"Did you know you wrinkle your nose when you get excited?"

"I do not."

"Look, you just did it."

"I did not. You're just trying to change the subject, Stoner!"

"I am not. . . . You were saying that Harrison came down here because of some personal failure, but you have no clue what the failure was."

"You were listening."

"Yes, and I'm listening for a helicopter. But I don't hear one. I think maybe I better go back and get some more wood. This could take all afternoon."

"I'm going to just scan through these journals. You know, his lost manuscript isn't nearly this pessimistic. Something must have happened over the years to change his mind."

After lunch Brady tossed a few more wet logs on the fire and helped her carry the lunch goods back to the cabin.

"If the chopper comes in before I get back, signal him in to land between the fire and the spring. That worked pretty well this mornin'."

She brushed her hair with her fingers and jammed her hands into her back pockets. "How do I signal a helicopter?"

"Wave your arms and point . . . I guess. Then get back because it sure kicks up a cloud of dust. I might go over and investigate where I found those diggin's. If there's enough gold, I might just winter it out in here. It couldn't pay much worse than cowboyin'."

"Really? You'd come in here by yourself?"

"Nah, I'd bring Capt. Patch with me."

"It seems funny for you not to have him now."

"Shoot, he refused to ride in that rental car of yours. Of course, staying with Heather and the girls isn't exactly roughing it for him either. Anyway, I'll be back in five minutes if I hear that helicopter."

"You'll find me right on the porch reading journals."

"I'll find you by the smell of that perfume."

"Do you like it?"

"Yep. It smells like spring wildflowers. What's it called?"

"You know . . . one of those crazy names. . . .

It's a real fresh smell, don't you — "

"Come on, Austin, what's it called?"

"Well, this one is Neglected Passion, but that doesn't mean that — "

"Desperate. This woman's sounding downright desperate. Good thing old James isn't here. He wouldn't have a chance."

"James?"

"St. Cloud. Didn't you mention a boyfriend by the name of James St. Cloud?"

"Oh . . . him. Well . . . that's really over and — "

"Be back in a few minutes, Lynda Dawn."

"Yeah . . . well . . . I mean, it's just perfume. . . ."

She kept mumbling to herself as he hiked back into the canyon packing the canvas wood-hauler over his shoulder.

Jimmy. I didn't call him! But I didn't say I'd call him. He's the one who huffed off to Palm Springs. But, of course, I did miss out on going to the wedding. Lord, Jimmy's just not my type. I need someone who's more confident of himself . . . someone who won't cramp me into a tiny . . . someone who is strong and . . . someone who is exciting, but not too . . . someone whose loyalty is legendary . . . someone who is looking after my best interests . . . someone sort of like . . . you know . . . but not so . . .

She dragged the box of ledger journals over to the chair on the porch and plopped herself down.

Don't weaken now, girl. By Monday you'll be back in the city with your wonderful life of editing books!

And by Tuesday he'll be calling someone new his darlin'.

Sitting in the mild fall sunshine in the isolated canyon, she took a deep breath and immersed herself in the blue sky.

It's almost like a tranquility transfusion. It makes you feel alone but not lonesome. I'll bet Harrison spent a lot of time just sitting and staring out into the canyon. Millions of people in the city live and die without ever once experiencing this. It's crazy. The frantic pursuit of riches robs a person of true wealth.

Get a grip, Austin. Soon you'll be quitting your job and moving off to Taos, New Mexico, to make pottery . . . or something.

Sorting through her green duffel bag, she pulled out a small unopened bottle of perfume. She stared at the label and smiled. *He wants spring wildflowers? He'll get Spring Wildflowers.*

She was well into the second journal when she ran across an entry that caused her to sit straight up. It was a poem written to a child, and scribbled in the margin were the words, "The baby would be about seven now."

A child? Harrison had a kid? Didn't he know if it was a boy or a girl? What did he do — abandon the mother? 1938? A seven-year-old? That's it! That's why he came down here! That's the dilemma! One of his Hollywood starlet girlfriends was pregnant, and he couldn't face it, so he took off!

But which one? This is the stuff tabloids are made of! Let's see . . . I think I read about Harrison and Peggy Hopkins Joyce . . . no . . . no, it was Garbo!

*Wasn't it? But she didn't have any kids . . . did
she? How about that blonde — what's her name? No
. . . she was with William Randolph Hearst. Oh,
it was probably some starlet no one can even remember.*

She began to skim quickly through the pages
trying to find some other reference to a child or
a marriage or a woman left behind. In the ledger
journal marked 1940++ she found a clipping from
a St. George newspaper announcing the Japanese
bombing of Pearl Harbor.

"Hey, darlin'!"

Startled, she looked up to see Brady Stoner dragging in another load of wood.

"Are you sleepin'?"

"Just lost in thought, I guess."

After building up the fire, Stoner hiked over
to where she sat in the shade of the porch. He
pushed his hat back and wiped the sweat off his
brow, smearing dirt across his forehead. Then he
sat down on the porch steps and rubbed his leg.

"Is it bothering you?" she asked.

"Oh, it sort of locks up and starts aching once
in a while."

"Maybe you should keep it elevated or something."

"It's all right . . . really. Did I ever tell you
about the time I got drug into a pen of bulls?"

"I don't want to hear about it. Bulls scare me
to death."

"Oh, it happened so quick I didn't have time
to get scared." He pulled off his hat and rubbed

his fingers through his hair. "Do you think the Mojave County coroner will actually make it today?"

"I'm beginning to have my doubts." She sighed. "What did you find back at the gold mine?"

"The ore looks promising. If I have time, I'll drag a load of it out here to the spring and see if I can pan it out. How about you? Have you found any nuggets in those journals?"

"Maybe. You want to hear something interesting? I think the reason Harrison came in here was to avoid the responsibility for making some girl pregnant."

"No kidding? He said that?"

"In a roundabout way."

"Why was that such a big deal? With his philosophy of no moral absolutes, it wouldn't bother him how many women were pregnant, right?"

"That's what he's wrestling with. It shouldn't bother him, but it does."

"It would sure nag at me, that's for sure. Say, are you thirsty? I can bring us a jar of that cold spring water."

"Yeah . . . thanks, Brady."

"No problem. That's what you hired me for, boss. I am gettin' paid for this, aren't I?"

"Sure. Didn't I read somewhere that cowboys work for a dollar a day?"

"Whoa! That was a hundred years ago!" He laughed and hiked toward the springs.

Several minutes later when he was on his way back, she shouted at him, "Brady, I found it! I found Harrison's conversion! Here it is . . . sometime in 1942!"

"What happened? What made him change?" Stoner handed her the jar.

She took a long drink and wiped her mouth with the back of her hand, wondering if she had smeared dirt across her face.

"Well, Pearl Harbor got him to start reading a Bible. Seems like he was searching for some predictions of what the end of the world would be like. He was sure this was the beginning of the end."

"And that led him to faith?"

"No, that led him to Bible reading, and that led him to the book of Mark, and that led him to belief in Christ."

"Right out here in the canyon with no church, no preacher, no evangelist, no one at all. This is big stuff, isn't it?"

Austin nodded. "Momentous. And to think I almost didn't fly back in here! I mean, if Gossman had been decent about the manuscript, I'd be back in New York."

"Who knows but that you have come to the kingdom for such a time as this?" Brady quipped.

"What wonderful philosopher said that?"

"I think it was a harem girl turned queen by the name of Esther. . . . Anyway, you read your journal. I'm going to lay here and take a little siesta. Holler at me if the fire is gettin' low."

"You can sleep right here on the porch?"

"It's softer than a city sidewalk."

"I won't ask you how you know that."

"Good." He grinned and pulled his black felt cowboy hat over his eyes.

Austin flipped through the journal looking for further signs of Harrison's new-found faith. By the summer of 1942 he was writing about the joys and delights of creation, and in December he talked of a long trip to Marlowe's store in Rincon to pick up typing paper and a typewriter ribbon that he had ordered on an earlier visit. Marlowe had only been able to get him a used ribbon, but he had plenty of paper and wrote that he would soon start working on "the book."

Most of the 1943 entries were almost devotional — lots of quotes from Psalms and poems setting out the majesty of God's creative power. When she flipped open the pages of the 1944 journal, she noticed that the entries stopped about April. Page after page of white space followed.

Did he get sick? Maybe he was working on the book. Maybe he started using another journal.

Sorting through the box of ledgers, she discovered that the next date was 1946.

What happened for a year and a half? He must have had something to write! It must be here somewhere.

Emptying the box completely, she pulled up the newspaper that lined the bottom of the crate.

V-J Day? This newspaper is probably worth something itself.

Tumbling out of the newspaper came three letters. All three were addressed to Shotgun Canyon Harry, R. R. #1, Rincon, Arizona.

The letters! These are the ones that old mailman talked about . . . two cents due.

A small scrap of paper dropped out of the first yellowed letter as she unfolded it. She reached to retrieve the scrap and began to read the letter.

Dear Marty,

What can I say? I've been alternating screaming at you and crying for the past two weeks since I received your letter. Of course I thought you were dead. The whole world thinks you're dead. I'm happy for you that you've come to peace with God.

There is no reason at this date to tell you of the torment that you've put us through. But we have survived and will survive without you. I will not tell anyone of your location. If they find where you are, then everyone will know!

Please do not write again. You've forfeited that privilege many years ago. Our lives are peaceful and settled without you. I assure you I will return all other letters unopened.

I have prayed every day for the past two weeks that God would forgive you. I'm sure He will. Perhaps someday I will be able to do the same.

Sincerely,
Grace

P.S. I might live to regret this, but I've enclosed a snapshot of Julie Ann. This was taken on her thirteenth birthday.

"No!" Lynda cried out. "No!" Looking down at the tiny black-and-white photograph, she continued to wail, "No . . . no . . . no!" She pressed the picture to her chest, and the tears poured down her cheeks.

Brady Stoner sat up so quickly his hat rolled out into the bare yard.

"Darlin', what happened? What happened?"

She just sobbed and tried to take a breath.

"Did you throw that shoulder out again? Lynda, what happened? Tell me . . . what's the matter?" he insisted.

He jumped to his feet and stepped toward her. She rose and dropped the letters to the ground. She wanted to stop crying, but the wails couldn't be contained. Finally she threw her arms around Brady's neck and laid her head on his chest.

"Darlin', it's okay . . . whatever it is, it's okay! Just relax, babe . . . just relax. Get your breath. I'll get you out of here to a doctor. . . . It will be all right. You can fly out with the coroner."

"No," she sobbed. "No!"

"No, what, darlin'?"

"Ha-Harrison's daughter . . . no!"

"Daughter? So he did have a kid. What's the matter with that?"

"The picture," she sobbed.

Pulling back from her grasp, he took her

clenched right hand. "Let me see the picture. Come on, Lynda Dawn . . . turn loose. Let me see it!"

Stoner pried her fingers back and took the photo. "Cute girl. So this is his daughter. Have you ever seen her before?"

Every time she opened her mouth to speak, she burst out in uncontrollable sobs. She could feel the tears rolling down her cheeks. Finally she took a deep breath and blurted out, "That's my mom!"

"What?"

"It's my mother, Brady," she cried. "That's her picture! I have one just like it at home. This letter is from my grandma!"

"Are you kiddin' me? Is this for real? Harrison is your . . . this guy was your mother's . . . he was . . ."

He slipped his arms back around her waist and pulled her tight. "It's okay, darlin'. . . . You go ahead and cry!"

She did.

He held her, and they rocked back and forth on the front porch of the deserted cabin in a place called Shotgun Canyon a hundred miles from nowhere . . . at the edge of the universe.

Finally she ran out of tears and pulled away.

"Could you get me a drink of water?" she whispered hoarsely.

"You got it, darlin'. Just sit down. I'll be right back."

By the time he returned from the spring, she had investigated the other two letters. Both envelopes contained unopened letters addressed to G. L. Ramsey, Box 62, Key Largo, Florida. They had been returned (with postage due).

Opening the letters, she read one that described Harrison's conversion. The second one pleaded with her grandmother to read the letters and write back to him.

"You doin' better?"

"I'm kind of numb."

"I reckon so. Have a drink of spring water."

"Thanks." She took a small sip and held the rest. "My mother died never knowing who her father was." She began to sob again. "I don't know why Grandma would never tell us."

"Kind of embarrassing for a person in her generation, I suppose."

"But my mother never could adjust . . . I think it ground away at her every day of her life. She always felt rejected. It was a big, black cloud that hung over her. I always figured that's why my dad took off. It was just too depressing to be around my mom. If only she knew. Why couldn't she live long enough to find out?"

"Lynda Dawn, I can't answer that. But all of this sort of takes a strange twist, doesn't it? I mean . . . you've been hot on this manuscript ever since that Fondue character came into the office — "

"And mentioned G. L. Ramsey! Harrison had told him to look up G. L. Ramsey, but Harrison knew Grandma was in Florida. . . . Why would he send Fondue to New York? Maybe he thought she was still alive . . . you know . . . that someone in the publishing house would know her and show her the book."

"Maybe so . . . or maybe that was the only name Fondue had to go with."

"Martin Taylor Harrison's my grandfather. Do you know what this is like? I mean, what if you suddenly found out Buffalo Bill was your grandfather?"

"Eh . . . well, I guess I'd drive out to Cody, Wyoming, and lay claim to The Irma."

"The what?"

"The Irma Hotel. It was Buffalo Bill's. Wait a minute, Lynda Dawn! If Harrison's your grandfather, then you're a legal heir, right?"

"I guess . . . if it all holds up. I don't know what it takes to prove who your grandfather is."

"If he's your grandfather, then that manuscript belongs to you, and you can publish it with any company you want."

She looked up at his excited brown eyes and rubbed her runny nose on her sleeve.

"Yes! But . . . but not just me. I mean, my sister and brother are in this, too!"

"Lynda Dawn, you discovered a lot more than a lost manuscript!"

He grabbed her around the waist and whirled her around as she laughed wildly.

"Is this incredible or what?" she shouted.

Suddenly he stopped spinning her around and hugged her tight, planting his thin, soft lips on hers. The kiss was warm, exciting, tentative. She wanted him to instantly stop — and instantly go on. She couldn't decide which.

Just as quickly he pushed her back. "Sorry, boss . . . I got a little excited."

"No . . . it's . . . Don't worry about it." She tried to explain, "I'm so excited I could kiss a rock."

"Oh, good," he groaned, "I'm glad it wasn't anything personal."

"No, no, I didn't . . . Brady, how dare you take advantage of me when I'm in a state of total confusion!" she chided.

"Take advantage of you? I . . . I had bigger kisses than that when a rodeo queen gave me a silver buckle."

"That's obvious!" She started to pout, then broke into a smile. "I've got to get my bearings. My whole head is just spinning."

"Just because I kissed you?"

"Dream on, Stoner. You aren't that good."

"But that kiss was . . . sort of good, right?"

"Oh, sure . . . in a cowboy kind of way." She picked up the letters and looked over them again.

"Well . . . this cowboy is going to . . . Anyway, I think I'll mosey back and dig a little in that gold mine. It looks like you need some time alone."

"Huh? What? Oh, yeah . . . thanks. This is . . . I can't . . . I've got to get to a phone and call my sister and brother and maybe . . . ." Her voice dropped off and faded to thoughts as Brady Stoner hiked out of the yard toward the north end of the box canyon.

Lord, You knew this all along. You led me here.

You're the reason I flew off to an unknown adventure, drove a truck across this place with an unknown cowboy, rode a mule down a dangerous cliff . . . It's all been Your leading. Thank You, Lord.

After about an hour of skimming through the rest of the ledger journals, she stood up, splashed her face with water from the jar, and walked out to the still-smoldering fire. Placing several more wet pieces of wood on the fire, she thought about walking back to where Brady was, but then turned south and strolled along the now-dry creek bed out to where the spring formed a waterfall until it dried up in the early summer.

Within a few minutes she found herself at the mouth of the canyon where the ledge trail began its ascent. Looking over the edge, she caught sight of the Colorado River far below.

Lord, I don't have any idea why it doesn't scare me now. It's like . . . like I know You're right here with me. It's beautiful. It's like something lifted up off me. . . . It's like a brand-new world. She stared out into the main canyon. *It's like . . . a helicopter!*

She raced back to the fire and put another log on it. Then she hollered toward the back of the canyon, "Brady! Brady! The coroner is here!"

She began to run back to the cabin, then spun, and trotted out toward the spring where she waited for the chopper to come close enough to guide it to the landing area.

Wild West Casino Tours? The coroner in Arizona rents a Wild West Casino Tours helicopter? They must have been called out to a search and rescue with

*their rig and had to rent this one. Lord, I sure hope
they find a body buried back in that grave. I'd hate
to have to pay for another . . . oh, but if — if Brady's
right, if the Harrison royalties go to his grandchildren,
maybe I can afford this trip!*

The helicopter hovered above the former garden
area. Lynda scooted back to the cabin to avoid
the swirling dust. The aircraft set down, and the
engine noise cut back but was not turned off. She
could see several men inside. Finally one wearing
a bright print shirt and dark glasses stepped out
and, with head bowed, ran toward her, carrying
something that looked like a briefcase.

"Are you Lynda Dawn Austin?" he shouted.

"Yes!"

"Well, it's a good thing you had that signal fire
burning. We would never have found this canyon.
Where's the cowboy?"

The man was stocky. He looked to be about
five and a half feet, had dark curly hair, and
sported a tattoo of a snake on his forearm.

Who is this guy? "You aren't from the coroner's
office, are you?"

"Coroner? Are you kiddin'? Did somebody die?
Now that would make a story. No, I'm from Channel 3 in Vegas. We want to do a television story
on you and that million-dollar manuscript. But we
understood a cowboy was going to be with you.
We want him in the story, too."

"He's . . . ah . . . around somewhere."

*Brady Stoner, you get your dirty Wranglers over
here right now!*

385

"We thought the story would look good on location. We'd like to tape over by the cabin. If you'll get the manuscript and the cowboy, I'll have the crew set up the cameras. It won't take more than ten or fifteen minutes. Then we'll be out of your hair."

"Eh . . . what station did you say you were from?"

"Channel 3 — KJED."

"Well, I think I need to see some identification."

"You're kidding. We spend all day trying to find you and then guarantee you a slot on the evening news, and you're asking for ID cards? Get real!"

She glanced over at the helicopter. Several sunglassed faces stared out at her. Searching for any sign of Stoner, she wanted to turn and run to the cabin.

"Oh . . . look, here comes Mr. Stoner! He'll see to it that . . ."

She turned her back to the man and watched Brady Stoner run on his bad leg toward them. He was waving his arm and shouting, "Darlin', get away from that slimeball!"

"What?" she hollered back.

"He's one of Trent's thugs!"

A strong, hairy, snake-tattooed arm suddenly clamped around her neck. She could feel the cold, hard steel of a gun barrel shoved against her neck.

"Stay where you are, cowboy! Unless you want your lover girl to take this .45 Mag point blank."

"Trent?" she called out as Stoner stopped in his tracks.

"He's one of the guys who pounded on me out behind the fast-food joint!" he called out. "What are you tryin' for, sport — twenty years to life?"

"Yeah, you really scare me, cowboy! You two are so dumb it's incredible. I can waste you, and no one would find the bodies in here for a hundred years."

She noticed Brady glance toward the helicopter. Straining to look, she saw a couple of men crawl out and begin walking toward them. She could hear the prop still thrashing the air.

"Trent, you've got to be the scumbag of Vegas!" Brady yelled. "Take your social misfits and get out of here!"

"Stoner, let's get something straight," Trent screamed. "We've got the girl and the gun, so we make the decisions!"

Brady kept his distance but looked right at her. "Are you all right, Lynda Dawn?"

"I'll survive," she replied in a less than commanding voice.

"Well, for heaven's sake, don't bite him. You'd get syphilis or AIDS or rabies!"

"You're pushing it, cowboy. I can blow her away right now." The stocky man waved the gun and gripped her tighter.

"Come on, Stoner, don't get Larry ticked off," Trent cautioned, staying about twenty feet away from both Austin and Stoner. "He's got a tendency to go wild when he gets really mad. All we want is that million-dollar manuscript. Go get that book, and we'll let the girl go."

"Why? That book's not worth a penny to anyone but Atlantic-Hampton. No one else in this country can publish it," Stoner shouted.

"You're wastin' my time, Stoner," Trent called. "That TV show 'True Story,' offered me five hundred thousand dollars for the manuscript."

"They can't publish it, can they?" Brady asked Lynda.

Trying to push the hairy arm away from her neck so she could breathe more easily, she called out, "No, but they can exploit it for a month of shows."

"Trent, turn the girl loose. We don't have the book here. She shipped it off to New York already."

"Not according to your interview in the newspaper."

"Tell them, darlin'. We certainly aren't dumb enough to bring Harrison's book back out here! Go ahead. Tell 'em."

"The manuscript is . . . well, you can't . . . even if it did happen to be . . . ."

"I don't believe you," Trent growled. "You didn't send it to New York, and you didn't leave it in your room at the Tropicanna. I know. I checked. Keep the gun on her, Larry."

Trent and the other man moved toward Stoner. Trent's companion had his hair cut so short he almost looked bald. He wore a black tank top and a dangling earring in his left ear. "Shoot her if she puts up a fight," ordered Trent.

"You won't shoot her," Stoner asserted, backing away from the men. "Harm her and you know for a fact that I won't tell you where that manuscript is!"

"That might be, but we don't have to make you talk, cowboy. We'll just see how long she wants to stand there and see you get your head bashed in!" The tall one with the short hair circled behind Stoner. He and Trent began to move in.

"Don't tell them anything, darlin'! I can handle this! You hear me — don't tell them anything!" Stoner hollered as he dove at Trent. The pasty-faced man tried to jump back, but the crack of the fist on his chin rang above the noise of the helicopter. She felt the hairy arm now almost choke her.

Spinning to face the man behind him, Brady ducked and caught a glancing blow to the right shoulder. Slamming a hard right cross into the man's stomach, he turned back and felt Trent's double-fisted roundhouse in the ear. He staggered back and dropped to his knees.

A heavy black leather boot crashed into his mid-section. He rolled toward the cabin away from the wild kicks of both attackers.

"Wait!" she yelled. "Wait!"

Trent glanced over at her. Stoner seized the moment. Leaping to his feet, he tackled Trent, and the two went rolling toward the helicopter. Before the other man could join the attack, Stoner straddled Trent's back and bent the man's right arm behind him almost to his head.

"Call him off, Trent, or I'll break your arm! You know I'll do it!" Stoner gasped.

"Shoot him, Larry!" Trent called out to the one holding Austin.

"You mean it?"

"Shoot him. He's breaking my arm!" Trent screamed.

The man released Lynda and pointed the .45 at Stoner almost fifty feet away.

"Don't hit the chopper!" the third man shouted as he backed away from the two on the ground. Austin slapped her hands into the gunman's face, digging her fingernails into cheeks, drawing trails of blood.

The man jumped back, fired wildly into the air, and dropped the gun. Clutching his face, he frantically knelt down to retrieve the revolver. Lynda sprinted toward the cabin. She got within a few feet of the porch when the man wearing the black tank top tackled her from behind and slammed her face first into the dirt. She struggled to pull free but was pinned down by the large man who smelled of cigarettes and sweat.

Austin heard Trent scream in pain and knew that Brady had kept his promise. She managed to see Brady run toward the man with the bleeding face, who was fumbling to grab the gun. The sideways view from ground level made an unreal angle. She could hear her heartbeat pound throughout her entire body.

Joe Trent was still screaming curses when the

stocky man picked up the gun and aimed it at a charging Brady Stoner. She could hear herself scream, "Don't shoot him! I'll get you the book. Let me up. Don't shoot him!"

Clutching his limp right arm, Joe Trent shrieked, "Get the book!"

The man on her back climbed off and yanked her to her feet. The one called Larry kept Brady at bay with the .45.

"It's on the porch. Let me go get it."

"What do you mean, it's here?" Stoner shouted. "You didn't bring it with you, did you?"

"Yeah," she confessed. "I thought . . . that it would be safer here. You told me not to let it out of my sight."

"I didn't mean for you to bring it back out here."

"Now you tell me."

"Go with her, Bobby!" Trent shouted to the man who clutched her arm with his powerful grip.

"Don't give it to 'em, darlin'," Brady shouted.

"They'll kill you," she cried.

"If I perish . . . I perish."

"I'll just grab it out of the — "

"Not without me, you aren't," Bobby growled.

She stepped up on the porch with the man right at her side. "It's in the green duffel bag."

"Bobby, get the manuscript!" Trent screamed, still standing halfway to the waiting helicopter.

Shoving her across the splintery wooden porch floor, the man yanked open the bag and pulled out a white manuscript box.

"Is this it?"

"That's it." She nodded.

"I can't believe you brought it back to the canyon!" Brady called out.

"It's just not worth it, Brady. They can have it. Now turn him loose, Trent!"

"You want me to shoot him, Joe?" Larry growled.

"No! Don't shoot him. We'll shove them both over the edge. Give me that book! We've got to make sure that's the right one."

Bobby stepped off the porch and handed the box to the limp-armed Trent, who cautiously approached the cabin.

As Joe Trent fumbled to take the lid off the box with his good arm, Lynda backed toward the open door of the cabin.

"Is that it, Trent?" Larry called out. "Is that the million-dollar manuscript?"

"Yeah . . . this is it!" He crammed the lid back onto the box. "You know, five hundred thousand dollars and Stoner shoved off a cliff — even with a broken arm, this is going to be a great day!"

Feeling the unpainted doorjamb behind her, Austin reached behind her back into the building and groped for the shotgun. She found the cold steel of the barrel and whipped the gun up to her right shoulder, pumping a shell into the chamber as she did.

The unmistakable sound of the shotgun caused Joe Trent and the other man to jump back away from the cabin.

"Drop it, Trent. . . . Drop the manuscript!"

He dropped the box and backpedaled away from her.

"Tell him to drop his gun!" she hollered.

"Forget it!" the gunman growled. "You shoot me with that shotgun, and you'll hit your lover boy, too. I ain't dropping nothin'!"

"You let Brady go, Trent, and I'll give you the manuscript," she bartered, keeping the Winchester model 12 pointed at the man with the broken arm.

Trent continued backing away from her. "Sure . . . sure, we'll trade, lady. . . . We'll trade."

"Keep the shotgun on Trent, darlin'. We don't have to trade them anything!"

Lynda followed them out into the yard without lowering the shotgun. "I said, let him go!"

"We'll let him go when you give us the book! Larry, keep that .45 on him."

Brady Stoner, face and knuckles smeared with dirt and blood, rested his hands on his hips. "Don't do anything you'll regret, Lynda Dawn. This thing is more important than you and me. You know it!"

"Keep spread out," Trent yelled to the others who now lined up about fifty feet from the cabin. "She can't hit more than one of us. Besides some New York editor couldn't hit the broad side of a barn! It's probably not even loaded."

"Come get the book, Trent," she yelled.

"You go get it, Bobby!"

"I ain't gettin' any closer to that buckshot."

"Larry?"

"I'm not puttin' down this .45!"

"Stoner, you go get the manuscript. Keep him covered, Larry! Go on, Stoner . . . go get that book!"

Brady limped his way toward her and stooped to pick up the boxed manuscript.

"Are you sure you want me to do this?" Under his breath he mumbled, "Shoot Trent, toss me the gun, and dive for the cabin door."

"Toss it to me, Stoner!" Trent hollered. "Toss that book over here."

"Come and get it, Trent!"

"Toss it to him, Brady," Lynda Dawn ordered.

"What?"

"You heard me. It's mine, and I say toss it to them!"

"Now you're makin' sense," Trent shouted. "Toss it here, and we'll fly out of here."

"Toss it high," she said softly to Stoner.

"Huh? Oh . . . yeah . . . are you sure?"

Lynda Dawn Austin nodded her head and yelled, "Pull!"

Stoner hefted the manuscript-laden white cardboard box, sailing it twelve feet above their heads. With all eyes on the flying box, none of the men saw Lynda lift the model 12, but the blast rocked their ears, and the box exploded into a rain of confetti like a ticker-tape parade.

An incredibly sharp pain stabbed her right shoulder when the gun recoiled into it and caused the tears to flow down her already smeared cheeks. Her right shoulder dropped low, but not before she pumped another shell into the chamber.

"You're crazy!" Trent screamed. "You just blew up five hundred thousand dollars!"

Brady Stoner grabbed the gun from her shaking hands and turned it on the others. "There's your manuscript, Trent!" he yelled at the stunned men who still stared at the pieces of paper floating in the warm canyon breeze. "Now get out of here!"

"Shoot 'em!" Trent yelled.

"Let's get out of here. There ain't no money in it now," Bobby called.

He and Larry began backing toward the helicopter.

"Wait! Give me that gun. I'll shoot them!" Trent screamed.

"Come on, Joe. It ain't worth it! All they have to do is hit the helicopter, and we'll never make it out." Bobby turned and began to run to the waiting aircraft.

Deserted by the others, Trent spun around and rushed to the helicopter. Brady took aim with the shotgun.

"Brady, no!" Austin cried out. "Please help me!"

He lowered the shotgun and stepped to her side. "Get in the cabin — against the far back wall!" he shouted over the increasing noise of the helicopter's revving engine. "They'll shoot at us! Get in there!"

She saw splinters fly from the wall of the cabin as Brady shoved her inside and dove in behind her. They heard no sounds above the roar of the helicopter, but bullets ripped through the thin-walled cabin. Then suddenly the helicopter was gone, its noise only a faint echo out in the main canyon.

"Don't bite your tongue, darlin'. . . . This is goin' to hurt."

"I know," she whimpered.

He grabbed her sagging right shoulder from behind and yanked it back against his strong chest.

She sobbed.

She struggled to catch her breath.

She thought she might pass out.

But she didn't yell or scream.

Or call him names — this time.

ELEVEN

"Why don't you rest up on that bed, and I'll be right back."

Lynda noticed blood trickling through the dirt on his face and the swollen left eye. She thought about what she must look like and made a feeble attempt to brush the dirt off her own face. "Where are you going? You look bad. You'd better clean up first."

"I need to step outside. Oh, don't worry about me. I've been hurt worse than this."

She bristled at the words. "Stoner, I'm sick and tired of hearing that phrase. If you were lying there dead, you'd manage to raise up on your elbow and say, 'Don't worry, I've been hurt worse.' "

A wide grin broke across his face. "You remind me of a bobcat."

"Why?"

"Purdy to look at, but a guy never knows when she'll lash out. I'll be right back."

She shook her head. "Well, cowboy, be careful. What if they circle around?"

"Why would they do that? There's nothin' here they want."

"Trent doesn't seem like the type who needs a logical explanation for his actions."

"You're right . . . but then I've known New York editors that aren't logical either. Take it easy for a minute. I won't be long."

"What are you going to do?"

"For one thing, I'm goin' to try and salvage some of that manuscript. I can't believe you shredded it like that!"

"Oh, so that's the illogical action of a New York editor?"

"It seemed radical. Didn't you say it would be better to have it published than tucked away somewhere? Even if the thing is illegally published, folks will read it, and it will have a powerful effect, right? I didn't think you'd blow it to kingdom come. Kind of drastic for a city girl."

"Drastic!" Her voice began to rise. "You call that drastic? You were the one who said I should let them beat you to death rather than give them the book. Come on, Stoner, no book is worth your life! Get real!"

Their conversation was almost at the shouting level.

"What's so extreme about that? You said it might be the most important book in the last fifty years! Aren't there some things worth risking your life over?"

"You don't have to yell at me, Brady Stoner. There's no one else around for a hundred miles, and you know it. I just have a hard time believing a rodeo cowboy is all that concerned over a literary masterpiece. It was . . ." Her voice began to lower. "It was very noble of you."

"Yeah . . . well, in case you thought I was just being heroic, it was more . . . you see, I . . . It's sort of like I just didn't want to lose."

"You didn't want Trent to think he could come in here and take something away from you. Is that it?"

"Trent took something away from me once before and . . . Well, you know the story."

"And you've never forgiven him for it?"

" 'After such knowledge, what forgiveness?' "

"You want to give me the chapter and verse for that?"

"T. S. Eliot, *Gerontion*. Look, I wasn't about to let Joe Trent leave here in victory."

"So you'd give your life?"

"Maybe. A man has to live with himself. If I had let Trent come in here and take that book away from you, I'd be miserable. Only a jerk like Trent can seem to forget about his past."

"Well . . . he didn't get the manuscript," she declared.

"That's right. We stopped him, didn't we? Of course, we don't exactly have it either — not in one piece."

"It was a good shot, wasn't it?"

"You're a surprising lady. Did you see the shock on Trent's face?"

"Not really. I was hurting from the recoil."

"He turned white as a sheet. I don't know if it was the shock of seeing five hundred thousand dollars blown to shreds or if he figured he would be the next target of the lady's wrath."

"I really . . . *really* want to keep that shotgun," she stated. "Did you feel the balance in that gun?"

"You know, when I was a kid huntin' birds up in the Owyhees, I once had a . . . Wait a minute. This is crazy. Your knees are shaking from the pain in your shoulder. I look like a buffalo ran over the top of me. We just blew up the most important Christian book of the twentieth century . . . and we're standin' here talkin' the merits of a model 12? I still don't believe you brought that manuscript out here to the desert and then minced it."

Lynda Dawn Austin reached up with her left hand and pulled Stoner's dusty black beaver felt hat off his head as she walked toward the door of the cabin. Looking in the broken scrap of mirror, she gingerly placed the hat on the back of her head. A few dried tears streaked her cheeks, and she tried to wipe them clean with her equally dirty hand.

Then she turned to Stoner. "I didn't blow up the manuscript, of course. Do you think I need some more perfume?"

"What did you say?" he gasped, following her out the door onto the porch.

"I said, 'Do you think I need some more perfume?' "

"No!" he shouted. "What do you mean, you didn't shoot the manuscript?"

"I shot a copy of the manuscript, not the original. You don't really think I'd shoot the — "

"A copy?"

"You have heard of photocopy machines?"

"But . . . but when? . . . where?"

"Well, there's this cute blonde named LeeAnne at the group reservations office in the Tropicanna. She thinks Brady Stoner has an 'awesome smile.' Well, she spent about an hour of her own time copying the manuscript."

"She did?"

"And she put the original in the hotel safe for me."

"She's a jewel."

"Yes, and I'm sure she'd appreciate your telling her that." Austin lifted her eyebrows as she teased.

"Wait . . . you mean to tell me you didn't bring the manuscript out here after all?"

"Just a copy. I'm not quite as ditsy as you thought."

"You mean I was gettin' myself beat to a pulp for some copy? Why didn't you tell me?"

"Oh, sure. I tell them it's not the original, and the next thing you know they'll be beating up on LeeAnne."

"But . . . but why didn't you just give them the copy to begin with?"

"Because . . . well," she stammered, "I wasn't about to let Trent take something that was mine. Losing stinks."

"Yeah, and just what's the chapter and verse for that, Miss Austin?"

"Eh . . . I think that's in *Bobby Knight's Basketball Handbook*, page 1, paragraph 1, line 1."

Suddenly Stoner began laughing.

She smiled and waited for him to stop and explain.

He didn't.

Finally she joined in.

"Look at us," he managed to say at last. "We're all banged up. We're out in the middle of the boonies. This is a pitiful sight. We could pose as Bosnian refugees . . . and what are we worried about?"

"Winning." She giggled.

"Yeah! This is insane. We just risked our lives so we could be winners!"

"We won, Stoner. We whipped Trent."

"And you're going to whip Atlantic-Hampton, too."

"Yes, I am."

"And maybe you'll even whip the indelible ghosts that haunted your mother and grandmother."

The smile fell off her face. She eyed the barely smoldering remains of the signal fire. Then she pulled off his hat and handed it back to him.

"You doin' okay with that?" he asked.

"It's hard to think about. I just keep remembering my mother, Brady. She was so unhappy. I don't think she ever really felt loved by any man."

He leaned over quickly and kissed her lightly on the cheek. In the bright light of the desert sun, his lips felt surprisingly tender.

"How about her daughter? Did she ever feel really loved by a man?"

"I . . . I guess I don't really know. Darn it, Brady, you always do that."

"Do what?"

"You force me to deal with things I've spent a lifetime hiding from."

"It's my gift," he asserted.

She sat down in the rickety chair on the porch and rubbed her sore arm. "I need a vacation," she announced.

"I thought this was a vacation."

"Brady, this has been the craziest, most confusing, disorienting . . . physically, mentally, spiritually exhausting two weeks of my life."

"Well, at least you weren't bored. I suppose we ought to pretend that coroner is still flying in. I'd better build up the fire."

Lord, I need a break. You've got to help me with this. I've got to talk to Atlantic-Hampton about the manuscript. I've got to talk to my brother and sister about our . . . grandfather. I've got to talk to James about Brady. I've got to talk to Brady about . . . Lord, this would be a horrible long-term relationship. All we've done is argue and make up for two weeks. He's so . . . so self-confident, so bullheaded, so . . . so tender.

Glancing up to make sure Brady Stoner wasn't watching her, she stepped over to the green duffel bag, pulled out a bottle of something called Wild Horses, and splashed a little behind both ears.

At four o'clock that afternoon they finally heard the Mojave County Sheriff's helicopter hovering above Shotgun Canyon. Stoner signaled it in. The coroner, a sheriff's deputy, and the pilot tramped across the former garden to greet them.

They described the attack by Joe Trent and gang. The deputy, using the radio in the helicopter, was able to get through to the sheriff in Clark County, Nevada.

Stoner then led the three equipment-toting men to the grave site.

Austin, choosing not to be present when the body was exhumed, stayed at the cabin. Sitting on the chair on the porch, she stared out at the massive, silent red, yellow, and orange walls of the canyon.

Lord, my whole world's changed in two weeks. If the manuscript gets published, my job will never be the same. If Harrison really was my grandfather, my family life will never be the same. If Brady . . . well, either way my love life will probably never be the same.

And it's a cinch my shoulder will never be the same!

It's sort of like . . . like You just plucked me up out of a routine and shuffled everything around. Nothing's the same. I thought I had every day of my life planned out, and now . . . now I don't even know what's going to happen tonight.

I'm not very good at this, Lord. I like everything planned. No . . . I don't. What I mean is . . . I like these last two weeks, but they make me nervous.

I feel like a puck at a Ranger game.

Maybe You could just give me a little more peace and order — and a little less excitement. That would be nice.

Real nice.

Maybe tonight Brady and I could sit out here on the porch and kind of talk things through real quiet like. Just the moon, stars, soft desert breeze, and a distant coyote's call.

Get a grip, girl. It's getting hard for you to tell the difference between real life and fiction.

But, Lord, we've got to talk about the two of us. I mean, I can't just fly off and say, "Write to me sometime." What if he really does like me? What if some of those darlin's are sincere?

Lord, help us to think this thing through. I don't want to be impulsive. We'll talk about it like mature adults. Discuss the pros and cons and then . . . then . . . Well, he'll probably ask me to marry him.

"Look, Brady," I'll say, "we can't rush into this thing. We really don't know each other yet. Perhaps you can come to New York, and we'll spend some time . . ."

Not! Brady in New York? Get real, girl!

I'll fly out for Thanksgiving . . . or Christmas. . . . Eh, maybe we could meet at . . . Denver . . . or Cheyenne! Yeah . . . and we'll have a nice dinner, er, supper — by candlelight. . . . And then we'll talk about . . . how much he misses me, and then he'll . . . or I'll . . .

"You're having delusions, girl!" her own voice

startled her. "You're acting like some high school sophomore!"

She stood up and began to hike out to the mouth of the canyon. "I'm beginning to sound more like Spunky Sasser than Lynda Dawn Austin!"

By 5:00 P.M. the men hiked back across the canyon carrying a long, black body bag. Brady Stoner swung over to where she sat.

"Was it him?" she asked.

"Well, there was a body of an old man. The coroner will have to run the checks on it. It's sort of hard to tell anything, if you know what I mean."

"I don't want to hear about it, Stoner!" she protested.

"Well, get yourself together. We're loading up and going out with the coroner."

"What? But . . . I thought . . . what about the helicopter coming in the morning?"

"We can cancel it and save you some bucks."

"But what will we do in Kingman?"

"They need to refuel in St. George first. We'll get off there, and they have plenty of room for all this gear."

"I thought . . . we could . . ."

"Don't try to carry any of these boxes. Just grab your purse and duffel. I'll get the rest. Come on, boss, let's load up!"

"But I . . ."

Stoner toted a box of papers with the typewriter perched on top toward the helicopter. After a hectic half hour, they had loaded up the crates, sacks, and shotgun and were lifting off from Shotgun Canyon.

Brady Stoner sat up front next to the pilot and spent the entire time with the headset on. Halfway through the trip he turned back to her and shouted that Joe Trent and the others had been arrested at a hospital emergency room in Las Vegas. She nodded her head, but she said nothing to anyone on the whole journey to St. George.

He didn't want to stay in the canyon. He was in a hurry to get out of there. Something's different. It's time to quit pretending, isn't it, Lord? We had a little reprieve, but this is truly the time to shake hands and say, "Drop me a card at Christmas time."

I don't know why we couldn't have stayed one more night. He gets to see those desert stars all the time. By this time tomorrow I can be smelling diesel fumes in the concrete canyons and listening to some rude cabby.

The airport at St. George suddenly appeared. Looking out across the tarmac, she was surprised to see Heather and Capt. Patch waiting for them.

"How did Heather know we were coming in?" she asked.

"We radioed ahead. It sure was nice of them to bring us out, wasn't it? Saved you $750!"

"Yeah . . . it was splendid." She sighed.

It took over an hour to explain everything to Heather and the girls. Well after dark they finally stored all Harrison's belongings in Heather's garage and left the St. George double-wide to walk out to Brady's pickup.

Watching him limp, Lynda walked toward the driver's side.

"You'd better let me drive, cowboy."

"Not with that bad arm of yours in a sling. I'm all right. It just aches a little. Come on, Capt., hop in there, boy."

When they got to Interstate 15 and began to head west, she cleared her throat. "Brady, can we talk seriously?"

"I've been thinkin' the same thing. It's about time we had a heart-to-heart talk."

"Yeah."

"Well . . . what's your advice to me?" he asked.

"Advice?"

"Yeah. Do you think I should enter a couple of little rodeos before I go up to San Francisco, or should I just wait and go into the Cow Palace cold?"

"Rodeo?" She sighed. "I don't want to talk about rodeo!"

"I know. Neither do I."

"You don't?"

"No, I want to talk about you and me . . . and if we're goin' to see each other again and how I feel about you and . . . and . . . But I'm scared to death to talk about it. That's why I've been avoidin' it like a swamp."

"Scared? A cowboy afraid?"

"Yeah. Is there something wrong with that? Look, since it's nice and dark in here . . . I'm scared to death you might not care two twits about me . . . and I'm . . . well, terrified that you might like me a lot."

"That terrifies you?"

"Yeah. I, eh . . . I know you figured this out a long time ago — I like being friendly with the ladies . . . but I'm not too good at gettin' real close."

They didn't look at each other for a moment.

He rubbed the stubble on his two-day beard. "Look, I've never told anyone some of this . . . so you've got to promise you won't go writin' it in one of your books or somethin'."

"I promise."

"Well . . . I'm scared to get too close to you because I don't know what you're expectin' out of me, and I'm pretty sure I couldn't deliver it, whatever it might be. Then you'd get real mad and tell me to get lost and never speak to me again. Lynda Dawn Austin, it would break my heart to think I'd never get to talk to you or visit with you again."

"It would?"

"Yeah. So what I was kind of thinkin' was . . . couldn't we . . . you know . . . be really good friends and not mess this up? Now I figure this doesn't make a lot of sense to you. That's why I was afraid to talk about it. I should have just shut up."

"No, please go on. Really!" she insisted.

"Well, darlin' . . . your life's in New York City, and mine . . . mine's on the rodeo road. That's all there is to it. But I surely would like it if sometime I could look up in the stands at Cheyenne or Red Bluff or Reno and see your wonderful smile. I'd like to think that after I missed comin' out of the chute at San Antonio and I'm sittin' in some truck stop eatin' a stale burrito, I could call you up and listen to that sweet voice that kind of makes my throat tingle when I hear it."

"It does?"

"Yeah, especially when you get real excited and forget that you're some big city editor. Someday, darlin', I'm going to take that gold buckle at the National Finals. And we'll have that Champion's Banquet, and I want you to be there on my arm."

"Really?"

"But don't you see? If we get serious about this, you'll hate me soon, and you'll hate rodeo, cowboyin', and the West in general. You'll tell me to get lost, and I'll never be able to talk to you again. But if we just stay friends, I can keep on pretendin' that someday maybe we'll get serious. If we're friends, then I can keep lookin' up at the stands just in case you're there. If we stay good friends, I can keep pretendin' that I have a chance at winnin' the World. A man can live on hope for a long time. It's kept me goin' for thirty years."

He was silent again, and she didn't know what to say.

"It's a tough thing to admit, Lynda Dawn . . . that I just might not reach any of the goals I've always set for myself. Look, I'm a mediocre bronc rider and a mediocre cowhand. I'll probably push myself until I get hurt real bad. Then if I'm lucky, I'll be like Salvador — livin' down in the Strip tendin' someone else's cattle. But when you're around . . . it's like the world's a bigger place, and there are important things to do, and maybe out there somewhere the Lord's got a job or two for me. I like that feelin'. Finding that book . . . well, I suppose it's the most important thing I've ever done. In fact, it might be the only important thing I've done!"

He rolled down the window, and she could feel the warm wind whip through the cab of the pickup as they watched a desert moon light up the sky.

"Could you look in the glove compartment and hand me one of those McDonald's napkins?"

"Oh . . . sure. Are you okay?" she asked.

"Yeah . . . it's just . . . I must have got a little dust in my eyes, that's all," he explained.

After a minute or two he cleared his throat. "Lynda Dawn, I've carried on and on. I've never talked to a lady like that before. You've been mighty nice to sit there and listen. 'Course, you didn't have much choice at sixty-five miles an hour. I'm through runnin' on like this. Anyway, what time does your plane go out tomorrow?"

"About 2:30, I think. Can you see me off?"

"It would break my heart if I didn't," he said softly.

The rhythm of the tires on the warm asphalt was the only noise she heard for several minutes.

"It doesn't seem fair. Why weren't you born a barrel racer from Roswell? Or Fallon? Or Oakdale?"

"Me, a barrel racer? That's about like you being an attorney for an advertising agency in New York."

"Talk about a depressing thought," he conceded. "Look . . . I'd like to hear what you have to say about you and me. I might as well hear the truth. I've been makin' way too big a deal out of this, havent I?"

"Brady . . . you . . . well, no. I'm really glad you said what you did. Only . . ."

"Only I embarrassed you, didn't I? Now you don't know how to tell me to get lost. Darlin', don't think you have to — "

"Stoner, would you please shut up for a minute. What you just told me makes a lot of sense."

"It does?"

"I think so. But it wasn't exactly what I thought you'd say. And now I have to rethink my speech."

"You had it all planned out?" he quizzed.

"Well . . . I thought we would still be out at the cabin tonight, and I figured we would . . . Anyway, how come you were in such a big hurry to leave? It's kind of like being brought home from a date early. I figured I must have had spinach stuck in my teeth or something."

"Eh . . . I didn't aim for it to be so obvious," he admitted. "It's just that I was thinkin' about this being our last night . . . and was afraid I'd . . . talk you into doin' something dumb."

She rolled down her window. Capt. Patch plopped his front paws in her lap and leaned his head out in the breeze. She patted him on the head and gazed out at the desert night.

"We've been together almost day and night for two weeks. Why did you think something might happen tonight?"

"Because I do dumb things after I win. Really, I'm a much better loser. I know how to be humble, to reevaluate, and set new plans and priorities. But when I win . . . well, anyway, we won big. You have the manuscript. You have the documents. You have a grandfather . . ."

"What did you win, Brady?"

"I made myself a thousand dollars, chased off Joe Trent and his hoods, and got to spend two weeks with the classiest lady I've ever known. No matter what my face looks like, I'm feelin' like a winner!"

"And that means you'll do dumb things?"

"Look . . . you're supposed to be the one . . . talkin'. How did the subject get back to me? Go ahead. Tell me this speech you were preparing."

"I can't."

"Why?"

"I need to think about it some more."

"Do you have to plan out everything you say?"

"Yeah."

"What happens if you don't?"

"I say dumb things that I spend years regretting. Look, Brady . . . let me have the night to sort out my thoughts. Everything's all scrambled up in my mind — Harrison, the book, my shoulder, you. This has been a crazy two weeks."

Lynda checked back into the Tropicanna, and Brady opted for the Motel 6 down the street. From eight to nine she was on the phone with her sister Megan. Then it was half an hour with her brother William.

At 10:22 P.M. room service brought up a taco salad. She ate about half of it, lay down on top of the bedspread, and fell asleep with the lights on.

At 6:30 A.M. a ringing phone startled her. She fumbled for the receiver and tried to remember when it was that she had turned off the lights and climbed under the covers, still fully clothed.

"Yeah?" she mumbled.

"Mornin', darlin'. Did I wake you up?"

"Brady . . . I'm still asleep. . . . What time is it?"

"Well, it's after daylight, that's for sure. I called Stacy, and she wants an exclusive interview before everyone and their brother tries to corner New York's hottest editor."

"Huh?"

"We've got a newspaper interview over at Stacy's office at 8:00 A.M. I'll be down and pick you up in about an hour."

"An hour! You're kidding!"

"Go take a shower, Lynda Dawn. You'll wake up. How's your shoulder this mornin'?"

"Oh . . . Brady . . . what did you say?"

"I said I'll meet you out in front of the Tropicanna in an hour. Look beautiful because she wants to take pictures."

"Is this a joke?"

"Bye, darlin'."

She listened as the dial tone hummed on the phone.

If I felt better, I'd kill you, Stoner. You don't call up a woman at 6:30 and tell her to be beautiful in an hour. You don't call up a woman at 6:30 A.M. for any reason on earth!

Somehow by 7:35 she stood out in front of the Tropicanna wearing a Western dress, boots, sunglasses, and an ample supply of Evening Desire.

The interview with Stacy took about an hour. She felt fully awake by the time they were through. Brady's eye was not nearly as swollen, and his face showed only slight signs of the fight the day before. He was wearing a long-sleeved white Western shirt buttoned at the neck. Watching him as he posed for the picture, she thought she was looking back into a hundred years of cowboy history.

He drove them to the sheriff's office to give a deposition for use in extraditing Trent and the others to Arizona on assault and attempted murder charges.

Leaving the county building, Austin felt the hot, dry desert wind blow across the asphalt parking lot.

"What now, cowboy?" she asked.

"Your plane leaves at 2:30?"

"Yeah."

"Well . . . I've got to phone Procom and check on some rodeo entries. Then I'd better call my folks up in Idaho again. They seemed to be worried about their baby. How about you? Do you need to call a few folks?"

"I talked to Megan and William last night."

"How'd they take the news about having Harrison for a grandfather?"

"My sister cried a lot."

"And your brother?"

"He's flying to New York with his attorney on Monday to be with me when I meet with Hampton, Gossman, and the others."

"That sounds great! I'll bet that shocks them."

"Yeah. My brother's a good guy. Like you in some ways."

"You've still got the rental to return," he continued. "Let's meet at the airport restaurant at one for lunch, and then I'll see you off." Stoner pulled back into the Tropicanna.

She patted Capt. Patch on the head and shoved open the pickup door. "I'll be there," she promised.

The next two hours flashed by as she made phone calls to the Harrison Museum in Key West, another to her sister, a third to Janie who had just returned from a Tokyo flight, and a fourth to Kelly Princeton.

Kelly's words echoed in her mind as she packed up. "Don't you come home without being engaged to that cowboy, girl! If you don't want him, Nina and I have first dibs!"

Sure, Kell, he's not your type. You couldn't deal with the uncertainties. Neither could Nina. She wouldn't ride a pony down that canyon. No way. In fact, very few women could get along with him. . . . I think I could . . . maybe.

She checked all her bags at the airport and got her boarding pass. Then she returned the car to the agency. It was 12:50 when she reentered McCarran International Airport and hiked past rows of slot machines to the first nice restaurant she found.

She spotted a familiar silhouette at a table near the window looking out on the tarmac.

"Hey, cowboy, I believe you're sitting in my chair."

"Excuse me, ma'am, this is your chair?"

"Hey, Stoner . . . I've listened to that George Strait song. You think I'm some city slicker that just fell out of a cab? I've been around, boy."

"Yes, ma'am!" He laughed. "Say, didn't we meet once at a dance hall in Cheyenne?"

"No way," she teased. "It was up at the Stampede in Calgary. I was drivin' the Chuck, and you were outriding at the time."

"What?" Brady took off his hat and waved it at her. "Where did you learn to talk like that? What do you know about chuck wagon racing?"

"Nothing." She scooted into a chair beside him. "I stole a *Pro Rodeo Sports News* from under the seat of your pickup. . . . Hey, this is a nice place. Do they have fresh red roses at every table?"

"Only yours. I bought them for you."

"Really? You bought me these flowers?"

"Yeah, but . . . you don't have to carry them on the plane. It might be embarrassing."

"Embarrassing? I'll carry them. Every woman will be jealous."

Brady Stoner insisted they order steaks for a celebration lunch. They spent most of the next hour laughing and reviewing the past two weeks.

They had finished dessert and were drinking coffee when Brady glanced at her reflection off the window and said, "I'm really glad you wore that dress, Lynda Dawn. I was figurin' you'd be all decked out in your editorial best."

"You don't like those clothes."

"Oh . . . no. They're . . . just fine. Only they remind me of where you're headed and where I'm not. You do know that you look mighty nice in a yoked dress and boots, don't you?"

"So I've been told."

"How come you're not wearing your sling?"

"Well, I've gotten used to the pain, I suppose. Anyway, I could never get a sling to look nice. How about you? How's your face?"

"It will heal. You gettin' anxious to get back to New York?"

"Well . . . I guess. Sort of. I mean, I want to get that manuscript business taken care of."

"You're really going to get it published, aren't you?"

"Yep. This whole thing — this trip out here and everything — it's like the Lord's been leading the whole way. Do you know what I mean?"

"I think so. Are we talkin' serious now, or do you plan on beatin' around the bush for another hour?"

"I knew you wouldn't let me stall much longer."

"I believe it's your turn, Lynda Dawn. Now how come you didn't want to tell me last night?"

She took a deep breath and then pushed her sunglasses to the top of her head. He leaned back and stretched his hands behind his head.

"I didn't say much last night because you caught me by surprise. I told you . . . I sort of plan out my whole life word by word — ahead of time, and you . . . well, Brady, you continually make me throw out the plans. I've always been afraid to just blurt things out. I always live to regret them, so I wanted to think about what you told me. That's all."

"Yeah . . . that's what I figured. Before I rambled on and on, you were just going to shake my hand and tell me goodbye, right? Then you got afraid of hurtin' my feelin's. Well, I guess I put you in a bind. It's just that — "

"Stoner, would you shut up! You told me it's my turn, and I've been practicing this speech all morning!"

"Yes, ma'am."

"I had no intention of telling you goodbye last night. What I had planned to tell you was yes."

"Yes?"

"Yes."

"Yes to what?"

"Yes to just about anything."

She could see her own blush in the reflection in the window.

"You're kiddin' me."

"I think you know me well enough to know that I'm not joking. But the truth of the matter is, all that you said last night made a lot of sense. I like having you for a friend, Brady Stoner. In less than two weeks you have become the most exciting and honorable friend I have in this whole world.

"This may be premature . . . but I hope that maybe we can be more than friends sometime. It would crush me if I did something to alienate you and break off our friendship. It really hit home when you talked about sitting in that truck stop thinking of me.

"Well . . . there are going to be days when I'm stuck in that little cubicle of an office up on the twelfth floor of 200 Madison Avenue when the load of work is about to crush me. And I'll stare out the window at the gray skies and the gray buildings and several million gray people in midtown Manhattan . . . and I'll want to be able to think of a strong, handsome cowboy who's mashing his black Resistol down on his head and grabbing tight to a bareback riggin', about to nod his head in some exotic place called Albuquerque . . . or Ellensburg . . . or San Angelo. I want to think that when the phone rings in the middle of the night, it just might be a lonesome voice drawling, 'Darlin', you were on my mind.' Darn it, Brady,

420

when ESPN announces the world champions early some December, I want to turn to the girls at Barton's and say, 'Hey, that's my Brady!'

"The truth is, I really need you for a friend, Brady Stoner. But I can't be sitting in a condo in New York worried about which waitress is swooning over your smile or those soft, brown eyes. You've got to be you, Brady. That's the friend I need. And I guess I've got to be me."

He took a napkin off the table and handed it to her. "I think you got a little dust in your eye, darlin'. I wouldn't want it to ruin your makeup."

She wiped both eyes and took a sip of ice water.

"Are you through with your speech?"

"I think so." She flashed a quick smile. "Now can we talk about you?"

"Sure."

"You entered those rodeos, didn't you?"

"Yep. I'm goin' to win 'em, too. Oh, I won't get to the finals this year. But next year I'll go hard and try to stay healthy. Then you'll have to fly out to watch me in the finals."

"I'll be there. Send me clippings during the year, okay?"

"Sure, but you'll have to keep me up on that manuscript. I bet you win some industry award or somethin'. Do they have that kind of thing?"

"Yeah, it's a big thing every year. Hey, if I win an award, Stoner, you have to come be my escort."

"A tuxedo and everything?"

"Yep."

"Can I wear my hat?"

"I'd be insulted if you didn't."

He glanced over at the clock on the wall. "You think it's time to get out to the gate?"

"I suppose. You don't have to wait any longer. I can get myself on."

"Of course I do. What if the flight's canceled and you have to spend another night here?"

"Then we'll both be in trouble, won't we?" She winked.

"Come on, girl!" He stood to his feet, jammed on his hat, and tugged at her arm. "Before I forget everything I learned in Sunday school."

They walked slowly through the terminal, looking into the shop windows, and teasing about which items they would buy for each other. Austin's leather purse was strapped over her left shoulder, and she carried the red roses in her right hand.

By the time they finally reached the gate, preboarding had already begun. He slipped the fingers of his right hand into her left.

"Can you call me Monday night after that meeting with Hampton?" he asked.

"Sure. Where will you be?"

"At home."

"Home? You mean up in Idaho?"

"Yeah, I need to rest up a couple more weeks. Then I'll rodeo a little in the northwest before goin' to San Francisco."

"I don't have your phone number."

"Here. It's on this envelope. That's my mom and dad's number."

"Is this a note for me?" She began tugging on the sealed envelope.

"No," he insisted, "you can't open this letter until after the plane takes off."

"Why? What is it?"

"A secret."

"Why can't I open it now?"

"Because you might tell me no, Lynda Dawn, and it would break my heart. I like livin' on hope. You know that."

"You can't expect me to wait until the plane takes off!"

"They're callin' your row. You better load up, boss. You're so organized that you wouldn't dare open it ahead of time."

"Oh, you really think you know me well, don't you?"

"Yep."

"Well, did you know I was going to do this?"

She threw her left arm around his neck and pulled his face down toward hers planting her lips on his. She felt his strong arms gently engulf her waist and draw her tight. His lips felt firm, warm, and tender.

Finally pulling back, she opened her eyes and looked into his smiling face.

"Yep," he said. "I knew you were goin' to do that."

She stuck out her tongue and then turned to hand her boarding pass to the attendant. Before entering the walkway, she looked back.

"Goodbye, darlin'. . . . Call me Monday."

"Goodbye, cowboy. Thanks for the ride."

Lynda Dawn Austin sat in row 17, seat A, holding red roses in her right hand and a sealed note in her left. She watched the asphalt roll beneath the plane.

She didn't even close her eyes this time as the plane took off. Instead, she studied the sunny Las Vegas landscape. She could see the glass pyramid of the Luxor, the lion's head at the MGM Grand, and smoke boiling up from the volcano at the Mirage.

Lord, down there has got to be the phoniest city on the face of the earth . . . and the most real relationship I've ever had in my life. How come I feel like a junior high girl leaving summer camp?

I want him, Lord. I want him for a forever friend.

Glancing down at the note in her hand, she took a big breath and carefully ripped it open.

Okay, Stoner, be nice to me.

There was a beautiful photograph of a mountain sunset on the front of the card, with two horses grazing in a green meadow. Inside were the words, "Whenever I count my blessings, you keep heading up the list." There was a little hand-drawn cowboy hat at the bottom of the page and an arrow pointing to the back of the card. She flipped it over and recognized his scrawling print.

Lynda Dawn,

You are formally invited to attend a Cowboy Thanksgiving Supper for Two at the Teton View Lodge, Jackson, Wyoming, on the Saturday after Thanksgiving. We'll have steak, buffalo chili, sourdough biscuits, deep-dish berry pie, boiled coffee — and all that. I've reserved us a couple of rooms for the night at the lodge.

The view of the Tetons is spectacular at sunrise.

I hope you can make it, darlin'.

Love,
Brady

P.S. Dress Western.

She stared out the window and felt a tear roll down her cheek.

I'll be there, cowboy.
It would break my heart to miss it.